GLOFF
THE HAT-TIPPER

'Just imagine! Me, a humble lop-ear; hat-tipper to Imbix Hoth, High Master of the Leagues of Flight! It's a great honour, I can tell you, but not what you'd call an easy job.

Far from it, in fact. There's low doorways to watch out for. Arches, bridges, jutting branches . . . Plus the strength of the wind. And then there's the movements of the wearer himself. Whether he likes to nod or shake his head or wave his arms about, we hat-tippers have got to be prepared for the lot.

You see, these important bigwigs in the leagues loves their high hats. The higher the hat, the more important the wearer – and the trickier it is for his poor hat-tipper. Now, my master Imbix Hoth, his hat is as high as they come and his temper is as sharp as them finger-spikes he likes to wear. Razor-sharp they are, and he's not afraid to use them. I should know. After all, I knew his last hat-tipper, old Sluggin.

Spotted the archway all right, did Sluggin, but forgot about the blustery day outside. The hat fell in the mud and so did Sluggin . . . Imbix and his finger-spikes saw to that! Sluggin never got up, which is when I got chosen.

Like I said, it's a great honour, but it's not an easy job . . .

THE DEEP WOODS

THE TWILIGHT WOODS

THE EDGELANDS

The Edge.

THE EDGE CHRONICLES

CLASH OF THE SKY GALLEONS

PAUL STEWART & CHRIS RIDDELL

CORGI BOOKS

CLASH OF THE SKY GALLEONS
A CORGI BOOK 978 0 552 55127 4

First published in Great Britain by Doubleday,
an imprint of Random House Children's Books
A Random House Group Company

Doubleday edition published 2006
Corgi edition published 2007

1 3 5 7 9 10 8 6 4 2

The Random House Group Limited makes every effort to ensure
that the papers used in its books are made from trees that have been legally sourced
from well-managed and credibly certified forests. Our paper procurement policy
can be found at: www.randomhouse.co.uk/paper.htm

 Mixed Sources
Product group from well-managed
forests and other controlled sources
www.fsc.org Cert no. TT-COC-2139
FSC © 1996 Forest Stewardship Council

Corgi Books are published by Random House Children's Books,
61–63 Uxbridge Road, London W5 5SA

www.kidsatrandomhouse.co.uk
www.rbooks.co.uk

Addresses for companies within The Random House Group Limited can be found
at: www.randomhouse.co.uk/offices.htm

THE RANDOM HOUSE GROUP Limited Reg. No. 954009

A CIP catalogue record for this book is available from the British Library.

Printed in the UK by CPI Bookmarque, Croydon, CR0 4TD

For Joseph, Anna, Jack, Katy and William

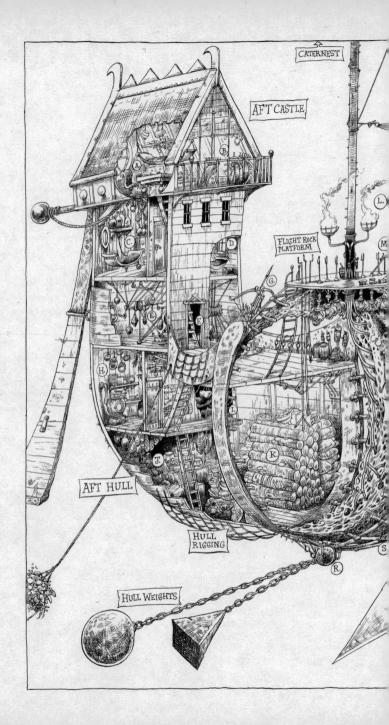

CATERNEST

AFT CASTLE

FLIGHT ROCK
PLATFORM

L.

M.

A.

B.

C.

D.

E.

F.

G.

H.

I.

J.

K.

AFT HULL

HULL
RIGGING

R.

S.

HULL WEIGHTS

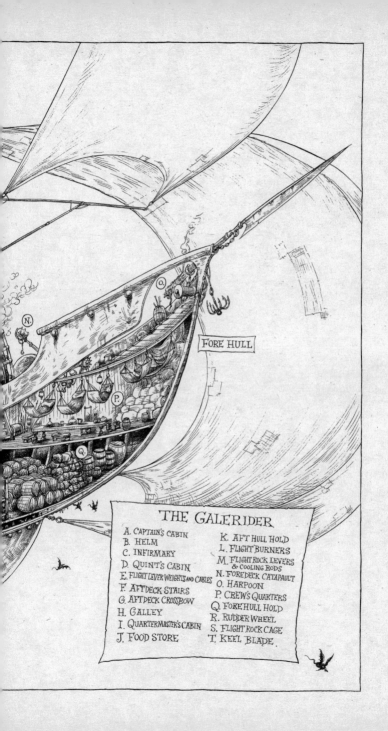

FORE HULL

THE GALERIDER

A. CAPTAIN'S CABIN
B. HELM
C. INFIRMARY
D. QUINT'S CABIN
E. FLIGHT LEVER WEIGHTS AND CABLES
F. AFTDECK STAIRS
G. AFTDECK CROSSBOW
H. GALLEY
I. QUARTERMASTER'S CABIN
J. FOOD STORE

K. AFT HULL HOLD
L. FLIGHT BURNERS
M. FLIGHT ROCK LEVERS & COOLING RODS
N. FOREDECK CATAPAULT
O. HARPOON
P. CREW'S QUARTERS
Q. FOREHULL HOLD
R. RUDDER WHEEL
S. FLIGHT ROCK CAGE
T. KEEL BLADE

INTRODUCTION

It is well to remember one thing about the Edge. Nothing is ever what it seems.

Nowhere is this truer than in the beautiful yet perilous Deepwoods. The fruit of the rosy heartapple, for instance, is sweet, juicy and fragrant, yet a single bite of its golden flesh is enough to strike its victim dead, the corpses round its trunk nourishing the treacherous tree and helping it to grow taller and still more alluring. Likewise wig-wigs. At first sight, these soft, fluffy, orange creatures look cute and harmless. But in an instant, they can part their fur to reveal jaws like bear-traps, and in frenzied packs they devour their prey in a matter of seconds.

Then of course there are the banderbears. With their great curved claws and huge glinting tusks, these massive monsters are indeed ferocious if provoked – yet take the trouble to look behind that terrifying exterior and you will find one of the wisest, noblest, most loyal creatures in all the Edge.

If the Deepwoods is a place of danger and deception, then other parts of the Edge are yet more treacherous.

The Edgelands for instance, with their howling winds and swirling mists, are home to the phantasms, wraiths and strange restless spirits that prey on any who stray there; while the seemingly beautiful and enchanting Twilight Woods are more dangerous still. Here, the eternal half-light of the forest robs those who enter them of their thoughts, their memories, their senses, their minds – and yet refuses to let them die, no matter how hideously decayed they become.

It is, however, beyond the Mire – a vast wilderness of shifting mud and towering dunes, deadly blowholes, sudden mudslides and loathsome scavengers – that perhaps the most insidious dangers of all lie. Here, where tribes and races from all parts of the Edge gather on the very lip of the world, are to be found the mighty twin cities.

Above is Sanctaphrax, the great floating city, with its ancient academies and learned scholars, its fabulous towers and astonishing viaducts. Below lies Undertown, a vast sprawling city of foundries, markets and sky-shipyards; of squalid slums, crowded taverns and magnificent palaces of unsurpassed wealth and opulence. In the twin cities, the unwary and uninformed do not last long. It is essential to keep your eyes and ears open; to learn how things are – and fast!

Learn, for instance, how the proud academics jealously guard their right to harvest the flight-rocks from the Stone Gardens, a place where trespassers face death. Learn also how the Leagues control everything and everyone in Undertown, and would control the sky

itself if only they could. To cross a high-hat leagues-master means death at the hands of a waif assassin – or worse. Yet there are a few who dare to challenge the Leagues of Undertown and their cosy relationship with the academics of Sanctaphrax.

These individuals are known as sky pirates – few in number, certainly, but brave, reckless and bold beyond measure. But the days of these swashbuckling sky pirates – tolerated by the mighty Leagues only because they use their services themselves in their bitter internal feuds and rivalries – may be numbered. The powerful Ruptus Pentephraxis, head of the Leagues of Under-town, and his scheming henchman, Imbix Hoth, Master of the League of Rock Merchants and High Master of the Leagues of Flight, wish to crush the sky pirates once and for all.

Listen in the refectories and cloisters of Sanctaphrax as professors whisper of it. Linger in the taverns of Undertown as sky pirates discuss it. Loiter at the gates of the sky-shipyards, where the yardmasters and their shipwrights talk of little else. There is danger in the air. A great showdown is coming; a reckoning. Everyone senses it. Yet the foundries and workshops bustle with industry as normal, the cradles of the sky-shipyards are full of ships under construction, and the academics await another rock harvest just as they always have.

But it is well to remember one thing about the Edge. Nothing is ever what it seems . . .

*

The Deepwoods, the Stone Gardens, the Edgewater River. Undertown and Sanctaphrax. Names on a map.

Yet behind each name lie a thousand tales – tales that have been recorded in ancient scrolls, tales that have been passed down the generations by word of mouth – tales which even now are being told.

What follows is but one of those tales.

CHAPTER ONE

EDGE WRAITHS

'Not even here in this place of ghosts and demons and half-formed things!' bellowed the wild-eyed sky pirate captain, his voice cracking as he struggled to make himself heard above the screaming wind. 'Not even here will you be safe from my vengeance!'

The sky ship bucked and swayed as it fought against the violent air currents which kept all but the most reckless or foolhardy from venturing over the lip of the Edge and down into the abyss below. For here, where the warm Mire mud cascaded down over the cliff face in huge oozing mudflows and met the icy air currents of the void below, gales and hurricanes and turbulent fog were whipped up into a frenzy.

'No matter how far down into these infernal depths you descend,' Wind Jackal raged, shaking his fist at the eternal gloom below, 'I shall hunt you down . . .'

'Father, please,' the young sky pirate by the captain's side protested, and laid a hand on his shoulder. 'The crew . . .'

Wind Jackal turned from the balustrade at the helm of

the *Galerider*, the look of glazed fury on his face giving way to a frown as he found the eyes of his crew upon him. There was Spillins, the ancient oakelf, high up in the caternest. Ratbit, the swivel-eyed mobgnome, his heavy jacket laden with charms. Steg Jambles, the harpooneer, with young Tem Barkwater, as ever, by his side. Sagbutt, the fierce flat-head goblin, his neck-rings gleaming. And Maris Pallitax, staring up from the fore-deck. They all shared the same expression – one of barely contained panic as they stared wide-eyed at their captain, looking to him for reassurance.

Only the newest member of the crew seemed immune to the terror of this fearful place he had brought them to. The Stone Pilot. Concealed inside the tall conical hood that she never removed, and silent as the day – only weeks earlier – when she had been rescued from the Deepwoods slave market, she tended the flight-rock, seemingly oblivious to all around her. The sight of the Stone Pilot applying the cooling rods and adjusting the blazing sumpwood burners which surrounded the flight-rock seemed to calm the captain, for he took the wheel from his son with a grim smile.

'Forgive me, Quint,' he said, running his hands over the flight-levers. 'It's just that, after all these years, he seems so close . . .'

A blast of wind hit the *Galerider*, making the sky ship shudder from stem to stern, and forcing Wind Jackal to feverishly adjust the hull-weights. His hands raced expertly over the bone-handled flight-levers on either side of the great wheel, raising this one a tad, lowering that one.

'Sky curse this infernal wind!' he snarled, scanning the mud-clogged cliff edge. 'I can't hold her much longer. We must find somewhere to tether . . .'

Suddenly, the strident voice of Spillins cried out from the caternest. 'Jutting rock at fifty strides!'

'Thank Sky,' Wind Jackal murmured, removing his right hand from the hull-weight levers for a split second; just long enough to put the carved tilderhorn amulet gratefully to his lips. 'Hold her steady as you can, Stone Pilot. We're depending on you. Tem! Ratbit!' he bellowed. 'Man the winch! Steg, prepare to descend.'

A chorus of voices and a flurry of movement erupted all round the sky ship as the crew hurried to do their captain's bidding, taking up their positions and getting to grips with the ship's heavy equipment. Ratbit barked commands at the young and lanky Tem Barkwater as the pair of them swung the winding-winch round until the great ironwood wheel was jutting out over the port side of the sky ship. Steg Jambles secured a leather harness round his midriff, seized the rope that dangled from the winch-wheel and attached one to the other.

'Jutting rock directly beneath us!' Spillins shouted down.

Quint and Maris scurried across the deck – skirting round Filbus Queep the thin-faced quartermaster, who had appeared from his quarters above the aft-hold – and peered over the side. Sure enough, there was the single jutting crag that Spillins had spotted, a small island of stillness and stability amidst the constantly shifting Mire. It stood proud of the oozing white mud, which swirled slowly round it, then poured over the edge in great globules that glistened for a moment, before disappearing into the eternal gloom below.

Quint turned and looked up at the flight-rock platform. The Stone Pilot was standing to the left of the great rock, her back towards him. Since the moment they'd first met, the mysterious figure had uttered not a single word. Yet the hunched urgency with which she worked now, feverishly pumping the rock-bellows and riddling the ashes from the roaring furnace, spoke louder than any words.

Every moment the *Galerider* hovered here, untethered over the void, it risked being swept away and lost for ever in Open Sky. But the Stone Pilot was a natural, whose skills seemed to grow with every passing day. Under her care now, the heated flight-rock was gradually becoming less buoyant and the *Galerider* was descending towards the jutting rock.

'Now, Steg! *Now!*' bellowed the captain, his hands leaping from lever to bone-handled lever as he fought to keep the sky ship hovering motionless in place.

Steg Jambles didn't need telling twice. He tested the rope with a quick tug – just to be on the safe side – before stepping off the side of the ship. Tem and Ratbit took the strain and, when Steg had gathered himself, began turning the pulley-lever. Slowly, carefully, they lowered the thick-set fore-decker down through the air towards the jutting rock.

At the balustrade, Maris gripped Quint's arm and turned to look up at him, her dark eyes glistening with a mixture of awe and excitement. Ever since Wind Jackal had plucked the pair of them away from Sanctaphrax those few short weeks earlier, she had seen so much: the snow-white desolation of the Mire, the treacherous glow of the Twilight Woods, the endless canopy of the Deepwoods from above – as well as the horrors of the slave market from which both the Stone Pilot and Tem Barkwater had been rescued. But this . . . this was the most chilling place they had visited so far, and she shivered with dread.

'The great void,' she murmured tremulously. 'The realm of ghosts and demons and . . . what was it your father said?'

'Half-formed things,' said Quint, staring down at the fore-decker dangling below.

'*Stop!*' Steg's bellowed command was just audible above the turbulent air.

Tem and Ratbit stopped turning the winch at once, and slid the locking bolt across. Far below, Steg gripped hold of a rough chunk of the jutting rock with one white-knuckled hand, while with the other, he unhooked the glinting rock-spike from his sky pirate coat.

'When you're ready, Master Steg!' Wind Jackal called out from the helm, battling to hold the ship steady, as the howling wind battered and buffeted it, seemingly from all sides at once.

Steg thrust the pointed end of the spur into a narrow crack in the rock then, with a great round-bowled hammer that he'd unhooked from his belt, he pounded

the spike into place with a flurry of colossal blows. As the sound of Steg's hammer blows rose up from below, Wind Jackal smiled grimly.

'Be ready with that tolley-rope, Master Tem,' he bellowed down at Steg's mate.

'Aye-aye, Captain,' Tem called back.

'Spike secured!' Steg's voice floated up from below. He had driven the metal spike deep into the crack in the rock.

'Tolley-rope, Master Tem!' Wind Jackal's command rang out.

Quint looked down to see Tem Barkwater lean out over the balustrade and hurl the length of thick rope down to Steg Jambles. It uncoiled as it dropped. One end was secured to a tolley-post at the prow, the other dropped into Steg's outstretched hands. With a deft turn, twist and threading through of the rope, he fashioned a perfect tilder-knot – so called because it was the type of knot used by slaughterer hunters to snare and bind any migrating tilder that happened past their hides – and slipped it over the head of the spike. He gave it a sharp tug. The rope closed round the shaft of metal.

'Tolley-rope secured!' he shouted. 'Pull me up!'

Tem and Ratbit jumped to the winch-handle and began turning. A moment later, Steg Jambles's tousled head appeared above the balustrade. He grinned.

'The old *Galerider* is tethered, Captain,' he said as he jumped down onto the deck. 'Should hold for a little while yet.'

'Let's hope so, Master Steg,' said Wind Jackal, descending the stairs from the helm. He turned towards Quint, his eyes blazing with a frightening intensity. 'I've waited many a long year for this moment,' he said. 'For your mother's sake, Sky rest her soul, and your dear lost brothers . . . Will you come with me and watch my back, Quint?'

'You know I will,' said Quint, clasping his father's arm and following him to the prow.

Maris gazed after them, the blood draining from her face. 'Sky protect you, Quint,' she said hoarsely, her voice little more than a whisper.

As Wind Jackal and Quint arrived on the fore-deck, Tem and Ratbit realigned the winding-winch and swung a second winch round into position next to it. Quint eyed the dangling harnesses warily, his courage beginning to drain away.

'Don't just stand there, lad,' Wind Jackal was saying, looking up as he secured the harness straps around his legs and waist. 'Get yourself buckled in. I need you, lad ... If anything were to happen, I want to know that you'll finish the job off.'

Quint nodded. 'You can count on me, Father,' he said, climbing into his harness. 'After all, I was there, too, remember.'

The pair of them climbed up onto the balustrade. Tem was manning Wind Jackal's winding-winch; Steg Jambles, Quint's. At a word from Wind Jackal, both he and his son stepped off the *Galerider* and into mid air.

Quint's stomach lurched. The harness tightened around the top of his legs as the winding-winch creaked into motion and the rope began to descend. He'd seen how the wind had turned and twisted the suspended Steg Jambles, but nothing could have prepared him for the sheer violence of the turbulent air. It hit him like a blow to the ribs and sent him spinning round and round.

'Stick your legs out, son,' he heard Wind Jackal calling across to him and, when he looked round, he saw his father bent double, his legs jutting forwards at right angles to his body.

Quint did the same. The spinning stopped and, as the rope continued to be let out, he found himself drawing level with the jutting rock the *Galerider* had been anchored to. A moment later, and the sheer rock face of the Edge itself was directly in front of him. He planted his legs squarely against the great wall of rock and, as the rope was released from above, began making his way down the vertical rock face in leaps.

The wind howled louder than ever down here in the perpetual shadow of the void beneath the Edge, and it was cold – so cold that, even though there was sweat running down his back, Quint's teeth chattered and his breath came in foggy puffs of air. Every so often, there would be a soft *ploff-ploff* sound from above him and a huge column of steaming Mire mud would whistle past him, breaking up as it did so and showering him and his father with a viscous, fetid-smelling spray.

Wind Jackal swung over towards his son and signalled for him to remain silent, before pointing to the gloom below. Quint glanced down. There, huddled in the shadowy darkness some fifty or so strides below him, were a series of vivid scars cut into the cliff face: jagged ledges, one above

another, covered with the remains of lufwood roofing, splintered and wrecked by the howling winds.

These must be the abandoned ledges of the ancient cliff quarry from the time of the First Scholars, Quint realized with a shudder. It looked as strange and ghostly as the priceless rock that was quarried there.

Quint ran his hand over the rock before him. Dark and grainy, rough to the touch and stained with the white Mire mud, it did not look anything special. He knew, however, that when it was polished, the rock was transformed into a shimmering, shining material that glowed from within, as though countless glisters had been sealed within it, like insects inside fossilized pine-sap.

Highly prized by the early architects of Sanctaphrax, the polished rock was the chosen material for decorating the increasingly ostentatious schools and academies which sprang up around the great floating city. It was used in small amounts to top towers or crenellate rooftops, or to provide a detail or two above an arch – and so it would have remained if it hadn't been for the Academy of Wind.

When its high professor at the time, one Aurelius Ventilix, heard that the School of Light and Darkness was to have its upper towers clad in cliff-marble – as the substance was commonly known – he decided that the Academy of Wind should not be outdone. Consulting with his architects and organizing what was to become the first of the Leagues of Undertown, he determined that every inch of his own school of learning would be clad in the priceless rock – even striking a deal with the cliff quarry to ensure that all consignments of rock slabs were delivered to the Academy of Wind and nowhere else.

Soon, the Academy of Wind had become the most spectacular building in all of Sanctaphrax. During the day, the polished walls swirled with ever-changing patterns of light, while at night the whole building glowed brightly, shining out like a magnificent beacon which could be seen for miles around. Mire travellers took to using it as a reliable landmark, while even migrating snowbirds were observed to orientate themselves by its light.

They, however, were not the only creatures to be attracted to the resplendent edifice. At first, the gatherings of tiny lights clustering close to the walls were dismissed as being glow-worms, fireflies, embermoths. It was only when their numbers grew that their true identity was revealed.

They were glisters.

Countless millions of the microscopic creatures – those elemental seeds of life, blown in from Open Sky and residing deep within the porous Sanctaphrax rock – were leaving their subterranean home and gathering all round the Academy of Wind. To those outside, watching, they made an attractive spectacle. Inside the institute, however, it was a different story. Surrounded by the mass of minute creatures which not only fed on emotions, but also affected them, those within the academy began to change – and not for the better.

The normally calm academic atmosphere was suffused with terror, rage and seemingly irrational displays of envy and despair. And all the while, the number of glisters clustered round the outer walls increased. Then one night, when the moon was full, a huge swarm of the minute creatures covered the academy, clogging its doors, its windows and gateways. From inside there came terrible sounds, howls of rage and screams of despair – listened to with awestruck terror by the academics from the other schools outside.

By the time morning dawned the next day, an awful quiet had descended upon the academy. When the noon-day bell tolled the hour, the academics outside could bear it no longer. Taking their courage in their hands, they broke down the doors to the academy – to reveal a bloodbath within. Driven mad by the glisters, the academics of the Academy of Wind had slaughtered each other until none remained alive.

Needless to say, the Sanctaphrax academics were appalled, and ordered the immediate removal of the cliff-marble cladding – not only from the Academy of Wind, but also from the upper towers of the School of Light and Darkness, the turrets of the Colleges of Cloud and Rain, and everywhere else the beguilingly beautiful polished rock had been used. The only place it remained was the West Wall of the Knights Academy.

The proud knights academic defied the other academies and refused to demolish their beautiful wall – indeed they rather enjoyed the way it kept their in-quisitive neighbours away. But few academics, even the knights academic themselves, would linger for long at the Great West Wall at night when its surface sparkled with tiny dancing glisters.

Quint, in particular, was wary of the place. After all, he had once ventured deep into the heart of the Sanctaphrax rock and had seen first hand what could happen when the reckless and the unwise meddled with these strange, beguiling creatures . . .

That aside, the horror triggered by the events that took place at the Academy of Wind was enough to put an end to the quarrying of the rock. Work stopped immediately and was never resumed, and the cliff quarries fell into disuse.

At Wind Jackal's signal, Quint followed him down the cliff face towards the quarry ledges, fifty or so strides below. When they landed on the first narrow ledge carved into the cliff face, Quint noticed that his father had unsheathed his sword. Grim-faced, he motioned for Quint to do the same, then began inching his way along the narrow cutting, which was no wider than a window ledge. Here and there, overhead, the remains of an awning – erected to protect the ancient quarry-workers from the howling wind and falling Mire mud – stuck out from the rock.

Not that it offered much protection now, for the jutting struts had snapped off and the lufwood planks were splintered and warped. Those that remained creaked and groaned and seemed to give the howling wind a new and sinister voice, as if the spirits of the long-dead stone masons were calling out a ghostly warning. Quint tried to shut out the awful noise as he crept along the ledge after his father, but in vain . . .

'Don't allow your harness rope to get snagged,' Wind Jackal hissed over his shoulder, 'or they'll never be able to winch us out of here.'

Following his father's example, Quint checked that the rope above his head was clear of the struts of the wrecked awning as he continued. At the end of the cutting, Wind Jackal paused for a moment, before swinging out across the cliff face and descending to the ledge below. Quint followed close behind, and again they inched along the narrow cutting, their backs pressed against the smooth, quarried surface of the cliff face. Down they went, from ledge to ledge, until the gloom thickened and the ghostly howling made speech impossible.

Quint gripped his sword tightly and felt the reassuring tautness of the harness rope tug at his shoulder. It was good knowing that up there, in the light, Steg Jambles was holding onto the other end. Three short tugs and the harpooneer would winch him out of this waking nightmare.

Ghosts and demons and half-formed things ... Quint swallowed hard as his father's words sounded in his head. How desperate was the one they hunted that he sought refuge in such a terrible place?

Still deep in thought, Quint felt his father's hand on his shoulder. They had come to the lowest of the quarry ledges. Below them, the cliff face sloped sharply away into an inky blackness, and in front of them, the narrow ledge ended beside a narrow crack in the rock face, like a gap in some huge stone curtain – deep, dark and only inches wide.

Wind Jackal raised the hilt of his great sky pirate sabre to his lips and kissed it, then, checking his harness rope, he stepped inside.

At the prow of the *Galerider* Tem Barkwater turned the winch-wheel, feeding out the rope as steadily as he could manage. Beside him, Steg Jambles was doing the same.

'How do you think they're getting on down there?' Tem murmured, his bony face wide-eyed with anxiety.

'Don't go concerning yourself with that, lad,' said Steg. 'The captain and his son have unfinished business to sort out down there. *Personal* business!' He fixed the gaunt youth with an unblinking stare. 'It's up to you and me to keep feeding this here rope out nice and steady until they're ready to come up.'

Tem nodded.

'And when they give three tugs on this rope, then . . .'

'We winch them up,' Tem blurted out eagerly.

Steg smiled. 'Like your life depends on it, Tem, lad. Like your life depends on it!'

The moment Wind Jackal and Quint stepped inside the narrow fissure in the cliff face, the howling of the wind was instantly shut out – only to be replaced with a dank and eerie stillness. Some way in the distance, a pale light was flickering. Quint's mouth was dry and gritty with Mire mud, and he could feel the blood thumping in his temples.

Just ahead of him, his father crept along the narrow tunnel between the two huge walls of rock, his sword held out in front of him, the rope from his harness trailing out behind. Carefully, silently, scarcely daring to breathe, Quint followed. He must watch his father's back, he told himself, be prepared to step in if he was needed; if something should go wrong . . .

The light grew brighter and Wind Jackal hesitated, then motioned for Quint to join him. Just ahead of them, some sort of chamber had been carved out of the tunnel wall.

At its entrance, stacked against the wall, lay a heap of ancient chisels, rock-hammers and quarrying tools,

while above them was a
row of hooks, from which
hung decaying cloaks,
frayed gloves and long,
pointed hoods that looked
for all the world like
long-dead, desiccated
woodmoths. Inside the
chamber, a hunched figure
was squatting beneath a
huge, ancient lamp – its
light pale and feeble as the
last of the tilder oil burned
itself out.

Quint glanced at his
father and was shocked to see a look of pure hatred
contorting his features. With a hideous cry, like that of a
wounded beast, Wind Jackal launched himself into the
chamber and brought his heavy sabre down on the
squatting figure in a savage, vicious sweep. There was
an explosion of blood and guts as the bloated, lifeless
sack disintegrated with the blow and Quint and Wind
Jackal found themselves covered in stinking tilder
entrails.

Wind Jackal stared for a moment at his son, his face
blood-spattered and shocked, before the lamp spluttered
out and pitched them into absolute darkness.

'Nothing but a tilder-leather sack, filled with blood . . .
Sky curse my blind thirst for vengeance!' Quint's father
groaned. 'I've led us into a trap . . .'

'Father, I . . . Did you feel that?' Quint's harness rope twitched and bucked.

In the darkness, Quint heard the weary sky pirate captain sigh unhappily. Then the harness rope twitched again, more violently this time, and from the direction of the tunnel came an ominous rustling, scratching sound . . .

'Three tugs!' said Tem. 'I felt them . . .'

'Me, too,' agreed Steg Jambles. 'Well, what are you waiting for?' He frowned at the young deckhand. 'Winch, lad! Winch!'

Tem leaped at the winch-wheel and began winding it furiously. 'I know, I know, you don't have to tell me,' he shouted over his shoulder to the harpooneer. 'As if my life depends on it!'

'*Whoooah!*' Quint cried out, as he found himself being dragged back towards the tunnel entrance – and closer to the scratching, snuffling sounds.

Behind him, Wind Jackal stumbled on the end of his own harness rope. 'Whatever you do,' he shouted to Quint, 'don't cut the rope, or we'll never get out of here.'

'What's out there?' Quint whispered, as he slid and slithered through the pitch-black darkness of the tunnel, like an oozefish on the end of a line.

'Only one way to find out,' answered his father, and Quint found something hard and shiny being pressed into his hand.

It was a piece of sky-crystal; Quint could tell from its smooth, round shape. He slammed it against the tunnel wall and it glowed in his hand with a warm, yellow light. Behind him, Wind Jackal did the same and together they held their glowing fists up above their heads as they approached the tunnel entrance, half running as the harness ropes dragged them ever faster.

There, blocking the narrow fissure, was a huge, white creature, its thin papery wings folded tightly behind it as it squeezed into the entrance. It had massive watery eyes that seemed far too big for its shrunken, skull-like head, and long, spidery hind-legs that stretched out towards them, glinting with long, needle-like talons. Thin spittle-like drool dripped from its jaws which, as Quint watched, seemed to dislocate as they opened to become impossibly huge.

'*Khhhaaah!*'

The sound it let out was long, harsh and rasping, a blast of air that came from the very depths of its angular body and was expelled with great force from its gaping maw. Its head darted from side to side, the tiny nasal flaps at the top of its beak-like mouth flickering furiously. It was the smell of fetid tilder blood that had drawn it into the tunnel, like a woodmoth to a candle.

'The neck!' Wind Jackal shouted. 'Aim for the neck!'

Quint gripped his sword and raised his forearm to fend off the lunging attack that instantly came. He felt the vice-like jaws crunch into his arm with the pain of a thousand hot needles, before swinging his sword in an upward arc.

A high-pitched shriek, choked off in mid-screech, followed by the sounds of crunching bone and the crumpling of papery wings, filled Quint's ears – before he found himself bursting from the tunnel's entrance at the end of the harness rope and swinging free in the dark, freezing air. Below him, the hideous creature tumbled away into the murky blackness, its glassy-eyed head separated from its body.

Some way behind him, Wind Jackal also swung clear of the tunnel, before rising up alongside Quint on the end of his own harness rope.

'Winch, you skycurs!' roared his father. 'Winch us out of here!'

In front of Quint, the quarry ledges and the rock face sped past in a blur as the violent wind howled once more in his ears.

From below there came more hideous screeches, as three more creatures swooped up out of the infernal darkness. Their papery wingspans were the size of sky ships, and their gaping jaws wide enough to swallow a full-grown hammelhorn whole. Yet for all that, their white bodies were skeletally thin, and looked as delicate as a spindlebug's. Round they circled, calling to each other, and coming ever closer to this tempting, dangling bait – so much tastier and more substantial than the dried-out morsels of carrion that the Mire mud filtered down to them in the depths below.

In their harnesses, Quint and Wind Jackal flailed desperately with their swords as the creatures swooped, dived and snapped at them with their razor-sharp teeth. Each time a creature glided past, Quint caught sight of its huge, swivelling eyes, the irises enlarging and contracting as if calculating exactly when and where to strike.

His arm was throbbing painfully now, and he was nearing exhaustion. How long could he keep these hideous creatures from the phantasmal depths at bay?

Quint glanced across at his father, dripping – like himself – with rancid tilder blood, and swinging his heavy sabre in a figure of eight in front of him. Above, the hull of the *Galerider* had come into view.

'Not far now,' he murmured to himself. 'Not far now . . .'

'*Waaaarch!*'

A creature – the pupils of its huge eyes fully dilated – managed to avoid the flashing blade and glanced past Quint, tearing his sky pirate coat at the shoulder with trailing talons as it did so.

'Winch! Sky take your souls!' Wind Jackal roared up at the sky ship as another of the creatures swooped and snarled above his head.

It glided round, its eyes wide and staring, and closed in for the kill. Then suddenly, as Quint was beginning to fear the worst, a bright arc of light shot through the air and straight through the papery wings of first one, then another of the vast flapping creatures. For a moment they seemed to hover in mid air, before bursting – like great paper lanterns – into brilliant flame and hurtling down into the blackness. With a screech of alarm, the third creature broke off its attack and fled back to the safety of the void.

Moments later, Steg and Tem were hauling Quint and his father on board, looks of shock on their faces as they saw the blood-spattered state of their faces and clothes.

'Edge wraiths,' said Filbus Queep the quartermaster, shaking his head. 'Foul creatures of the void . . .'

'But what happened to them?' Quint asked, clambering out of his harness with the help of Tem.

'Harpoon dipped in flaming sumpwood tar,' said Steg proudly.

Quint looked up to see Maris smiling down at him, trying hard to conceal the look of fear and concern on her face.

'It was Mistress Maris's idea, and it worked a treat,' Steg continued. 'Now, with your permission, Captain, perhaps we can get out of this accursed place.'

But Wind Jackal wasn't listening. He was standing at the balustrade, gazing down into the bottomless void, his eyes glittering from beneath a mask of dried tilder blood.

'This isn't over,' he muttered through clenched teeth. 'In fact, this is just the beginning . . . !'

·CHAPTER TWO·

GLAVIEL GLYNTE

As he approached the heavy, studded leadwood door, the young sky pirate captain paused, raked his fingers through his unruly thatch of thick fair hair and set a bicorne hat of polished leather on his head at a jaunty angle. Adjusting his neckerchief and smoothing his ornate frock coat, he glanced up at the tavern sign creaking rhythmically as it swung back and forth in the cold northerly wind. The sign, like the tavern itself, had clearly seen better days.

The ornate ironwork was rusty, the hinges warped, while the painting itself – an image of a glistening green vine writhing over a pile of cracked skulls and bleached bones – was faded and flaked. Despite all this, the menace in the picture was unmistakable.

The tarry vine was a parasite. It lived in symbiosis with the fearful bloodoak in the darkness of the Deepwoods, its roots sunk deep into the blistered bark of the tree. Attracted to warm-blooded creatures, it would lassoo prey, drag it to its host and deposit it into the bloodoak's great mandibled maw. Then, as the tree crushed the life out of its victim, the vine would gorge itself on the hapless creature's blood.

The Tarry Vine tavern had been aptly named, the sky pirate thought ruefully as he stepped inside the huge slab of a building, with its rows of dimly glowing windows and shuttered roof garrets. For here, in the bustling backstreets of Undertown, the twinkling lights of those windows and roof garrets, and the heady aroma of woodhops escaping from the gently smoking brew-chimneys above, snared unsuspecting passers-by and dragged them inside with a grip as tight and unyielding as any Deepwoods tarry vine. Once inside, as the young sky pirate knew only too well, the tavern's very own version of the bloodoak awaited . . .

'Well, well, well, if it isn't my old friend, Thaw Daggerslash!' came a gruff voice.

A portly gnokgoblin in a high-collared jerkin lounged on a large, ornately carved throne beside a heavy tapestry curtain. A tallow lamp above his head cast a feeble yellow light over the narrow chamber.

'Evening, Jaggs,' said Thaw Daggerslash coolly, unbuckling his sword and handing it over.

The gnokgoblin scratched his belly and looked the sky pirate slyly up and down.

'Covered in Mire mud, I see,' he leered. 'Been trying your luck at pearl-hunting, have you? A bit desperate for a fine young sky pirate captain, I'd have thought. Haven't got a nice cosy sky ship yet, then?' Jaggs gave a throaty chuckle and threw the sword onto the untidy pile at his feet.

The young sky pirate forced himself to smile in reply. 'Thanks for your concern, Jaggs, old mate,' he said. 'Mire-pearling is for mugs. I've got bigger oozefish to fry.'

The gnokgoblin raised his heavy eyebrows in sarcastic surprise, then leaned across and drew back the tapestry curtain, with its woven pattern of writhing tarry vines.

'Too high and mighty to sign on as crew,' Jaggs taunted as Thaw pushed past him. 'You dress up as a sky pirate captain and think you are one. Well, I'll tell you this for nothing, it's not as easy as that – frying oozefish or no frying oozefish!'

'We'll see, Jaggs, old mate,' the sky pirate called over his shoulder as he knocked on the door in front of him.

It swung open and he stepped inside. Instantly, he found himself engulfed in the seething, heady atmosphere of the most notorious tavern in all Undertown.

A deep, rumbling cacophony of conversation was overlaid with intermittent explosions of noise: bellowing voices, raucous laughter and snatches of rousing songs. There was back-slapping and boot-stamping; there was ladle-sloshing, trough-sluicing and tankard-clunking; and the constant clatter of huge kegs being rolled over the floor, as the serving-goblins replaced the empty ones with full ones.

And as each fresh barrel was tipped into the foaming drinking troughs, so the nutty aroma of fresh woodale would join the more pungent odours of the hall. Acrid tallow smoke from the dim lanterns, roasting ironwood acorns from the hanging braziers, and the strange, musky smell of wet sky pirate coats slowly drying in the warm air,

as their owners sat hunched over the quaff-tables, slumped at the drinking-troughs or jostled each other at the huge ale vats.

Wizened quartermasters, burly deckmates and harpooneers, swaggering sky pirate captains and their hulking bodyguards – every size, shape and type of sky pirate seemed to be represented in the high-gabled, cavernous drinking hall. Thaw Daggerslash took a deep breath and, with as much swagger as he could muster, made his way through the throng.

A gangly mobgnome brushed past him, a tray of brimming tankards balanced on her upraised hand.

'You there,' he said, seizing her by an arm. 'Is Glaviel Glynte in tonight?'

The mobgnome spun round, a look of irritation in her eyes – which melted away when she found herself looking into the kind, noble face of the handsome young sky pirate captain.

'The tavern master, sir?' Flustered, she blushed and lowered her gaze. 'I . . . I think . . . that is to say . . .'

'Yes?' Thaw smiled at her.

'You could try the garrets, sir.'

The mobgnome turned and pointed up, past the rows of kegs lining the second and third storeys, towards the upper balconies, far above their heads. As she did so, the tray balanced on her hand wobbled and threatened to tumble to the floor. Thaw steadied it, his hands brushing against hers. She blushed all the more fiercely.

'Good luck, sir,' she said, and with that, scurried away.

Turning on his heels, Thaw Daggerslash headed for the stairs that led up to the balconies, passing through the huddled clusters of sky pirates as he went. Mingling together in the Tarry Vine tavern, there seemed to be members of every tribe and clan in the Edgelands – mobgnomes, cloddertrogs, brogtrolls, slaughterers, waifs and goblins of every type, from lop-ears and hammerheads, to long-haired and tusked.

In stark contrast, Thaw Daggerslash himself was a fourthling – and proud of it.

Unlike the tribes and clans of the Deepwoods, who identified closely with their own kind and shared fierce loyalties and cherished customs, fourthlings could not clearly be categorized. They weren't goblins or trogs, waifs or trolls, but often had shared ancestors who were all of these and more. Kobold the Wise, leader of the

Thousand Tribes centuries before the floating city of Sanctaphrax was even dreamed of, had named these outsiders fourthlings – for the blood of the tribes from all four corners of the Edgelands mingled in their veins.

Ever since then, fourthlings had made their way in the world without the benefits of clanship and tribal protection. Instead, they worked and lived amongst their Edgeland neighbours, becoming slaughterers or woodtroll timberers as the occasion presented. The trogs and the goblin tribes of the Deepwoods refused to have anything to do with fourthlings, but in the great melting pot of Undertown, these same fourthlings prospered.

They became sky pirates and Sanctaphrax professors, leaguesmen and merchants. Here in the bustling city, tribes lost much of their importance, and power and influence was gained through guile and cunning, not clan loyalty.

Yes, Thaw Daggerslash was proud indeed to be a fourthling.

There was a smirk on his lips as he turned the corner of the long flight of stairs and, doubling back on himself, continued past the stacks of giant kegs onto the high balconies. Up there, where the rafters divided the broad ledge-like floor into garret alcoves, the light from the overhead lamps was at its brightest – though, paradoxically, it was also where the darkest shadows were cast.

Thaw Daggerslash made his way along the upper balustrade, glancing into the individual garrets, where only the most important sky pirate captains – and the occasional high leaguesman – could be glimpsed, sitting at low tables in furtive conversation. He was halfway along the balcony when he heard the unmistakable nasal voice of Glaviel Glynte.

'And I'm telling you,' the tavern keeper was saying, 'if you haven't paid up in three days, then the *Mistmizzen* goes back to the boom-docks.' Thaw could hear the sound of him cracking his knuckles, one after the other. 'What's more,' he hissed, 'I'd rather rip out its flight-rock and sell it on to the Leagues; I'd rather turn its timbers into furnacewood before I ever let you captain her again. Do I make myself clear?'

'C . . . c . . . crystal clear,' came the stammered response.

'Glad to hear it,' snapped Glynte. 'Now, get out!'

Thaw stood back as the hapless sky pirate captain scurried past him, head down and cheeks burning. It couldn't be easy for a captain to have his cherished sky ship threatened with destruction like that – but then, Thaw realized, he must have known the risks when he first came to the Tarry Vine tavern in search of a loan. He was probably lured by the thought of adventure and riches, snagged by the tavern's promise, only to find himself in the clutches of the grasping bloodoak himself, Glaviel Glynte.

Glynte was well known for backing ambitious captains whom other more cautious tavern keepers had turned down. But if they didn't deliver on his investment, Glaviel Glynte was notorious for destroying a sky pirate as completely as a bloodoak devours its prey.

Thaw sighed thoughtfully. Now he was in the same situation as so many ambitious young sky pirates before him, coming cap in hand to this fearsome tavern keeper. That, he told himself, was as far as the similarity went. He would honour his debts, he'd make sure of it – for Thaw Daggerslash had no intention of allowing Glynte to destroy him. Thaw was going to captain a sky ship of his own and make his fortune.

Perhaps one day, he thought with a smile, he'd be as rich as the tavern keeper – for Glynte was rich. Very, very rich.

He, like so many other Undertown tavern keepers, had acquired his wealth by investing in sky pirate ships and then taking a hefty cut of the profits. From modest beginnings, he had built up a successful empire and now boasted a share in more than fifty separate vessels – as well as a magnificent palace in the Western Quays.

There were many who were jealous of his wealth, not least amongst the leaguesmen, but since the Tarry Vine tavern was a safe haven for all sky pirates – particularly when the Leagues were indulging in one of their perennial purges – the sky pirates, in turn, offered him their unqualified protection. In the skies above the Edgelands, league ships and sky pirate ships engaged in a constant struggle, but on the streets of Undertown, an uneasy truce was tolerated by all sides.

'Next!' Glaviel Glynte's voice barked out.

The character before Thaw – a short lugtroll with a squint – started back and suddenly scuttled away, apparently losing his nerve right at the last moment. Now at the front of the line, Thaw stepped forward into the small garret.

'Sit down, sit down,' Glynte told him impatiently without looking up.

Thaw did as he was bid, stumbling slightly as he moved, for the stool, bathed in shadows, was lower than he'd anticipated. It was also positioned so that the lamp above him shone directly in his eyes. Glynte ignored him. Hunched over a vast leather-bound ledger, a scratchy quill in his right hand, he was busy transferring one column of numbers into the next. Beside him was his assistant, a tousle-feathered, beady-eyed shryke, who sat motionless and stared unblinking into mid air, an overbearing seen-it-all-before attitude about her.

Thaw could feel his confidence ebbing away as the tavern keeper continued to ignore him. He cleared his throat and leaned forward on the low stool, and was about to say something when Glaviel Glynte abruptly looked up.

'What can I do for you?' he asked in a low, silky voice, with just a hint of menace.

The tavern keeper's politeness disarmed Thaw momentarily.

'I need ... That is, I would like ... I mean, if you ...'

Glaviel Glynte laid his pen down and fixed the callow sky pirate with an intense stare. Beside him, the shryke matron turned her own unblinking eyes on him. Thaw swallowed hard.

'Spit it out, son,' said Glynte. 'We haven't got all day, have we, Sister Horsefeather?'

The bird-creature shook her head from side to side while maintaining her unbroken gaze on Thaw's face.

'Sorry sir,' said Thaw. 'It's just . . . I need a loan. A small loan. Just enough to get me started.' He took a deep breath. 'I need to recruit a crew and equip a sky ship . . .'

'You *have* a sky ship?' Glynte's eyes narrowed.

'Not exactly . . .' Thaw wavered under the intensity of two sets of piercing eyes. 'I mean . . . I could have . . .'

Glynte and Horsefeather exchanged knowing looks. The shryke opened her beak.

'The tavern keeper isn't interested in "not exactly"s and "could have"s!' she rasped. 'Do you have a sky ship, or not?'

Thaw blushed furiously and looked down at his feet.

'No, not yet . . .'

'Then the tavern keeper can advance you fifty gold pieces – enough for a simple sky barge and one deckhand,' clucked Horsefeather. 'And you can leave your fine notions of being a sky pirate captain for when you're a little older. Take it or leave it.'

Ignoring the shryke, Thaw turned to Glaviel Glynte, his scalp itching with frustration.

'Fifty gold pieces,' he said bleakly. 'But . . . but I was hoping for at least ten times that amount. I need the loan to get the crew on my side, then . . .'

'Sky ship first, boy,' clucked the shryke. 'Then money for crew. Do you want the barge or not?'

'But . . .' began Thaw.

The tavern keeper slammed the flat of his hand down on the table-top. 'Next!' he bellowed.

'So what *were* we doing out there at the cliff quarries?' Tem murmured.

'Yes, Quint,' whispered Maris, 'why did your father sail to such a terrible place?'

The three of them were sitting in the far corner of the Tarry Vine at a long, old table, its dark surface pitted and scarred with the carved names of generations of sky pirates. Opposite them were the other crew-members: old Spillins the oakelf, Ratbit the mobgnome and Sagbutt the flat-head, Steg Jambles the harpooneer, and Filbus Queep the quartermaster, engaged in their own hushed conversation.

Wind Jackal was sitting at the head of the table, his brow furrowed and his eyes glassy, lost in dark thoughts of his own. Of the crew of the *Galerider*, only the Stone Pilot was absent – but then she never liked coming ashore, preferring instead to go below deck to her cabin, where she would curl up in her hammock in the darkness, and dream.

'Perhaps you should ask my father that question,' said Quint, looking across at the sky pirate captain.

All eyes turned to Wind Jackal, who was tracing the long-forgotten names carved on the ancient table with his forefinger.

'I thought he was dead,' Wind Jackal said slowly. 'Perished in that terrible fire that killed my beloved family, and from which only my son Quintinius escaped . . .'

His eyes glistened, but behind the tears there was a frightening intensity to his gaze. Quint reached out and patted his father's arm.

'Turbot Smeal!' Wind Jackal almost spat the words out, so laden with hatred they seemed to be.

Around the table, the crew-members nodded their heads reverently. Everyone knew of the terrible fire that his ambitious and vindictive quartermaster had started in Wind Jackal's house when the young sky pirate captain had been away.

It had blazed ferociously, spreading and engulfing half of the buildings in the Western Quays before fire sky ships had finally managed to quench the flames with water scooped from the Edgewater River. By the time the fire was doused, however, it had already taken the lives of his wife, Hermina, five of his six sons and their nanny. When he returned, only Quint – at five years old, his youngest – was there to greet him.

'I swore there and then that I would avenge the death of my loved ones; that I would find Turbot Smeal and bring him to justice . . .' Wind Jackal's eyes blazed. 'Justice! Pah! What justice was there that scum like him would understand?'

His voice took on an ice-cold clarity. 'There in the smoking embers of my home, I planned what to do with him when I caught him. I would hang, draw and quarter him. I would drench him in blood, tie him up in the Stone Gardens and leave it to the white ravens to pluck out his eyes, his tongue, his still-beating heart ... I wanted him, drowned, burned, garotted, beheaded, sky-fired ... Anything! I wanted to see him die!'

He paused and, clasping the sides of the table, stared round into the circle of faces, one after the other. And, one after the other, those faces looked back down at the table, pained and embarrassed, and unable to respond. Quint's heart thumped. His face was flushed.

'F ... Father,' he began, and reached again for Wind Jackal's arm.

This time the sky pirate captain brushed him aside.

'But it wasn't to be,' he said, his voice as cold and sharp as a newly forged sword. 'And why not? Because that filthy, low-down, no good son of a gutter vulpoon was already dead.' He snorted. 'Burned himself to death in the fire, didn't he?' A small, unpleasant smile tugged at the corner of his mouth. 'At least, that was what everyone believed. There were even eye-witness reports that said he'd been seen on fire, trying to flee through the blazing streets.'

The crew, who had been looking away, turned back.

'And I believed them for so long,' he said. 'Until one afternoon, twelve years after the fire, almost to the day, a ratbird arrived with a message telling me I'd find the miserable wretch in an obscure slave-market clearing in the middle of the Deepwoods.'

Maris gasped involuntarily.

Wind Jackal sighed. 'The ratbird died in my hands, and the note was unsigned. But I had to find out if it was true . . .' He looked across at his son. 'That's why I picked you up and took you from the Knights Academy, son. Oh, I know I snatched you from your studies, putting on hold that great day when you might set forth on a stormchasing quest to the Twilight Woods – and for that I am truly sorry. But I needed you with me. This was a family matter . . .'

Quint nodded, but Maris could see that he was troubled.

'Of course, things didn't work out the way I had hoped, and we got distracted by that business with the Stone Pilot.' Quint and Maris both smiled. 'But when we got back to Undertown, an old Mire pirate told me of a rumour he'd heard that Smeal had found a new hide-out . . .'

'The cliff quarry,' Tem breathed.

'Just so,' said Wind Jackal. 'And *that* was why we went down there, Quint and I, to get our revenge once and for all.' He shook his head. 'Yet once again we were thwarted. It was a trap. Smeal must know we're on his trail. He laid an ambush – leading us down into the quarry, then luring those foul wraiths to devour us.' His eyes took on a steely intensity as, once again, he surveyed the gathering around the table. 'But thanks to you, my loyal crew, we survived to continue the hunt.'

Quint swallowed anxiously. Maris cupped his hands in her own beneath the table-top, and squeezed.

'I intend to hunt him until I catch him,' Wind Jackal said, his voice now a deathly quiet whisper. 'I shall never give up – and if you value me as your captain, you will follow me in this quest. If not, you are free to go, right now . . .'

The crew glanced at one another. None of them had ever seen their beloved captain in such a state before. Spillins smiled half-heartedly. Steg Jambles picked up his half-empty glass of woodale, raised it to his lips – then returned it to the table, untouched.

'We're with you,' said Maris, breaking the silence.

Under the table, Quint squeezed her hand.

'Wind Jackal!' came a cheery voice from the staircase. 'How *are* you?'

Everyone turned, relieved, to see the young sky pirate Thaw Daggerslash coming down the stairs from the upper balconies. Smiling broadly, he nodded in turn at the assembled crew.

'It's good to see *all* of you,' he said. His gaze lingered on Quint and Maris. 'You must be the son I've heard so much about,' he said. 'And you . . . Who might this beautiful young lass be?' he asked.

'My name is Maris. Maris Pallitax,' said Maris a little stiffly. 'My father used to be . . .'

'Most High Academe,' Thaw Daggerslash broke in. 'Linius Pallitax. I met him once ... A wonderful academic and kind-hearted to a lowly sky pirate.'

Maris melted. 'He was kind to everyone he met, no matter how grand or humble.'

'Such a tragic loss,' said Thaw, his face etched with concern. He turned to the captain. 'But Wind Jackal, my old friend, I couldn't help noticing a certain tension in the air. If there is anything wrong ...'

Wind Jackal shook his head. 'Crew business,' he muttered. 'Nothing that need concern you.'

Thaw Daggerslash's pleasant smile didn't falter. 'Of course not, of course not,' he said amiably. 'But you know, if you ever need a second-in-command, I'm still available.'

'You're a talented sailor, Daggerslash,' said Wind

Jackal, 'and one day, you'll make a fine captain – if you only have the patience to work your way up. Besides, as I told you before, I have a son . . .'

'True, true,' Thaw Daggerslash smiled, giving Quint a pat on the shoulder. 'And I'm sure he'll do you proud, Captain Wind Jackal, sir.'

'No hard feelings, then?' said Wind Jackal, handing the young sky pirate a tankard of woodale.

'No hard feelings!' said Thaw with a laugh.

He took the tankard and drained it in one go, before slamming it down on the carved table. He looked up at Wind Jackal, suddenly serious.

'One day,' he said, '*my* name will be carved on this table, next to yours, Captain Wind Jackal, by Sky it will!'

Wind Jackal smiled and raised his tankard in salute. 'I'll drink to that,' he said.

'Back again, are you?' sneered Glaviel Glynte, his left eyebrow arched high.

Beside him, the bird-creature clucked with amusement.

'What's it to be, then?' said Glynte. He picked up his quill and dipped it in the ink-pot before him.

'I've decided to take you up on the offer of the sky barge,' said Thaw Daggerslash. 'And a crew of one . . . It sounds exactly what I need just now.'

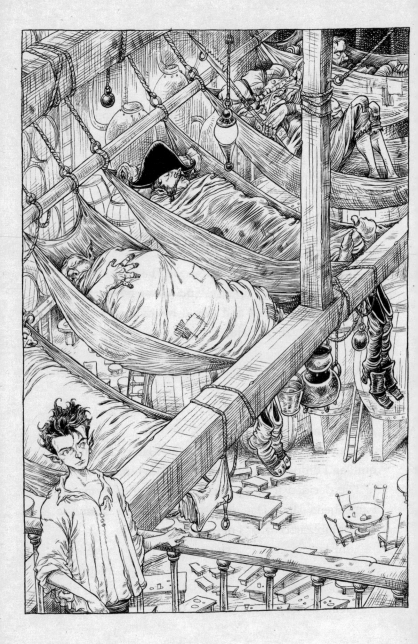

CHAPTER THREE

Turbot Smeal

The rafters high up above the drinking hall of the Tarry Vine tavern were festooned with hammocks of every shape and size. Grubby spider-silk sheets, which could accommodate several crews, swayed gently beside the hanging-pockets favoured by waifs, oakelves and the lighter sleepers, while in the garret alcoves, captains and quartermasters enjoyed all the privacy that a hanging-drape could provide.

There was, however, no escaping the snuffling, snoring and muttered sleep-talking of the hundreds of sleeping sky pirates. And yet, as their growling snores mingled with the warm woodhop-scented air that rose up from the brewing cellars far below, a heady, hypnotic atmosphere was created that induced sleep in all but the most troubled occupants of the rafters.

Quint lay on his back, staring upwards. Above him, the two sides of the steeply sloping roof came together in the shadows, looking, he mused, like the upturned hull of a great sky ship. On either side of him, the crew of the

Galerider added their snores to the general rumbling hum – a sound answered by the tiny batowls that nested in the gaps between the joists.

Next to him, Ratbit smacked his lips together noisily, and rolled onto his other side. Sagbutt let out a rasping snort, while further down the line of hammocks, Spillins muttered something in his sleep and gave a small, high-pitched giggle.

Quint glanced across at the garret alcove, where Maris was sleeping. The faint glow of her tilder-oil lamp had faded an hour earlier and, from behind the spider-silk drapes, nothing stirred. Quint turned over in his hammock and pulled his greatcoat around him with a shiver. Despite the warm air and sonorous snoring, he could still feel the dreadful chill of the cliff quarry, and whenever he closed his eyes, the hideous shrieking face of an edge wraith seemed to loom at him out of the darkness.

Sleep, he thought miserably, seemed impossible, even in this warm, safe place.

Just then, from out of the darkness there came a long, agonized groan – like that of a tilder, a hunter's crossbow bolt buried in its neck, breathing its last. Quint sat up. There it was again, coming from behind the curtain of the garret alcove next to the one where Maris was sleeping.

Quietly, Quint climbed out of his hammock and tiptoed along the narrow rafter to the safety of the garret balcony. He paused for a moment outside the alcove, only to hear the terrible groan once more. Quint pulled back the curtain and stepped inside.

'F . . . Father?' he whispered. 'Are you all right?'

Wind Jackal was standing at the tall, narrow garret window, the shutters of which he'd thrown open. A chill, swirling wind plucked at his heavy sky pirate coat and ruffled his hair. At the sound of Quint's voice, Wind Jackal slowly turned, the moonlight catching one side of his face and throwing the other into deep shadow. Beneath his brows, his eyes glinted.

'He's out there, somewhere,' he said in a low voice, scarcely above a whisper. 'The very thought of it is like a swarm of snickets gnawing at my innards.'

Wind Jackal turned back to the window, where Quint joined him.

'Father,' Quint began again, laying a hand on Wind Jackal's arm. 'I'm worried about you . . .'

Wind Jackal surveyed the roofs and towers of the sleeping city spread out before him. 'Surely you, of all people, understand,' he shot back, his voice almost a snarl. 'I have to destroy Turbot Smeal . . . I *have* to!'

Quint nodded, but his grip on his father's arm tightened. 'What I don't understand . . .' he said slowly, not daring to look at Wind Jackal's face. 'What you never told me, and

I've always been afraid to ask is . . . why? *Why* did Turbot Smeal murder my mother and brothers?'

Wind Jackal continued to stare out into the night, his face a silvery mask in the moonlight, as impassive as one of the statues on the top of the Sanctaphrax Viaduct. For a long time he said nothing. But when, at last, he spoke, his voice was a low monotone, as if he was battling to keep the rage and sorrow from exploding out of him, like an over-cooled flight-rock.

'I have never spoken of it, Quint my son, because I believed that Turbot Smeal was dead,' Wind Jackal began. 'I didn't want to dredge up memories almost too painful to bear. But now I know he's alive, it's only right that you should know the whole story . . .'

He paused for a moment, then continued, never once looking at his son standing beside him.

'The crew of a sky ship is like a living body,' Wind Jackal said. 'Arms and legs, hands and feet, stomach, heart – all working separately, but together. All different. All essential . . .' He nodded slowly. 'There must be a captain. The head. Someone to take control, to make decisions . . . And then the captain needs a strong right hand – someone he can trust with his life if he has to, someone who'll stick with him, come what may, and watch his back . . . For years, I had Garum Gall, the most faithful cloddertrog a captain could wish for, and when he passed on to Open Sky . . .' Wind Jackal paused.

'You've got me, Father, *I'm* your strong right hand.'

For the first time since Quint first entered the garret alcove, Wind Jackal looked him straight in the eyes.

'I've got you, Quint, that's right.' He smiled gravely, then went on. 'The *left* hand,' he said, 'should be a fighter. Preferably a goblin, like Sagbutt. Not too smart, but a ferocious warrior in tight quarters. And the arms and legs are the fore-deckers, the harpooneer and his mate – Steg Jambles, Ratbit, Tem Barkwater. Strong and tireless, and highly trained. Then there are the eyes – Spillins the oakelf. And just as important, the heart. The stone pilot, without whom no sky ship could ever come to life and take to the skies. And finally, Quint, there is the stomach . . .'

Saying this, Wind Jackal paused and swallowed hard as he struggled to keep his feelings under control.

'The stomach of any sky ship is the quartermaster – and like any stomach, it grumbles and growls and demands to be fed. But it is just as vital as all the other parts. And just as a stomach nourishes the body, so a quartermaster nourishes a sky ship, ensuring it is well-provisioned, its cargo-hold is full and its voyages are profitable. It takes special qualities to be a good quarter-master – strong contacts in the leagues, an eye for a bargain and . . .'

Again, Wind Jackal swallowed hard.

'Utter ruthlessness . . . And Turbot Smeal was the greatest quartermaster of them all!'

Quint looked uneasily at his father, but Wind Jackal seemed to be lost in a world of his own.

'The Leagues of Undertown!' He spat out the words as if they were an ancient Deepwoods curse. 'They seek to control and exploit everything that comes in or out of this great city of ours, their greedy fingers in every Undertown pie. Nothing escapes their influence.

'There are the great Leagues – the Blood Leagues, for example, which deal in livestock; the Leagues of Construction, which control all building work; the Leagues of Plenty, which trade in manufactured goods of all kinds, and the Leagues of Toil, which control all those who sweat in the workshops making those goods – not to mention the accursed Flight Leagues, whose leaders seek to control all who would take to the skies!'

Wind Jackal scowled, his twisted face white with rage. Quint flinched involuntarily.

'Each of these great leagues is divided into smaller leagues,' Wind Jackal continued. 'For instance, the Flight Leagues incorporate all kinds of minor leagues such as cage-forgers, sail-spinners, rope-teasers, clinkers and corkers, welders and weighters . . . All the trades needed to build a sky ship.

'By forming into leagues, they believed they could control everything, but they forgot one thing. Each other!'

Wind Jackal paused for a moment to let the words sink in.

'Every league competes with every other league,' he went on, his voice low and scathing, 'whatever fine words the leaguesmasters utter about "sticking together" and "the common good"! They just can't help themselves. No league ever misses an opportunity to get one over on its rivals – but they can't ever be *seen* to be doing it. Oh, no! That wouldn't do at all. Which is why they need *us*, Quint, my son.'

Quint nodded. 'Sky pirates,' he breathed.

'Aye, lad,' Wind Jackal agreed. 'Free and unbowed and answerable to no leaguesmaster in a ridiculous high hat.' He sneered. 'Of course, they hate us and try to stop our ships and seize our cargoes, but at the same time, they need us to do their dirty work – such as raid their rivals' league ships or disrupt one another's trade.

'No leaguesmaster – high or low – would ever admit it, but without sky pirates to carry out their nasty little underhand practices and take the blame, the Leagues of Undertown would descend into open warfare. And that, Quint, my son, would be bad for business! Which brings me back to Turbot Smeal, greatest quartermaster of them all.'

Wind Jackal shook his head and gazed out over the rooftops of the sleeping city. Quint's mouth was dry, and there was an uneasy fluttery feeling in the pit of his stomach.

'Turbot Smeal ... Turbot Smeal ...' Wind Jackal's voice dripped with hatred as he spoke the quartermaster's name. 'I was a young sky pirate captain putting my first crew together when he sought me out. Said we would be good together. And although, even back then, his small yellow eyes and bleached complexion made me shudder, there was something he had to offer. He had useful contacts in the leagues all over Undertown. There seemed to be no swindle or underhand deal that Turbot Smeal wouldn't get wind of – no one he couldn't flatter or deceive to get a better deal or gain an advantage.

'Almost as soon as we teamed up, Turbot kept the *Galerider* busy, and the profits began rolling in. I made sure Garum Gall, my right hand, kept a close eye on Turbot, and even credited myself with curbing some of the loathsome quartermaster's worst excesses. Slave-trading, for example. Turbot Smeal knew, no matter what the profit, that I would never, ever deal in slaves. But timber, fine pelts and Deepwoods goods of every kind – we shipped them all and, thanks to Turbot's contacts, the leagues left us alone.

'Of course, there was a price to pay. There always is, with the leagues. The price was to accept commissions from different leagues when the occasion warranted it, to raid their rivals' ships. And we were good at it. There wasn't a league ship in the sky that would dare to take on the *Galerider* in a fair fight.

'We grew richer. I met and married your mother, Hermina, and a year later our first son, Lucius, was born, followed by Centix, then Murix, and Pellius and Martilius. And, last but not least, you, Quintinius . . .' The trace of a smile flickered across his face. 'We moved to the opulent palace in the Western Quays – and life was good. I counted myself the luckiest person alive . . .

'At the same time, my old friend Linius Pallitax was prospering also, his career in Sanctaphrax going from strength to strength. Together we actually thought we might be able to change the way things were done in the two cities – reform the leagues and academies and bring Undertowners and academics closer together.' He laughed bitterly. 'What fools we were . . .'

'Not fools,' said Quint fiercely. 'Just unlucky . . .'

'Aye, son, perhaps you're right,' said Wind Jackal. 'And yet I should have known that someone as rotten as Smeal could never be changed. I remember the look of leering greed and triumph on his face when he came to me with what I took to be one of the finest deals he had ever brokered – one that would not simply put money in our pockets, but might actually do some good . . .

'Following long talks with Purlis Havelock, Leaguesmaster of the League of Furnace Tenders, Smeal had agreed that we would raid a slave ship owned by Meltus Drail's League of Stokers and Smelters, since the latter had been undercutting their prices by using cheap – and illegal – slave labour. The poor wretches were to be shut up in the Stokers and Smelters' sewer workshops and worked to death. I was happy to agree to the deal on the strict understanding that the slaves should be released by us back in the Deepwoods.

'Smeal muttered darkly about profits and waste of valuable time, but the League of Furnace Tenders were paying us handsomely to ruin their rivals, and at last he, in his turn, agreed.

'So, anyway, the day arrived. Hot and humid it was, as I recall, with ominous, dark purple banks of cloud rolling in from Open Sky. The ambush was due to take place in the morning at six hours on the borders of the Deepwoods and the Twilight Woods. We arrived at the site the night before, weighed anchor in a leadwood grove and cut down branches, which we used to camouflage the vessel before settling ourselves down for the long night ahead.

'And it was a long night, Quint. Long and unpleasant. I've never liked spending the hours of darkness out there in the Deepwoods, and that particular night there was a dry lightning storm which crackled and flashed hour after hour, without a break. It lit up the dark forest, casting eerie shadows and setting the forest creatures off with their hideous screeching and squawking like the spirits of the dead. By Sky, Quint, my thoughts became bleak – and yet, as ever, day was on its way.

'By five hours the lightning had subsided and the sky was beginning to brighten up with the first glimmering light of dawn. I began to shake off my despond and look forward to the approaching encounter. And sure enough, at half off the appointed hour, Spillins – the eyes of the *Galerider* – spied the slave ship approaching from the top of the caternest.

'A blackwood vessel it was – nameless, dark and sinister, and in need of urgent repair. Certainly no one who didn't already know would have suspected the valuable cargo it held as it sailed across the sky from the

Deepwoods to the Stoker and Smelter leaguesmen awaiting them in the foundries on the Mire side of Undertown. We made no move until the rickety sky ship had passed overhead. Then, emerging from our cover and discarding the branches that had concealed us, the *Galerider* attacked with full force.

'A harpoon attached to a rope was launched from our prow. It skewered the vessel's port-side and held it fast. Then, by turning the winch-wheel and tightening the rope, we drew the other ship alongside us.

'The cowardly leagues crew didn't put up much of a fight once I'd called for stave-hooks and tolley-ropes and given the command to board. It was all so easy.

'Too easy . . .'

Wind Jackal fell still, as if the weight of memories was too much to bear. He groaned and, in the silvery moonlight, Quint saw his father hold his head in his hands.

'We rounded up the crew of the slave ship and sent them packing in the two open rubble tenders that served as lifeboats on the battered vessel. Then I was just about to open the hold and free the poor unfortunates held there when all at once Spillins, telescope raised, announced that there were two more league ships approaching. And fast!

'Of course, with half our crew on the *Galerider* and half on the slave vessel, I was in a very weak position. It was only when Spillins shouted down the names of the two league ships – the *Forger of Triumph* and the *Smelter of Woes* – that I realized these were vessels belonging to the League of Furnace Tenders. And indeed, raising my own

telescope, I saw Purlis Havelock, the master of the League, himself, at the helm of the lead ship.

'I had an uneasy feeling, but as yet, no reason to suspect anything might be amiss. They drew along-side, one to the *Galerider*'s port-side; the other on the starboard-side of the slave ship. They had us penned in like tilder in a cage. Havelock started to engage me in pleasantries. About the weather, the Deepwoods, a job well done ... Then, while we were chatting, I noticed that something was happening on the other league ship.

'Havelock's leaguesmen had boarded and, so far as I could make out, were taking the slaves – frightened-looking woodtrolls – out of the slave ship and placing them in shackles, ready to transfer them to their league ship. I bellowed at them to stop, only for Turbot Smeal to countermand my order from his position next to Havelock. I remember his weasel words to this day.

'"Relax, old friend," he smirked, waving the leaguesmen on. "We can't afford a wasteful trip to some woodtroll village who knows where. This way, we get double our fee and Havelock here takes the wretches off our hands . . . "

'"Not if I have anything to do with it!" I roared, suddenly aware that Smeal must have brokered a separate deal with the leagues.

'Unsheathing my sword in a flash, I sliced through the tolley-rope that tethered the *Galerider* to Havelock's *Forger of Triumph*, bellowing to Ratbit on the other side of the sky ship that he should do the same to the harpoon-rope binding us to the slave ship. Then, having commanded Ramrock to cool the flight-rock, I slammed the flight-levers across, raising the hull-weights and giving full head to the sails.

'We soared up into the air, turned in mid air and – our weapons drawn and ready – swooped back down in a broad arc towards the second league ship before a single slave could be taken on board. It was Purlis Havelock's turn to be outraged.

' "In the name of the Leagues," he roared. "*Attack!*"

'Suddenly, the decks of both league ships were bristling with weapons, and arrows and crossbow bolts were flying through the air at the *Galerider*. Meanwhile, on board the slave ship, Steg Jambles and the great cloddertrog twins, Grim and Grem, had launched into action. While Steg did his best to steer the slave vessel away from the second league ship, the cloddertrogs threw themselves at the leaguesmen who had come aboard and made short work of them . . .

'But it was still two to one, and despite the *Galerider*'s superiority as a sky ship, the league ships had come well-armed and prepared for a fight. I had to think fast. Then it came to me – a little trick I'd seen snowbirds do to draw prey from their nestlings. So I feigned a broken wing . . .'

'You did *what*?' said Quint, intrigued.

Wind Jackal smiled grimly. 'I pushed one of the flight-levers right across,' he explained. 'The mainsail fluttered, flapped and collapsed. Purlis Havelock couldn't believe his luck.

' "We've got him!" I heard him bellow triumphantly. "Move in for the kill!"

'Suddenly, as the *Galerider* hovered in the air, a sitting wood-duck, there were league ships coming at us from both directions. I pretended to panic, tugging at the supposedly broken flight-lever, all the while keeping an eye on the position of the league ships. I knew that

Ramrock would be doing the same. Then, when they were only strides away, their weapons raised ready for the final onslaught, I bellowed to the stone pilot . . .

' "LIFT!"

'It was the command my faithful old pilot, may Sky rest his spirit, had been waiting for. He tugged on the drenching-lever, chilling the flight-rock in an instant and catapulting us high up into the sky. A moment later, from below us, there came a deafening *crash!* as the two league ships slammed into one another. I looked over the side to see the *Forger of Triumph* sliding off to the west, while the *Smelter of Woes* — which had had a gaping hole punched in its side and half its hull-weights severed — was spinning helplessly round and round as it plummeted down out of the sky towards the treacherous Twilight Woods, from which its hapless crew would never emerge.

'It was all too much for Havelock. He never even considered the thought of engaging in a fair fight between the two of us. No, so far as he was concerned, the battle was already over. With a bellowed command to his crew, he and his league ship swung round in the sky and beat a hasty retreat, back towards Under-town, where he would have time to plot his revenge.

'For our part, we swooped back down to the rickety slave ship to finish off the job we'd started. Grim and Grem were waiting for us, bloodied but triumphant. With a tolley-rope secured from the stern of the *Galerider* to the prow of the slave ship, we set out on the long voyage back to the Deepwoods to return the woodtrolls to their distant village.

'I've never seen such rejoicing as I saw that day when we arrived back and reunited them with their families – nor received such genuine hospitality as we were given there in that wonderful village. I tell you, Quint, woodtrolls are among the finest, noblest tribes to be found anywhere in the Deepwoods. I made some fine and true friends amongst their kind and, believe me, if you are ever in any trouble out in the Deepwoods, you can do a lot worse than seek out a woodtroll village . . .

'Anyway, after a great feast put on in our honour, it was high time for us to return to Undertown. We left the slave ship with them to deal with as they saw fit, and set sail. I hadn't laid eyes on Turbot Smeal since just before the battle with the league ships, when he'd cosied up to Purlis Havelock. I suspected he'd jumped ship and taken his chances with the leaguesmaster, but I fully expected that he'd come grovelling back when the *Galerider* docked in Undertown.

'How wrong I was . . .'

Wind Jackal's voice suddenly faltered and Quint could see the muscles in his father's jaw tense as he gritted his teeth to continue.

'We ... we saw the smoke ...' he said, his words now choked with emotion. 'As we approached Undertown; thick dark columns that coiled up into the sky and formed a menacing pall over the city. And as we got closer, it was clear that the whole of the Western Quays were ablaze.' He swallowed. 'I ... I steered a course along the Edgewater River. It was chaos below me, the streets filled with noisy crowds desperately fleeing the flames, while the air above them throbbed and hissed with the sound of the fire sky ships loading up their great barrels with river water, flying to the blazing rooftops and attempting to quench the insatiable fire.

'As I sailed further along, the more the devastation increased, and I knew that ... that ... the fire must have begun close to our home ... I came down lower in the sky, scouring the row of buildings ... And ... then I saw ... you ...'

'Me,' said Quint softly.

'Curled up in a ball on the top of a roof ... Not our roof, for that had already collapsed. No, you had some-how made it along to the neighbouring buildings ...' He groaned softly. 'All curled up you were ... Curled up and motionless ... And ...'

'You slid down a tolley-rope and landed beside me,' said Quint, tears streaming down his face. 'I remember. You scooped me up in your arms and held me close ... So close. I ... I remember the sound of your heart pounding in your chest. So loud. So fast ...'

Suddenly, Quint felt Wind Jackal's hand on his shoulder, and he looked up into the gloomy silver light

to see his father's face convulsed with pain.

'Oh, Quint,' he moaned, and lowered his own head so that it rested on his son's chest. 'Can you ever, ever forgive me?'

'Forgive *you*?' Quint whispered.

'It ... was all my fault. I should have realized how evil, how twisted Turbot Smeal was. How he would go to any lengths to punish me for crossing him. If only I had returned immediately, perhaps ...'

'You can't know that, Father,' Quint tried to reassure him. 'You saved those woodtrolls from certain death ...'

'And lost my family in the process.' Wind Jackal's voice was harsh and bitter. 'And now I shall make him pay! I shall make Turbot Smeal pay for destroying my family!'

His eyes were blazing now with an intensity that

seemed almost unhinged. Quint stepped forward and embraced him.

'Aren't you forgetting, Father,' he said. 'You still have me.'

From the garret alcove next door, there came a short gasp, and the faint sound of a tilder-oil lamp being snuffed out.

·CHAPTER FOUR·

THE SKY-SHIPYARD

'Come on, you two,' said Wind Jackal, pushing his seat back noisily over the stone-flagged floor. 'We'd best make a move.'

Quint glanced across at Maris. Her face was ashen and drawn, and there were dark rings beneath her eyes. It was, he thought, almost as if she'd slept as badly as he had the night before – although when their eyes met, Maris gave Quint a reassuring smile. In front of her, the plate of tilder sausages and snowbird eggs had barely been touched, but at Wind Jackal's command, she stood up and drew her cloak about her. Pushing his own plate away, long since cleared of its sausage and eggs – not to mention mopped clean with toasted blackbread – Quint got to his feet and followed Maris and his father.

The great drinking hall of the Tarry Vine tavern was deserted. The floor was dirty and sticky, and the air was shot with glittering dust as shafts of light from the high narrow windows cut through the stillness and fell on upturned tables and discarded drinking vessels. The sky pirates, whose loud snoring had set the tavern's rafters trembling during the night, had all risen just before dawn as the ale vats were being filled, and slipped away into the sprawling alleys and lanes of Undertown.

The crew of the *Galerider* had followed – each with errands to perform. Steg Jambles and his constant shadow, Tem Barkwater, were buying rope and rigging in the chandlery sheds. Ratbit the mobgnome and Spillins the oakelf had set off for the weavers' district in search of spider-silk sails, whilst the quartermaster, Filbus Queep – with Sagbutt the flat-head goblin as protection – was visiting one of his contacts in the League of Taper and Tallow Moulders.

Quint, Maris and Wind Jackal were the last to leave. Tossing a gold coin into the apron pocket of a mobgnome maid, the sky pirate captain placed his great bicorne hat firmly on his head and stepped out into the early-morning sunshine. Quint and Maris followed him.

The street was already busy. A heavy lugtroll laboured past, pushing a barrow loaded with crates of pungent pickled tripweed, followed – as if in a convoy – by a dozen others, pushing loads of tangy woodsaps, barrels of sourmash, round creamy hammelhorn curds and clotted sides of tilder meat, clouds of bloodflies buzzing overhead. Behind them – the hems of their gowns rolled up and fastened to avoid trailing in the mud – stood several fussy-looking leaguesmen in low, three-pronged hats, busy ticking off lists of produce on barkscrolls.

From the opposite direction came a gaggle of milk-maids. These sallow-skinned gabtrolls, their quizzical eyes bouncing on the end of stalks as they peered over the heads of the crowd, waddled along awkwardly, slopping buckets balanced at either end of yokes which straddled their shoulders. Every twenty strides or so, they waved the long-handled ladles they carried and called up to the windows on either side of the street in beguilingly soft, mellifluous voices.

'Pure milk! Pure milk! From hammelhorns ... pastured in lullabee groves!'

'Mind your backs! Mind your backs!'

A pair of slaughterers with sallowdrop switches in their blood-red hands were approaching, driving two huge tethered hammelhorn bulls along the narrow cobbled street. Quint and Maris darted into a mud-churned alley out of the way and waited for them to pass, before running to catch up with Wind Jackal, who was striding ahead, seemingly oblivious to the bustling crowd. From behind them came the sounds of angry voices, and Quint glanced round to see the two slaughterers being confronted by a leaguesman, whose face seemed to be turning even redder than theirs as he shouted.

'Where do you think you're going with those?' the leaguesman was bellowing, as the gabtroll milkmaids stopped to gawp over his shoulder.

'The League of Gutters and Gougers...' began the first slaughterer.

'Oh, no, you don't. Not without the permission of the League of Haulers and Herders!' the leaguesman thundered, his three-pointed hat seemingly quivering with outrage. 'You *know* that!' he added, and held out a stubby hand.

As Quint turned away, he heard the distinctive *clink clink* of coins mingle with the cries of 'Pure milk!' behind him.

Undertown, he thought. Throbbing, thronging, heaving, sweating, stinking, hustling, bustling Undertown. During his time in the Knights Academy, high up in lofty Sanctaphrax with its mannered rituals and arcane traditions, he'd put aside all thought of the place. Now, back down in the gritty day-to-day life of the seething city, it was as if he'd never been away.

With the rickety stores and ramshackle dwelling-towers on either side closing in, the street seemed to become more crowded than ever. Quint had to push and shove his way through, to keep up with his father, whose bicorne hat bobbed above the heads of the crowd. Maris stumbled alongside him, her hand gripping Quint's arm tightly, and a look of barely concealed alarm on her face. For whereas Quint was used to the streets of Undertown, Maris – born and raised in the floating city of Sanctaphrax – had only ever lived there and in the refined grandeur of Undertown's Western Quays. The raucous clamour of the rough quarters of Undertown was entirely new – and deeply disturbing – to her.

All around, the air throbbed with noise. The clatter of iron wheels on stone cobbles, the snorting of livestock and jangle of tack. Bellowed greetings and sobbed good-byes, curses and oaths, and the cries of the street-traders, announcing their wares. And in amongst the cacophony of noise was the hum of odours, dark and pungent, as honeymead, sour milk, woodsmoke and hammelhorn dung created an ever-changing symphony of smells.

'Over here, Quint, lad!' bellowed a familiar voice. 'Keep up!'

Up ahead, Wind Jackal had turned the corner, and was striding down a broad avenue leading to the tall, often windowless, clap-board buildings that lined the Edgewater River.

'We'll take a sky ferry,' he called over his shoulder.

'What's the hurry?' panted Maris, looking up at Quint, the rings beneath her eyes darker than ever.

'I don't know,' shrugged Quint, 'but at least he seems a bit more cheerful than he was last night. Come on, or he'll leave us behind!'

Maris laughed and hurried after Quint as they ran down the avenue. All around, there were groups of leaguesmen clustered together, their tall, three- and four-pronged hats swaying as they nodded or shook their heads, like ironwood pines in a storm. Here by the waterside, the wharf-towers and warehouses groaned with the accumulated riches of the Deepwoods, laboriously flown in by sky ship. There were deals to be done, cargo to be traded and fortunes to be made – very little of which would ever filter down to the milkmaids and herders of the crowded alleys behind the avenue.

Quint and Maris joined Wind Jackal on one of the many small wooden jetties that stuck out over the river like the prickles on a woodhog's back, few of the high-hatted leaguesmen giving them so much as a second glance as they passed by. Then the three of them picked their way along the narrow platform, taking care to dodge the cluster of small boats that bobbed about their heads. At the far end, which jutted out high over the muddy Edgewater, a gnokgoblin was leaning against a boarding-post, the end of a tolley-rope in one hand.

'The sky-shipyards,' said Wind Jackal. He produced a coin from his pocket and placed it in the gnokgoblin's hand.

'Right away, Captain,' he replied. 'Jump aboard, sirs, miss.'

Maris went first, climbing up the knotted rungs that stuck out from the post on both sides. At the top, she clambered across into the flat-bottomed vessel tethered there. Quint followed, with Wind Jackal and then the gnokgoblin bringing up the rear.

Settling himself on a small bench, the gnokgoblin raised the sail, slipped the tolley-rope from the mooring-ring and the little sky ferry – the *Edgehopper* – leaped up into the air. Quint and Maris looked around them as they rose higher and Undertown fell away beneath them. Suddenly, the maze-like streets and alleys took on a certain order, and the broad sweeping curve of the great Edgewater River as it sliced through the city could be seen. Below, in the dirty swirling water Quint saw shoals of oozefish swimming in neverending figures of eight, while ahead, the glass dome of the magnificent Leagues Palace – home to Ruptus Pentephraxis, the High Leaguesmaster – glinted in the bright early morning sunshine.

Despite its patched sail, its creaking timbers and the primitive flight-cauldron, filled with flight-rock rubble, that just managed to keep everything aloft, the vessel was in expert hands. It sped like an arrow from the east to the west bank of the river, and then made its way along the curve of the Edgewater. Past breweries and mills it went, and on over the foundry district, with its vast metalworks and factories, with tall smoke-belching chimneys, cramped workshops and cobbled inner courtyards, where heaps of raw materials were piled high beside crates of finished goods.

A little further to the north, on the edge of the foundry district, Quint could see the distinctive outline of the sky-ship cradles; huge cage-like structures which soared up into the air from square towers, high above the neighbouring rooftops. These elegant pieces of scaffolding were the structures that supported the sky ships being built in the great sprawling sky-shipyards beneath them. It was towards the sky-ship cradles that the *Edgehopper* was heading.

Wind Jackal turned to the gnokgoblin pilot and pointed down below. 'Just over there will do fine,' he said with a smile.

'Aye-aye, Captain.' The gnokgoblin leaned down hard on the little vessel's tiller.

Quint felt his stomach lurch and, for a moment, regretted his hearty breakfast. The *Edgehopper* swooped down out of the sky and glided to a halt in a large courtyard surrounded by tall square towers on all sides. With the sky ferry hovering a couple of strides above the ground, the gnokgoblin motioned for his passengers to disembark. Stepping to the ground after Quint and Maris, Wind Jackal tipped his bicorne hat to the pilot.

'Excellent flying,' he said, tossing the gnokgoblin another coin.

'Learned my trade as a "leaguer",' the pilot laughed, pocketing the coin. 'But I just couldn't take to being ordered around by high hats the whole time. This way, I can be my own boss . . .' He swept the *Edgehopper* back into the air. 'Just like you, Captain!'

The gnokgoblin laughed again as he flew away, back towards the Edgewater River.

'Throwing your money around, I see,' came a terse, hoarse-sounding voice, and Quint turned to see a leaguesman in a high four-pronged hat, standing at the ornate entrance to one of the towers.

His rich robes were gathered and fastened above the ankle and he wore 'mire-paddles' – flat, wooden shoe-protectors for splashing through the muddy streets. A great cluster of the charms and amulets beloved of leaguesmen formed a cluttered ruff around his neck, and in one hand he carried a long thin 'leagues-cane'; a walking-stick that could be unsheathed in an instant to reveal a razor-sharp sword.

Wind Jackal tipped his hat. 'Yardmaster Hollrig,' he said coolly. 'Just come to find out what your shipwrights have to report on the *Galerider*.'

Thelvis Hollrig, high-hat yardmaster in the League of Sky Shipwrights, smiled to reveal teeth filed down to points – the very latest Undertown fashion.

Quint shuddered.

'Hummer!' The yard-master clicked his fingers. A moment later, a harassed-looking clerk came bustling out of the tower clutching a sheaf of barkscroll plans. 'The *Galerider* berthed with us ... the day before yesterday?' Thelvis Hollrig glanced at Wind Jackal, who nodded.

The clerk, a thin grey goblin with white tufted ears, fished a pair of grubby-looking spectacles out of his waistcoat pocket and began examining the barkscrolls. As he did so, Quint looked around. When the *Galerider* had limped in to dock here, after the terrible voyage to the cliff quarries, it had been the middle of the night. The shipyards had been quiet and deserted, with the cradles and ship towers nothing more than dark silhouettes against the sky.

Now, in the morning sunshine, it was as if some giant had disturbed a nest of woodants and sent them scurrying here and there with twigs and leaves to repair their home. Yet instead of woodants, the tiny figures high up in the sky cradles, dangling from sky barges and tenders, or balancing on thin swaying ladders that snaked up from the tops of the towers, were shipwrights and boat-builders. Tree-goblins, oakelves, waifs and mobgnomes, skilled in woodcraft and with a head for heights, they swarmed over the great timber carcases of the sky ships, carrying ironwood struts rather than twigs, and lufwood decking instead of leaves.

'*Galerider* . . . *Galerider* . . .' the clerk muttered. 'Ah, yes, here we are . . .' He pulled out a barkscroll plan and traced the ink lines with a finger. 'West Tower . . .'

He looked up and Quint, Wind Jackal and Maris followed his gaze. High above, nestling in a sky cradle at the top of the West Tower, was the *Galerider*.

Her sails were gone and the rigging – both from the mast and the hull – had been uncleated and taken off. The rudder, the harpoon and the balustrades had also been removed, while at the stern there was a massive hole right through the ship, light streaming in from the other side, where extensive repairs were being made to the hull.

'Considerable cloud-limpet and sky-fungus damage to the stern, brought to a crisis by storm damage,' the clerk read from the barkscroll in a monotonous voice. 'Localized storm damage to sails, rigging and winding-ropes ... Storm damage to outer timberwork ... And to hull-weights and alignment mechanism ...'

The yardmaster smiled his pointy-toothed smile. 'What in Sky's name were you doing out at the cliff edge, Captain? You must have realized what damage those winds can do ...'

'I had my reasons,' said Wind Jackal, his brow furrowing.

'No report on the flight-rock, as your stone pilot has refused our shipwrights access at the present time.' The clerk concluded his report and looked from Wind Jackal to the yardmaster, and back again.

High above their heads, Quint could just make out the small defiant figure of the Stone Pilot in her tall conical hood, standing on the flight-rock platform with her arms folded in front of her.

'Yes, well,' said Thelvis Hollrig, tapping his leagues-cane briskly on the ground. 'Leaving aside the issue of re-boring and trimming the flight-rock, I'm afraid your sky ship needs a lot of work, Captain, which – as I'm sure you'll understand – will not come cheap ...'

Wind Jackal nodded grimly.

'If you'll just follow me to my chambers, we'll discuss the delicate matter ...' The yardmaster smiled and

motioned for Wind Jackal to follow him inside.
'Of payment.'

As Thelvis and his father made their way to the
yardmaster's chambers, Quint and Maris were left to
wander round the shipyard. Far above them, massive
cranes and towering derricks, as lofty as ironwood
pines, twisted and turned, their luffing-jibs extending
and contracting as they swung round. Suspended from
their great hooks were gigantic wooden structures and
metal casings, which flew through the air as the crane-
operators raised and lowered the winch-cables, moving
each separate segment of the new sky ships into position
with extraordinary accuracy. Then, when a bellowed
command from below had confirmed that the pieces
were in place, a work team of sky-shipwrights swarmed
over the sections, joining one to the other.

'They look like woodants,' Maris commented.

Quint smiled. 'That's just what I was thinking,' he
said. 'Only a moment ago . . .'

Each sky ship was made up of three main parts. The
wooden prow, the metal flight-rock cage and platform,
and the helm. It was only when these three parts had
been bolted, riveted and dove-tailed together that the
final additions could be made. Maris and Quint circled
the yard, gazing up at the towers, one by one.

In one cradle, a bowsprit and figurehead were being
added to the prow. At another, a vast rock-sling was being
bolted into place above the flying-jib. Further along, a
main-mast, complete with rigging-eyelets and caternest,
was being secured to the central part of a ship, while at yet

another of the towering cradles, the aft-castle and rudder were being mounted simultaneously above and below an impressive helm of finest redoak.

'So many sky ships,' Maris said in wonder. 'And each one different.'

Quint nodded. 'That's 'cause they all have a different purpose,' he told her. 'That one there, for instance,' he said, pointing up to a double-master to his left, 'must be a league ship. Or rather it will be when it's finished. See how heavy and low-slung the wheelhouse is. It can hold a huge cargo, and it's particularly stable in bad weather. And look at the flight-rock cages . . .'

'There are four of them,' said Maris.

'Precisely,' said Quint. 'For four smaller flight-rocks. Once again, to aid stability. At the expense of speed and manoeuvrability,

of course. In fact, this type of league ship is notoriously slow and cumbersome . . .'

'But doesn't that make them easy prey for . . . well, for sky pirate ships?' said Maris.

'Not necessarily,' said Quint. 'Look up there, just above the rudder casing – can you see those hooks?'

Maris nodded.

'They're for fire-barges,' he said. 'Half a dozen of them. Small and fast, and usually packed with goblin "leaguers" – they can be used to fight back if the vessel's attacked.' He paused and looked round. 'And that ship there,' he said, pointing to a small, sturdy craft with a solid-looking metal sphere where the flight cage should be. 'That's your typical tug. Staple of the league fleet . . .'

Maris frowned. 'It hasn't got a sky cage,' she said. 'What's that huge round casing for?'

'Rubble,' said Quint. 'Flight-rock rubble. The bits and pieces from old, broken flight-rocks; chips and splinters . . . Occasionally robbers will break into the Stone Gardens and take buoyant rocks before they're ready . . . Old, new; all the bits end up as rubble, which is put inside the sealed metal cases. No use for a sleek sky pirate ship, of course, but for a league tug, they work well enough. And over there . . .'

'I was awake last night,' said Maris, interrupting Quint and changing the subject, her dark-ringed eyes suddenly serious.

Quint turned to her. 'You heard . . . ?'

'Everything,' she said. 'I heard both of you. I know all about the fire . . . About Turbot Smeal . . .'

Quint swallowed hard. 'Then you know why my father came for me. What's driving him on . . .'

Maris nodded. 'And why he took such a risk with the *Galerider* out there at the cliff edge,' she added, gripping Quint's hands. 'This hunt for Turbot Smeal,' she said, 'it's forcing him to take terrible risks . . . Are you sure it's worth it, Quint?'

Quint looked down at his feet. 'He's my father,' he said miserably. 'And I'm his right hand. Where he goes, I must follow.'

'And me, Quint?' said Maris, forcing him to look her in the eyes. 'What am I?'

Quint smiled and returned the squeeze on his hands. 'You're my friend, Maris . . .'

Just then, there was the sound of the *tap-tap-tapping* of a leagues-cane and heavy footfalls, and into the sky-shipyard strode three individuals.

The first was a colossus of a leaguesman, as broad as he was tall. He had a patch over his left eye, a shaved head, the scalp mottled and uneven, and a thick, grizzled moustache. He wore heavy boots, gleaming gauntlets and a broad belt worn so tight it accentuated his huge paunch, and from which hung a collection of weapons – a long-sword, a dagger, a sling, a ball and chain. Over his shirt and breeches, thick leather armour plates protected his neck, his chest, his shoulders and shins.

Quint gulped. It was none other than the High Leaguesmaster of Undertown, Ruptus Pentephraxis, himself, the highest of the high-hats – even though, on this occasion at least, his head was bare. Quint shook his head unhappily. He knew that Ruptus and Wind Jackal had a history of violence and enmity between them that went back for years.

Beside the High Leaguesmaster, his companion tapped his long elegant leagues-cane impatiently. Small where Ruptus was large, thin and puny where Ruptus was huge and strong, his pinched face was swarthy, with piercing green eyes and black side-whiskers which had been waxed into sharp points. He was wearing long flowing robes with a high, jagged collar, and had metal spikes at the end of each of his thin bony fingers which glinted menacingly in the sunlight.

Finger-spikes, Quint knew, were favoured more highly than rings by certain leaguesmasters, and these especially ornate points, glinting in the sunlight, could belong to only one person.

Imbix Hoth was his name.

For years Master of the League of Rock Merchants, he had recently also been appointed High Master of the entire Leagues of Flight – although there was some debate as to *how* this had happened. What was not in question was the fact that in Undertown he was now second in importance only to the High Leaguesmaster himself. Imbix Hoth controlled the trade in flight-rocks. Without his co-operation, no sky-shipyard could survive for long. Behind him stood a weedy, lop-eared goblin gripping a long, forked hat-pole, with which he supported his master's extremely tall four-pronged hat.

The two high-hat leaguesmasters strode past Quint and

Maris, treating them as if they didn't exist, before stopping at the chiselled entrance to the yardmaster's tower. Behind them, the lop-eared goblin delicately prodded his master's hat, which swayed slightly, and then winked over his shoulder at Quint and Maris. Ruptus Pentephraxis pounded at the tower door with one immense fist, and the startled face of Hummer the clerk appeared.

'Tell your master that the High Leaguesmaster is here, and that I've brought someone who can solve that little problem we've been having.'

'Yes, sir, right away, sir. *Do* come in, sir,' grovelled the clerk.

The two leaguesmasters entered, the lop-eared goblin tipping off Imbix Hoth's high hat just in time, and catching it in one hand as he followed them inside.

'High-hats and their hat-tippers!' said an amused-sounding voice. 'Don't you just love them?'

'Excuse me?' said Maris. 'I . . . Oh!' she smiled. 'It's you!'

Thaw Daggerslash stood before them, smiling broadly, his hands on his hips. 'It is indeed,' he said. 'Mistress Maris Pallitax,' he said, extending a hand in greeting. 'It's so good to see you again.'

Maris smiled and held out her own hand, which Thaw took and turned over, before planting a light kiss on the back of it. Maris blushed furiously, which made the young sky pirate smile even more broadly. He was wearing a shabby stained apron and torn canvas trousers rather than his splendid embroidered frock coat, and his fair hair was messy, with flecks of sawdust and woodchips in it.

'And Master Quint,' said Thaw, turning his disarming smile on him and clapping him warmly on the back. 'Excellent to see you again, too, my young friend.' He frowned. 'What brings you here?'

'The *Galerider* is being repaired,' Quint explained.

'Is it now?' said Thaw. 'Little wonder, after the battering she must have taken out there at the cliff edge.'

'You heard about that?' said Quint.

'The sky-shipyards are abuzz with talk of it,' Thaw replied, his face suddenly concerned. 'Whatever possessed your father to sail there?'

This time it was Quint who blushed, but Maris was quick to come to his rescue.

'And you, Captain Daggerslash,' she said sweetly. 'What brings *you* here?'

'Me?' said Thaw, with an embarrassed laugh, smoothing

down his apron and shaking the sawdust from his hair. 'I have come to take possession of a beautiful sky vessel of my very own. One that, due to a temporary shortage of funds, I've had to repair largely by myself!'

Thaw put two fingers to his lips and gave a short, piercing whistle. The next moment, a small and rather battered sky barge appeared from behind one of the sky-ship cages and slowly descended towards them, the port-side bow markedly lower than the starboard. As it drew closer, a shaggy-haired albino banderbear – little more than a cub by the look of him – peered down.

'Wuh-wuh!' he grunted, straightening up, and let a long rope uncurl from the side.

Thaw saluted theatrically. 'As you see,' he laughed, 'the *Mireraider* is a real beauty! And my crew – all one of him – awaits.'

He grabbed hold of the rope and pulled himself up on board.

'Farewell, Maris. Farewell, Quint,' he shouted back as the sky barge rose again. 'We're off to seek our fortune as wreck-raiders. Wish us luck!'

'Good luck!' Maris shouted after him.

As the tiny craft dis-appeared behind the roof-tops, Quint turned to Maris. 'He's going to need all the

luck he can get,' he said. 'Wreck-raiding is just about the most dangerous thing any sky pirate can undertake.'

'It is?' said Maris, shaking her head. 'But he seemed so light-hearted and happy . . .'

'And brave,' said Quint. 'A true sky pirate captain!'

'Talking of true sky pirate captains,' said Maris, with a little smile, 'here comes your father.'

Quint looked across, to see Wind Jackal emerging from the tower. He looked serious, but by no means as grim and troubled as Quint had feared. As Hummer scurried out behind him, Wind Jackal turned to the clerk and shook him by the hand.

'Tell the yardmaster we have a deal,' he said. 'I'll send my quartermaster round to sort out the details.'

Hummer nodded and returned inside.

'A deal, Father?' Quint asked tentatively.

'Aye, Quint, lad,' said his father, a relieved look on his face. 'Full repairs and refitting of the *Galerider* in return for a voyage to the Deepwoods for a consignment of bloodoak timber.'

'That's wonderful, Father,' said Quint, relieved to hear that Wind Jackal had returned to his sky pirate trade, rather than tormenting himself with thoughts of revenge. 'And when are we setting sail?'

'Tomorrow morning,' he said. 'Just as soon as . . . Sky above!' he exclaimed, as a ratbird flew in and landed on his shoulder. 'Hello, boy!' he said. 'I recognize *you* well enough!'

'Nibblick!' Quint exclaimed at the sight of his pet. 'I've been wondering where you'd got to. I was afraid we'd lost you to those cliff storms.'

The little creature chirruped and squeaked and, with a flutter of its wings, flew across from Wind Jackal's shoulder to Quint's outstretched finger.

'Look,' said Maris, 'I think he's got a message.'

'He can't have . . .' Quint frowned and looked more closely. Sure enough, sticking out of the little capsule strapped to the ratbird's leg, was a corner of paper. He unscrewed the top and pulled out the message.

'What does it say?' asked Wind Jackal.

'. . . Oh, nothing,' said Quint, shakily.

'Let me see,' said Wind Jackal.

'Really, it's nothing,' said Quint. 'It's . . .'

'Then let me see.'

Reluctantly, Quint handed over the message. His father read it out loud, his voice taking on the same cold, vengeful edge as it had had the night before. Blookoak consignment or no bloodoak consignment, he knew that Wind Jackal would be unable to ignore the mysterious message the ratbird had brought him.

If you wish to find the one you seek, meet me in the Sluice Tower at midnight.

A well-wisher.

97

·CHAPTER FIVE·

THE WAIF ASSASSIN

Quint's finger traced idly round the letters carved into the table-top. F ... O ... The tip of his index finger circled it once, twice, before moving on. X. He sighed.

'Rain Fox,' he murmured, and wondered who he could have been, this long forgotten sky pirate captain who had carved his name on the tavern table. Had he been rich and successful, with a magnificent sky ship and a loyal crew? Or, Quint mused darkly, had he been like most sky pirate captains – short of money, unsure of his crew, harassed, careworn, and continually looking over his shoulder. Probably he'd ended up being 'festooned' – left at the top of a Deepwoods tree by a mutinous crew, and replaced by a younger, more ambitious captain.

Who knows? All that remained of Captain Rain Fox now was a series of deep scratches in the surface of the scrubbed lufwood.

Quint stared down at the ancient carving, just one of

hundreds that covered the tables in the Tarry Vine tavern. Across from him, where Maris sat dozing fitfully, was Quint's father's name – *Wind Jackal* – carved in elegant letters with a curling flourish beneath it. How different from most sky pirate captains his father had always seemed: cheerful, calm and determined, his emotions under control and his actions well thought out and decisive.

How he had come to admire and depend upon his father's judgement, Quint thought with a sad smile. It made it all the more disturbing and worrying to see how this search for Turbot Smeal had consumed him with hatred and blinded him to dangers that the great Captain Wind Jackal, who had once carved his own name on this lufwood table, would never have ignored.

And now this new message, as mysterious as the others, had arrived just as things looked as if they might be getting back to normal. Quint looked down at his lap, where the tiny body of his ratbird lay, stiff and lifeless. He stroked the soft fur between Nibblick's tufted ears, and tears filled his eyes. The ratbird had died in the sky-shipyard within minutes of delivering its message, from the same slow-acting poison that had killed the first one his father received. It was a common way for gossips and schemers to cover their tracks. 'Messages of no return' they were called – but that didn't make it any easier to bear.

Quint slammed his fist down on the table. 'Damn you, Smeal!' he snarled.

Maris woke with a start. 'You're beginning to sound

like your father,' she said with a yawn as she stretched her arms. 'Speaking of whom, has he come back yet?'

No sooner had Quint, Maris and Wind Jackal returned to the Tarry Vine tavern from the sky-shipyard, than his father had left again, ordering the two of them to stay behind.

'Wait here for the crew!' he'd barked as he strode out, his face drained of all colour. 'I'll be back as soon as I can.'

So they'd sat there, at the carved table, for hours. Maris had dozed off, while he, Quint, had been left to brood . . . He looked up at his friend.

'No, not yet,' he said, in a tired, listless voice.

'I just don't get it . . .' Maris began.

'Don't get what?' said Quint, stroking Nibblick miserably.

'This message . . .' Maris said with a frown.

'It's a trap, just like the others,' Quint said darkly. 'Think about it, Maris. First the slave market, then the cliff quarries, and now the Sluice Tower. Don't you see? They're all convenient, out-of-the-way places to set traps. Turbot Smeal is a fugitive. All Undertown – not just those who lost loved ones in the great fire of the Western Quays – would cheerfully kill him as soon as look at him, so he *has* to hide. In his evil, twisted way, he blames my father for his fate, so what does he do? He lures Wind Jackal to him . . .'

'You mean . . .' said Maris, staring at him.

'Yes,' said Quint. 'Turbot Smeal himself is sending these messages.'

He looked down at the little ratbird in his lap. 'I don't know quite how, but he is, I'm sure of it. And he's lying in wait, like a fat woodspider at the centre of a spider-silk web.'

The crew started returning to the tavern as late after-noon was slipping into early evening, and the sun was sliding down behind the rooftops. Ratbit and Spillins were first back. They'd not only managed to find the spider-silk sails that Wind Jackal had requested, but had had them delivered to Thelvis Hollrig's shipyard, where they were to be rigged ready for the follow-ing morning's departure.

'Drove a real hard bargain, we did,' Ratbit was saying, his swivel-eyes wandering round the gathered company as he sat down at the large lufwood table. 'Eight sails for the price of four.'

'And there's enough material over to re-line my cater-nest,' Spillins added, a broad smile across his wrinkly old face. 'Fair chilled to the bone I was, up there. It'll stop those draughts whistling through . . .'

'No more than you deserve, old timer,' said Ratbit, slapping his companion on the shoulders.

Quint was about to ask whether either of them had seen Wind Jackal, when Spillins turned and peered at the main entrance to the tavern. His rubbery smile grew wider.

'Evening, shipmates!' Steg Jambles announced jovially, as he strode across the floor.

The others looked up at him in surprise – before bursting out laughing.

'Steg, you old rogue!' Ratbit exclaimed, looking him up and down. 'I thought you were meant to be buying new ropes and rigging . . .'

'And so I did,' said Steg. '*And* delivered them to the shipyards . . .'

'So, the chandlery sheds are selling fine jackets as well now, are they?' said Spillins.

'You look as elegant as a leaguesmaster in all that finery!' Ratbit teased him.

Steg looked down and plucked at the new jacket he was wearing. It was a deep red, tapered at the waist and high-buttoned, with clam-pearl fastenings and a dark fromp-fur trim at the collar and cuffs.

'If you think *I* look good,' he said, turning and raising a hand towards Tem Barkwater behind him, 'then take a look at the lad here,' he said.

Blushing furiously, Tem shambled forward and stood there, stooped and awkward, shuffling his feet.

'Wonderful!' cried Maris, clapping her hands together. 'Tem, you look magnificent!'

Tem lowered his head bashfully. He was wearing a thick jerkin and a tilder skin jacket, heavy canvas leggings and stout boots which, unlike Steg's foppish jacket, looked practical and hardwearing. But it wasn't these that caught the eye. Instead, it was the broad hammelhorn felt cap with the upturned brim which the youth wore at a self-consciously jaunty angle that drew attention to itself. It was bright, flaming crimson and several sizes too big, and Tem was clearly in need of his very own hat-tipper to stop it slipping down over his reddening face. Gazing at the floor, he pulled the extraordinary headgear off and held it behind his back.

'And you've had a haircut!' said Maris.

'No he hasn't,' said Steg. 'He had his ears lowered!'

The crew burst out laughing – and Tem, blushing all the more furiously, rubbed his hands over his unruly mop of thick, freshly cropped hair.

'Having fun, I see,' came a soft, insidious voice behind them, and everyone turned to see Filbus Queep the quartermaster standing there; the great flat-head goblin, Sagbutt, standing at his shoulder.

'Productive day, Queep?' said Steg Jambles, his face becoming serious.

The quartermaster nodded as he took his place at the table. 'I've secured a contract with the League of Taper and Tallow Moulders,' he said. 'A particularly lucrative contract, I might add, since none of our fine leaguesmen are brave enough to undertake such a task.'

'Which is?' asked Steg.

'We're to deliver a cargo of candle-wax to the Great Shryke Slave Market . . .'

'But we're meant to be picking up a consignment of bloodoak timber,' Quint butted in.

Queep swivelled round and fixed the youth with a piercing stare. 'Indeed?' he said, narrowing his eyes. 'Blookoak timber, you say?'

'Yes, it was agreed this morning between my father and Thelvis Hollrig,' Quint explained, 'to cover the cost of the repairs to the *Galerider*.'

'I see . . .' said Filbus Queep, taking out a small notebook and a stub of ironwood charcoal. He opened the book and scribbled some calculations. 'That should work out very nicely . . .' He smiled thinly. 'Repaired sky ship – faster journey time – more hold capacity . . . . Tallow to slave market. On to Timber Glades. Blookoak to Undertown . . .' He snapped the little book shut and looked round the table. 'Equals a healthy profit!'

'I'll drink to that!' roared Steg Jambles, raising a tankard of woodale.

The others raised their own tankards and drank a toast, as Maris and Quint exchanged glances. Queep wiped woodale foam from his mouth and looked at Quint.

'Anything wrong, Master Quint?' he asked.

Quint traced a finger over Rain Fox's name on the table. 'There's been another message,' he said quietly.

All eyes turned to him.

'Smeal?' said Queep bitterly.

Quint nodded.

'Not again!' the quartermaster muttered, removing his steel-rimmed glasses and polishing them slowly on the front of his shirt. 'Don't get me wrong,' he said. 'If Wind Jackal were to decide to go off on his own in pursuit of Smeal, then I would be the first to give him my best wishes.' He paused to replace his glasses and pushed them up his nose. 'Yet if he wishes to continue as captain of the *Galerider*, then I think we, as crew, have the right to expect his undivided attention.'

Steg gasped. ' "*If he wishes to continue as captain*",' he repeated. 'Queep, this is mutinous talk.'

'On the contrary,' Queep responded, 'I am merely pointing out the duties of a captain. If those duties are not fulfilled, then the individual forfeits his right to remain captain.' He shrugged. 'It is the way sky pirate captains have been deposed and replaced ever since sky pirate ships first took to the sky.'

All round the table, the crew nodded sagely. Quint looked down at the table, angry and embarrassed. It was Maris who broke the awkward silence.

'Wind Jackal is trying to bring a former quartermaster to account for his treachery,' she said. 'Now, it seems, his current quartermaster is set on turning his crew against him.' She stared furiously at Filbus Queep.

'Is this true?' came a sonorous voice.

Everyone looked round at the newcomer, a mixture of shock and guilt plastered across their features. Spillins blanched, while Steg Jambles turned woodbeet-red. Both of them looked away. Ratbit held the captain's gaze, but couldn't stop blinking.

'Well?' said Wind Jackal.

'Just heard you received another message,' said Filbus Queep silkily, his voice low and eyebrows raised.

'Did you now?' said Wind Jackal.

He headed for the largest chair at the table – a wooden armchair with interlocking tarry vines carved into the upright back – and sat down. Then he looked at each of the crew-members seated round the table, one by one, his gaze lingering just long enough to make each of them uneasy.

'Have I ever let you down?' he asked, his eyes now darting round the circle of crew-members. 'Have I?'

A couple of them shook their heads and looked down,

unable to hold his gaze. Steg Jambles, blushing, cleared his throat.

'All the years we've sailed together, haven't I always looked out for you?'

Tem Barkwater scratched the back of his neck. Ratbit, elbows up on the table, supported his forehead on his hands.

'Spillins,' said Wind Jackal. 'You've been in my crew longer than any of the others. 'On all our raids and battles, have I, as captain, ever left a crew-member behind?'

'N . . . no,' the oakelf stammered.

Wind Jackal turned to Ratbit. The mobgnome wilted under his intense stare.

'That time we were ambushed in the lufwood glades – I came back for you on prowlgrinback, remember?'

'I'll never forget it, sir,' Ratbit replied.

'Sagbutt,' said the captain, turning his attention on the flat-head. 'Do you remember down in the boom-docks, when you foolishly turned your back on that leagues-man and were clubbed unconscious? Eh? We ended up losing half our cargo, didn't we? Did I turf you off the *Galerider*?'

'No, sir,' the flat-head grunted.

Wind Jackal's eyes scanned the table.

'Steg, you fought with me at the Battle of Wilderness Lair. I know your heart is true.'

Steg nodded. There was a painful lump in his throat.

'And you, Filbus.' Wind Jackal's penetrating gaze rested on Filbus Queep. 'Surely you remember the oath you made to me when I rescued you from that group of

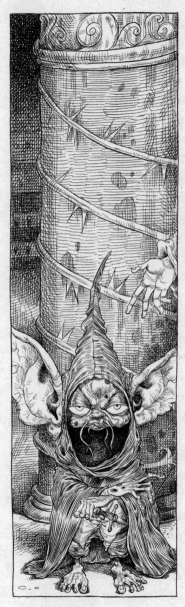

murderous under-professors in Sanctaphrax?'

'Yes, Captain,' the quartermaster muttered. 'I pledged to follow you wherever you led until I could repay the debt I owe you ... You have my loyalty, Captain.'

Wind Jackal nodded and sat back in his chair. 'Good,' he said. He twisted the end of his moustache thoughtfully. 'As you've heard, I have received another message, and I have engaged the services of a waif to help.'

As he spoke, a small individual dressed in a hooded cloak stepped out of the shadows and approached the table. He stood at Wind Jackal's right side.

'This is Menisculis,' said Wind Jackal.

The sky pirates looked at the waif before them with a mixture of fascination and revulsion. There were many waifs living in Undertown, and of all kinds – ghost-waifs, nightwaifs, flitter-waifs; waterwaifs, with their green-tinged skin and webbed fingers; pale, mottled grey-waifs, dangling barbels hanging down from the corners of their wide, fleshy mouths ... The thing they all had in common was that they could read the minds of other creatures – apart, strangely, from other waifs who did not wish their minds to be read. It was their mind-reading abilities that made waifs so valuable, and yet so mistrusted. Menisculis was – as they could all tell from his large eyes and fluttering, almost transparent, ears – a night-waif; the best mind-readers of all.

'This morning,' Wind Jackal told them, 'while I was at the sky-shipyard, I received a message of no return.'

Quint swallowed hard.

'Despite what some of you may want ...' He glanced at Maris and Quint. '... I am not going to let the matter rest. I intend to get to the bottom of this business once and for all. And Menisculis, here, should ensure that.'

'*Indeed I shall.*' The waif's whisper sounded in every head gathered round the table.

'I hate it when they do that,' grumbled Steg to Tem in a half-whisper.

'I must check this message out,' continued Wind Jackal, 'and I'm going to need all of you to do it.' He looked round. 'Are you with me?'

The crew climbed to their feet and looked their captain steadily in the eye as the tiny waif's ears twitched and trembled.

'*They're with you, Captain,*' Menisculis's voice sounded in everyone's head.

The captain motioned for everyone to sit down, and picked up his tankard of woodale.

'So, Steg,' he said, his eyes sparkling. 'What exactly is that you're wearing?'

Maris turned to Tem as the last of the crew followed Wind Jackal out of the tavern, her eyes moist with frustration.

'When he said he was going to need all of the crew, I thought he meant it!' she said with a gasp of exasperation.

Tem looked at her uneasily. 'But . . . but the captain said he needed us to stay here,' he told her. 'To send help if they didn't return . . .'

Maris snorted. 'And you believed him!' She shook her head. 'Don't you see, Tem? He's trying to protect us . . . Well, if he thinks we're just going to sit here and do nothing, he's got another think coming!'

Tem swallowed. 'He has?'

'Certainly,' said Maris. 'Grab that new hat of yours, Tem. It'll keep your ears warm! . . .'

Oh, Maris! Maris! Maris! Quint thought as he followed his father down the foggy street outside the Tarry Vine tavern. Please don't do anything stupid!

He'd noticed that look in her eyes when he'd turned at the tavern door to wave her goodbye – a look he'd seen so many times before. In the Palace of Shadows when her father, Linius Pallitax, had made her promise not to go down inside the Sanctaphrax rock . . . On board the

Cloudslayer when he himself had suggested Maris be dropped off before the vessel journeyed out into Open Sky . . . It was a look – not of defiance exactly, but of absolute determination. A look that appeared compliant, but which Quint knew was saying, 'You may think I've heard and understood and will do as I am told, but sadly you are wrong.'

Still, there was nothing Quint could do about it now. They made their way down to the riverside, through the thickening fog and crossed the Edgewater in one of the huge, nameless river-coracles that plied their trade both day and night. Wind Jackal, Quint and the waif, Menisculis, sat at the front; Steg Jambles, Spillins and Ratbit in the middle; while Filbus Queep and Sagbutt sat at the back, either side of the ferry-pilot. Stout and surly, and with a large growth on the side of his pointed chin, the lugtroll pilot spoke not a single word as he slowly but steadily winched his passengers across.

At the far side, Wind Jackal settled up, then led his crew away from the riverbank and into the filthy sprawl that was East Undertown. Once, the area had been relatively thriving, with tenement-towers and back-to-back shacks shooting up to offer cheap housing for those who worked in the factories and foundries nearby. Now, decades later, those same buildings had fallen into disrepair, and as the thick air squeezed its way down the narrow street, there was a neverending succession of curious noises – creaking timbers, slipping roof-tiles and groaning foundations – as though the fog itself was eating away at the buildings and hastening their decay.

For the fogs that rolled in from the Mire on the westerly winds were notoriously dense. What was more, as they passed over the foundry district, they gathered up the smoke and soot and noxious fumes belching out from the chimneys, and churned the whole lot into a foul-smelling miasma that dirtied every window, stained every stone a poisonous shade of yellow and filled the eyes and lungs of everyone unfortunate enough to live there. As Quint strode after his father, over ground that turned from cobblestones to mud – his eyes streaming and jacket pulled up over his mouth in an attempt to filter out the foul air – he became aware that all around them, the foggy night was filled with the sound of coughing.

'*It's this way.*' The nightwaif's voice, clear as a bell, sounded in the crew's heads. '*We turn left at the end of this alley, just after the building with the broken windows.*'

Behind Quint, Filbus Queep and Ratbit shuddered and muttered under their breath about 'nasty, creepy little waifs', while ahead, Wind Jackal strode on.

From far off at the top of a distant tower – maybe in the Western Quays, or possibly even up in Sanctaphrax – there came the muted sound of a heavy bell chiming quarter off the hour.

'Fifteen minutes till midnight,' said Wind Jackal, a hint of anxiety in his voice.

'*It's all right,*' the waif's voice sounded in Quint's head. '*We're here.*'

'Thank Sky for that,' Quint heard Wind Jackal mutter, while behind him, the rest of the crew were whispering, outraged by the intrusion in their heads.

'*Turn left.*'

They did as they were told. A moment later, as they rounded the corner, the air abruptly cleared as the currents swirling up from beneath the jutting rock caused the fog to fray and peel away from the Edge itself. Here the city of Undertown met the edge of the cliff and disgorged the filth and foul waters of its industry from sewer pipes, down into the void below. Just ahead, stark against the night sky, was the dark silhouette of the building that housed the biggest sewer pipe of all: the Sluice Tower.

The broad, squat tower was divided into three main floors – the upper two, studded with numerous windows.

The topmost rooms were set inside the steep, tiled roof; the lower ones were behind plastered walls which had chipped and peeled so many times they looked like badly blistered skin. The third and lowest part of the building consisted of the foundations that hugged the edge of the jutting rock, and out of which the vast sewer pipe emerged. Normally, a mere trickle of water and waste ran from this ancient sewerage conduit, but on occasions, when storms had threatened to flood Undertown, the gates inside the Sluice Tower were opened and a mighty torrent would gush from the pipe until the waters had subsided and the danger of flooding passed.

The Sluice Tower and the great pipe it was built over stood at the entrance to the dark, verminous world of the sewers of Undertown. Here, desperate denizens – the lowest of the low – eked out a filthy existence alongside muglumps and Mire vermin of every description. In such a world, the impoverished Undertowners who inhabited the dank, fetid rooms of the Sluice Tower were considered fortunate.

Wind Jackal raised his hand and the crew behind him came to a halt. All, that is, except for the waif, who crept forward and crouched down beside the Sluice Tower's outer wall. The little creature pressed its long thin fingers to the blistered wall and began fluttering and twitching its ears as it listened.

'Take up positions. I want the Sluice Tower sealed,' Wind Jackal ordered. 'Sagbutt, the front entrance. Queep, the back. Steg and Ratbit, I want you to watch the drain-covers – I want no nasty surprises coming up from the sewers. And Spillins, an overview. Get yourself up onto the roof. If you see anything amiss – anything! – I want you to sound the alarm.' He turned to Menisculis.

The waif glanced back at him with its huge eyes. 'Many voices,' he said. 'I can hear the thoughts of a trog female, who is with child and hungry, but terrified that her father might find her . . .'

His ears swivelled round.

'And here, a pair of gnokgoblin brothers. They were in service to a leaguesman ... *Ha!*' he cried. 'Ruptus Pentephraxis, no less! And they have stolen from him. A sizeable amount of gold ...' He paused and shook his head. 'But wait. One is planning on blaming it all on the other and making off with the lot ...'

The ears trembled and swivelled some more.

'Oh, and here. Up on the top floor ... Sad, sad thoughts. A lugtroll, fresh to Undertown. She believed the streets were paved with gold, yet now she has to forage in the rubbish dumps just to find enough to live on ...' He paused. 'She misses her mother, back in the Deepwoods. Her grandmother.' He gasped. 'Her daughter ...'

'Keep listening,' Wind Jackal said, 'for dark thoughts; perhaps murderous ...'

The waif raised his hand, and hissed. 'Wait, Captain,' he whispered. His ears swivelled round, so that both of them were pointing downwards. The fluttering increased.

'Down in the sewer pipe itself,' the waif said. 'Dark thoughts ... Evil thoughts, Captain ... There is one waiting, brooding on the past but with plans for the future ... But the hate ... It is powerful, Captain ... Making it hard for me to read his thoughts.'

Wind Jackal drew his sword and motioned for the crew to take their places. He then looked hard into the waif's eyes for a moment. Menisculis nodded slowly. Turning away, Wind Jackal whispered to Quint tersely.

'Follow me.'

They crept over to the boundary wall beside the Sluice Tower and climbed it. Standing on top, Quint looked down into the yawning abyss on the other side.

'How far does it go down?' he wondered out loud.

'For ever,' said Wind Jackal, as he eased himself down onto the far side of the wall. 'So you'd better not slip!'

Heart thumping, Quint followed his father and the waif down the outer wall, picking out handholds and footholds by the shadows cast by the low moon. Then, shifting across to his right, he grasped hold of the lip of the huge sewer pipe, and swung round inside, landing with an echoing splash at the bottom. His father was waiting for him. The waif, Menisculis, was nowhere to be seen.

Quint drew his sword as quietly as he could and followed his father inside. Somewhere ahead in the gloom, he knew, the mysterious message-sender was waiting. Wind Jackal's waif had heard him. He'd heard the hatred in his thoughts; hatred so intense that it could only belong to Turbot Smeal, couldn't it? Quint touched the small furry body of his ratbird in his greatcoat pocket, and felt a surge of hatred of his own.

All around them, water dripped, the sound echoing round the cavernous pipe. Far ahead of them, glowing in the moonlight that bounced its way along the tunnel, were the bars of the sluice-cage, glinting like teeth, the odd branch or plank wedged between them like trapped food. And behind that, black and heavy, the sluice-gate itself, closed – all except for a tiny gap at the very bottom through which the tiny trickle emerged.

From above their heads, filtering through the air-ducts and pipework, they could hear low conversation, laughter, snoring, as those in the upper storeys far above whiled away the long night.

'Captain Wind Jackal, at last!' came a strange lisping voice from the shadows ahead. 'I have a message for you . . .'

Just then, from behind him, there was a flurry of movement, and a waif threw himself at Wind Jackal from a shadowy recess, high above their heads. As he dropped down through the air, Quint caught sight of the dagger in his hand glinting . . .

'Father!' he cried out.

But Wind Jackal had already seen his attacker. A fraction of a second before the waif would have landed on his back

and embedded the blade in his throat, the sky pirate captain leaped to the floor and rolled over, dragging his son with him. As he fell, Quint heard something whistle over his head.

'*Aaaiiii!*'

The screech echoed down the long tunnel and back again. Then, silence.

For a moment, Quint remained where he was, crushed against the bottom of the wet pipe, his father's arm holding him down. He raised his head and peered ahead.

'Wh . . . what happened?' he gasped.

There before him were two waifs. One was dead, a dagger in his hand and another dagger embedded in his chest, from which thick black blood was pouring. Kneeling down next to him was Menisculis.

Quint scrambled to his feet, helped by his father.

'I . . . I don't understand,' said Quint. 'Where is he? The one you heard?'

'*What I heard,*' said Menisculis, looking round, '*was this waif assassin here, throwing his thoughts . . .*' He nodded admiringly. '*And very good he was, too.*'

He leaned down, pulled his dagger from the assassin's chest, wiped it on his trousers and returned it to its sheath at his belt. Wind Jackal laid a hand on Quint's shoulder.

'It's as I suspected all along, Quint, my lad,' he said. 'Another one of Smeal's traps. But this time, thanks to our waif friend here, we outwitted him.'

'You knew it was a trap all along,' sighed Quint, a huge wave of relief washing over him. 'I wish you'd said something before. Maris and I were so worried! . . .'

'*He couldn't say anything,*' Menisculis's voice sounded in Quint's head, '*or you would have given the game away to this waif assassin here. As it was, the hatred in your thoughts was a perfect cover for me, Master Quint, to assassinate the assassin.*' A thin whispery laugh sounded in Quint's mind, making him shudder.

Quint looked across at his father, who was smiling grimly. In the distance there came a low rumble.

'Father!' Quint gasped. 'What . . . what's that noise?'

Coming towards them like rolling thunder was a rumbling, rushing, roaring sound.

'Water!' cried Menisculis.

The next instant, there was a grinding sound of metal against stone. The sluice gate was being raised. The noise from beyond became tumultuous. Quint turned and peered into the darkness of the tunnel – and then he saw it. Bubbling, frothing, foaming; a vast torrent of water hurtling down the pipe towards them.

'Run!' bellowed Wind Jackal.

But it was already too late. The wall of water surged towards them, picking them up and tossing them forward as it gushed towards the end of the tunnel. Menisculis disappeared from view; then Wind Jackal, his arms still waving frantically. Then Quint himself went under, and was rolled over and over, unable to see, unable to breathe . . .

Oh, Maris, he thought. Maris . . .

All at once, he burst out of the pipe, like a bubble from a bottle of sparkling winesap, out into the open air.

Falling . . . He was falling . . .

Thunk!

And then he was falling no more, but was trapped in some kind of net, with the water still pouring over him, passing through the holes in the net and down, down, down into the endless void beneath the Edge. Beside him lay Wind Jackal. From far above them, Quint heard a familiar voice cry out and, looking up, he saw the small sky ferry – the *Edgehopper* – hovering overhead. It rose up above the Sluice Tower and away from the torrent of water still gushing from the pipe. The faces of Maris and Tem, worried but smiling, peered down at them.

'It's all right,' Maris shouted back. 'We've got both of you! You're safe.'

Quint gripped his head in his hands and moaned softly. By the look on Wind Jackal's face, and on those of the crew who now appeared at the cliff-edge wall, they heard it, too. In the *Edgehopper*, Maris and Tem exchanged shocked looks with the gnokgoblin pilot and buried their heads in their folded arms.

Far below, falling into the endless night, yet in all of their heads, was the voice of the nightwaif, Menisculis, crying out to them – but growing fainter by the second.

'*Help me! Help me. Help . . .*'

·CHAPTER SIX·

IMBIX HOTH

'Halt!' The gruff command cut through the cold, early morning air. The academic-at-arms, in the heavy armour of a rock guardian, levelled his crossbow at the leaguesmaster in the high hat before him. 'Nobody enters the Stone Gardens while the rock harvest is in progress!'

The guard was tall, but slightly built, with piercing grey-blue eyes and a shock of brown, curly hair that fell down over one side of his wide forehead. He was also young, yet the look in those eyes, betraying the dark horrors he had witnessed, seemed to belong to someone twice his age. Behind him, fifty of his comrades stood shoulder to shoulder, their full-length shields emblazoned with the red oval insignia of the Knights Academy.

Imbix Hoth looked the academic-at-arms slowly up and down, his high hat wobbling and being steadied by his lop-eared goblin hat-tipper. The armour, he noted, was scuffed and dented, and the row of shields were scratched and pitted by sword blows and crossbow bolts.

'I heard all about the Battle of the Knights Academy,' Imbix purred, with a smile that revealed a mouthful of small, stained peg-like teeth. 'And how Sanctaphrax lost many of her best academics-at-arms in that bloody fight . . .'

He raised a hand of razor-sharp finger-spikes and waved the young academic-at-arms dismissively aside.

'So, since you're obviously new and this is your first harvest,' he said, 'I'll forgive you your insolence in stopping me entering the Stone Gardens.'

The leaguesmaster took a step forward – then stopped, outraged, his eyebrows shooting upwards, when the young academic held his ground.

'Perhaps I didn't make myself clear,' he said coldly.

Behind him, the eight massive Undertown shrykes of his bodyguard were getting restless. Dressed in full-length black cloaks and gleaming spiked helmets, they clacked their beaks and hissed with irritation, the ruffs of feathers at their necks standing on end.

Stretching back from the gates of the Stone Gardens in the direction of Undertown was a line of some fifteen huge stone-wagons, teams of shaggy hammelhorns in harness. The wagoneers, who had been standing around stamping their feet and blowing on their hands in the chill of the early dawn, now all turned to watch the confrontation unfolding before them.

'Just one word from me,' hissed Imbix Hoth, no longer smiling, 'and my shrykes will rip out your insolent heart and feast on your liver!'

'There'll be no need for that,' came a slightly breathless voice. 'Let the Master of the League of Rock Merchants through, Captain, there's a good fellow.'

The stone marshal, Zaphix Nemulis – a high professor in the violet and white striped robes of the Academy of Wind – pushed past the academic-at-arms, who was still blocking the entrance to the Stone Gardens, and ushered Imbix and his bodyguard inside with a flurry of apologies and excuses. As the shrykes strode past, one leaned towards the young guard, who had now lowered his crossbow, and spat a stream of green bile at his feet. The watching wagoneers – leaguers from the League of Rock Merchants – chuckled and went back to checking their hammelhorns' harnesses and preparing their grappling-poles for the harvest to come.

Just two hours earlier, as the first blinding darts of light had broken over the horizon and shot the mist-drenched Stone Gardens with long, stark shadows, a great multitude of white ravens had taken to the sky. High above Undertown the birds had flocked, thousands of them, breaking the dawn silence with their piercing cries as they headed for the great floating city.

'*Waaark! Waaark! Waaark!*'

Round the Raintasters' Tower and Loftus Observatory they had wheeled, alerting the Sanctaphrax academics to the fact that a rock harvest was imminent. Their screeching din had woken even the deepest sleepers, who had tumbled from their beds with the rest, quickly dressed and, still bleary-eyed, headed for the Stone Gardens.

Down in Undertown, this discordant din that had rudely torn every trog, troll, goblin, waif and shryke from their slumbers was known as *the chorus of the dead*. It was common knowledge that when the venerable academics of Sanctaphrax died, they were taken to the Stone Gardens to be laid out at the top of the stone stacks, where their earthbound bodies were consumed by the white ravens. To the superstitious Undertowners, it seemed logical that the spirits of those deceased entered the rocks. After all, what other reason could there be for the ghastly howls that filled the air when those same rocks finally broke free of the stacks as they floated up towards Open Sky?

The thought of it all filled them with dread. On that particular morning – with the marked exception of the drivers of the stone wagons, who had no choice – the Undertowners had remained in their beds, curled up beneath their covers, where they fingered the lucky amulets around their necks, murmuring prayers and incantations as the terrible chorus rang out. In starkest contrast, Sanctaphrax itself was a hive of activity as professors, under-professors, apprentices and acolytes streamed from the schools and academies, descended in crowded hanging-baskets, and hurried to the harvest in carts, carriages and barrows.

They arrived in the eerie Stone Gardens not a moment too soon. The high stacks of rock were already 'singing' – a low, mournful humming sound that confirmed what the white ravens roosting on the topmost rocks had felt with their sensitive claws. The huge boulders were ripe at last.

In time-honoured fashion, the schools and academies quickly spread out, gathering round their own rock stacks – rock stacks that the most venerable amongst them had watched mature over many a long year. From almost imperceptible bumps in the Edge rock they had grown into the towering stacks of a dozen or more boulders, one on top of the other, in ascending size. Forming a circle round their chosen stack, teams from the individual schools – mistsifters, raintasters, cloud-watchers, fog-graders, and numerous others from all the major and minor academies – raised their eyes skywards and waited expectantly. The rock bailiff, Silenius Quilp, marched through the gardens, excitedly shouting orders.

'Prepare the rock nets!' he bellowed. 'Fire up the braziers! Be ready with those rock callipers!'

At his command, the academics raised canopies of nets – each one fringed with a line of glowing sumpwood fire-floats – on the ends of long poles. They manoeuvred them high over the stacks, and waited. Beside them, apprentices stoked lufwood braziers furiously, while under-professors heated the huge, two-man rock callipers to a white-hot glow. Then, at the rock bailiff's cry of '*Silence!*', all fell still.

In the early light of the morning, apart from the eerie stone song, the only sound to be heard was the far-off squawking of the white ravens perched at the top of the Loftus Observatory. Gradually though, as the seconds passed, the low drone of the rocks became louder and more plaintive, like the mournful lament at a goblin wake, until one after the other, the uppermost rock on each stack gave a long low howl as it wobbled and shook, and then slowly rose up.

'Harvest!' roared the rock bailiff, rushing through the Stone Gardens, waving his staff above his head. 'In the name of Sanctaphrax, harvest!'

At the sound of his voice, the academics leaped into action. The 'net-tenders' pulled their poles free, and the great circular nets closed round the rising rocks, weighted by the fire-floats. For a moment, the huge boulders hovered above the stacks. Then, one by one, fringed by the warmth of the glowing floats, they slowly sank.

As the rocks approached the ground, the 'rock-fasteners' surged forward with their glowing callipers and seized the floating boulders in their fiery jaws. Great hisses of steam rose like storm clouds and, as the rock-fasteners held them tight, the rocks' mournful howl was extinguished.

All round the Stone Gardens the same procedure was being enacted. At a towering rock stack beside the Edgewater River, a team of cloudwatcher under-professors from the prestigious College of Cloud – each one wearing a scuffed, worn tilder-leather apron that betrayed their years of experience – netted and clamped their rock with both speed and precision. At the rock stack next to them, a team of fog-graders from the minor Academy of Fog was faring less well. Cobbled together only that morning, the group was a hotch-potch affair, ranging in age from callow apprentices to an elderly professor in his nineties who, despite his experience, was slow and so shaky that the others had to snatch his pole away from him before he got it tangled up in the net.

Meanwhile, in the eastern-most part of the garden, a group of seven young apprentice raintasters, their deep blue hoods pulled up over their heads, had set to work with enthusiasm. They'd raised their poles and positioned the net as they'd been shown, and when the rock had risen up from the stack, it had been caught and warmed, until it slowly descended once more.

But then, as two of them clamped the rock with the heated callipers, they noticed that something was badly wrong. The apprentice on the brazier bellows hadn't pumped them hard enough. The charcoal hadn't blazed hot enough, which meant that the callipers themselves had glowed red rather than white-hot. So, while all around them, the clamped rocks from other stacks had fallen silent, their own rock had continued to howl like a wounded tilder.

Worse than that, it began to rise up off the ground. The raintasters swarmed round their embattled rock-fasteners, concern plain on their faces. Twenty years it had taken for the rock to reach maturity. Twenty years! Pushing up from the ground, growing larger and lighter while those above it had been harvested, one after the other. Twenty whole years – about to be wasted, because of one moment of carelessness.

'For Sky's sake, don't let it fly off!' one of them cried as he fell on the rock and tried wrestling it back to the ground.

'The net! The net!' another one shouted, but by now half of the sumpwood burners had burned out, and there wasn't enough heat to keep it grounded.

Suddenly, a College of Rain under-professor from one of the other stacks came hurrying across, a pair of white-hot callipers that he'd pulled from his own brazier grasped in his hands.

'Take the other end,' he bellowed to the apprentice closest to him.

The youth leaped to do as he was told, and together the pair of them clamped the callipers round the rock. There was a hiss, a sigh and a cloud of steam – and finally the rock fell still. A cheer went up from the others.

'Thank you, sir,' they cried. 'Thank you.'

The under-professor nodded. 'Next time, heat your callipers properly,' he said. 'And always have a spare set at the ready.' He chuckled. 'The College of Rain hasn't lost a flight-rock for twelve harvests, but you lot came mighty close, I can tell you.' He nodded towards the distant gates. 'Now, take your rock, and join the grading queue.'

Soon a great procession of academics was making its way back through the Stone Gardens. The groups from each academy and school clustered round their own individual rocks, tending them with glowing tapers, fire-floats, torches and lanterns of every description – anything to keep the new-born flight-rock warm. Back through the now silent stacks, already beginning to welcome the returning white ravens, the academics marched in triumph, and on towards the Reckoning Bench.

There they were greeted by the rock bailiff, Silenius Quilp of the School of Light and Darkness. He was red-faced and breathless after his exertions, but smiling broadly. Beside him on the tall, ironwood bench sat the stone marshal, Zaphix Nemulis of the Academy of Wind, twitching slightly and adjusting his spectacles as he opened the giant ledger that was balanced on his knees. And to his left, standing stiffly upright, his arms folded, was Imbix Hoth, the Master of the League of Rock Merchants.

As the first academics – a group of under-professors from the College of Cloud – approached the bench, carefully tending their flight-rock, Imbix smiled, and his small, reddish eyes glinted greedily. Behind him, his black-feathered shrykes craned their necks and stared with unblinking yellow eyes.

'Diameter?' the stooped, wispy-haired rock bailiff enquired as the group of cloudwatchers reached the bench.

'Three strides, twelve,' came the reply.

Quilp frowned over the top of his half-moon glasses. 'Are you sure?' he queried. 'Looks like three strides, *thirteen*, to me.'

The cloudwatchers with the callipers clamped firmly round the rock held it steady while an under-professor took a measurement with a copper measuring rod.

'Three strides, thirteen,' he confirmed.

'I knew it,' said Quilp, turning to Zaphix the stone marshal with a smile of satisfaction. Although Silenius Quilp had never made it beyond sub-Under-Professor in the prestigious School of

Light and Darkness, his skills in the Stone Gardens were legendary.

Zaphix entered the measurement in the ledger on his balanced knees.

'Right, now attach it to the weighing-basket,' Quilp instructed.

The cloudwatchers eased the net across to the weighing-basket, and secured it in place. As the rock cooled slightly it began to pull the basket upwards, which in turn tugged on the hook beneath it and caused the needle at the centre of the measuring dial to swing round. Silenius Quilp crouched down and squinted at the callibrations.

'Eight hundred and sixty-three,' he read off.

Zaphix dipped his snowbird quill in the tiny pot of black ink and wrote the number in the column next to the diameter.

'Which means . . .' Quilp muttered under his breath, a complicated mental calculation involving the diameter of the rock times air temperature plus humidity, divided by the square root of its negative weight . . . 'Flight grade . . . third class,' he announced. 'A real beauty.'

Zaphix scratched away in the ledger before turning to the leaguesmaster, his eyebrows raised.

'For such a rock?' Imbix Hoth purred, his finger-spikes tapping down on the table-top. 'Twelve refectory tables of finest lufwood,' he said, 'and the College of Cloud's cellars filled with vintage sapwine.'

The under-professors bowed to the leaguesmaster

stiffly. They were clearly delighted with the price they'd obtained for their flight-rock but, as Sanctaphrax academics, they were hardly going to let a leaguesmaster, however lofty, see the pleasure on their faces.

'Sold!' announced the stone marshal, and entered the details in the ledger.

'Next!' the rock bailiff's voice rang out.

A group of mistsifters stepped confidently forward, the long sleeves of their checkerboard robes fluttering in the breeze. The rock they tended was massive, more than twice the size of the cloudwatchers', but as Silenius Quilp was weighing it, he frowned and pointed to a fissure which ran, like a livid scar, halfway up the rock's surface.

'A rupture, I'm afraid, Professors,' he announced to the mistsifters as Zaphix scratched in the ledger.

They turned to Imbix, who smiled ruefully. 'Pity,' he muttered. 'Over-ripe . . . So close and yet so far . . .'

'Fit only for rubble, I'm afraid,' said the stone marshal, shrugging his shoulders.

'A vat of woodale,' Imbix announced. 'Take it or leave it.'

The mistsifters bowed as stiffly as the cloudwatchers before them, their faces – behind the metal noses they wore – betraying no emotion.

'Next!'

The procession of harvested flight-rocks continued until well into the morning, with the academics accepting the leaguesmaster's bids for their rocks. Occasionally a group of older professors would hold out for more by standing silently, until Imbix added a gilded looking-glass or an ornamental wall-hanging or two to his bid. But most of them just accepted his offers.

And why shouldn't they? After all, the academics were being amply rewarded. A single flight-rock, for instance, had provided the Academy of Gloom with enough candles to last for a year, while a harvest of four rocks had ensured the Institute of Ice and Snow supplies of feathers, quills and down for decades to come. The leaguesmaster's offers were invariably generous, lavishing upon them everything they could want, and more.

It was, of course, in his best interests to do so. Without the Sanctaphrax academics' expertise, built up over generations, together with the white ravens to whom they offered up their dead, there would be no harvest. On occasions in the past, Undertowners had attempted to harvest flight-rocks for themselves – those, that is, who were not terrified by the ferocious white ravens and the disturbing eeriness of the gardens – only to find that the skill of the 'net-tenders' and 'rock-fasteners' was not easily matched. What was more, those who had succeeded in securing a flight-rock had then had the academics-at-arms to contend with, making their chances even slimmer.

Naturally, the Leagues of Undertown understood this only too well. It was the reason they furnished the Master of the League of Rock Merchants, Imbix Hoth, with all the luxuries they could, for him to shower on the academics in return for the precious flight-rocks which, it seemed, only the academics could successfully harvest. By selling the flight-rocks only to the League of Rock Merchants, the academics of Sanctaphrax avoided undignified haggling and squabbling with the Leagues of Undertown, and were able to retreat to their floating city with all the provisions and luxuries they could possibly need.

It was an arrangement that suited them and Imbix Hoth very well indeed. The leaguesmaster guarded his position jealously and saw to it that anyone who sought to take his place met with an unfortunate end – usually from the razor-sharp tip of a shryke's talon.

At last, with the sun now high up above the rock stacks and the hammelhorn wagons at the gates of the Stone Gardens all carefully loaded with their precious cargo, Zaphix Nemulis closed the ledger and put away his snow-bird quill. The last of the academics – an irascible bunch of fog-graders who had haggled silently for ages – finally settled for twenty bales of tilder cloth and eighty barrels of pickled oozefish, before shuffling off after the departing academics-at-arms. Now, the Stone Gardens were peaceful once more, with only the desultory calls of the roosting white ravens breaking the stillness.

'Sanctaphrax thanks you, Leaguesmaster,' said,
Zaphix, 'for your generosity.'

'As ever, I am pleased to be of service.' Imbix smiled
with a slight bow that almost caught his hat-tipper
by surprise.

The leaguesmaster ignored the flustered prodding of
the hat pole, and took the stone marshal by the arm.

'Now, on a more personal note . . .' He glanced
around furtively. The rock bailiff had packed away
his equipment and was hurrying off to catch the
noon-day baskets. 'Shall we take a little walk,
Stone Marshal?'

Zaphix smiled smoothly and fell into step with the
leaguesmaster as he walked. Behind him the razor-sharp
talons of the black-feathered shrykes clicked on the rock
as they followed.

For a few minutes they walked through the Stone
Gardens, neither of them speaking. Past the freshly
harvested rock stacks and the smaller 'infant' stacks,
they went; over rubble that had fused itself back into
the rock surface and on between budding stone
mounds that were about to sprout. Soon, they were
nearing the very edge of the gardens – indeed the
very edge of everything; where the rock stuck out and
the Edgewater River cascaded down into the yawning
void below.

As the bright yellow sun had risen higher in the
sky, it had slowly burned off the fog that enveloped
the Stone Gardens through the morning. Now, with
the distant bell at the top of the Great Hall softly

chiming midday, all that remained were wispy snakes of mist that wound their way round the bottoms of the stone stacks and the ankles of those walking between them. And as they approached the tapering slab of jutting rock in the farthest corner of the gardens, with the yellowy-blue sky all round them, it felt to Zaphix Nemulis as though he was walking through the air.

They came to a halt in front of the very last stone stack. The leaguesmaster and the stone marshal looked up.

'How is it coming along?' asked Imbix, his voice silken and his eyes glinting greedily. 'How big is it exactly?'

'Now, now, Imbix, it doesn't do to hurry such things,' said the stone marshal. 'Ten strides, and still growing, by my latest measurements.'

'Excellent! Excellent!' cackled the leaguesmaster. 'But I need it to grow bigger still!'

'Yes, so you keep telling me,' said the stone marshal, being careful to keep all irritation from his voice. 'And as I have told you before, Imbix, delaying the flight of a mature rock is a very tricky business indeed . . .'

'A business for which I'm paying you handsomely!' snapped the leaguesmaster.

'Yes, indeed you are, Imbix. Now take a look here . . .' said the stone marshal smoothly, trying to deflect the leaguesmaster's attention from the small fortune in marsh-gems and mire-pearls he'd already parted with. 'I have drilled a small hole through the stonecomb . . .'

He pointed above their heads to a tiny hole in the surface of the huge boulder at the top of the stack.

Imbix followed his gaze, his brow furrowing.

'It leads to the very heartrock at its centre,' said Zaphix. 'A minute crystal of stormphrax in a length of glowworm skin has been inserted,' he explained. 'The skin has now rotted away, and in darkness, the storm-phrax weights the rock down sufficiently to allow it to grow untroubled. It can be removed later, when . . .'

'Ingenious,' Imbix Hoth broke in. 'But can you make the rock bigger?'

'Given time,' said the stone marshal.

'I need it now,' snapped Imbix.

Zaphix Nemulis nodded. 'I'll do my best,' he said, 'but I can make no promises . . .'

'Get it to fifteen strides and you shall be as rich as a leaguesmaster!' Imbix declared, his finger-spikes digging into Zaphix's arm.

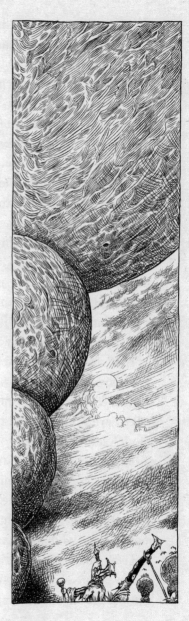

Just then, from behind them, one of the shrykes gave a loud hiss and leaped behind a small stone stack. Imbix and Zaphix turned to see it emerge a moment later with a struggling mobgnome clutched in its talons.

'What's this?' screeched Imbix Hoth furiously. 'A spy? A traitor? What have you heard? Speak up!'

'Calm yourself,' Zaphix Nemulis interrupted, eyeing the unfortunate creature, who was clutching a grubby sack in his trembling hands. 'It's just some poor wretch in search of rubble by the look of it. I'll give him a reprimand and send him on his way . . .'

'No!' Imbix silenced him. 'The mobgnome is mine!'

Eyes blazing, the black-feathered shryke threw the mobgnome at the leaguesmaster's feet.

'Have mercy, sir,' the mobgnome whimpered, wringing his hands together. 'I . . . I gathered a little rubble, just chippings . . . My sky ferry's on its last legs . . .'

'That's as may be,' said Zaphix, icily.

'Twelve mouths to feed, my wife has,' the mobgnome wailed. 'Twelve hungry mouths . . .'

'Yes, well now there'll be one fewer for her to worry about,' said Hoth, raising a spiked hand. 'Shrykes!' he shrieked, his raucous voice slicing through the air like a rusty blade. 'Deal with this vermin!'

A blood-curdling shriek went up as, in a flurry of black plumage, the eight shrykes fell on the hapless mobgnome, who disappeared beneath flashing talons and stabbing beaks. When the bloody flurry was over, all that was left of the mobgnome was a red stain on the rocky ground.

'That,' said Imbix Hoth, as the shrykes fell into formation behind him, 'is how I deal with rock-rustlers.' He glanced across at Zaphix Nemulis, his narrowed eyes as bloodshot as those of the shrykes under his command. 'It is how I deal with *any* who cross me.'

CHAPTER SEVEN

THE BANE OF THE MIGHTY

Quint glanced across at Maris. She was staring straight ahead, her face in profile, with that look of steady determination on her face that he knew so well.

What was it? he wondered. The arch of her eyebrow, the delicate line of her chin – or perhaps the way her mouth curved up ever so slightly at the corners? Whatever it was, Quint had come to depend on that look, to seek it out whenever he needed courage or reassurance. Of course, he knew that beneath that expression there lurked the same worries, fears and confusion that he himself felt, but the fact that Maris seemed so determined not to show her emotions somehow always made him feel better.

The day hadn't started well. Quint had committed the tiny body of Nibblick, his ratbird, to Open Sky – sending a small bundle of blazing lufwood chippings up into the morning sky from his window.

Maris turned and caught him staring at her, forcing Quint to look hurriedly away, his face reddening. The broad street leading to the sky-shipyards was lined with stalls and workshops, and teeming with Undertowners.

As usual, the rock harvest had thrown everything into disarray. For most Undertowners, what with the white ravens and the *chorus of the dead*, the day was just beginning. They'd spent almost the entire morning inside, their doors locked and windows shuttered. Stores and stalls that should have opened at dawn had remained closed; in the foundries and factories, no one had turned up to relieve the night-shift; while the streets themselves – normally thronging with merchants and pedlars, barrows and carts – had been all but deserted.

It wasn't until eleven hours, when the white ravens had finally abandoned their terrible din and begun to return to the Stone Gardens, that the superstitious Undertowners, rich and poor alike, had ventured from their mansions and palaces, their hovels and dens. They'd emerged, blinking, into the sunlight and glanced furtively around. Then, fingering their charms and amulets gratefully, they'd muttered heartfelt thanks to Open Sky that they had been spared by the spirits of the dead, and that their harbingers – the white ravens – had returned to the eerie Stone Gardens. Now at last, they were able to get on with the concerns of the living.

Suddenly, the shops were open and the markets

were trading. The air filled with the sounds of business – raised voices, bidding and bartering; chain-rattle and hammer-blow, and the crack of the hammelhorn-drivers' whips as they urged their beasts of burden on.

Just up ahead, Captain Wind Jackal and his crew made their way through the crowds, attracting long looks and furtive glances as they did so. Resplendent in their heavy greatcoats, bedecked with their compasses, telescopes, parawings and grappling-hooks, they each carried a sky chest upon their shoulders – huge tilder-leather and lufwood trunks packed with their personal belongings – in readiness for the long voyage ahead.

They looked magnificent, thought Quint.

It was an opinion that seemed to be shared by the Undertowners, judging from the warm smiles and approving nods the sky pirates attracted. The only exceptions were the odd, scowling faces of low-hat leaguesmen as they crossed the street to avoid them.

A bevy of portly gnokgoblin matrons, one with a prowlgrin pup crushed beneath a fleshy arm, smiled broadly as Quint and Maris squeezed past them. Quint smiled back, proudly.

All at once, the air was shot with the moist odour of the Mire. Quint peered in through a narrow doorway on his left to see a plump mobgnome perched on a tiny stool, his legs going up and down as he operated a foot-treadle. On the spinning platform before him, a pot was slowly taking shape as his large hands smoothed and teased and caressed the mound of white clay.

Next to the potter's, its squat façade decorated with hooks from which mugs, jugs, vases and vats were suspended, was a tall thin carpentry works. A stack of window frames stood on one side of the entrance; a dozen or so doors on the other. The air smelled of wood-pine and scorched timber, and the high-pitched squeal of a circular saw forced the two goblins – one buying and one selling – to conduct their haggling at maximum volume.

Quint turned sideways to allow an oncoming line of lugtrolls – a heavy roll of ornate carpet resting on their left shoulders – to get past, just as the sounds of angry voices rang out.

He looked across at where the shouting was coming from, to see a red-faced flat-head goblin driver standing up at the front of his immobile hammelhorn cart, waving his fist. In front of him was a prowlgrin-drawn carriage, its mobgnome driver looking equally angry, and in front of *him*, a long covered wagon, three hammelhorns in harness, impatiently pawing the ground and tossing their curly-horned heads from side to side.

Outside the gates of the sky-shipyard, all traffic had come to a standstill, and even those on foot were unable to continue any further.

'Make way! By order of the Leagues!' a voice bellowed, and Quint glimpsed the high hat of a leagues-master bobbing above the growing crowd.

As he spoke, the noise of the heavy metal wheels trundling slowly along the cobbled road became apparent. It was a low, ominous rumble, below the general hubbub of voices, and felt as much as heard. The metal pots and pans, kettles, cauldrons and watering-cans hanging out on display at the front of the ironmonger's clinked and chimed, while opposite, suspended from a hook outside his store, the leather-worker's great red and blue passionbird shuffled about on its perch, flapping its wings and squawking indignantly.

Next to Quint in the crush, Maris looked steadily ahead. Leaning over towards her, he whispered softly into her ear.

'Sorry,' he said.

For a moment, Maris seemed to ignore him.

The huge stone-wagons, which had been loaded  with harvested flight-rocks back in the Stone Gardens, now trundled into view, like great buildings on wheels. The crowd broke into wild cheering as the teams of hammelhorns were urged on by the wagoneers. The gates of the sky-shipyard slowly swung open and the first of the mighty wagons turned off from the convoy and clattered inside. The rest of the wagons continued on down the broad street towards the other sky-shipyards, the high-hat leaguesmaster and his shryke bodyguard leading the way.

'I'm sorry, too,' said Maris, looking Quint in the eye for the first time that day. Her face softened. 'It was wrong to sulk – it's just that I was angry that you didn't speak up for me . . .'

Quint took her hand and squeezed it gently. Around them, the crowd was ebbing away as it followed in the wake of the stone-wagons.

'I should have,' Quint admitted, 'but you and Tem disobeyed orders by following us last night . . .'

'We saved your lives!' said Maris, that look of determined defiance returning to her face. 'Without me, Tem and Duggin the ferry pilot, you would have been washed away, both of you, just like . . .'

She paused, and her face drained of all colour. Quint shuddered.

That night, they had all returned in silence from the Sluice Tower, the hideous, despairing cries of Menisculis the waif echoing in all their minds. Back at the Tarry Vine, Wind Jackal had taken the ferry pilot aside and, while the rest of the crew had made their way up to the rafters, had had a long conversation with him. When Wind Jackal finally joined the others, they were all in their hammocks – all, that is, except for Quint and Maris, who were waiting expectantly outside the captain's garret alcove.

'Did you thank Duggin?' Maris began excitedly. 'He's a brilliant pilot, he . . .'

Wind Jackal silenced her with a thunderous look.

'Never disobey an order of mine again,' he told her slowly.

'But . . .' Maris's face fell. She seemed at a loss for words and turned to Quint, her eyes appealing to him to say something.

Quint bit his lip and looked down at his boots. It was the cardinal rule of any sky-ship crew: *Never disobey a captain's order*. There was nothing he could say.

Tears were now filling Maris's eyes as she turned back to Wind Jackal.

'Now get to bed, both of you,' he said, entering his garret alcove and pulling back the curtain. 'It's late. Get a good night's sleep. We'll set sail at noon.'

Maris had gone to bed without a word. Quint had pulled off his wet clothes, flopped gratefully into the soft hammock and, totally exhausted, fallen into a deep, dreamless sleep. At dawn, they'd been woken by the screeching and squawking of the white ravens circling round the top of the tavern roof. And as the crew had packed up their sky chests, and polished and checked their equipment, Maris had studiously ignored Quint.

Quint noticed of course, though if he was honest, he wasn't sorry. He wanted to block out all memory of the terrible night before – the icy sewer water, the waif's cries, and the thought that Turbot Smeal was still out there somewhere.

Instead, he busied himself along with the others, preparing for the journey ahead, the old excitement that he always felt before a sky-ship voyage returning in waves as he burnished his breast-plate, buttoned up his greatcoat and buckled on his parawings. At last, they were leaving the crowded, turbulent streets of Undertown for the freedom of the vast sky and the immense, unknowable majesty of the endless Deepwoods beyond. Quint could hardly wait!

And now, here he was, outside the gates of the sky-shipyard where the *Galerider* awaited its crew.

Quint smiled at Maris. 'Let's put the last few days behind us – Sanctaphrax, Undertown, the cliff quarries, the Sluice Tower – and make a new start. The sky awaits us, Maris . . .'

Maris smiled back, her eyes twinkling with excitement. 'Then I, for one, wouldn't want to keep the sky waiting!' she laughed, and together they hurried after Wind Jackal and the rest of the crew, who were just entering Thelvis Hollrig's sky-shipyard behind the great lumbering stone-wagons.

Inside, the place was in uproar, as the sky-shipwrights and their teams of workers hurried to put the finishing touches to the various vessels in the sky-ship cages above. Some were climbing ladders; some were winching cargo – with two mobgnomes who had taken on more weight than they could manage suddenly soaring up into the air, squealing with terror, as a huge leadwood crate came hurtling down in the opposite direction. Shinning over the jutting gantries, crawling along the luffing jibs; dashing from one place to another, with slopping buckets and over-filled boxes and baskets and crates . . .

'Mind your backs! Mind your backs!' panted a red-faced cloddertrog just ahead of them.

Lumbering across the yard, a crimson flag clutched in his huge hairy hand, he was warning everyone thereabouts of the line of luggers trotting behind him, a freshly varnished mast clutched to their chests. Or rather, *trying* to . . .'

Crash!

The team of pitch-sloppers never stood a chance. Staggering backwards out of the shadowy winch-dock, a weighty wooden vat of steaming black tar suspended from ropes between them, they collided with the end of the mast.

The pitch-slopper at the front tripped, fell – and brought the rest down with him. The tar – fresh from the heating-brazier and as runny as tildermilk – slopped over the side, scalding the hapless goblin who had fallen and spilling out over the ground. It turned viscous and sticky in an instant. One after the other, the goblins following behind fell into it – and there they remained. Each time one of them managed to pull an arm or a leg free, it was by levering himself against one of the others, who then got *his* arms and legs stuck. Little by little, the tar spread to every bit of the struggling goblins – bodies, boots, hands and hair. And, as it cooled, it bound them together in a great sticky ball . . .

Meanwhile, the luggers had fared little better. Knocked off balance, they'd spun round in a huge circle, staggering and stumbling as they tried desperately not to drop the precious mast. In one uncontrolled sweep, they scythed down a troupe of sail-setters, smashed into a hammelhorn delivery-cart and knocked against a row of long ladders, all leaning up against a sky-ship cradle – then fell over, with the great mast across their chests, pinning them all to the ground.

The ladders fell in all directions, sending half a dozen hull-riggers hurtling downwards and leaving another six hanging on by the tips of their fingers, shouting for help . . .

In the midst of all this chaos, beside the huge stone-wagon, the yardmaster Thelvis Hollrig stood impassively. One bony hand fingered the cluster of charms and amulets at his neck, the other tapped his long thin leagues-cane on the ground. Beside him, Hummer the grey goblin clerk twitched his white tufted ears and scratched away at a sheaf of barkscrolls.

'Twenty flight-rocks!' Thelvis tutted through his sharpened teeth, casting an eye over the contents of the stone-wagon. 'And all but one of them fit only for light-galleys and rubble-barges! Hummer! Have the "nine-strider" taken to the launch cradle.'

'Yes, Yardmaster,' Hummer nodded. 'And the other flight-rocks?'

'They can be assigned later. We've got a triple-decker leagues-galleon awaiting a flight-rock, and I've promised our good friends in the League of Beamlaggers and Boardlayers a launch this afternoon – or had you forgotten?'

'No, Yardmaster.' Hummer shook his head.

'Well?' Thelvis tapped his leagues-cane on the ground.

'Yardmaster?' said Hummer.

'What are you waiting for!' thundered the yardmaster, unsheathing the sword concealed in the cane and waving it at the grey goblin. 'Unload it now!'

'Yes, Yardmaster!' gulped Hummer, dropping his sheaf of barkscrolls, stooping to pick them up – and dropping them again. 'You heard the yardmaster!' he barked in turn at a group of rock-handlers gathered round a brazier nearby. 'Unload the nine-strider!

The rock-handlers – large cloddertrogs in heavy gloves, aprons and hoods – bustled over, grasping glowing callipers.

'Careful! Careful!' yelled the grey goblin as the cloddertrogs tugged back the netting that covered the stone-wagon and grasped the huge round boulder beneath. 'Don't let the others escape!'

The netting was secured and the cloddertrogs trooped off through the shipyard, carrying the great floating rock above their heads, while on either side their companions ran blazing torches over its pitted surface. Catching sight of Wind Jackal and his crew, the yardmaster sheathed his sword and sauntered over.

'Captain Wind Jackal,' he said. 'All packed and prepared to set sail, I see.' Thelvis Hollrig flashed his sharp-toothed smile. 'You'll find your sky ship fully repaired and provisioned, and awaiting you at the North Tower.'

He pointed with his cane, before reaching out and grasping Wind Jackal's arm conspiratorially.

'And, Captain . . .' Thelvis muttered softly, his small eyes narrowing. 'Remember our little deal is strictly hush-hush. Don't want any of the Leagues of Plenty getting to hear of it. We've got a big launch this afternoon, so slip away quietly during that if you can, there's a good fellow.'

Wind Jackal nodded and pulled his arm free of the yardmaster's bony grasp.

'You heard the yardmaster, you scurvy skycurs!' he shouted, with a laugh. 'The *Galerider*'s ready and waiting for her crew!'

Spillins, Steg Jambles, Tem Barkwater, Ratbit, Filbus Queep and Sagbutt the flat-head goblin gave a heartfelt cheer and followed their captain as he strode through the bustling sky-shipyard. Maris and Quint caught the yardmaster's eye as they followed in their turn. The glinting smile he shot back at them made Quint shudder.

'Good luck out there in the endless Deepwoods,' Thelvis Hollrig called after them. 'Bloodoaks, shrykes, gloamglozers ... Rather you than me!' He chuckled to himself.

'Don't listen to him,' said Maris, her face once again determined and brave.

Quint smiled back at her. 'It's so good to have you with us,' he said.

Reaching the North Tower, they craned their necks back and gazed at the sky cradle above.

Far up at the top of the tower was the *Galerider* – and it looked magnificent. The varnished wood and the polished metal gleamed like new. The spider-silk sails that Spillins and Ratbit had delivered were in place and almost glowing in the lowering sun – with a corner of the extra sailcloth sticking out from the top of the reappointed caternest glowing brightest of all. Steg and Tem's ropes and rigging, fresh from the chandlery sheds, had been secured to the mast, hull and deck-cleats, and now whispered softly as the gentle breeze blew through them.

The biggest difference, however, was the body of the sky ship. Not only had the gaping hole disappeared, but all trace of the cloud-limpet and sky-fungus damage – made so much worse by the terrible storms they'd faced at the cliff edge – had been totally removed. Master carpenters and expert polishers had done their work well and now, freshly plugged, trimmed and varnished, the hull of the magnificent sky ship gleamed in the afternoon sun.

Pushing open the leadwood doors, Wind Jackal entered the tower, leading the others up the spiral staircase and out onto the gantry at the top of the tower. Then, one by one, the crew climbed the bars of the sky cage that encased the *Galerider*'s hull, and stepped over the balustrade onto her deck. There, as Wind Jackal – the last to board – joined them, they were met by the Stone Pilot and one other.

'Duggin!' exclaimed Maris, delightedly seizing the gnokgoblin ferry pilot's hand and pumping it up and down. 'What are *you* doing here?'

'Duggin here has accepted my offer to join the crew,' said Wind Jackal. He smiled kindly at Maris. 'Since he proved himself to be such a brave and resourceful sky-sailor last night.'

Maris blushed.

'The *Edgehopper*'s lashed to the fore-deck, Mistress Maris,' said Duggin, beaming from ear to ear. 'So it's both of us coming on this here voyage!'

'We're glad to have you,' said Wind Jackal, and the crew all nodded – especially Tem, who seemed as delighted as Maris at this new addition to the *Galerider*'s crew. 'Now, to your stations, all of you,' said Wind Jackal, 'and make ready to set sail!'

The crew did as their captain ordered. Ratbit headed for the aft-deck, Sagbutt for the gunwales, while Steg Jambles and Tem Barkwater hurried to the fore-deck, where they were joined by Duggin, who checked that his sky ferry was properly secured. Maris went below deck to check on the ship's medical supplies, following on the heels of Filbus Queep, who was eager to inspect the cargo of tallow. And while Spillins eagerly climbed the mast, exclaiming with delight as he jumped down into his refurbished caternest, Quint joined his father at the helm, his heart racing.

Just then, from a sky cradle on the West Tower, there came the long, sonorous sound of tilderhorns being blown.

'Must be the launch Hollrig was getting so excited about,' said Wind Jackal. 'We'll let them get all the cheering and horn-blowing out of the way, and then we'll slip quietly away.' He called across, 'All ready, Stone Pilot?'

On the flight-rock platform, the Stone Pilot – all facial expression hidden behind the great hood – nodded vigorously.

Quint unhooked his telescope and trained it on the West Tower. A league ship, still in its shipyard cradle, was silhouetted against the bright sky. All round the balustrade of the newly fitted vessel – both fore and aft – the heads of its crew could be seen, looking down. Some of them were waving. At the centre, on either side of the mast, the rock-burners were blazing with such intensity – sending super-heated air down a series of pipes and pistons into the very heart of the rock – that the great flight-rock itself was glowing.

Below the cradle, at the top of the tower, stood a leaguesman – the Master of the League of Beamlaggers and Boardlayers. He was as wide as he was tall, and dressed in clothes with so many ribbons and frill, that he looked almost like a shryke standing there, the wind ruffling his feathers. His high hat, as beribboned as everything else, glinted in the light of the burners and, as it swayed in the breeze, was constantly being prodded back into position by his hat-tipper.

'It is my honour, my privilege, my duty – as ritual decrees,' the leaguesmaster bellowed down at the listening crowd above the roaring of the burners, 'to introduce this . . .' He swept a flapping arm flamboyantly behind him. 'To introduce this, the latest addition to the leagues-fleet, to the sky . . .'

Quint focused his telescope on the ornate lettering at the magnificent vessel's prow. Below, on the gantries of the West Tower, leaguemen in high, mid and low hats now prepared to raise them in salute.

'*Bane* . . .' Quint read, '*of the* . . .'

'*Bane of the Mighty!*' roared the leaguesmaster, seizing his high hat and waving it above his hairless head.

As he spoke the words, the vessel's stone pilot – wearing the dark, domed helmet with the single eye-slit favoured by most league stone pilots – took a step forward. Then, reaching up, he gripped the two drenching-levers with both his hands and pulled them sharply down. Ice-cold sand and gravel poured from the sluice-tanks above, saturating the new, white-hot nine-strider in an instant.

As it made contact, the flight-rock hissed so loudly there were some in the crowd who covered their ears. Thick clouds of billowing steam poured out of the rock, rolling across the deck and over the balustrades, swallowing up the crew as they went. And deep within the clouds, the rock could be seen rapidly changing colour – white to yellow, orange to crimson, purple to black . . .

Creaking and cracking noises filled the air as the flight-rock – which had gone from super-heated to super-cooled in a matter of seconds – bucked and strained inside the shipyard cradle.

The crowd held its breath.

The next moment, there was a loud *clang*, followed by a louder *thud*, and all at once, like a giant mire-clam, the great cradle snapped open.

Crack! Crack! Crack!

Three short, sharp reports echoed out as, in rapid succession, the temporary anchor-hooks snapped, one after the other. An instant later, the air trembled with a tremendous *whooshing* sound as the sky ship abruptly hurtled up into the orange-tinged sky so fast it was as though it had been expelled from a giant catapult.

'Sky be praised!' the leaguesmen bellowed as the crowd erupted into deafening whoops and cheers.

'Stone Pilot!' Wind Jackal called across to the flight-rock platform. 'Give us lift . . .' The Stone Pilot turned, lowered the burners and pushed the cooling-rods into place. The flight-rock took the strain. As it did so, Steg Jambles reached over, pulled the slip-knot to untie the tolley-rope, and the *Galerider* rose steadily and gracefully into the air.

'*Whoooaaahh!*'

Behind them, the roaring crowd bellowed with excitement as the *Bane of the Mighty* completed its upward rush, levelled out and, as graceful as a caterbird in flight, swooped back down through the sky. No one on board the *Galerider* looked round.

Instead, airborne at last, with the wind in their hair and the low sun to the west shining in their eyes, they slipped quietly out of the sky-shipyard and headed off towards the Deepwoods, far, far beyond the distant horizon.

·CHAPTER EIGHT·

GALERIDER

High up at the very top of the great ironwood mast, Spillins the oakelf scanned the horizon, his gnarled fingers idly caressing the silky lining of the caternest in which he sat. The spider-silk was strong, yet soft to the touch. It plugged those annoying gaps in the worn threads of the old caterbird cocoon perfectly – gaps through which, for longer than the old oakelf cared to remember, the icy winds of the Edgeland sky had whistled and howled, chilling him to the bone.

But not any more, Spillins thought, with a smile. Now, with its spider-silk lining, the old nest was almost as good as new.

He continued to scan the horizon with his huge oakelf eyes. Despite the seventy summers they had seen, those eyes had never let him down, still able to spot a hover-grub on a copperwood leaf at a thousand strides.

Spillins ran his fingers over the outside of the cocoon, picking thoughtfully at the matted strands of cater-thread. Spun by glittering caterworms in the Lullabee

Groves of his youth, the cocoon had once shimmered and sparkled with turquoise lullabee light. He had found it just after a caterbird had hatched, and – as was his right – had carefully cut it down. Then, because he had his own caterbird cocoon at last, the young Spillins was able to leave his small and secretive clan in the Lullabee Groves and go out into the wide world beyond, to seek his fortune.

Some oakelves found remote, uninhabited places to hang their cocoons, and concentrated on honing their gifts of inner-sight – such as fortune-telling, by determining the coloured aura of those who sought them out. Others hung their cocoons near villages and settlements and offered their inhabitants the benefit of their wisdom and the insights that came from sleeping in a caterbird cocoon.

But not Spillins.

No, he'd chosen the path that only the most adventurous oakelves chose. He'd hung his cocoon, not from a living tree, but from a dead one – the mast of a sky ship. And he'd found no shortage of masts to choose from, for although every sky ship had a caternest, few could boast that theirs was a genuine caterbird cocoon with a resident oakelf.

Spillins had chosen the newly built *Galerider* as home for his cocoon. It was a choice he never regretted. By day he sailed the sky, while by night he dreamed the special dreams of a caterbird.

'Ah, dreams,' Spillins whispered yearningly, his fingers teasing the wispy strands of the cater-thread.

He remembered the very first dream he'd had in the

new, sparkling cocoon. He'd found himself soaring across the sky, gigantic purple-black wings tipped with white beating powerfully up and down. And his eyes . . . What wonders they had seen. For wrapped up in his caterbird cocoon, he was no longer Spillins the young oakelf. No, he was a great caterbird, soaring majestically across the sky.

'Nigh on sixty years ago it was when I first climbed up here,' he murmured, glancing up from the caternest at a passing flock of snowbirds. 'Scarce seems possible. Sixty years – and three sky pirate captains!'

Hurricane Razorflit had been the first; a vain and impetuous leader who'd met his end on the point of a shryke's serrated lance. Then Rain Quarm, who was more cautious, but prone to violent rages – and hadn't lasted long. It was after he had been festooned that the crew had voted unanimously to take on the dashing young captain, Wind Jackal. Spillins smiled. He could still see him as he'd been that day when he'd taken command. The confidence in his step, the fire in his eyes – and his aura, the most wonderful shade of blue, like a summer sky after the sun has set but just before the first stars have risen . . .

Spillins took a sharp intake of breath as something occurred to him. The last time he'd seen the captain, his aura hadn't been blue at all, but a poisonous shade of green . . .

Far below, on the flight-rock platform at the foot of the mast, the Stone Pilot reached up and pulled the burner-lever down two notches. The flames shrank in on themselves and turned from yellow to the palest of orange. A moment later, responding to the subtle drop in temperature, the flight-rock gained buoyancy and the *Galerider* lifted a little in the air.

The Stone Pilot stood back for a moment, as if assessing the adjustment that had just been made – but the expressionless conical hood gave nothing away. Turning from the burners, the Stone Pilot grasped a clutch of cooling-rods in a gauntleted hand and held them up to the light to examine them.

Long and thin, the cooling-rods were not simply smooth poles. If they had been, there would have been an insufficient area of metal to cool the rock quickly. Instead the long shafts had a series of small

metal discs welded into place at regular intervals along them. While remaining slender enough to slide into the outer stonecomb of the rock, the extra surface area ensured that, when chilled, the rods cooled even the most overheated of flight-rocks effectively.

The Stone Pilot removed a wire brush from a hook on the mast-mounting. Then, sitting down on a small, three-legged stool on the cluttered flight-rock platform, she grasped the brush in one gauntleted hand, the first of the cooling-rods in the other, and began to scrape vigorously at the particles of rock-dust which had fused themselves to the metal.

A flock of snowbirds passed overhead, their mournful cries lost in the vast expanse of sky, and a shudder seemed to pass through the seated figure. For a moment, the scraping ceased while the Stone Pilot checked that the conical hood was securely fastened and the thick greatcoat and fire apron were buttoned up and strapped securely. Beneath the heavy fireproof clothes, it was impossible to tell anything of the individual beneath, which was exactly the way the *Galerider*'s stone pilot liked it.

Most sky ship stone pilots kept themselves to themselves, seldom spoke and devoted almost all their attention to the notoriously difficult business of tending the flight-rocks in their care. But even the most dedicated pilots occasionally took off their conical hoods and set foot on the ground. The *Galerider*'s stone pilot was different. A constant figure on the flight-rock platform – at all times and in all weathers – the Stone

Pilot never took off the conical hood, apron and gauntlets of the profession, or uttered so much as a single word.

As mysterious in her own way as the great flight-rock she tended, the secret of the Stone Pilot's identity was known only to the *Galerider's* crew, the brave young sky pirate who had rescued her and his friend Maris.

'Down a tad, Stone Pilot!' The sound of Quint's voice, calling from the helm, broke into the Stone Pilot's thoughts.

Laying the brush and the cooling-rod aside, she jumped to her feet and hurried across to the bellows, which she pumped up and down. The burners flared and glowed brighter, heating the rock just enough to bring it down a little lower in the sky. The Stone Pilot returned to the stool and sat down again. Below, the flight-rock hissed and whistled in its cradle, while above, the sails billowed and tugged at the creaking mast.

Inside the heavy conical hood, it was dark, quiet and safe . . .

'Why have you stopped, Sagbutt?' demanded Filbus Queep. '*I'll* tell you when to stop.'

'Eyes sting,' the flat-head goblin complained.

'The mighty Sagbutt, deck-warrior and league-slayer,' said Filbus scornfully, 'defeated by a couple of woodonions!'

'Not a couple,' Sagbutt grunted. 'Lots!'

'Well I'm sorry about that,' said Queep, 'but I *need* lots.'

Sagbutt groaned miserably and wiped his red, streaming eyes on his filthy apron.

'That's the thing about woodonion broth,' Queep said. 'It requires woodonions. The clue, Sagbutt, is in the name. *Woodonion* broth.' He glanced up from the triangular chopping board, where three small piles – one of blue-thyme, one of fossweed and one of nibblick – filled each of the corners. 'And don't smash them, Sagbutt. *Slice* them! There's a good fellow . . .'

Above their heads, the low beams of the *Galerider*'s galley were festooned with pots, pans, jugs and cooking utensils of every description: ladles, whisks, sieves, hanging-scales, wooden spoons and spatulas; rolling-pins, mallets, hatchets and heavy chopping-knives. In the corner, by the low cabin door, a small stove glowed purple, the buoyant lufwood inside jumping and jostling as it burned. Filbus Queep the quartermaster loved the *Galerider*'s galley. He loved its order, its neatness, its precision.

'A place for everything, Sagbutt, and everything in its place,' he would say. 'Just how I like it.'

He especially liked the galley when, as now, it was hot and humid and laden with the delicious fragrances of cooking food; when the air was thick with steam that billowed out from a bubbling cauldron and hovered in clouds just below the low ceiling.

Filbus Queep picked up the boardful of herbs, swivelled round on his heel to the cauldron behind him, and swept them all into the boiling water with the back of his knife. Instantly the fragrance was released from

the aromatic leaves. He added a slurp of winesap, slammed a heavy lid on the cauldron and pushed the whole lot to the back of the stove to simmer. Then he poured a little oil into a pan and put that on the heat at the front instead.

'Woodonions, Sagbutt,' he said, without turning round.

The flat-head picked up his own chopping board and, eyes and nose still red and streaming, shuffled to the quartermaster's side.

'Excellent, excellent,' said Queep, tipping the woodonions into the smoking oil. They hissed and spat as they landed, before settling down to a soft sizzle. 'Smell that, Sagbutt,' said Filbus Queep, leaning over the pan and breathing in deeply. 'Doesn't that make chopping all those woodonions worth it?'

'Sagbutt like onions raw,' growled the flat-head, wiping his heavy cutlass on his tunic. 'Sagbutt like *every-thing* raw – tilder, hammelhorn, snowbird . . . 'Specially snowbird guts – nice and raw and steaming . . .'

'Yes, yes,' said Filbus. He shook his head. 'Sometimes I don't know why I bother . . .'

The quartermaster wiped the steam from his spectacles, placed them back on his nose – and noticed the weapon in the flat-head goblin's hand. His face darkened.

'Please, Sagbutt, my dear fellow,' Filbus said, eyeing the cutlass with evident distaste. 'Your sword . . .'

Sagbutt looked at the fearsome blade in his hand, its surface scarred and pitted from battles too numerous to recount.

'The one you cut off heads with; gut snowbirds with . . .' Filbus was frowning furiously. 'Clean your fingernails with. You didn't use it to . . .'

The flat-head goblin smiled broadly to reveal a mouth full of glistening white fangs, and nodded his flat, tattooed head.

'Yes,' he laughed, 'Sagbutt did. Sagbutt used *Skullsplitter* to chop woodonions . . .'

'And you double it back on itself, like so,' said Steg Jambles, 'slip the tide-ring into place. So . . . Then bend it back the other way, and . . .' He tugged the rope firmly, then looked up at Tem and grinned – his teeth, yellowed by years of chewing slipwood bark, gleaming in the afternoon sun. 'There,' he announced. 'One nether-fetter, fully repaired.'

Tem Barkwater nodded, impressed. 'You made it look so easy,' he said.

'It *is* easy,' said Steg. 'Once you get the knack.' He unfastened it, removed the tide-ring and frayed up the end of the rope once more. '*You* have a try,' he said, handing it over.

Tem took the rope and tried to do exactly what Steg had shown him. The pair of them were sitting on upturned barrels on the fore-deck. With his tongue sticking out of the side of his mouth as he concentrated, Tem smoothed down the rope's frayed threads, twisting it, turning it, doubling it back . . . But he was all fingers and thumbs. The rope seemed to squirm with a life of its own, and when he attempted to pull the tide-ring into place, the whole lot slipped out of his grasp.

'Sky curse it!' he shouted, his cheeks burning red with embarrassment and frustration.

'Easy, lad. Easy,' said Steg Jambles, patting his young protégé on the shoulder. 'Let's try that again . . .'

He paused. Tem Barkwater was staring down at the coil of rope at his feet, its threads now fanned out in eight unknotted strands like a . . .

'Whip,' breathed Tem, his face ashen-white.

Steg Jambles bent down and carefully picked the rope up and threw it into the shadows beneath the fore-deck gunwales.

'Perhaps that's enough for one day,' he said, and looked at Tem with concern. The lad was trembling, his bony knees knocking against each other.

Quint had first encountered him in the Timber Glades, pale and gaunt, and tethered to a whipping-post, being flogged. Having repaid the cruel wood merchant with a good hiding of his own, Quint had untied the youth and brought him on board. That was three months ago. Since then, the lad had never spoken of his past, nor of how he'd come to be punished so cruelly. Now, it seemed, he was about to speak. Steg sat down on the empty woodgrog barrel and waited.

'My brother Cal and I were tricked by the wood merchant,' Tem said in a quiet, hoarse voice.

Overhead, a flock of snowbirds let out their mournful cry. Tem didn't seem to notice them. His eyes were still fixed on the spot on the deck where the frayed rope had been.

'Go on,' said Steg.

'He said he'd teach us woodcraft and timbering, but that's not what he wanted us for . . .'

'No?' said Steg, willing Tem to continue.

'No,' said Tem, his quavering voice barely audible. 'We were to be bait.'

'Bait?' said Steg, puzzled.

For a while Tem didn't say anything. Then he looked up and stared into his friend's face. His eyes had a haunted look. He cleared his throat.

'Of all the trees in the Deepwoods – lufwood, lullabee, scentwood, stinkwood, sallowdrop – it is the bloodoak that the merchants prize most highly,' Tem began at last. 'That was the one the wood merchant wanted to cut down for its timber.' He snorted. 'The most dangerous task in all the Deepwoods. To chop down the mighty bloodoak you must distract the terrible tarry vine that feeds it, distract it with . . .' Tears sprang to Tem's eyes.

'Bait!' said Steg again, appalled.

Tem nodded. 'The wood merchant and his gang . . . They would tie us up at the end of long pieces of rope,' Tem told him, the words faltering and faint. 'Drive us into the forest, in those dark, fetid places where they suspected they might find bloodoaks – keeping at a safe distance themselves of course . . .

'Then – *whoosh!* – suddenly out of nowhere, the vines would appear, wrapping themselves around an arm or a leg, or worst of all, our necks, and yank us forwards . . .' He swallowed hard. 'When they felt the tugging on the rope, the loggers were supposed to run to us at once, cut the vines and cauterize them with blazing torches before they had a chance to sprout three vines where one had been before.

'But . . . but . . .' he stammered, close to tears. 'They didn't care about us, Cal and me . . . We . . . we didn't matter. We were expendable. Sometimes the vine would drag us all the way to the tree . . . over the bleached bones of the bloodoak's victims . . . Sometimes we were lifted up and dangled over the stinking maw of the tree, before they . . . they . . .' He had clamped his hands over his ears. 'Oh, I can still hear those mandibles slavering and slurping and clacking – and the awful *stench* . . .'

Steg Jambles laid a comforting arm round the lad. 'There, there, Tem, lad,' he said. 'Better to speak of such things than brood over them . . .'

'Then one day, I was sick. The merchant left me behind in the Timber Glades. Just took Cal. When he got back, he was furious. Accused me of slipping my brother a knife, to help him escape. He dragged me over to the whipping-post and began to flog me with his whip – eight knotted lengths of copperwood twine . . .' Tem shuddered, then turned to Steg. 'But I didn't care!' He was smiling now, although tears coursed down his face.

'You didn't?' said Steg.

'No,' said Tem, his eyes sparkling. 'Because Cal, my brother, had escaped!'

*

Below the fore-deck, in the gloom of the cargo-hold, Ratbit the mobgnome perched at the top of a tall stool. The simple oil lantern he was holding was set so low, it cast no light but a dull orange glow which illuminated the sour expression on his face.

'*Galerider* just repaired and fresh out of the sky-ship-yard,' he complained, 'and still the little sky pests find their way in . . .'

Just then, the ship lurched to starboard, and from somewhere in the storeroom, Ratbit was sure he heard the sound of scratching. He fell still, cocked his head to one side. But there was nothing – nothing, that is, but the low buzz of the ratbirds chattering and the ship's timbers creaking . . .

'One little chink and Sky knows what slips through,' he complained. 'And before you know it, the cargo is blighted, and the profit's gone . . .'

Critch! Critch!

There it was again. The mobgnome turned the lantern's adjustable lighting-pin. It raised the wick and the cargo-hold was filled with light. There was a sound of scampering – and then silence. Lantern in his left hand, trigger-crossbow in his right, Ratbit slipped down off the stool and crept through the great storeroom, flashing the light up each of the narrow aisles between the stacks of crates.

'Come out, come out, wherever you are,' he whispered, his voice low and sing-song.

The ship gave another lurch and Ratbit leaned forward to steady himself. Beneath the floorboards, in the dark bowels of the ship, the ratbirds twittered and squeaked.

'Getting turbulent,' said Ratbit. 'Come in to shelter, have we?'

Critch! Critch! Critch!

He spun round, just in time to see a long scaly tail disappear down the aisle behind him. He peered down the narrow gap. And there, scurrying away, was a scrabster – one of the more destructive examples of Edgeland skyvermin. Gelatinous beneath an opaque, bleached shell, the creature had a whiplash tail, three clawed mandibles and a dozen or so spindly legs. Ratbit raised the crossbow and fired. There was a thud as the bolt embedded itself in the floor – the scrabster froze, squeaked, then scampered away between the crates, unhurt.

'Damn you to Open Sky,' Ratbit cursed, turning sideways on to slip down the aisle.

Two hundred crates were stacked tightly together in the cargo-hold beneath the fore-deck, each one containing a thousand candles made from the finest hammelhorn-rendered tallow, the best that the League of Taper and Tallow Moulders could produce. They burned for hours, smelled sweet and produced no drips of wax. The shrykes loved them. Unfortunately, so too did scrabsters. In the worst infestations, entire cargoes could be consumed.

Suddenly, as Ratbit turned a corner, there was the creature just ahead of him, crouching down on its spindly legs, its beady black eyes glinting back at him from the shadows.

'*There* you are,' Ratbit purred, before loosing a second bolt. But the scrabster darted off before the bolt had even landed. 'Sky curse you!' he shouted as he slipped another bolt into the chamber and primed it.

Scrabsters were just one of the verminous creatures that could infest a well-stocked sky ship. Hull-weevils, bow-worms, hullrot- and mire-clams all floated, hovered or sailed on the air currents in the hope of finding a free ride on a passing sky ship. Ratbirds usually picked most of them off and kept the hull and cabins clear, but in a well-stocked cargo-hold, you had to be on constant guard . . .

Ratbit caught the sight of movement out of the corner of his eye. Slowly, silently, he twisted round, raising lantern and crossbow as he did so. And there, not half a dozen strides in front of him, was the scrabster. This

time, however, it was not looking at *him*, but rather at a
narrow crack in the side of a
crate, as if trying to determine whether it was
wide enough to squeeze
through.

It was a large specimen,
fat, clawed and oozing
gelatinously out of its
knobbly shell which, Ratbit
thought, rather suggested that
it had already started on the tallow candles. Its black
eyes extended on the end of thin stalks and glinted in
the lantern light as they peered into the hole in the
crate. A moment later – having made up its mind – it
raised one claw to the splintered wood and cut round
its edges.

Ratbit pulled the trigger, firing the crossbow bolt. It
sped through the air with a soft whistle and embedded
itself in the right flank of the revolting creature. For a
moment, nothing happened. Then, as if a lightning bolt
had passed through its body, the scrabster twitched and
jolted, green ooze pouring from the wound as it emitted
a strangulated high-pitched squeal.

The next instant, it flipped over and its claws went
limp.

'That'll learn you,' Ratbit murmured.

He crossed over to the dead creature, seized its tail
and pulled it free of the crate. Then, holding it up, he

inspected it by the light of the lantern – and gave a low groan. An empty egg sac hung down from beneath the creature's shell. From behind him there came tiny scuttling sounds in the shadows.

'Young'uns,' Ratbit growled, reloading his crossbow. 'This means war . . .'

In the small cabin on the port-side of one of the central rudder-cogs, Maris pulled open the storm shutters and let the light in.

'That's better,' she said brightly, turning to Duggin the gnokgoblin. 'Now we can see what we're doing.'

She opened the sumpwood trunk that hovered in front of her and searched its velvet-lined compartments. They were full of small bottles and stoppered phials that clinked musically as she rummaged.

Tweezel the spindlebug had taught Maris everything she knew about cures and remedies. Her father's old butler had had a medicine for every occasion. Tinctures for rashes, potions for aches and pains, poultices and salves for cuts and burns, grazes and bruises. Many was the time that he had patiently and methodically cleaned and dressed a cut or scratch that she'd picked up at the Fountain House School in the floating city.

It seemed so far away now, Maris thought . . .

Duggin peeled the poultice-dressing from the nasty-looking bump above his left eye and smiled. '*Galerider*'s a lot bigger than what I'm used to, Mistress Maris, but to be hit by a swinging jib-sail – an old ferry pilot like me – why, it makes me blush . . .'

'You'll get used to the *Galerider*,' said Maris, gently. 'I have. Now, hold still . . .'

She took the dressing from the gnokgoblin, reached into the trunk and pulled out a small pot of salve. As she unscrewed the pot, a sweet herbal fragrance – at once fruity and peppery – filled the small cabin. Duggin licked his lips.

'That smells good,' he said.

Maris laughed. 'Certainly better than the smell of frying woodonions coming from the galley.'

'What is it, though?'

'Hyleberry,' said Maris. 'It's excellent as a salve for burns and bruises – and Welma, my old nurse, used to make jam from it as well. Absolutely delicious . . .'

Her eyes took on a distant look once more. Long ago, when they'd first met in her

father's palace, Quint had burned himself, and she'd tried to soothe the burn by smearing hyleberry jam on his fingers. Her nurse, Welma, had been furious – not that she'd wasted the jam, but that Quint had been fiddling with the lufwood stove in the first place. But he was being brave, trying to protect her, just as he always did . . .

'What are you thinking about?' said Duggin, dragging Maris back from her memories.

'I . . . I was just wondering how you got to be a sky ferry pilot,' she lied, her cheeks reddening. She busied herself with the hyleberry salve.

'I joined the leagues as a young'un,' said Duggin. 'But being a leaguer and taking orders from high-hats wasn't for me. So then I got work on a rubble-barge in the boom-docks. Stayed there for ten years, and earned enough to get a sky ferry of my own built.' He smiled at Maris. 'Ten long years, they were. But the *Edgehopper* was worth every day of it.'

Maris smiled back and, leaning across, removed a roll of bandage from one of the chest's velvet-lined compartments. She placed the end of the bandage gently over the gnokgoblin's bruise. Next, taking care not to make it too tight, she wound it round his forehead and tied it behind his rubbery ear.

'And now you're a sky pirate,' she said. 'Just like the rest of us.'

A flock of snowbirds flew high over the stern of the *Galerider*, their plaintive mewing cries filling the sky.

'Never thought I'd live to sail in a sky pirate ship,' said

Duggin, joining Maris at the small cabin window, 'and see snowbirds flying high over the Deepwoods.'

Maris adjusted the gnokgoblin's bandage which had slipped down over one eye.

'If you want to live any longer,' she laughed, 'next time you see a jib-sail, duck!'

In the ornately decorated main cabin, high in the aft-castle of the *Galerider*, Wind Jackal stood before the great 'Captain's Desk'. With its edges and corners covered in inlaid calibrations of tilder ivory, and its leather surface tooled with flight paths and tether-points, the desk was a template on which to place the sky charts of tracing-parchment.

Wind Jackal flattened out a roll of parchment on the desk before him and weighted it down at the corners with four polished ironwood pinecones. Then he opened one of the broad, flat drawers of the desk and surveyed the array of glistening gold dividers laid out carefully upon its velvet lining. Each divider was set to the particular distance a sky ship could sail from 'tether to tether'.

Depending on cloud and weather conditions, a sky ship could sometimes sail for days over the Edgelands before needing to descend and tether itself to the anchor rings, rocky crags or ancient ironwood pines that dotted the time-worn flight paths which led to the great markets of the Deepwoods. At other times, a sky ship would go barely a hundred strides at a time in the teeth of ice gales or driving storms – a course charted by the smallest dividers in the drawer.

Of course, a sky ship could always soar off high into the sky, far higher than its tether chain – yet only the most desperate or foolhardy captain would risk his vessel in Open Sky. No, it made sense to judge your flight carefully from tether-point to tether-point, keeping low over the endless canopy of Deepwoods forest, and inching closer each day to the remote hammelhorn runs, timber yards or . . .

'Great Shryke Slave Market,' Wind Jackal murmured, picking up a large divider and walking it, point to point, across the expanse of parchment spread out before him on the Captain's Desk. Twenty tetherings at least, he thought, and that was only if the weather held . . .

He glanced across the cabin at the barometer on the wall and shook his head.

The needle was still falling. There was definitely a storm imminent – and it looked like a bad one. The last thing he wanted now was to get blown off-course. After all, it was hard enough plotting a path to the great market at the best of times – one could sail for weeks tracking the routes the slavers had taken.

That was the thing with shrykes. Always on the move. They would arrive at a particular part of the forest, set up their roosts – killing the trees and enslaving all who lived in the surrounding area – then, when the forest around had been stripped bare, they would up sticks, pack everything onto the backs of their prowlgrins and move on. In good weather, a voyage to the slave market could take weeks. In bad weather, with an ill wind and worse luck, a voyage could take years . . .

Wind Jackal laid down the divider and sat back in his tooled tilder-leather chair. Hands folded behind his head, he looked up at the ornately panelled ceiling and sighed a long, weary sigh. All his life he'd thrilled to the excitement of skysailing. He'd relished the challenge of plotting a course, calculating when to risk everything and when to sail safe and treetop close . . . But somehow, on this voyage, the joy had gone out of it. The charts, the dividers, the barometer were no longer his friends. Ahead seemed to lie only storm clouds and foreboding and . . .

'Turbot Smeal,' he murmured coldly.

Wind Jackal had barely slept for days. Every time he closed his eyes, the quartermaster's evil face would loom up before him. Even here in his cabin with its panelled walls and polished instruments, with the great Captain's Desk inlaid with tilder ivory and clam-pearl, with its sumpwood hammock and fire-crystal lanterns – the place he felt most at home in the whole world – the spectre of Turbot Smeal hovered. He heard his nasal voice in the whispering of the sails, his laughter in the creaking of the hull, and sometimes when he looked in the mirror it was Smeal's sneering face he saw, overlaid upon his own.

He leaned forwards and clasped his head in his hands. His stomach churned and his heart was thumping.

Just then, outside the broad windows, a flock of snow-birds flew past, their haunting cries filtering through into the cabin. Wind Jackal groaned and put his hands over his ears. It wasn't the cry of the snowbirds he could hear, but Turbot Smeal's mocking laughter . . .

Up at the helm, Quint stared ahead as the *Galerider* soared across the sky, the setting sun in his eyes and the cold wind on his face. His nimble fingers danced over the bone-handled flight-levers, constantly adjusting the sails and hull-weights to keep the *Galerider* on an even keel.

He had what sky-sailors called 'the touch' – the instinctive ability to know precisely which of the twenty-four levers – each one attached to its own sail or weight; each one set differently – to move in order to compensate for every wind eddy or temperature shift. Now he could steer the *Galerider* almost without thinking, as if the great sky ship with all its different crew-members was simply an extension of himself.

Quint loved the feeling he had when he stood at the helm, the flight-levers beneath his fingers. It was as if, here at the topmost deck of the sky ship, he was protecting all on board: his father, hollow-eyed and distracted as he pawed over the sky charts in the great cabin; Maris, as she tended to cuts and scrapes in the aft-store cabin she'd turned into an infirmary.

Down in the depths of the cargo-hold, Quint could hear Ratbit cursing and stamping about as he hunted cargo vermin, while up at the prow, Steg Jambles and young Tem Barkwater were deep in conversation. Tem seemed to be laughing and crying at the same time ... Up from the galley came the smell of frying woodonions and the sound of raised voices. Queep and Sagbutt were having another one of their furious arguments. Quint smiled. What an odd couple the small quartermaster and the great hulking flat-head goblin were – always shouting at one another, always fighting. And yet Sagbutt would lay down his life for Queep without a second thought.

The haunting cry of snowbirds rang out, and a great flock, in arrow-head formation, passed over the sky ship, a thousand strong. It was one of the great sights of the Edgeland skies and Quint never tired of it.

Just then, the wind swung round and gusted from the north, cold and strong, buffeting the starboard-side of the sky ship. Quint's hands automatically moved to the mainsail and neben-hull-weight levers.

Down on the flight-rock platform, the Stone Pilot was cleaning the cooling-rods.

'Down a tad, Stone Pilot!' Quint called across, and the Stone Pilot jumped up and hurried across to the bellows.

Within seconds, the combination of the burners and bellows had raised the temperature of the flight-rock just enough to bring the *Galerider* down the required dozen strides in the sky. The Stone Pilot was a natural, Quint thought with a smile – though he wondered if he would ever truly understand what went on in that head of hers, hidden beneath the great conical hood.

High above him, at the top of the mast, Quint could see the head of Spillins poking out of his beloved caterbird cocoon. The oakelf look-out was stroking the caternest with one gnarled hand almost as one might stroke a pet fromp or a friendly hammelhorn. Spillins was the oldest member of the crew. What sights those great dark eyes of his must have seen, Quint marvelled . . .

Just then, the oakelf's high, urgent voice rang out. 'Storm on the horizon!' Spillins cried. 'Approaching fast! . . .'

·CHAPTER NINE·

STORMLASHED

Wind Jackal lowered his telescope. 'Time is of the essence!' he reminded the crew in a booming voice. 'Make her stormtight. I want everything lashed down.'

He pulled down hard on two of the bone-handled levers, simultaneously staying the mainsail and lowering the stern-weight. The *Galerider* slowed and, as he raised the large starboard hull-weight, it swung round so that the stern was lowered and the prow pointed upwards.

'I'm waiting!' Wind Jackal's voice rang out. 'Let me hear those reports!'

Steg Jambles and Tem secured the second boomsail they had been struggling with and turned their attention instead to the winch-drives, drawing in the sail-sheets and tying them off as fast as they could. Sagbutt worked feverishly on the aft-deck, fastening the tolley-ropes and securing the nether-fetters, while Duggin – his head still bandaged – helped Ratbit as best he could with the rigging-locks.

'Storm at ten thousand strides and closing,' Spillins called out from the caternest high above their heads.

'Report!' Wind Jackal repeated, his hands tensed over the flight-levers.

At the flight-rock platform, the Stone Pilot had just finished preparing the drenching-tanks and chilling the cooling-rods. Now she was pumping the bellows, heating the rock as much as she dared. Quint hurried past her, with Maris close behind. The pair of them had battened down the hatches on the aft-deck to prevent the rain from getting in, having already secured those on the fore-deck. Meanwhile, Filbus Queep was down below, lashing the tarpaulins in the hold and unfastening the hull-shutters, just in case it did. A heavy downpour, sluicing unchecked off the deck and cascading down the stairs, could fill the bowels of a sky ship in minutes – with the watery ballast ruining the cargo and rendering the vessel all but unsailable.

Quint and Maris arrived at the helm, gasping for breath.

'Hatches battened down!' Quint made his report.

Beside him, Maris bit her lower lip nervously, her face drained of all colour.

The sky pirate captain nodded. 'Secure yourselves!' he told them grimly.

Quint did as he was told. He fastened the long tether-rope around his waist and then, since Maris appeared frozen to the spot, one around her waist too, and tied them both to the balustrade.

Maris shook her head as she stared ahead, her eyes wide and unblinking. 'I've never seen anything like it,' she whispered.

'Father knows what he's doing,' said Quint, resting his hand on her shoulder. 'And the *Galerider* hasn't let us down yet.'

Despite his confident words, as he watched the wall of cloud rolling towards them, Quint's own heart began to quicken. It was dark and turbulent, a boiling mass of charcoal grey exploding out of itself, each fresh excrescence tinged with purple and orange and shot with dazzling flashes of iridescent white. All round them, the mighty Deepwoods forest had changed colour. It was as though a dark yellow filter had been placed across the sun, leaving everything beneath it gloomy, yet malevolently glowing. The canopy of leaves below them surged and swirled like a mighty ocean swell, threatening to swallow up anything that dropped into its raging depths.

'Eight hundred strides,' Spillins shouted down.

'Sail-sheets secure, Captain!' Steg Jambles's hoarse voice rang out.

'Aft-deck secure!' growled Sagbutt.

'Rigging-locks secure!' Ratbit joined the chorus.

There was a pause.

'Queep!' roared Wind Jackal. 'You're keeping us all waiting . . .'

Pouring down from the base of the approaching cloud was torrential rain. From where they were, it seemed to be moving in soft rippling waves, like the fringe of a vast velvet curtain. Where the cloud neared the ground, it looked, Maris thought, almost as though it was dissolving. In starkest contrast, high up in the sky, the top of the dark cloud was silhouetted against the pale yellow sky, so clearly defined that it might have been cut out with a knife.

'Five hundred strides . . .'

Wind Jackal clenched and unclenched his fist over the flight-levers, his eyes steely and jaw set. He raised his head and bellowed above the deafening roar of the oncoming storm.

'*Queep!*'

All at once, the wind stopped blowing. The rolled sails stopped creaking, the rigging, which a moment earlier had been whistling, fell still – and the quartermaster's voice echoed up from the depths of the ship loud and clear against the eerie silence.

'Below decks secure!'

'What's happening,' Maris whispered, looking about her.

'It's the lull,' Quint replied.

'The lull?'

Quint shook his head. There was no time now to tell her about the anomalies of cloud-walls and storm-winds – about how at a distance, the wind of an approaching storm came *from* it, pushing everything in its path away; but how, closer to it, the wind reversed, and sucked everything *towards* its churning turbulence – and how, strangest of all, in between the two, the air was absolutely still.

'It means the storm's about to strike,' he whispered,

trying to sound calmer than he felt.

'Stone Pilot!' Wind Jackal called across to the flight-rock platform. 'Chill the rock . . . *Now!*'

Without a word, the Stone Pilot raised both arms, took hold of the drenching-levers and tugged. Chilled earth and sand dropped onto the glowing rock. Then, while it was still pouring down, she seized the ice-cold cooling-rods and thrust them into the rock itself. There was a splutter, a hiss and a powerful jet of stream.

The next moment, the *Galerider* shot up into the sky with such force that everyone on board felt their stomachs sink down to their toes. Back at the helm, Wind Jackal stood tall and erect, his hands clasping the rows of flattened flight-levers, while beside him, Quint and Maris gripped onto the balustrade. Ahead of them, the wall of black and grey cloud flew past in a blur. Higher and higher the sky ship flew, rising above the billowing stormclouds, and as it rose, the vessel began to shake and creak ominously . . .

On the flight-rock platform, the Stone Pilot stood over the flight-burners, as tense as a mire-heron waiting to strike an oozefish. The colder the rock became, the faster it rose – and the higher the *Galerider* climbed. Soon the sky around them would be so cold that, if they weren't careful, it would be impossible to re-heat the flight-rock and come down again. At that point, the *Galerider* would 'hurtle', and they would be doomed. They were all in the Stone Pilot's hands now.

At the helm, Wind Jackal remained erect and motionless, betraying none of his feelings as the *Galerider* continued to climb. Suddenly, above the sound of the rushing air, there came a screeching and squawking and Maris looked over the balustrade to see the air filled with countless ratbirds. They were streaming out from the bottom of the hull, a long ribbon of them that fluttered and flexed – before darting off down towards the ground.

'We must be close to hurtling,' Quint muttered. 'The ratbirds can sense it . . .'

The Stone Pilot must have sensed it too, for she ratcheted up the burners, which flared brilliant yellow in the thin air. As if in reply, the flight-rock seemed to give out a sigh which, as the burners set to work, rose to a low hum, then a steady whistle, rising in pitch and intensity.

Maris turned to Quint. 'We're slowing down,' she said, her voice breathless in the thin air. 'I can feel it. I . . .' She gasped. 'We've stopped!'

Quint nodded, but said nothing. As he wrapped his sky pirate greatcoat more tightly round him against the blistering cold of high sky, he knew that the *Galerider* was still in great danger. It was one thing to bring the flight-rock under control and prevent it hurtling. But quite another to remain here, hovering in the freezing air of high sky long enough for the terrible storm below to pass . . .

Shivering herself, Maris stared all round, her eyes wide with a mixture of excitement and awe. From one side of the sky to the other, the air was crystal clear. Only down at the far horizon was there any hint of colour – and that, the faintest smudge of yellowy-pink. She leaned against the balustrade and, craning her neck, peered down.

There, far below her now, was the top of the storm-clouds. Dazzling white and as fluffy as bolls of wild woodwool, the whole lot was in movement, with wisps of mist swirling above the rest like the steam in a cauldron of hot bristleweed broth.

'It's so beautiful,' she sighed, her breath coming in thick billowing clouds of white steam. She looked at Wind Jackal, then at Quint. 'What happens now?' she breathed.

'We wait up here as long as we can,' said Quint, trying to stop his teeth chattering. 'And hope the storm has blown past when we descend. Button up your greatcoat, Maris, it's going to get very cold . . .'

Maris, though, was not listening. '*Look!*' she gasped.

But Quint had already seen. As the *Galerider* had climbed higher, so the temperature had continued to drop. Now it had become so cold that sky-frost had

struck. As though one of the painters up on the viaduct walkway had applied a snowy wash, the entire sky ship was abruptly turning white – starting up at the top of the mast and rapidly moving down.

'Oh, my!' Spillins cried out in alarm, as his caternest was suddenly touched by the thick, crunchy layer of whiteness that turned the downy spider-silk lining as hard as marble.

Down the mast it ran, and along each and every rope and folded sail. The sailcloth, normally so soft and pliable, turned instantly stiff and inflexible, and fragile as glass. Round the hull the frost went, cracking and creaking as it turned the black rigging white. Even the glowing flight-rock began to cool once more – and though the frost melted as quickly as it formed on the flight-rock's cage, the intense cold ensured that it re-froze as rows of jagged icicles that became thicker and thicker with every passing second.

Wind Jackal shook his head. 'You've done your best, old girl,' he muttered, patting the *Galerider*'s wheel.

They had tried to hover above the storm. It hadn't worked. Now, there was only one thing they could do.

'To your stations!' he bellowed. 'Prepare to descend! We're going to have to stormlash, lads!'

Instantly, there was a flurry of movement on the flight-rock platform. With the ice building up on the metal rock cage, the flight-rock had already begun to cool. If they didn't act immediately, the *Galerider* would hurtle for certain. Wielding a huge sledgehammer each, Tem and Steg climbed over the rock cage, slamming the heavy tools at the great icicles one by one, until they shattered and fell away with the sound of splintering glass.

Meanwhile, the Stone Pilot pumped the heavy brass bellows for all she was worth. The flames of the burners roared as they turned from orange, through yellow, to a white so intense that when Maris turned away, she saw an afterglow of pink wherever she looked.

As the flight-rock itself began to glow, its buoyancy dwindled and a shudder ran through the frozen timbers of the *Galerider*. The next instant, the sky ship began its descent, heading back down through the crystal sky towards the billowing cloud far, far below. And as it dropped, the frost began to thin and melt, the rigging slackened and the sail-rolls thawed.

'Crew, to your storm stations!' roared Wind Jackal, adjusting the flight-levers with practised fingers. 'It's going to get pretty rough down there, lads. But hang on,' he told them, 'and be ready to stormlash when we get down to tree level.'

Quint reached across to take Maris's trembling hand, and squeezed it warmly. 'Don't worry,' he whispered as he untethered himself – though whether he was reassuring her or himself, he couldn't tell.

Steg and Tem climbed up from the flight-rock cage and raced back down to the fore-deck to prepare the grappling-hooks. Sagbutt and Duggin hurried from the aft-deck, making their way respectively round the port and starboard bows of the sky ship, hurriedly unleashing the rigging-locks and re-attaching them with a ten-point increase in the slack. Quint helped Filbus Queep and Ratbit check the tolley-rope and attach it to the heavy storm anchor. Meanwhile Duggin hurried to the bow to check that his beloved sky ferry, the *Edgehopper* was still securely lashed.

Up at the helm beside Captain Wind Jackal, Maris held her breath as the *Galerider*'s descent accelerated. As it did so, the timbers creaked and the fittings rattled . . .

'Cloud at a hundred strides depth,' Spillins's voice rang out. 'Fifty . . . thirty, twenty, ten . . .'

As they abruptly dropped down into the storm, Maris let out a cry of alarm. Everything had changed in an instant. The thick cloud was moist and clammy on her skin, and her nose twitched at a familiar smell . . .

'Toasted almonds,' she whispered, as the sound of rushing air filled her ears.

She looked round about her. But apart from the faint glow of the two flight-rock burners, each one surrounded with a soft, fluffy halo, she could see nothing.

The *Galerider* was falling; tumbling down through the thick air, pitching now to port, now to starboard, while its hull bucked – prow down, prow up, like an unbroken prowlgrin frantically trying to throw its rider.

'. . . and tether the staysail to . . .'

'Help me with . . .'

'Get that rope tied more tightly or . . .'

The snatches of muffled orders filtered back from the decks below her. Beside her, she could hear the flight-levers click and squeak, as Wind Jackal ran his fingers over them; raising, lowering . . .

The buffeting winds hammered against the sky ship from all sides, sending shock-waves pulsing through the entire vessel. The rigging whistled and groaned, and slapped against the hull. The mast creaked and splintered. And behind them, from somewhere high up in the aftcastle, an ominous knocking sound got louder and louder as a loose nether-stanchion banged against the rudder, over and over.

Then, all at once the cloud abruptly curdled and cleared, and Maris found that she could see the rest of the ship. There was the fore-deck, the misty figures of

Tem and Steg, Quint and Ratbit, now lashed to the gunwales. On the flight-rock platform, the hooded figure of the Stone Pilot was tirelessly working the bellows, while just below her, on the fore-deck, Duggin, Queep and the great hulking figure of Sagbutt crouched beneath the *Edgehopper*.

Whoopf!

The cloud returned, thicker than ever, and the *Galerider* began pitching and rattling as though the whole vessel had been clasped in the jaws of a vast sky monster that was shaking its head to and fro. All round her, Maris could hear wood cracking and sailcloth tearing.

'Prepare to stormlash!' Wind Jackal bellowed. 'Man the tolley-ropes!'

Maris pushed her windswept hair out of her eyes and looked down.

Suddenly, the clouds cleared again. Quint was rushing up the staircase onto the helm. Behind him, Filbus Queep and Sagbutt were struggling to control a large triangular sail which, its tether rope frayed and snapped, was flapping out of control. And behind them – far, far down over the side – she caught a glimpse of the green forest, hurtling up to meet them.

'Tree canopy at five hundred strides and closing,' Spillins shouted from the caternest.

'Take the wheel,' said Wind Jackal, stepping aside. 'When we hit tree height, lock the hull-weights into position, and hold her level.'

Quint nodded and took the wheel of the *Galerider*, his face a grim, expressionless mask. The clouds flashed past – now thick as tilder blankets, now thin as gauze.

'Sure you can handle it?' Wind Jackal looked into his son's eyes.

'I'm sure,' said Quint, in a hoarse voice.

'Good lad,' said his father and, brushing past on his way down to the aft-deck, he whispered to Maris, 'Stay with him.'

Maris smiled as bravely as she could. The next moment, her smile turned to a gasp of terror as the port bow of the *Galerider* was suddenly struck with such force that it keeled right over. If it hadn't been for the rope Quint had tied about her waist, she would have been thrown off the helm, over the balustrade and down to the forest below.

With the wind came the hail – huge balls of ice the size of snowbird eggs which hammered the stricken vessel, beating out a deafening tattoo against the port-side of the wooden hull.

'Prepare to cast the storm anchor!' Wind Jackal bellowed above the pounding clatter as he struggled down the stairs to the aft-deck, arm raised so that his heavy sky pirate greatcoat might afford some protection. 'We'll be at tree level any moment now . . .'

'Three hundred strides to the tree canopy!'

As the wind howled and wailed round them, like a choir of mad banshees, the sky vessel's descent eased, but the storm still buffeted and pummelled the *Galerider*, making her buck and shudder.

The hail gave way to rain – torrential, driving rain that lashed the deck, followed almost immediately by lightning. Great crackling explosions of dazzling light that roared and thundered around them, making the *Galerider* dip and lurch even more alarmingly. Suddenly, there came a deafening *crash!* as a jagged spear of lightning found its mark.

'Tem! Tem!' Steg Jambles's voice cried out. 'Over here, lad. My leg's trapped.'

'Hold on, Steg!' Tem shouted. 'I'm coming!'

The youth battled his way across the bucking deck. Down on his knees, the rope round his waist keeping him from being tossed from the ship, Tem crawled desperately towards his comrade. But it was heavy work. For every two strides he went forward, he slipped back one . . .

'Tree canopy, two hundred strides!' shouted Spillins.

'Sagbutt! Queep! The storm-anchor winch!' Wind Jackal roared from the aft-deck. 'On my command, let it go!' Turning, he raised a hand and shouted across to the flight-rock platform. 'Stone Pilot,' he bellowed. 'Prepare to give us lift . . .'

The Stone Pilot nodded back, but Maris could see the difficulty she was in. With the platform as unstable as the rest of the sky ship, tending the flight-rock was proving far from easy. Even so, as Maris watched, the hooded figure managed to grasp a clutch of cooling-rods and stagger across to the burners, twice falling heavily in the process.

Beyond, on the fore-deck, Tem reached Steg Jambles, to find a large winch-wheel had broken free of the harpoon-casing and was lying across the harpooneer.

'I can't feel my leg,' Steg muttered. 'I can't feel it at all.'

'I'll get you out of here,' said Tem, shifting around and readjusting his tether-rope. He reached down, seized the winch-wheel and took the strain. '*Urrgh!*' he grunted.

But it was no use. The heavy ironwood disc was far, far too heavy.

'Ratbit!' Tem shouted. 'Help me!'

With a great effort, the mobgnome crawled towards Tem across the fore-deck. Together, the two of them seized the heavy winch-wheel – struggling to keep their footing on the slippery, sloping deck as the *Galerider* continued to pitch and lurch.

'One, two, three . . . Heave!' cried Tem.

The two of them pulled with all their might. The winch-wheel shifted – not much, but just enough for Steg to pull his leg free.

'Thank Sky,' he groaned as he rubbed his calf tenderly. 'It's all right, I think,' he said.

With Tem for support, he struggled to his knees and, trying hard not to slip with the torrential rain lashing down, crawled back to the gunwales beneath the flight-rock platform.

'Bruised,' he said. 'But nothing broken . . .'

'One hundred strides!' The oakelf's voice rang out. 'Ninety . . . eighty . . . . seventy . . .

The *Galerider* shuddered as another stormcloud hammered into it, sending the Stone Pilot sprawling. The cooling-rods shot out of her gauntleted hands and tumbled down into the forest below.

'Lift!' Wind Jackal cried. 'Give us lift, Stone Pilot!'

'Sixty . . . fifty . . .'

With the drenching-tanks empty and the cooling-rods gone, the Stone Pilot had no option but to turn the burners down to their minimum setting. But it was a dangerous strategy. If the gale-force wind should snuff out the flames, then they were lost.

'Thirty!' cried Spillins. 'Twenty! Ten!'

'Storm anchor away!' Wind Jackal bellowed.

At the anchor-winch on the aft-deck, Filbus Queep released the winding gear, while Sagbutt, his muscles glistening and popping with the strain, heaved the heavy anchor – an immense ball of polished copper-wood – over the port-side of the *Galerider*.

There was the sound of splintering wood as the anchor crashed down through branch after branch of the trees in the forest canopy below. Suddenly, the tolley-rope attached to the anchor went taut – just as the flight-rock steadied the ship's descent. Now, as the *Galerider* hovered momentarily above the tree-tops, like a tilder-bladder balloon, the storm winds really hit it hard, sending it spinning round and round.

'Grappling-hooks!' bellowed Wind Jackal as everything turned into a sickening blur. 'Stormlash! Or we're lost!'

At the prow and at the stern, the crew launched their grappling-hooks as the treetops spun past at a dizzying speed. First the prow hook caught fast on an immense sallowdrop tree and the *Galerider*'s spin was brought to a shuddering halt. Then Sagbutt and

Duggin managed to snag a giant blackwood on the port-side and lash their tolley-rope down.

'Prow, secure,' Ratbit bellowed back above the sound of the roaring wind and hissing rain.

'Aft, secure,' shouted Duggin from the other end.

The rain was still pouring down and the wind was blowing at hurricane force, whipping the leafy boughs all round them into a frenzy, like a storm-swept sea. Even the huge sallow-drop tree – which had probably stood there for several hundred years – was swaying back and forwards, creaking and splintering as it did so.

Returning to the helm, Wind Jackal surveyed the scene for a moment, then shook his head. 'We're stormlashed,' he said. 'But the storm's still not reached its peak.' He frowned. 'The safest option is to disembark till it blows over.'

'Disembark?' said Maris and Quint together, horrified by the thought.

'It's a risk we'll have to take,' said Wind Jackal quietly. He raised his head and bellowed to the rest of the crew of the *Galerider*. 'Prepare to disembark!'

Quint untied the rope that had prevented him from being swept overboard, then turned to help Maris with hers.

'You go first, son,' said Wind Jackal. Quint nodded. 'And take Maris with you.'

Quint did as he was told without further question. With Maris behind him, he climbed down from the helm – taking care not to lose his footing as the sky ship lurched and rolled. At the fore-deck, he unfurled the rope-ladder coiled up by the balustrade, and dropped it over the side. It hung down in the air like the lolling tongue of a halitoad, swaying in the rain-drenched gale.

Slowly, carefully, he lowered himself down the ladder, rung after perilous rung, until the upper leaves of the blackwood tree started slapping against his legs. Lower he went, coming a moment later to an immense, almost horizontal branch, with another one growing out of it, which he could hold onto. He eased himself across and looked up.

'Come on, Maris,' he called, his heart thumping. 'You can do it . . .'

As he watched her climb down the rope-ladder, gripping tenaciously as she took the slippery rungs, one after the other, Quint realized all over again just how brave she was. When she reached the branch, he held out a hand for her to take, and felt a wave of relief as she grasped it.

He glanced up to see Tem Barkwater just climbing over the balustrade.

The tall, lanky youth was about to put his foot on the top rung, when there was a loud, crackling sound up in the sky, far, far above their heads. Quint and Maris both turned to see a vast and dazzling bolt of lightning come

hurtling down through the mist and cloud. It punctured
the thick air, leaving a trail of steam in its wake and . . .

Crash!

The point of the bolt skewered the ironwood mast of
the *Galerider*. The newly varnished wood smoked and
flared – but, as the torrential rain beat down, there was a
hiss and the flames were extinguished before they could
take hold.

As the lightning faded, a great rumbling noise started
overhead, which suddenly exploded with ear-splitting
loudness. And as it did so, Quint saw the flight-burners
on the *Galerider*'s flight-rock platform flicker and go out.
The flight-rock gave a long loud hiss as the freezing rain
hit it.

The next instant, there was the sound of splintering
wood and Maris and Quint felt violent tremors as the
grappling-hooks were torn from the branches of the tree.
As they looked helplessly on, the *Galerider* was swept up
and away into the turbulent storm.

Maris turned to Quint as it disappeared.

'Oh, Quint,' she whispered. 'What *now*?'

·CHAPTER TEN·

THE ANGLER

For a few moments, Quint said nothing. He was frozen in a crouching position, one arm round Maris, the other clutching the overhanging branch above. His face betrayed no emotion as his dark indigo eyes stared unblinkingly at the boiling black clouds into which the *Galerider* had vanished.

Beside him, Maris pulled her coat tightly around her as the wind howled and the rain lashed down, making the branches of the huge tree buck and bow. Dazzling lightning bolts illuminated the tangle of branches and leaves, which trembled and shook a moment later as colossal claps of thunder broke.

'What *do* we do now?' Maris shouted as the rumble died away.

'There's nothing we *can* do,' replied Quint, his eyes still fixed on the horizon. 'We must stay here until the storm passes, and pray . . .'

'Pray?' Maris questioned, the word snatched away by a blast of wind so violent, it tore the silvery heart-shaped leaves from the surrounding branches, pitching them into the maelstrom.

'Pray that the *Galerider* survives,' Quint told her, his voice loud above the tumult of the storm, 'because we don't stand a chance out here without her.'

Just then a great jagged bolt of lightning came crashing down out of the sky. It filled the air with thick mist and the tang of toasted almonds – and struck a tree some thirty or so strides to their right. As the blinding light faded, the turbulent sky seemed even darker than it had been before. Night was falling – and fast.

'How long do we have to stay up here?' asked Maris.

Quint shrugged. 'We're safer up here than down on the forest floor,' he said. 'The Deepwoods are dangerous enough at the best of times, but at night . . .' He shuddered. 'Better lash ourselves down and try to get as comfortable as we can.'

The rain continued to fall as Quint made preparations for the long night ahead. He swung the coiled rope from his shoulder and, having secured one end to the overhanging branch above, tied the other end around Maris's waist. For himself, he used his grappling-iron, plunging the sharp barbed hooks into the bark and then tying the stout line at the other end to his belt.

'Now, give me your parawings,' Quint said, turning to Maris, who was soaked to the bone and shivering uncontrollably.

With trembling fingers, Maris did as she was told, taking care not to let the wind tear the precious wings from her grasp as she did so. She leaned across to Quint, who had also removed his own, and pushed them into his outstretched hands.

Quint set to work, his fingers, stiff with cold, battling with the fiddly cords and strings. Using the hooks at the outermost edges of the wings, he secured the two sets of parawings to the branch above his head. Then he reached across and, by twisting the shoulder-straps round, managed to tie the pair of them together. He motioned Maris to join him beneath the dangling wings.

She crouched down beside him, her eyes wide with a mixture of curiosity and unease.

Next, reaching up, Quint tugged on the two release-levers. The black spider-silk wings instantly unfurled and billowed out. Quint grasped one of the outstretched wing-tips, Maris grasped the other, and together they

pulled the two ends round to form a bell-shaped tent, which Quint knotted securely in front of them.

At last, they were out of the driving rain and wind. Quint slumped down next to Maris and let out a weary sigh.

'Try to get some sleep, Maris,' he said, putting an arm round her and feeling the shivering begin to subside. 'We'll need all our strength tomorrow if we're to light a beacon.'

'A beacon?' said Maris, stifling a yawn. 'But how . . . ?'

'First, we'll have to climb an ironwood pine. The tallest we can find,' Quint said. 'Then we set fire to the top – the resin in the pinecones burns for days – and just hope that the *Galerider* spots it. That is,' he added glumly, 'if the *Galerider* isn't already a pile of shattered timbers by now . . .'

Quint felt Maris's hand close over his own and squeeze it tightly.

'Try not to think about it,' she whispered. 'And get some sleep yourself. It'll all seem much better in the morning . . . it always does . . .' she added with a wide yawn.

After a while, from beside him, there came the sound of gentle snoring and Quint became conscious that Maris had nuzzled up close, her breathing soft and regular as she slept. He wrapped his greatcoat around her and cushioned her head on his shoulder. All around him, mingling with the rush and roar of the storm, he could hear the nighttime sounds of the forest creatures.

Quint shrank into himself, his skin cold and clammy with fear. Many was the time the *Galerider* had anchored for the night in the Deepwoods, securing its tolley-ropes to the anchor-rings, rocky crags or ironwood pines that lay along the flight paths. But on those occasions, he'd been inside his cabin, tucked up in his hammock, the air filled with the reassuring sounds of the rest of the sleeping crew.

Here, inside this makeshift parawing tent that flexed and strained with the battering wind, it was different.

He felt exposed and vulnerable. Razorflits screeched as they wheeled through the air; rotsuckers flapped past on padded wings, their lamp-like eyes scanning the forest. Fromps coughed, quarms squealed, manticrakes gibbered and croaked, while somewhere far, far away, a solitary banderbear yodelled out to the storm-filled sky . . .

Although Quint had no memory of dropping off to sleep, he must have, for the next thing he knew, a loud *winnik-winnik-winnik* call was dragging him back to consciousness. He opened his eyes and peered blearily out of the tent to see a sleek lorrel in a nearby treetop calling to the early morning dawn as it groomed its golden fur.

He looked down to see Maris fast asleep, her head in his lap. 'Maris,' he whispered. 'Maris, it's morning . . .'

Maris's eyes snapped open. 'Wh . . . what . . . where am I?' she said.

Quint untied the parawings, which fell open to reveal the Deepwoods outside. Maris sat up. The rain had stopped and, although the wind was still blowing hard, it was no longer a threat to the trees – or to themselves. As she looked about her, however, Maris noticed various bare patches in the surrounding canopy where some of the greatest trees had come crashing down, bringing others with them.

Everything – from the leaves and bark, to the sky itself – gleamed and glinted, as though the heavy downpour had burnished the entire forest. Up above their heads, the remnants of the great gathering of stormclouds skudded quickly across the sky. One moment, the sun beat down; the next, everything was cast in shadow.

'The Deepwoods,' Maris breathed. 'They're . . . they're beautiful.'

'They might be beautiful,' said Quint, as he unhitched the parawings and separated them. He slipped his own over his shoulders, and helped Maris on with hers. 'But remember, Maris, the Deepwoods are deadly. We have to find an ironwood pine, and that means climbing down to the forest floor and trekking. When we do, you must promise me . . .'

'Promise you what?' said Maris, wide-eyed.

'That you'll stay close to me. We must keep to the shadows – and don't touch or eat or drink anything, no matter how hungry or thirsty you get.'

'But—' Maris began.

'Nothing!' insisted Quint, seizing her by the shoulders and staring into her eyes. 'Not a dew-filled seedpod, not a succulent delberry . . . Nothing at all! The Deepwoods cannot be trusted!'

Maris stared back into Quint's eyes, so full of concern and anxiety. She nodded slowly.

'I promise,' she said.

Without further delay, they began climbing down the huge blackwood tree, leaving those great gnarled branches where they'd weathered the storm. Quint went first, finding handholds and footholds on the broad pitted expanse of the trunk, and pausing on branches to help Maris down after him. Occasionally, she would slip – but Quint's reassuring hand was always there in an instant, gripping a wrist or an ankle to steady her.

The lower they got, the easier the climb, as the broad trunk of the blackwood tree became ever more gnarled and encrusted with handy knots and whorls. Maris began to relax, and paused now and again to look around.

'Oh, Quint, what are *they*?' she asked as they passed a bough full of tiny hovering birds of iridescent green.

'Emerald mossbirds, I think,' said Quint. 'Though sky pirates call them skull-peckers.'

'What a horrible name for such beautiful birds,' said Maris, resuming her descent.

Quint smiled, and decided not to tell her about the unfortunate habit they had of pecking out the eyes of any creature foolish enough to venture onto their nesting branch.

'What's *this*?' Maris asked a moment later, pointing at the long thin insect running across the branch by her hand. She giggled. 'Look at all its little legs going!'

'A hairy thousandfoot,' Quint replied, adding matter-of-factly: 'And they can strip the flesh off a finger in seconds . . .'

Maris gave a small yelp of alarm and quickly withdrew her hand as the orange and grey mottled creature disappeared into a crack in the blackwood bark.

As they got closer to the ground, the forest around them became darker and colder, with the low sun unable to penetrate the depths of the forest. Finally, they reached the base of the tree, where the great gnarled roots fanned out from the huge trunk and sloped down towards the shadowy forest floor below. There, they disappeared deep into the rich earth, anchoring the mighty blackwood tree securely enough to withstand all but the most ferocious Deepwoods storms.

Quint paused and peered down into the gloom. Anything could be down there, lurking in the shadows – packs of voracious wig-wigs with their fluffy bodies and knife-like teeth; poison-tentacled hoverworms or death-breathed halitoads . . .

He took a deep breath, grasped Maris's arm and quietly slid down a long, snaking root towards the forest floor. Their feet hit the mossy ground with a soft *ploff* at exactly the same moment, and they tumbled forwards. Instantly, Quint sprang to his feet and grasped Maris's arm once more, pulling her into the shadows beneath a cluster of huge toadstools. He glanced around furtively, then motioned to Maris to follow him.

'Keep your eyes and ears open, and stay close!' he instructed, before setting off at a brisk pace. 'And try to touch as little as possible. Flowers can sting, thorns can poison, vines can scratch and snag . . .'

Maris hurried after Quint, her face taut with fear.

'And as for the creatures,' Quint continued, skirting round a clump of milkwort fronds, 'they're best avoided, however small and innocent-looking they may appear.

Remember, Maris, out here in the Deepwoods, nothing is what it seems!'

Maris stared about her, Quint's ominous words echoing inside her head. It was difficult to imagine that it was quite as dangerous as he maintained. The shadowy undergrowth was shot with shafts of dazzling sunlight. Magnificent treetrunks were everywhere, some with sleek silvery bark, some with velvety golden bark, and some with dark rough bark out of which grew mossy fronds, multi-coloured lichens and delicate blooms that fluttered in the fading wind.

There were banks of moonbells and dewdrops, tumbledown-furze and comb-bushes which, as the wind blew, filled the air with soft music – an ever-changing chorus of delicate chimes and plangent humming. And the smells! Every footstep they took brought new ones – the sweet fruity aromas of limeweed and woodapple blossom, laced with the the sour odour of stinkwood and decay.

So much beauty, thought Maris, as she followed Quint through a small glade and back into the undergrowth, yet shot with so much danger . . . Suddenly, out of the corner of her eye, she saw a flash of blue.

'Quint,' Maris said, her voice hushed and urgent. 'Look over there. Lemkins!'

Quint followed her gaze, to see three lemkins – their bright fur glinting in the shafts of sunlight like sapphires – frolicking together in a clearing just ahead. Over and over they tumbled, pulling one another's ears and tails, and chirruping with delight.

'Just like Digit,' Maris whispered. 'You remember Digit, my little lemkin pet? He died last winter – and I still miss him . . .'

Suddenly, in the blink of an eye, one of the lemkins shot through the air, as if sky-fired, and disappeared into the shadows beneath a comb-bush. The bush shook violently, as though it was alive, and the air filled with a hideous wheezing sound. The other two lemkins raced up the nearest tree, making their distinctive *whaa-iiii kha-kha-kha-kha* calls of distress.

'Run!' Quint shouted. 'It's a halitoad!'

Maris stared at the comb-bush as its broad serrated fronds parted and a hideous creature with warty skin and bulging eyes waddled out into the sunlight, its mottled chest inflating like a tilder-bladder balloon, and its long

sticky tongue licking its gaping needle-fanged mouth.

Quint grabbed her arm and, dragging her with him, dashed across the clearing as fast as he could. They had just entered the surrounding trees when, from behind them, they heard a rasping blast as the halitoad exhaled.

'Hold your breath!' Quint told her, as he pulled his collar up to cover his mouth and pinched his nose shut.

Beside him, Maris did the same, and the pair of them continued running through the trees until their lungs were bursting. Then, unable to go a step further, they tumbled to the ground and sucked in a lungful of air.

'*Urgh-gh-gh* . . .' Maris gagged, and began spluttering with disgust as a foul and fetid stench caught in the back of her throat. '. . . That *smell* . . .' she cried, her eyes watering.

Quint nodded grimly. 'The halitoad's breath is fatal. Any closer and we'd be as dead as that lemkin,' he said. 'We were lucky. Very lucky.'

Looking around, Quint set off again, with Maris close beside him.

They went deeper into the woods and as they did so, although the sun was now much higher in the sky, when the canopy closed above their heads, the forest floor became as dark as in the middle of the night.

'All these trees,' Quint muttered. 'Blackwood, redoak, leadwood and lullabee; sapwood, sallowdrop and weeping-willoak . . .' He shook his head. 'Yet not a single ironwood pine.'

They went on in silence, trudging through the dense undergrowth, their feet sinking into the thick mattress of fallen leaves. Maris had no idea how long they trekked through the gloom, avoiding the enticing sunlit glades that looked so beautiful, but were so deadly.

Then suddenly, up ahead, there was a shaft of light. Golden beams of sunlight were streaming down from above. As they approached, Maris and Quint saw that a line in the forest had been cleared. The reason became apparent as they got nearer. A huge tree had come down in the previous night's storm and, as it fell, it had taken a dozen or so others with it.

'Typical,' Quint snorted, as they approached the gigantic trunk.

'What?' said Maris.

'First ironwood pine we find,' he said, 'and it's lying on its side.'

Together, they made their way cautiously to the edge of the vast pit where the tree had been been uprooted and looked down. The taproot of the colossal tree had gone down into the earth almost as far as its trunk had grown up, and now the hole it left was immense. Dark and smelling of rot and fungus, the rainwater which had collected like a small lake at the bottom glinted in the sunlight.

As Maris looked down at it, she suddenly realized how thirsty she was. Her mouth was dry and gritty, her throat hurt and she could still taste the faint but disgusting halitoad-breath tang on her tongue. She'd do anything to wash it away.

'No,' said Quint firmly, as if reading her mind. 'We can't risk it. The water might look clear, but it could contain rust-blight or spore-worms . . .'

'Spore-worms?' Maris shook her head and turned away. 'No, on second thoughts, I don't want to know,' she said weakly.

Quint laid a hand on her shoulder. 'I know it's hard,' he said gently, 'but we have to go on. If we find an ironwood pine and climb it, then we'll be able to gather some rainwater at the top, where it'll be pure . . .'

'*If* we find an ironwood,' said Maris miserably, drying her eyes. 'But what if we don't?'

'We must,' said Quint firmly, helping her to her feet. 'One thing's for certain, we can't stay here much longer . . .'

He pointed ahead at the dappled sunlit clearing. Strange Deepwoods creatures were emerging, drawn to the light – and the promise of an easy meal.

Small translucent cray-spinners, with diaphanous wings and eyes at the end of long swaying stalks, were twisting in the dappled light. Large dust-flies and tentacled

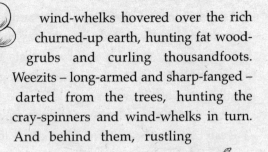

wind-whelks hovered over the rich churned-up earth, hunting fat wood-grubs and curling thousandfoots. Weezits – long-armed and sharp-fanged – darted from the trees, hunting the cray-spinners and wind-whelks in turn. And behind them, rustling

through the trees, came larger predators with their sights set on the weezits . . .

There were armour-plated hoglets, sharp-tusked and quick; and gladehawks with hooked beaks and massive talons. While Quint and Maris watched from the shadows, they swooped from above and snapped from below, as they took their place in the food-chain.

Quint turned and set off in the opposite direction as a troop of whooping silver-backed quarms swung through the trees and launched themselves at the hoglets.

Maris clasped her hands over her ears as the air filled with ferocious shrieks and frenzied snarls, and hurried after him. Over and under the fallen trees the pair of them scrambled, and back into the depths of the forest. They darted between thickets and scrabbled through tangled undergrowth; they picked their way over stepping stones in broad, shallow streams which Maris yearned to drink from, but that Quint forbade with a frown and a shake of the head. Soon they were hot and panting, with sweat beading their foreheads and trickling down their backs – and still there wasn't an ironwood pine to be found.

Far, far above their heads, the sun was sinking lower in the sky and the light that managed to break through the forest canopy was casting ever-longer shadows . . .

'It'll be night soon,' said Quint, stopping and wiping his face with his sleeve. 'We'll have to climb the first big tree we come to, whatever it is, and wait till morning.'

Maris sighed and let her head drop. 'I'm so tired, Quint,' she murmured. 'And hungry, and thirsty . . .'

But Quint wasn't listening. He was staring into the

gloom at the gnarled roots and trunks of the trees around them, as if assessing how difficult each one might be to climb, and how long it would take them.

Maris looked away. How sick she was of this terrible place, with its beautiful glades and hideous creatures. How she longed to be back on the *Galerider*, sitting down to a bowl of woodonion broth and a tumbler of sweet rainwater from the aft-deck water butts . . .

She paused. There, just within reach, was a large red woodsap, nestling in the leaves of the forest floor. It was smooth, ripe, without a blemish – and sitting there just waiting to be picked up. Maris's mouth began to water uncontrollably. She knew just how deliciously succulent it would taste.

She looked up. Quint was a few strides away, staring up at the tumbling, curled root-stack of a tall sallowdrop tree.

She knew she shouldn't . . . But what harm could it do? A large, red, juicy woodsap which had just dropped from a branch far above . . . If *she* didn't pick it up, then it was sure to be snatched and devoured by some Deepwoods creature at any minute . . .

With a trembling hand, Maris stretched out towards the woodsap. Her clammy fingers closed around the ripe fruit . . .

Quint turned and shouted. 'Maris! No!'

She tried to lift the woodsap, only to discover that it was strangely heavy. She tugged at it greedily, Quint's desperate voice roaring in her ears.

'*No! No! No . . .*'

Suddenly, the forest floor erupted from beneath Maris's feet as a massive scaly creature rose up on thin spindly legs. At the same moment, Maris realized that the sweet, succulent woodsap clenched in her hand was in fact attached to a thick, knotted tentacle rooted in the creature's broad, mud-coloured forehead. As she dangled from it, five enormous eyes opened and focused on the tempting morsel which had taken the bait. The creature opened its cavernous mouth and, with a whiplash jerk of the tentacle, tossed its victim high into the air.

Maris cried out with terror as she fell back towards the gaping maw. Then, just as she was about to be swallowed whole, a huge black ironwood pinecone shot through the air and embedded itself in the creature's gaping gullet with a fleshy *spplafft!*

227

The creature's jaws snapped shut. Maris landed with a heavy thud on its forehead and skidded off. The five eyes bulged and the tentacle with its woodsap-lure shot up straight in the air as the creature began to gurgle and choke on the heavy pinecone now lodged in its throat.

On the forest floor, gasping and winded, Maris looked up to see the hideous monster stumble forward on its long, spindly legs, a long broad fin of a tail swishing wildly behind it. Then, with a long, despairing gurgle, it slumped to the ground with a flat-sounding *splat* and lay motionless. The decoy woodsap on the end of the tentacle fell lifelessly at Maris's feet.

She turned away from it in disgust, bile rising in her throat, only to see Quint, hands on his hips, beaming down at her delightedly.

'Wh . . . wh . . . what *was* that?' she gasped.

'A landfish,' smiled Quint, helping her to her feet. 'An angler by the look of it – but no match for a well-aimed ironwood pinecone . . .'

'Pinecone?' said Maris in a dazed voice.

'First thing that came to hand!' said Quint, with a delighted laugh. 'Look over there. There are hundreds of them beneath that . . .'

'Ironwood pine!' she screamed with joy, gazing up at the most magnificent tree she had ever seen. 'It was right here all the time!'

She hugged Quint excitedly and the two of them did a little jumping jig for a few moments. The light had faded now to a grey dusk, which was darkening by the second. Quint and Maris stopped and craned their necks back.

The base of the ironwood pine's trunk was ten times wider than the grandest tower in Sanctaphrax; a hundred times wider than the *Galerider*'s mighty mast; a thousand individuals it would take, each one clasping the hand of the next, to encircle it. And tall! The tree soared up into the sky, dwarfing all the others about it, before spearing the lofty canopy and standing proud above the rest.

Maris turned to Quint, her face suffused with happiness. 'I'll bet there isn't a taller ironwood pine in all of the Deepwoods,' she said.

'You could well be right,' said Quint, standing with his hands on his hips looking up at the tree. 'There's just one problem.'

'What's that?' said Maris, suddenly serious.

Quint smiled at her. 'The long, long climb ahead!'

·CHAPTER ELEVEN·

THE BEACON

They started straight away. The huge ironwood pine, in contrast to the blackwood, was surprisingly easy to climb. The bark of the tree was rough and scaly, and provided convenient foot- and hand-holds.

'It's as easy as climbing a staircase!' said Maris in wonder, as they made their way up the trunk, soon leaving the darkening forest floor far behind.

'Maybe so,' said Quint, 'but be careful of the resin.'

He pointed to cracks in the slab-like bark, from which a thick amber substance oozed in great globules.

Maris peered at one of the glistening drops of resin seeping from a deep fissure to her right. The great shimmering globule was almost as big as she was, but that wasn't what made her gasp. No, what took her breath away was the sight of a rotsucker – its thin snout outstretched, its bat-like wings frozen in mid-flap, and its glowing eyes dim and unseeing – entombed within the resin.

As she followed Quint up the huge trunk towards the

first of the branches high above, Maris saw countless other Deepwoods creatures which had got trapped in the treacherous resin, from tiny woodants and termites, to plump quarms and bony weezits, all frozen in mid-step, flap or hop, and strangely beautiful in their amber prisons.

'It reminds me of the collections in the Palace of Shadows,' said Maris, pausing to marvel at a razorflit caught in the act of swallowing a giant woodmoth. 'Yet nothing in my father's palace was half as exquisite . . .'

'Or as deadly,' added Quint. 'We'll be safe when we get up to the branches.'

He took Maris's arm and guided her away from a large column of resin, just as a glistening drop – as big as a fist – fell from the end, like wax dripping from a can-dle. It disappeared into the shadows below with a sticky sounding *plopff!*

Now that the sun had dropped low in the sky, down below them, the forest floor was in darkness. Only by climbing higher, up towards the light that still brightened the sky, could they prolong the day.

'I'm so thirsty, Quint,' Maris rasped as she followed him up the rough bark 'steps' of the trunk.

'I know,' said Quint softly. 'But just hold out a little longer if you can.'

Maris looked up at the first of the arched branches high above, spanning the air like the vaulted ceiling of a mighty palace hall, and shook her head miserably. 'I'll try,' she whispered.

Although the ironwood had seemed easier to climb at first than the gnarled and slippery blackwood, the pine tree was far, far larger. This made the distance from its base to the first of its huge branches a daunting climb and, since the slab-like bark was becoming more and more fragile the higher they went, increasingly dangerous.

In fact, all the trees of the great Deepwoods forest were different from one another. With the passing years, the bloodoak – a flesh-eater – grew broader rather than taller, its mandibled jaws stretching to take in ever-larger prey. The lullabee, knobbly and irregular, with branches sprouting every which way, grew in a robust yet haphazard manner; while the branches of the blackwood would divide and sub-divide, becoming more and more dense with every season. Then there was the redoak, a graceful tree with diamond-shaped leaves that would turn bright crimson at the end of every frost. Growing continuously, the redoak's branches sprouted from the central trunk, one after the other, almost like a spiral staircase.

And then, of course, there was the ironwood pine itself. In contrast to most of the other trees, it had distinct growth spurts. For several years the trunk would grow tall and straight. Then, triggered by an upsurge of sap, branches would appear in a ring around the circumference of the trunk. Once these had become established, with massive, dark-green pinecones nestling between the dark-green needles, the trunk would grow again. As it did so, extra branches would grow, so that the lower rings could have anything up to a hundred branches radiating out from the trunk. This number diminished the taller the tree became, until at the top, there was a ring of merely three or four small branches.

'I reckon that's a good fifty years we've just climbed,' Quint announced as they finally reached the first ring of branches, each one the size of a blackwood tree.

'You mean, *strides*?' said Maris.

Quint shook his head. 'Years,' he said, 'judging by the height of the trunk. You know, the ironwood grows a new branch every twenty years or so. There must be a hundred branches in this first ring alone – not counting all the branches in the rings above. I'm telling you, Maris, this tree must be ancient . . .'

Maris looked up at the rings of branches above her head.

'Older than my grandfather,' she mused. 'My great-grandfather, my great-*great*-grandfather . . .'

'Maris, this tree is so big, it's probably older than the great floating city of Sanctaphrax itself.'

Maris's eyes widened. 'Older . . . than . . .' Her voice faded away to nothing as she sat down on the huge branch and, for a moment, forgot just how thirsty she was.

'Come on,' said Quint. 'We need to go on a bit further.'

Dragging herself wearily to her feet, Maris followed close behind Quint as he continued up the tree. They passed circles of branches, followed by long stretches of trunk, followed by more circles of branches, as they forged their way further and further up the tree. It was so immense that it was home to countless creatures that never left it – insects, grubs, birds and beasts, for whom the great ironwood pine was their entire world.

There were colonies of wood-wasps living in huge papery lantern-like constructions that swayed beneath the branches; there were flightless urchin-birds with spiky dark-green feathers and needle-thin orange beaks that hid themselves away among the brushes  of pine-needles, and scaly creatures with long twisting tentacles that probed the air from crevices in the bark. And eyes . . . Lots and lots of eyes. Wide discs of green, narrow yellow slits and blood-red dots – all glinting in the half-light as she hurried past.

They had climbed just beyond the top of the forest canopy when Quint turned to her at last. 'We'll camp here for the night,' he told her, unclipping his parawings.

With a sigh of relief, Maris unclipped her own and watched as Quint secured the parawing tent to one of the myriad smaller branches that sprouted from the massive one on which they stood. Then, without saying a word, he pulled his knife from his belt, reached up and cut through the stalks of half a dozen of the small, pale-green pinecones that hung in clusters from the branch overhead. He handed them to Maris.

'Break them open,' he instructed her. 'Then peel the individual kernels. *They're* what we're after.' He climbed to his feet. 'But whatever you do, don't eat them!'

While Maris got to work, Quint set off along the main branch. After a few minutes, the branch forked, and forked again, each new branch bristling with great brushes of fragrant pine-needles. Quint clambered out over one of these springy mattress-like brushes, until he reached the very tip. He could go no further. All round him was the forest canopy, golden and gleaming in the evening sunlight.

Quint sniffed the air and his nostrils filled with a delicious, tangy smell – a cross between limeleaves and woodhoney. A broad smile spread across his face.

'Better than I could have hoped for,' he murmured as he reached out and parted the pine-needles at his feet to reveal a clutch of yellow, ball-shaped mushrooms clinging to the underside.

Taking care not to slip, Quint lowered himself so that he was seated astride the branch. He slipped his hands inside his greatcoat, unbuckled his tooled breast-plate and pulled it free. Then, having wedged it upside down between his knees, he reached out and took one of the balls of fungus in both hands. With one short, sharp jerk, he twisted it to the left. There was a soft *crack* and a lingering *squellp* – and the fungus came free. He laid it down gently inside the hollow of the breast-plate, before returning his attention to the rest of the cluster.

Squellp! Squellp! Squellp!

A little while later Quint returned and placed a heavily laden breast-plate in front of Maris.

'What are *they*?' she asked, not sure whether to be delighted or horrified.

Quint smiled as he unfastened the small metal cup from the side of his belt. Then he selected the largest of the mushrooms and, holding it over the cup, gently squeezed. As he did so a clear liquid streamed down into the cup and the air filled with a juicy perfume. When the cup was filled

almost to the brim, Quint handed it to Maris.

'Try that,' he said.

Maris raised the cup tentatively to her lips. Then, wincing slightly, she took the smallest of sips. Her face lit up with an expression of absolute joy. Throwing back her head, Maris drained the cup in one go.

'That is *delicious*! What is it?' she asked, as she stuck her hand out for a second cupful.

Quint selected a second fungus, and squeezed it dry. 'It has many names. Kobold's tears. The gift of Riverrise. Cloudtree juice . . .' he said, as he forced the last drips out of the spongy fungus and passed the cup back to Maris. 'But what we sky pirates call it is sky nectar.'

She drained it quickly, and wiped her mouth on the back of her hand. 'Sky nectar,' she said. 'I've never tasted anything better!'

'It's pure rainwater trapped in the fibres of the fungus,' Quint explained. 'The spores give it that sweet taste. Of course, the fungus also grows lower down, but it's dangerous to try it there. *Anything* could get mixed up with the rain. No, it's only up here, above the canopy where the rain first lands, that it's safe to drink.'

He looked down at the pile of ironwood pine-kernels she'd peeled. 'Excellent work,' he said.

Maris beamed.

Quint leaned forward, picked up one of the golden, heart-shaped kernels, inspected it – then popped it in his mouth. '*Mmm!*' he sighed. 'Like tilder sausages flavoured with orange-grass and nibblick . . .'

'What?' Maris exclaimed. 'But you told me not to eat them . . .'

'Did I?' said Quint innocently. He took a handful of the pine-kernels, and ate them, one after the other. A smile spread across his face. 'Absolutely delicious.'

'You . . . You . . .' Maris cried out.

Quint laughed. 'You'd better tuck in, before I eat the lot,' he said.

'Oh, Quint, that *is* good,' said Maris, a moment later. 'Meaty. Spicy. Succulent . . .'

She reached forward for another one. And then another, and another, before washing them all down with some more freshly squeezed sky nectar.

Maybe it was because she had been so hungry and thirsty. Maybe it was the relief of escaping from the terrors of the forest below with its pusfrogs and slither-worms and wig-wigs, and who knew what else besides. Or maybe it was just sitting there in that huge ancient tree that had survived and prospered for countless centuries, and whose branches not only protected them, but also provided this generous feast . . . Maris would never know. What she *did* know was that the simple meal she shared that evening with her friend, Quint, high up above the dark forest, was the most delicious she had ever tasted in her entire life.

'Perfect,' she whispered.

Far away, the sun – now a great wobbling crimson ball – sank down behind the distant trees. As it did so, the low streaks of cloud down near the horizon turned to bright yellows and oranges, pinks and purples, while the sky behind them was stained a deep red that spread out like spilled winesap on a tablecloth.

A soft wind blew, rustling the leaves at the tops of the forest canopy as it passed across the majestic sweep of the endless Deepwoods, and filling the warm air with a mixture of aromatic scents – oakmint, lyptus-balm,

blue-thyme, and the herby fragrance of the ironwood pine itself. A flock of snow-birds circled in the sky, before swooping down towards the tall lufwoods, where they would roost for the night. A giant caterbird flapped its way across the darkening sky . . .

Slowly but surely, the darkness of the night moved across the firma-ment, like a great black blanket. Stars came out, bright and twinkling in the moonless sky. The cries of the night creatures grew louder as fromps and quarms, febrals, goremorps, manticrakes and so, so many others joined the rousing chorus – a great symphony of sound that swirled round the forest and rose up into the sky.

Up on the huge branch, Maris and Quint settled down to sleep in the parawing tent, Quint's sky

pirate greatcoats pulled up round their ears and buttoned tightly. Bone-tired from their climb, but well fed
and watered, they fell in moments into a deep, heavy
sleep that not even the Deepwoods could disturb.

Maris dreamed of the Palace of Shadows – her former
home in the great floating city of Sanctaphrax. She
dreamed she had lost her pet lemkin and was searching
for it through the great rooms of the palace, each one full
of cabinets and curiosities and ornate furniture. But
something was wrong. From the cupboard doors and
bureau drawers, amber resin oozed. It was spreading
over the marble floors, and she was running through
room after room. But the more she ran, the slower she
moved as the resin trapped her heels, then rose to her
knees, her waist, her neck . . .

Beside her, Quint was dreaming of the sky-shipyards.
He was looking up at a sky cradle. And there was the
Galerider, newly repaired and perfect in every detail. He
was climbing the tower; emerging at the top. The
Galerider's crew was waving to him . . .

They were all there, Ratbit, Steg Jambles, Tem
Barkwater, Sagbutt, Filbus Queep and the Stone Pilot . . .

And there was his father – shouting, trying to tell him
something. But Quint couldn't hear . . .

He reached out to grasp the *Galerider*'s tolley-rope, but
a gnarled hand snatched it from him and pushed him
away. It was a hooded figure with no face – though
Quint knew at once that it was Turbot Smeal. He felt a
hot rage boil up within him as he drew his sword and
lunged at the figure, only for it to disappear.

Suddenly, the *Galerider* rose up into the air, only it wasn't the *Galerider* any longer. It had turned into a land-fish! A huge monstrous angler, with Turbot Smeal as its lure, whirring high above its horrible grinning head . . .

'Quint! Quint!' Maris's voice sounded. 'Wake up! You're having a bad dream!'

Quint opened his eyes to see Maris's concerned face staring into his own. He sat up and ran trembling fingers through his hair.

'Sorry,' he said. 'Did I wake you?'

Maris smiled ruefully. 'Actually, no, I was having a bad dream myself,' she admitted.

Quint unhooked the parawing tent and peered out.

'Talking of bad dreams . . .' he said, looking out at the great expanse of forest rolling off to the distant horizon, 'we'd better break camp and get to the top of this tree . . .'

'The beacon?' said Maris.

Quint nodded. 'There's just one thing, though,' he said.

'What's that?' Maris turned to him.

'I've never lit an ironwood pine beacon before.'

Following a brief breakfast of pine-kernels and sky nectar, Quint and Maris set off shortly after dawn on the long climb to the very top of the ironwood pine. A brisk wind had got up. It swirled round them, tugging at their fingers and plucking at their clothes.

They climbed for several hours, passing ring after ring of broad branches; century after century of growth. And as they climbed, the trunk narrowed, the rings of branches became thinner and closer together, and the amber resin no longer oozed from the bark. Here, instead, it was set solid in small fists of gleaming fiery colour.

Maris paused and snapped a small piece from the bark. It was smooth as glass, yet curiously warm to the touch, and not at all sticky. She slipped it inside her pocket and patted it, 'for luck', she whispered.

'This'll do,' Quint announced finally.

Maris looked up. Half a dozen strides above their heads was a huge clump of pinecones; beyond that, the very top of the tree, which ended with the needle-clad apex of the great trunk, pointing up at the sky like a giant finger.

'Here, take my knife,' said Quint, pulling it from his belt and handing it to Maris. 'I want you to strip the trunk and these main branches here of every twig, every pinecone, every pine-needle. We need to make a fire-break, to stop the fire at the top of the tree spreading down to the branches below. And while you're doing that, I'll climb up and prepare the treetop for firing.'

Maris nodded and set to work. Hacking determinedly, she turned her attention to the trunk, chopping off all the protruding bark and leaving it as smooth as a well-whittled stick. Climbing past Maris, Quint clambered up to the next ring of stubby branches where the great clump of dark-green pinecones – each one the size of a banderbear head – were clustered.

The sun was high in the sky now, sending dazzling rays out across the forest. Above him, a woodteal puffed out its speckled chest and sang, its voice pure and mellifluous.

Quint turned his attention to the clump of pinecones. He eased himself slowly up towards them. Then, with his legs wrapped round the tree-trunk as tightly as if he was riding a prowlgrin, he reached up. While his left hand supported the first of the giant pinecones, his right hand swung the sword round. He ran the edge of the blade deftly down the ridged and knobbly surface in a zigzag line.

For a moment, apart from a tangy whiff of pine that wafted into the air, nothing happened. Then, where the blade had passed, the dark-green skin peeled back a tad and thick, deep red resin began to well up like blood. It gathered in the corners of the line, which got fuller and fuller, until it started running down the surface pinecone in two glistening red blobs.

'Thank Sky!' Quint murmured, smiling with relief that a theory he had only ever heard about from old sky pirates in Undertown taverns actually seemed to be working.

Emboldened, he seized the pinecone once more, and scored the skin with a whole series of zigzag lines. Then, with resin coursing all down the outside of the cone, he turned his attention to the next one, and the one after that, until the whole clump of giant pinecones – each one with a dozen or more wounds to their skin – oozed and dripped the deep red, intoxicatingly scented resin.

'*Criss-crossed the cones, I did,*' Quint could hear the old captain, Storm Weezit, saying to his father in the

Tarry Vine tavern. *'Then I lets the resin drip – but not too much mind . . . Next, I strikes these here sky-crystals . . .'* Quint could remember the crystals held in those gnarled old sky pirate's hands – hands that were scarred by horrible burns . . .

Quint closed his eyes and took a deep breath. He couldn't stop now. The two of them had come too far . . .

Balancing precariously on a broken-off stump, Quint rummaged in the pockets on either side of his greatcoat and pulled out the two yellow sky-crystals. As they came together they glowed brightly. Then, taking one in each trembling hand – and before he could have any second thoughts – Quint struck them together.

Clack!

From the branch ring below, as Maris watched, it all seemed to happen in slow motion. The spark – glinting like a shooting star – dropped down through the air towards the dripping red pinecone. She was waiting for it to land before bursting into flames, so it came as a surprise when, with an inch to go . . .

WHOOF!

The vapours ignited with a loud explosion, and all at once the whole cluster of pinecones was ablaze. Quint, thrown back by the blast – his arms flailing, his mouth open, his eyes shut – was falling, falling, falling, until : . .

Crack!

He hit the ring of branches on which Maris stood.

Maris fell to her knees beside him. She stroked his cheeks, his forehead, the line of his jaw – the black soot that covered his face coming off on her fingers.

'Quint,' she said urgently, as scalding drops of the crimson resin plashed all round them. 'Quint, are you all right? Tell me you're all right . . .'

Quint opened his eyes. 'I . . . I'm all right,' he whispered, but as he looked up at the blazing fire at the top of the tree – the bright roaring flames reflected in his eyes – it was impossible to ignore the look of terror in his expression.

'Oh, Quint,' Maris gasped, her heart overflowing as she seized his hands. 'Fire . . . I'd forgotten how terrified you are of it.' She squeezed his hands warmly. 'It must have taken a lot to climb up there and . . .'

'It had to be done.' Quint swallowed, sat up and looked around. 'The fire break?'

'I've stripped everything. The branches, the trunk . . .'

'Good work,' Quint managed to smile as he stroked the smooth wood.

Maris helped him to his feet, and the pair of them stared up at the burning pinecones above. Now that the sticky coating of volatile resin had burned off, the inner cone was burning – but far less dramatically.

Apart from a patina of small, pale purple flames which flickered over the surface, the main indication that the fire had not gone out was the white smoke pouring out of the top of each of the pinecones in the cluster. Thick and as pungent as incense, the individual coils of smoke wound round each other, plaiting themselves together, before flying off into the sky as a great swaying column.

'It seems to work,' said Quint, watching the smoke rise higher and higher.

'Seems to work?' said Maris. 'Quint, it's fantastic. I bet it's visible in Sanctaphrax itself!'

Quint turned to Maris. 'It's not Sanctaphrax that we need to see it,' he said. 'It's the *Galerider* – that is, if she's still sky-borne . . .'

But Maris wasn't listening. Instead she was staring over Quint's shoulder, a look of horror on her face.

'Quint!' she cried. 'Your parawings! Take them off! Quick! They're on fire!'

A jolt ran through Quint's body as he tore at the straps of his parawings. The red lines and splashes of resin from the pine-cones which streaked the wings smouldered and burst into flames as Quint struggled free from them and flung them away in horror. The flaming parawings landed on a branch below them, then slipped off, further down the tree. For a moment, nothing happened. Then, there came the unmistakable whiff of pine smoke coiling up towards them – and a moment later, a branch some twenty or thirty strides below them burst into flames.

Maris gasped. 'Quint,' she said, her voice tremulous with fear. 'We're trapped.'

Quint swallowed hard. Above them, the treetop blazed furiously, spitting and cracking and burning down towards the firebreak. Below them, the fire took hold, sending thick smoke coiling upwards. The gathering flames started to rise.

'There's not much time,' said Quint urgently. 'Use your parawings – you'll have to fly off to another tree.'

Maris leaned forwards, then wrapped her arms round Quint and hugged him fiercely. 'I'm not going anywhere,' she said. 'Do you understand, Quint? I am *not* going to leave you . . .'

Suddenly overwhelmed with the thick smoke coming up from below, she collapsed into a fit of coughing. Above, the great cluster of pinecones crackled and fizzed; below the fire crept inexorably up the trunk, coming closer and closer towards them . . .

'Maris . . . Oh, Maris . . .' he whispered, his voice rasping as he tried not to cough. 'For Sky's sake, save yourself, Maris . . .'

·CHAPTER TWELVE·

THE SWARM

The instant the flight-burners were snuffed out, the flight-rock had gone berserk, battering away at the bars of the cage as the storm winds froze the rock's surface and turned it super buoyant.

The grappling-hooks gave way, one after the other, as a series of sickening jolts convulsed the stormlashed vessel and tore the *Galerider* from its moorings. In an instant, the mighty sky ship was plucked from the tree-tops and tossed into the raging night, as if by a giant hand. The last thing Captain Wind Jackal saw as the helm spun from his grasp were the shocked faces of Quint and Maris staring up at him, open-mouthed, from their perch in the blackwood tree.

What followed had been like a nightmare – a nightmare from which the crew of the *Galerider* could not wake up. A universe of cracking wood, flying splinters, beams, pulleys, ropes and sailcloth stripped from the vessel and hurtling past their heads. There was nothing they could do but tether themselves to the nearest spar, gunwale or balustrade, and hold on with all their might, their muscles clenched and protesting as the great sky ship was blown across the sky in the clutches of the storm, rainlash and windhowl echoing in their ears.

But it couldn't go on, Wind Jackal knew that. Out of control, the *Galerider* was being torn apart by the gale-force winds, but the minute they released their icy grip, the flight-rock would send them hurtling up into Open Sky for good. All was lost. Wind Jackal fought the rising desire to release his tether and give himself up to the storm and oblivion.

Was that Turbot Smeal's mocking laughter he could hear, rising out of the howling winds?

'No!' Wind Jackal roared into the teeth of the gale. 'It shall not end like this!'

But what was that? Wind Jackal forced himself to look up, icy rain stinging his face like frenzied woodwasps. There, through the driving rain and roaring wind, a hooded figure, hunched and bowed, was slowly, painfully, hauling itself across the juddering flight-rock platform.

As Wind Jackal peered across from the helm, the muscles in his arms aching and his fingers numb, the Stone Pilot reached out – a short axe in her gauntleted hand – and flailed at one of the squat barrels of wood-pitch lashed to the mast. The barrel splintered and its black contents shot out of its ruptured side, splattering the hooded figure. Monstrous now in a thick, congealing coat of woodpitch, the Stone Pilot rolled off the flight-rock platform and down onto the rock cage.

What was happening? Wind Jackal had never seen anything like this. Had the Stone Pilot gone mad; abandoned hope as he himself so nearly had?

The next instant, there was a spark as the blackened figure brought a sky-crystal smashing down on the bars of the cage, then an explosion of light ... The hooded figure burst into flame before Wind Jackal's horrified eyes, and remained, clamped to the bars of the rock cage like a giant fire float.

The flight-rock responded instantly to the intense heat of the burning woodpitch, sucking in the warmth and plunging the *Galerider* back down towards the swirling treetops. Seizing the opportunity given to him, Wind Jackal slammed the flight-levers either side of him as far forward as they would go. In answer, the sky ship's descent grew less steep – but they were still coming down perilously fast, the storm still driving the *Galerider* on.

The jagged tree-line was rising to meet them. It was their only chance, Wind Jackal knew that.

If the blazing torch that was the Stone Pilot could only cling to the rock cage for a few seconds more, the flight-rock would pull them down into the dark forest below and the *Galerider* would have to take her chances in the tangle of branches and tree-trunks.

Better the Deepwoods should have them, thought Wind Jackal, than this accursed storm. The Deepwoods had taken his son, now let it take him!

Suddenly they were down amongst the trees, the howling wind replaced by thrashing branches which tore at the speeding sky ship from all sides. A mighty lullabee was looming up before him, tall, solid, its great branches reaching, grasping. Wind Jackal ducked . . .

Then all was blackness.

Wind Jackal's eyes snapped open.

He was half-standing, half-kneeling; his tether rope lashed to the helm's balustrade stretched taut. The rope was frayed and close to snapping, but it had held, and Wind Jackal felt a wave of relief wash over him. Without this length of plaited woodvine, carefully woven and repaired by Ratbit the mobgnome, he would have been blown away by the terrible storm of the night before.

Wind Jackal squinted up into a clear blue sky, then down at the deck of the *Galerider*. It had been a savage landing, but he'd had no choice – and they'd been lucky, Wind Jackal could see that plainly. The great lullabee tree had stopped the *Galerider* dead, but not before the sky ship's razor-sharp keel had sliced through deep into the trunk of the unfortunate tree. Now they were wedged tight in the cleft of the shattered wood, high above the forest floor.

Becoming aware of a hissing sound, Wind Jackal glanced over to the flight-rock platform. The noise was coming from the softly glowing flight-rock. He saw that the flight-burners were burning steadily and – slumped below them in a blackened, smoking heap across the rock cage – was the hooded figure of the Stone Pilot.

'Crew, report!' Wind Jackal roared, untying his tether and hurrying down from the helm, across the aft-deck, towards the flight-rock platform.

'Tem, tethered and safe, Captain!'

'Steg, tethered and safe!' The voices rang out from the fore-deck.

'Spillins, tethered and safe!' called the oakelf from the caternest.

'Sagbutt, safe!' The goblin's growling call sounded from behind Wind Jackal in the shadows of the aft-deck gunwales, followed by, 'Duggin, tethered and safe!'

'Queep, tethered and safe, Captain – though Sky alone knows how . . .' came the quartermaster's voice from below deck.

Wind Jackal reached the steps to the rock platform and raced up them. At the top, he fell to his knees in front of the Stone Pilot. The black pitch had burned itself out and was now a thick, brittle crust coating the Stone Pilot's protective clothing. Black soot covered the conical hood, covering the eye-pieces and making it impossible to tell whether the person beneath was dead or alive.

A low groan told Wind Jackal that the Stone Pilot had managed to survive her terrible ordeal. She must have dragged herself up from the rock cage and, with the last of her strength, relit the rock burners. Below them, the warm flight-rock continued to wheeze contentedly. By her selfless actions, the Stone Pilot had saved the *Galerider*. Carefully, Wind Jackal lifted her in his arms, the heavy overalls creaking and crackling as he did so, and carried her back to the aft-cabins, despite her weak protests.

'You've done well, Stone Pilot,' he told her. 'You've saved us all. Now you must let us tend you.'

They met Filbus Queep at the door to the aft-cabins, and Wind Jackal passed the Stone Pilot to him. Duggin hurried over to join them.

'Take the Stone Pilot to the infirmary cabin and do what you can for her,' Wind Jackal commanded.

'Aye-aye, Captain, we'll take care of her,' said Duggin, ushering Filbus through the door.

'Hyleberry salve,' muttered the quartermaster, disappearing with the gently moving bundle. 'And plenty of it . . .'

Wind Jackal turned to find Steg Jambles, Tem and Sagbutt the flat-head goblin standing in front of him on the aft-deck. They looked miserable and downcast, Steg clutching an injured arm, Tem's face battered and bruised, and Sagbutt's right eye blackened and almost closed. The *Galerider* had fared little better.

'Report, Mister Jambles,' said Wind Jackal.

'The mast's badly cracked above the sail-ring, but Spillins reckons it should hold. The aft-hull's holding up, but the fore-hull's taken quite a battering. The main-braces to the rock cage need shoring up before we can attempt a launch, Captain . . .'

'Take Tem and Ratbit and see to it right away,' said Wind Jackal. 'The sooner we get skyborne the better. We're sitting snowbirds here . . .' He paused. 'What's wrong?'

Wind Jackal looked from face to face.

'It's Ratbit, Captain,' Steg Jambles began, swallowing hard. 'I'm afraid we lost him . . .'

'Lost him?' Wind Jackal frowned. 'You mean . . . ?'

Steg nodded. 'He'd tied himself down to the high gunwale on the fore-deck, but his tether must have failed,' he said. 'We found this . . .'

Tem stepped forward and held out a frayed length of woodvine rope. Wind Jackal took it and examined the splayed-out strands at the end of the rope for a moment.

'Sky blast it!' he muttered. 'He was always checking and repairing everyone else's tether ropes, making sure they were good and strong. Took hours over it, he did, yet when it came to his own . . .'

Wind Jackal threw the frayed rope to the deck in disgust and slammed his fist down on the port balustrade. He hated losing a crew-member, especially one as resourceful and loyal as the mobgnome.

'That's the way he was, Captain, you know that,' said Steg sadly. 'Always thinking of others before himself, was old Ratbit.'

'And friendly,' added Tem. 'Made me feel welcome when I joined the crew, right from the start . . .'

'Very brave,' Sagbutt grunted. 'Slight of build, but big of heart.'

Wind Jackal turned back to his remaining crew-members and took off his tricorne hat. Bowing his head, he raised a hand to his heart.

'Sky bless Ratbit, our loyal crewmate, and watch over him until that final voyage when we shall all meet again in Open Sky.'

'Open Sky,' repeated Tem, Steg and Sagbutt, their own heads bowed.

'Open Sky,' said Filbus Queep, his hat in his hand as he stepped through the aft-deck door and joined them. The quartermaster smelled strongly of aromatic hyleberry. 'I've done my best for the Stone Pilot, Captain. The hood and apron offered some protection, but she has severe burns to her arms and lower legs, and is running a temperature . . .'

Just then, Spillins's voice rang out from the caternest above. 'Figures moving through the forest, Captain! Lots of them . . .! To the east . . . And the north . . . south . . . *and* west!'

Wind Jackal slammed his hat back on to his head.

'Steg, you and Tem shore up those braces. Nothing fancy. Just make them strong enough to withstand the launch. Move!'

He spun round and thrust a pair of gauntlets into the quartermaster's hands.

'Filbus, you'll have to take the Stone Pilot's place. Just keep those burners alight and douse the rock on my command . . .'

'I'll do my best,' said Filbus uncertainly, climbing the steps to the flight-rock platform. 'What do you think is out there, Captain?'

As if in answer, there came a whirring sound, followed by three splintering thuds as three black barbed arrows embedded themselves in the mast just above the quarter-master's astonished head. Sagbutt leaped up onto the flight-rock platform, tore an arrow from the mast and held the ragged flight feathers to his nostrils.

'Pah!' he spat in disgust, flinging the arrow away. 'Goblins . . . Grey goblins, Captain.'

Wind Jackal groaned. Grey goblins were renowned for their single-minded tenacity in battle. Small and wiry, individually they were nowhere near as strong as a ham-merhead or a flat-head, but what they lacked in strength and stature, they more than made up for in naked aggression. Agile, fast and spectacularly violent, they specialized in mass attacks, known as 'swarms'. The effectiveness of a swarm depended on complete fearless-ness – which was aided by the lullabee-grub juice they swigged from the flat bottles that hung from their necks before and during an attack.

'Ten strides and closing, Captain. From all sides!' came Spillins's report.

'Sky damn me, if I give up a hold full of tallow to grey goblins!' roared Wind Jackal. 'Swarm or no swarm. Sagbutt, can you defend the decks until I get us out of here?'

Sagbutt gave a snaggle-toothed leer and drew his sword.

'Sagbutt pleased to oblige!' he replied, stroking the blade. '*Skullsplitter* chop woodonions for too long . . . Now for some *real* work!'

Wind Jackal hurried to the helm and began setting the flight-levers, as the forest floor below filled with hideous shrieks and ear-splitting howls, and the great lullabee tree began to tremble. Almost in the blink of an eye, like frenzied woodants, grey goblins burst from the undergrowth in their hundreds, surrounded the base of the tree and began to clamber up its knobbly trunk. Moments later, their feet pattered up the sides of the *Galerider*, making a sound like hailstones in a skystorm.

'Prepare to repel boarders, Sagbutt!' shouted Wind Jackal, drawing his own sword. 'Report, Steg! Are the braces secure?'

'Just a moment longer, Cap'n,' came the harpooneer's harassed reply.

Suddenly the fore-deck was awash with grey goblins. Small, quivering and long-limbed, each one wore a battered leather jerkin and carried a rudimentary wooden shield and short serrated sword, equally suited to stabbing or hacking. Round their necks, gleaming in the sun, were round flat flasks that clinked against their breast-plates.

With a howl of rage, Sagbutt spread his massive legs wide and swung a great flashing arc with *Skullsplitter*. The fore-deck exploded in a ring of spattered blood as the first wave of goblins lost heads, limbs and bodies.

Whirr! Crunch!

Sagbutt swung again and a second wave of grey goblins was mown down like glade-wheat before a scythe. All around, the shrieks and howls intensified, but

the crowd of grey goblins gathered at the *Galerider*'s sides seemed now to hesitate before the fearsome flat-head's blade.

'Braces secured!' Steg's voice could just be heard rising up from below the fore-deck.

'Now, Filbus!' Wind Jackal roared, and the quartermaster doused the warm rock. With a creaking and splintering of wood, the *Galerider* lurched and battled with the lullabee tree to break free. A bloodied Sagbutt looked up at Wind Jackal, a great smile on his broad face.

'Sagbutt repel boarders, Captain,' he beamed. 'Sagbutt . . . *Urrrghh!*'

Suddenly, the flat-head goblin's eyes bulged and his tongue lolled out of his mouth, followed by a stream of blood, as a black barbed arrow pierced his throat. Sagbutt – the smile frozen on his face – toppled forwards onto the blood-stained deck as the *Galerider* broke free of the tree and soared up into the air in a steep climb.

The grey goblin swarm clinging to the sides of the sky ship fell away in howling shrieking clumps, like Mire mud from a mudshoe, until only one or two remained, their small angry faces contorted in fear.

'No!' cried Filbus Queep, flinging off his gauntlets and rushing down from the flight-rock platform – only to skid on the bloody gore-drenched decking. Sliding to a halt on his knees, the quartermaster cradled the flat-head's great head in his lap. 'Sagbutt, old friend, speak to me,' he moaned, rocking backwards and forwards.

'Sagbutt go . . . to Open . . . Sky . . .' croaked the flat-head, his eyes glazing over. 'Sagbutt wait for you there . . . We cook great feast together . . .'

'Yes,' said Filbus. 'Yes, Sagbutt, old friend, we'll cook great feasts together . . .' The quartermaster bowed his head, his body shaking with barely suppressed sobs.

'*Filbus! Look out!*' Wind Jackal screamed from the helm as the *Galerider* soared high into the sky above the Deepwoods.

The last remaining grey goblin had hauled himself up the hull-rigging and onto the deck and now stood over the quartermaster, his serrated sword raised above his head, poised to strike. Too late, Filbus, his eyes streaming with tears, looked up – to see the blade descend.

Without a sound, the quartermaster slumped forwards over his flat-head friend, mortally wounded. Their blood swirled together on the twisted deck.

With a shout of rage, Wind Jackal raced down to the fore-deck, his sword flashing in his hand, only for the grey goblin to leap over the high gunwale and fall howling to his death.

Moments later, Steg Jambles, Tem and Duggin – who had left the Stone Pilot sleeping fitfully in the infirmary cabin – found Wind Jackal standing over the two fallen crew-members, amidst the carnage.

'Clear the deck and find some lufwood decking,' he said simply, his face impassive, before striding back up to the helm.

Tem Barkwater turned to Duggin, his face drained of all colour. 'Sagbutt . . . Queep . . .' he murmured. 'Gone!'

Duggin shook his head. 'I thought Undertown was dangerous. I had no idea that it could be so . . . so *wild* out here in the Deepwoods.'

Steg Jambles glanced round at Wind Jackal. The captain couldn't have failed to hear the two crew-members' words, yet his face – set like a mask – betrayed no emotion as he gripped the helm. Steg knew, however, that with Quint and Maris out there somewhere, the dangers of the Deepwoods would be uppermost in Wind Jackal's mind.

With nimble fingers, the captain brought the *Galerider* round and headed back in the direction they had been blown from the previous night. Through the afternoon they sailed – pausing only briefly for a short funeral ceremony and to release the hastily constructed lufwood raft which, blazing fiercely, carried the bodies of Sagbutt the flat-head goblin and Filbus Queep the

quartermaster off into Open Sky. Then it was on again, soaring across the sky in search of Quint and Maris. The shrykes would have to wait for their consignment of tallow candles.

As darkness fell, the crew exchanged uneasy glances. It was rare indeed that a sky pirate ship didn't anchor for the night. But Wind Jackal clearly had no intention of interrupting the search.

'We fly on,' he announced from the helm.

Thankfully, the sky was cloudless and clear that night, and as he adjusted the flight-levers, Wind Jackal made calculations in his mind, desperately trying to retrace the chaotic storm flight of the previous night. If he could just get them back to roughly the same area . . .

The sky pirate captain chewed into his lower lip. Would the lad have managed to set a beacon? he wondered. It was his only chance of being found.

'Look out for a fire,' he called up to Spillins.

'Aye, Cap'n,' came the oakelf's reply as he trained his telescope on the horizon.

As the first blush of dawn touched the distant horizon to the east, Wind Jackal stifled a yawn. He was exhausted – yet he would not give up. If his calculations were correct, then they should be close to the area where Quint and Maris had been festooned. Yet as the sun rose higher, and the golden light spread out once more across the endless canopy of leaves, the hope of finding them seemed more remote than ever.

Steg brought him a simple breakfast. Black bread and pine-brew.

'You must eat, Cap'n,' Steg said, holding out the steaming bowl.

Wind Jackal shook his head, his red-rimmed eyes never straying from the horizon for a moment.

Just then, Spillins's voice shouted down excitedly from the caternest. 'Smoke!' he cried. 'A column of smoke, down on the horizon at twelve degrees!'

Without the least expression registering on his face, Wind Jackal adjusted the flight-levers and steered a new course, heading now directly for the white column of smoke. Everyone was up on deck by the time they approached the fire.

'It *must* be a beacon,' Steg was saying to anyone who would listen. 'A forest fire would have spread . . .'

As they drew closer, however, it was clear that the fire generating so much smoke was out of control. Bright red embers were flying up into the air, while the top of the vast tree was swathed in roaring flames. As Wind Jackal brought the sky vessel lower, his crew trained their telescopes on the distant blaze.

Suddenly, everyone was shouting at once.

'There they are, on that branch!'

'I can see them!'

'*They're not moving . . . !*'

Wind Jackal tried his best to manoeuvre the *Galerider* round as he came in, but with the roaring flames threatening at every moment to lap against the flapping sails, he couldn't get any closer. The fire was blazing both above and below the two unconscious figures. If they weren't plucked away in seconds, then they would certainly perish – if they weren't already dead . . .

'Duggin!' he shouted across at the gnokgoblin. 'Could you take the *Edgehopper* in closer than this?'

'I'll give it my best shot, Cap'n,' he shouted back.

Together with Steg and Tem, Duggin unlashed the small sky ferry. Moments later, with Duggin at the tiller and Wind Jackal before him, the small vessel leaped

up into the sky, circled round the mast of the *Galerider* –
held in place by Spillins at the helm – and swooped
down into the lofty inferno.

The heat was appalling, singeing their hair and
scorching their skin. As they came in as close as
Duggin dared, Wind Jackal threw himself from the
side of the ferry and onto the branch. Flames lapped
at his fingers as he tied ropes around Quint and
Maris's chests.

'*Now*, Duggin!' he hollered.

The gnokgoblin, who had been hovering just above
them, pulled on the tiller and the sky ferry soared up
into the air. As the bodies slipped away from the
branch, Wind Jackal seized the two ropes, and held on
for dear life. The heavy weight made the little
vessel list precariously to one side – but Duggin
managed not only to level up, but also to continue
round, and off towards the waiting sky pirate ship.

As they came in to land on the fore-deck of the
Galerider, Wind Jackal jumped down a moment early,
so that he could steer the two unconscious bodies
gently down onto the floor. He loosed the slip knots
and knelt down beside them.

'Quint,' he whispered. 'Maris. Open Sky shall not take
you! Not after all the others . . . Speak to me! Speak to
me . . .'

·CHAPTER THIRTEEN·

SISTER SCREECHSCALE

The tallow candle sputtered and smoked. Its yellow light flickered, flared – and went out, plunging the small wickerwork tally-lodge into total darkness. Sister Screechscale the tally-hen blinked round blindly, her beak clacking with irritation.

'Feckle! Feckle!' she squawked. 'Where is that scrawny insult to an egg? *Feckle!*'

'Coming, mistress of my heart,' cooed a timid-sounding voice in the darkness, accompanied by the *scritch-scratch* of clawed feet descending a ladder.

'Don't you "mistress of my heart" me, you moth-eaten excuse for a shryke-mate!' shrieked Sister Screechscale. 'How am I expected to do my talons in the dark? Get me another candle!'

'One of the new ones from Undertown, dearest one?' cooed the shryke-mate's voice close to Sister Screechscale's ear.

'No, one of the rotten old ones from the league ships that burn too fast and smell of putrid ooze-fish!' Sister Screechscale clucked sarcastically. 'Yes, Feckle, of course one of the new ones! And be quick about it!'

'Yes, light of my life,' Feckle cooed back at her as he rummaged about in the dark, opening and closing various drawers and cupboards. 'Ah, here we are!' he exclaimed at last. 'So *these* are the candles you were telling me about – the ones the sky pirate captain traded for the banderbear . . . ? Shall I light one for you, my perpetual joy?'

'No, I'll do it. I don't trust you with fire, feather-brain,' snapped Sister Screechscale, snatching hold of a thick, waxy smooth candle in the dark.

She reached forward, brushing past the ledger and tally-discs on the desk in front of her as her clawed hand felt for, and found, the candlestick holder. Then she stuffed the new candle into the half-molten remains of the one that had just burned out.

Next, muttering under her breath, she reached into the pocket of her apron and pulled out a flint-stick, which she struck. The hissing flame illuminated the room with a watery pale-green light. Sister Screechscale leaned forward again and touched it to the tallow wick. It spat and sparked, before settling down to a soft golden flame.

'So what was I saying?' she clucked, as she settled herself back down on her perching-stool.

She picked up the whetting-stick, running it down the

talon of her first finger, slowly, rhythmically. Once honed, her already vicious hooked, yellow claws would be razor-sharp weapons that could stab a wilful prowlgrin-mount in its haunch or slice through an impudent goblin slave's neck with the careless ease of a hot blade through tilder-grease.

'You were telling me about the new candles, my supreme bliss,' cooed the tiny mottle-feathered shryke-mate, hopping onto a lower perch beside the tally-hen.

'Yes, that's right,' said Sister Screechscale, inspecting the talon she'd been filing under the light. It glinted malevolently. She lowered it to the table, tapped three times on the surface, then scored a line through the already scratched wood, before setting to work on the second talon.

Outside the small wickerwork tally-lodge, stretching out through the treetops like the web of some monstrous spider, were the wooden walkways, hanging-cages, domed turrets and shingled cabins of the Great Shryke Slave Market. Far beneath the lofty canopy, where the sun could not penetrate, lines of lanterns provided the only light – an oily, smoke-stained half-light. Here, like insects stuck in spider-silk, were razorflits, rotsuckers, fromps and quarms, lorrels and lemkins, peering from between the bars of crowded cages. Here, too, amid shrieks and howls and a constant stifling stench, auctions continued through the night on the great canopied platforms suspended from the trees.

Goods of all kinds could be traded here, from mire-pearls to tallow candles – but the commonest currency was life itself. Trogs, trolls, waifs, oakelves and goblins sold as slaves to trogs, trolls, waifs, oakelves and goblins who were not. To enter this savage web, and not be ensnared, the trader of whatever type needed one thing – something only a tally-hen like Sister Screechscale could provide . . .

A precious white cockade: a fresh briar lily whose petals slowly turned from white to yellow to brown, before crumbling to dust in three days. Unless replaced, the wearer could be enslaved, which meant – as the Great Slave Market hustled and bustled – that Sister Screechscale's cockades were in constant demand.

Despite the dangers, the Great Shryke Slave Market was popular. After all, where else could a leaguesmaster find his pampered wife the pet lemkin she'd been pestering him for? Where else could a rogue slaver buy himself a hammerhead bodyguard? Where else could ill-gotten marsh-gems and mire-pearls be traded for an illicit banderbear pelt, no questions asked? And where else could you gamble on how long any creature might last in the terrible Wig-Wig Arena?

Inside the glowing tally-lodge, the tally-hen started work on her third claw, the whetting-stick gliding softly round the curve of the talon as she carefully manicured it.

'Well, anyway,' Sister Screechscale clucked, 'it's like I said. There's something afoot, mark my words, Feckle. They're up to something, those Undertown leagues – all the gossip and rumours, I've been hearing. All the tittle-tattle. Besides, I can feel it in my tail feathers, Feckle. They've got it in for those sky pirates . . .

'Not that that's anything new. But what is new is how these high-hat leagues types have been buying up spider-silk, timber and foundry goods like their lives depended on it. Only the finest quality, mind, not the usual rubbish they're content to sell to those whey-faced Undertowners back there at the Edge. No, they'll only buy the best. And when you ask them what they need triple-woven spider-silk or seasoned bloodoak for, they clam up tighter than a mire-clam.

'Still, as long as they keep supplying the market with slaves, then who am I to complain?'

She tapped the table-top with the third nail. Then, not quite satisfied that it was as sharp as it could be, resumed the painstaking filing. Her eyes narrowed.

'It's the other stuff I object to – stinking candles, shoddy cooking-pots, glittery fabric that rots in a season ... I mean, do those high-hat leaguesmen think we hatched in an Undertown back alley? Downright cheek, I call it!

'Not like the goods the sky pirates bring. Always the finest quality ... But then, they take pride in their trade. Take this candle, for instance – beautiful quality, as fragrant as a forest glade and twice as golden! The only trouble with sky pirates is they won't deal in slaves – not even if their lives depended on it. It's well known. So you can imagine my amazement when this young sky pirate captain taps on the tally-lodge window the other day, and tells me he wants to sell a banderbear!'

Sister Screechscale tapped the third talon down on the table once more. This time, the sharpened point punctured the varnish with ease. She squawked with satisfaction and moved on to the fourth and final talon.

The thumb-claw of her right hand. Her favourite!

It was the talon that had seen more action than all the others put together. More, even, than the battle-spurs on her powerful feet. If ever she was troubled during her work – when a visitor to the tally-lodge got belligerent, or a guard called to her to help out

274

with some disturbance on the hanging-walkways, then the thumb-claw of her right hand was always at the ready.

Not for her the jointed flails or hooked staves beloved of the other shrykes. No! With her left hand gripping her adversary – and to the accompaniment of an ear-splitting screech – she would slash out with that right-hand thumb of hers, splitting her victim open from sternum to sacrum, before devouring the steaming guts that spilled out . . .

She used it now to scratch an irritating itch buried deep in the ruff of feathers at her neck.

'At least, he *looked* like a sky pirate captain. Tall, strong-looking and handsome, with a fine frock coat and polished bicorne hat, he really dressed the part. Blond hair and flashing blue eyes, he was a real charmer. Introduced himself as Captain Daggerslash – Thaw Daggerslash, out of Undertown. Tells me this story about how he'd run into trouble mire-pearling over the mud-dunes, and it was all he could do to get his crippled sky barge to within five hundred strides of the market. Came the rest of the way on foot – though you wouldn't have thought it to look at him. Reckon the half-starved banderbear cub he had in tow had carried him most of the way . . .

'Anyway, he gives me this flashing smile and says he's looking for a very good friend of his, Captain Wind Jackal of the *Galerider*, who, he has it on good authority, is running a shipload of the finest tallow candles into the market. Have I seen him?

he asks. I say no, but as every sky pirate knows that Sister Screechscale gives them special rates on white cockades, I says I'm sure he'll enter the market through my tally-lodge, and no mistake.

'Then he tips his hat to me, all respectful-seeming, leans in close to the tally-lodge window and whispers in my ear-feathers so his banderbear can't hear.

' "How about taking Hubble, here, off my hands, sister?" he says. "Fine albino banderbear. One cockade and thirty gold pieces. What do you say? Help a poor sky pirate down on his luck?"

' "One cockade and *ten* gold pieces," I reply, quick as a flash. I knew that I'd get a good price for the banderbear down at the Wig-Wig Arena – and an albino one would

go down well with the crowd, even though the wig-wigs would be sure to rip it to pieces.

'You could tell he didn't like my offer, but there was nothing he could do. I had him over a barrel.

' "It's a deal," he says with a little smile, then he looks all concerned and caring, and whispers, "Only don't let on to poor old Hubble that I've sold him. It'll hurt his feelings. I'll tell him to stay with you until I come and fetch him, and he'll be as meek as a tilder fawn."

' "It's all the same to me," I say, and hand him a cockade and ten gold pieces.

'Captain Daggerslash whispered in the banderbear's ear. Then, giving me another of those dazzling smiles, he sauntered off into the market as if he hadn't a care in the world.'

Sister Screechscale resumed the filing, carefully honing the two sides one stroke at a time, so that the point of the claw wouldn't end up off-centre.

'Sure enough, later that day, who should appear at my tally-lodge window, but none other than Captain Wind Jackal and his crew. And what a sorry-looking bunch they were, to be sure. There was a dark-haired girl and a young sky pirate who looked like the captain, both with haunted, dark-ringed eyes; a worried-looking harpooneer and his young mate, together with a ragged gnokgoblin who said he was going back on board to look after their stone pilot, who was ill.

'The captain himself had a face like thunder, but was polite enough. I sold them all cockades, and mentioned that Captain Thaw Daggerslash was looking for his good friend, Captain Wind Jackal.

'At the sound of his former master's name, the banderbear jumped to his feet, and dashed forward from where he'd been sleeping behind the tally-lodge, only to find that I'd tethered his left leg to the gate-post while he slept. He began to make a terrible fuss, waving his arms and yodelling in that way that

they do. I should have taken him off to the arena straight away, but I'd been so rushed off my feet all morning, and you, Feckle, were off having your neck-ring repaired . . .'

Sister Screechscale exchanged the whetting-stick for a buffing-pad – a stuffed pouch of wild tilder leather dipped in blackwheat oil – and began to polish the freshly honed claws vigorously, one after the other.

'Well, blow me to Open Sky, if Captain Daggerslash doesn't come running down the walkway!

'Just as well. I was about to call the guards to deal with the banderbear . . . I'm embarrassed to admit that I hadn't sharpened my talons in a while, and I didn't like the look of those tusks.

'The young sky pirate and the girl are trying to calm the banderbear while Captain Wind Jackal says, all high and mighty-sounding, "What's the meaning of this! This banderbear is a sky pirate. Not a slave!" and draws his sword.

'It's all threatening to turn pretty nasty, I can tell you. And here's me with blunt talons and not a guard in sight.

'Well, I know as well as the next shryke how touchy these sky pirates can get about slaves, but the fact was I'd bought the banderbear fair and square, and I was about to say as much when Captain Daggerslash arrives, out of breath and blowing like a beached oozefish.

' "Captain Wind Jackal!" he exclaims. "Thank Sky I've found you! Hubble and I were sky-wrecked some five hundred strides or so from here. I left Hubble here while I went in search of fellow sky pirates, only for some wretch to sell him to this fine upstanding shryke-sister when my back was turned!"

'As he said this, the handsome rogue winked at me. Wind Jackal lowered his sword.

' "Sister," Daggerslash said, catching his breath and giving me a theatrical bow. "I have no doubt you purchased my loyal shipmate in good faith, and I would reimburse you this instant if I hadn't lost a small wager in the Wig-Wig Arena. But if my friend here, the great Captain Wind Jackal, is willing to purchase Hubble's freedom, then he shall earn my undying gratitude."

'Again he winked, and I had to admire his bare-faced audacity.

'Sure enough, Captain Wind Jackal stepped forward and cleared his throat. He seemed embarrassed to have unsheathed his sword so readily.

' "Sister, I apologize if I was hasty," he said. "I'm running a shipload of tallow candles. If you'll accept a crate, perhaps we can consider this matter closed?"

'Well, I'm not one to look a gift-prowlgrin in the mouth, I can tell you. A crate of the finest tallow candles, straight from Undertown? Why, I'd have been lucky to get a quarter of their value for the skinny bander-bear pup, and I knew it. Besides, with those blunt talons of mine, I wasn't about to pick a fight, now was I?'

Sister Screechscale chuckled to herself and tapped the thumb-claw against the table-top, then scraped it, making a deep straight line and leaving a trail of splinters in its wake. The point was perfectly honed. No one who fell into her clutches now would stand a chance.

'So I kept my beak shut and took the candles. Thaw Daggerslash and the banderbear went off with Captain Wind Jackal and his crew. That young rogue was laughing and joking as if he hadn't a care in the world, Feckle. But then I'm not complaining, because Thaw

Daggerslash taught me a valuable lesson . . .'

'What lesson is that, pride of my nest?'

'To keep my wits sharp,' clucked Sister Screechscale, 'and my talons sharper!'

·CHAPTER FOURTEEN·

THAW DAGGERSLASH

'Hauling up the log-baits, I see,' came a cheery voice from the direction of the fore-deck of the sky ship.

Quint looked up – his brow furrowed and beaded with sweat – and smiled as he saw Thaw Daggerslash descending the steps from the flight-rock platform to join him on the aft-deck.

'Here, let me help,' Thaw offered, taking the chain from Quint and reeling it in, hand over hand.

After a few moments, the lufwood log attached to the end of the long chain appeared at the balustrade. Its surface was crawling with air-borne creatures of every type. Clusters of transparent mist-barnacles clung to the knotty bark beside wind snappers, whose curved claws were withdrawn into their flat white shells. And oozing from the wood itself, their bodies rhythmically convulsing, were gelatinous sky worms with long tentacles that entwined in great wriggling clumps.

The log, trailed on the end of the chain in the sky ship's wake, had attracted the strange drifting creatures of Open Sky that would otherwise have attached themselves to the *Galerider*'s hull. Regular log-baiting was essential to keep a sky ship flight-worthy, but lowering and hauling the logs was back-breaking work.

'This was Ratbit's job,' said Quint sadly. 'He loved hauling the log-baits in and examining what they'd caught . . .'

'Can't see the attraction myself,' said Thaw, with a flashing smile. 'Ugly little blighters, the lot of them, if you ask me.'

The handsome young sky pirate grasped the seething, squirming log-bait with long iron callipers and unhooked it from the chain.

'Shame about Ratbit. Heard he was a fine deckhand and cargo steward,' said Thaw, his piercing blue eyes suddenly serious. 'The sort of crew-member a captain hates to lose . . .'

Quint nodded. 'We *all* miss him,' he said. 'Ratbit was a good friend.'

'Pity about the quartermaster, too – and the goblin,' said Thaw, absentmindedly turning the log-bait round on the end of the callipers, and reaching into his pocket for his sky-crystals. 'To lose a deckhand is unfortunate,' he mused, 'but to be forced to "earth" your ship, and then to lose a quartermaster of Filbus Queep's reputation, along with a fearsome fighting goblin . . .'

'What are you trying to say?' said Quint, feeling his cheeks beginning to flush.

'Oh, nothing,' said Thaw lightly. 'Your father's just been very unlucky, that's all.'

He shot Quint a dazzling smile and struck the sky-crystals against the iron callipers. A spark sprang across to the lufwood log-bait, which fizzled for a moment, before flaring with a bright purple flame. Thaw released the callipers' grip, and the burning log, together with its wriggling passengers, shot up high into the sky, before disappearing into the clouds.

'Ratbit always separated the hull-vermin from the innocent wind creatures before he sky-fired a log-bait,' said Quint quietly.

'Did he indeed?' said Thaw, handing Quint the chain and clapping him heartily on the back. 'What a very fine deckhand old Ratbit was, to be sure!' He paused for a moment. 'Better hook up another log and lower it, there's a good fellow. I've grown very fond of the *Galerider*,' he added. 'I'd hate her hull to go unprotected.' He laughed and strode off towards the door to the aft-cabins.

Once inside, Thaw Daggerslash quietly climbed down the ladder and stood for a moment outside the infirmary cabin, his head cocked to one side as he listened to the soft murmur of voices within. Then, reaching into one of the pockets in his greatcoat, he pulled out a small, silver salve-box and tapped it lightly on the lid, before knocking on the cabin door and entering.

The figure of the Stone Pilot – looking impossibly small and fragile without the heavy apron, gauntlets and hood – lay in a sumpwood cradle tethered to the cabin wall. Hyleberry-infused cloth covered her from head to foot, her intense dark eyes glittering through a narrow slit in the bandages. Beside her sat Maris, a small kettle in her hands. The kettle bubbled as she warmed it over a

tallow candle, and an aromatic steam rose from its long spout.

'How are my favourite crew-members today?' Thaw smiled warmly. 'I was just passing, and wondered whether you might like this.'

He held out the silver salve-box. At the sight of the handsome young sky pirate, Maris broke into a beaming smile of her own and visibly flushed. Beside her, the Stone Pilot gave a muffled sigh and raised a white mittened hand in greeting.

'Oh, how thoughtful, Captain Daggerslash!' Maris exclaimed, taking the salve-box and flipping the lid open. 'Cloudberry balm! Perfect for easing inflammation of the joints . . .'

'And cooling fever,' Thaw went on for her, 'especially when burn-related. I should know!' he added with a laugh. 'I've picked up a fair few burns just lately.'

From the sumpwood cradle, the Stone Pilot gave a small groan and tried to sit up.

'Please, my dear Stone Pilot!' said Thaw, kneeling down beside her. 'Don't distress yourself. I might be a little clumsy with the flight-burners, but your beloved flight-rock is safe and well in my care, I assure you.'

He patted her lightly on the arm, seemingly oblivious to her shiver of pain at his touch.

'Now, you must concentrate all your efforts on getting well, and not worry about a thing. After all . . .' Thaw shot a dazzling smile at a blushing Maris. 'You have the finest nurse anyone could wish for – she has the expert touch of a gabtroll, but twice as soft . . .'

'You're very kind, Captain Daggerslash,' said Maris quietly, refilling the little kettle with aromatic sallow-drop water and placing it back over the candle.

'Alas, a captain no longer,' said Thaw, getting up and giving them each a low bow. 'But perhaps, one day, a captain once more.'

He left the small cabin and closed the door quietly behind him before pausing as he caught the unmistakable smell of burning tilder sausages. Thaw hurried up the ladder and made his way to the *Galerider*'s galley, bursting through the door.

'Tem Barkwater!' he exclaimed with a hearty laugh. 'If it isn't my favourite galley-slave! Now, let's see if we can't rescue these sausages before they all turn to charcoal . . .!'

The *Galerider* rose on the warm air currents, the patched spider-silk sails ragged but billowing as they filled with the following wind. The damaged ironwood mast – lovingly bound by Spillins – creaked and groaned, but held firm as the mighty sky ship sailed on, lighter now after delivering her cargo of tallow candles to the Great Shryke Slave Market.

At the *Galerider*'s centre, the warm flight-rock wheezed fitfully as the steady burners kept its temperature constant. Without the expert hand of the Stone Pilot to tend it, the rock had become a dull, lifeless thing, keeping the great sky ship airborne, but little else. At the helm, the figure of Captain Wind Jackal stood erect and vigilant. Given the inadequately tended flight-rock, his job was all the more exacting. His fingers moved constantly across the flight-levers on either side of the ship's wheel, making adjustments, not just for the hull-weights, rudder and sails, but for the dormant flight-rock as well.

It was ceaseless work, but Wind Jackal refused to leave his post even for a moment. The *Galerider* was his ship and the crew was his responsibility. This voyage had tested his captaincy to the very limit, and there had been times when even he – the great Captain Wind Jackal – had felt his resolve weakening and his courage failing. He had lost three brave and loyal crew-members, and the memory of their deaths would haunt him for the rest of his days, he was certain of that.

But he was a sky pirate captain, and such tragedies had to be accepted. What he found harder to take; what made his heart contract within his chest as if grasped by the icy talons of a shryke-sister, was the dark panic of almost losing his son, Quint, together with Maris, the daughter of his best friend. The seemingly endless hours that had passed when he'd thought they were lost for ever had been, without a shadow of a doubt, the blackest of his life.

Even after their rescue, the memory of that black despair nagged away at Wind Jackal. It made his hands tremble over the flight-levers; it drenched his body in a cold clammy sweat, while lighting a fiery furnace in the pit of his stomach that seemed to consume his strength from within. But just as he fought with the wheel and flight-levers to keep the *Galerider* on a steady course, so Wind Jackal fought the raging panic within himself, and gradually, as the seconds turned to minutes, and the minutes turned to hours, he felt his sanity slowly returning, while the sky ship sailed on over the endless Deepwoods.

For three days they journeyed, sailing by day and anchoring up by night, and leaving the stench and misery of the shryke market behind them like a bad dream. Up over the high ridges they'd climbed, across the lakes and the glade country beyond, towards the great Timber Stands of the woodtrolls and deep forest clans. As the sun rose on the fourth day and a fair wind filled the *Galerider*'s sails, Wind Jackal felt his spirits start to rise lift.

'Report, Master Spillins!' he shouted to the oakelf, who, ever since they'd left the slave market, had kept to his caternest as determinedly as he, Wind Jackal, had kept to the helm.

'Timber Stands on the horizon, Captain,' Spillins announced. 'Can't see any pathways yet, but I'll keep looking.'

'One path leads to all!' Wind Jackal called back, his spirits lifting all the time.

The ancient Timber Stands of the Deepwoods forest – where lufwood, lullabee, blackwood and a thousand other trees were to be found – were ringed by the settlements of the deep forest clans. Gnokgoblin colonies nestled high in ironwood pines, mobgnome camps were dotted amongst blackwood groves, and slaughterer villages lay beside forest glades and pastures – all offering goods to trade, and a shelter from the dangers of the Deepwoods. But of all the many settlements, it was only those of the woodtrolls that offered the prize Wind Jackal was seeking.

Their great villages of buoyant-wood cabins were unmistakable from the air, marked out as they were by myriad criss-crossing paths, each one worn down by countless woodtroll feet. Each village was connected, one to the other, in a great snaking progression that wound round the highest and richest of the Timber Stands.

Here, timber of the highest quality was to be found. Seasoned and stored, sometimes for centuries, it was renowned throughout the Edge. And like woodbees to a honeybush, the sky ships of the leagues and the sky pirates alike would cluster round the villages, seeking this timber out.

Behind him, from the balustrade on the stern side of the upper cabins where Duggin's sky ferry, the *Edgehopper*, was lashed, came the sound of voices in conversation.

'Ah, Duggin, my fine fellow!' Thaw Daggerslash's cheerful voice was unmistakable. 'Repairing your excellent fine craft, I see.'

'She might not look much to a fine sky pirate such as yourself,' came Duggin's voice, 'but the *Edgehopper* means all the world to me . . .'

'I'm sure she does, Duggin. I'm sure she does.' Thaw gave a laugh. 'I say, have you seen that blasted heap of fur and bones that masquerades as a banderbear?' he added. 'Can't find the dratted beast anywhere . . .'

'If you mean Hubble,' said Duggin stiffly, 'then I last saw him with Quint, who was trying to talk to him. Poor creature's been neglected if you ask me . . .'

'Not my fault, I assure you, Duggin,' said Thaw smoothly. 'It was that damned sky pirate I was fool enough to recruit to go with Hubble and me on our mire-pearling voyage. Seemed capable and experienced enough, but he pulled the wool over both our eyes. Turned out he was poisoning Hubble behind my back, so that when he festooned me, poor Hubble was too weak to resist. Took my sky barge and left the two of us to fend for ourselves in the Deepwoods, Sky damn his eyes!'

'I . . . I'm sorry,' Duggin mumbled. 'I didn't realize . . . Thought you had . . .'

'Don't mention it, Duggin,' said Thaw Daggerslash good-naturedly. 'After all, a good sky pirate captain learns from his mistakes. Just ask Captain Wind Jackal . . .'

At the helm, Wind Jackal's hands tightened round the wheel, and he swallowed hard.

'Pathway below, at a hundred strides, Captain!' Spillins the oakelf's quavery voice sounded from the top of the mast. He shrank back into the comforting darkness of his caternest.

The path stood out from the dark green of the forest like a vivid tear in a velvet curtain, winding its way into the distance. All Wind Jackal had to do was follow its course and they would come to a woodtroll village. Spillins felt a warm glow seep through his chest and stir his heart with a dull ache.

Oakelves and woodtrolls were ancient friends. They had a natural feeling for each other's customs and beliefs, and Spillins knew that he'd receive a warm welcome amongst the woodtroll cabins that lay somewhere up ahead. For the first time since the moment in the slave market when he'd initially laid eyes on the young sky pirate, the old oakelf began to feel better.

As to what had happened to Thaw Daggerslash, Spillins didn't like to think about it. But whatever it was, it had been enough to turn the handsome young sky pirate's aura a hideous, boiling, corrosive purple, the like of which the oakelf had never seen before in all his days.

Just then, from the deck below, came Thaw's good-natured laugh as he greeted Quint and Hubble the banderbear. Spillins shuddered, curled up in a tight ball and covered his ears.

'Maris!' called Quint, leaning over the aft-deck gunwales. 'Come and look at this!'

Maris appeared at the door to the aft-cabins and joined Quint, squinting down through the hazy air as the *Galerider* slowly descended. Unlike the endless expanse of unbroken green that they had been sailing above for so long, the forest below them now showed all the signs of woodtrolls. Trees had been felled on either side of a narrow track – a track which had been made by generations of woodtroll feet. And, as the sky pirate ship drew closer, the wisps coiling up from the distant cabin chimneys revealed themselves to be the purple-tinged smoke of lufwood, the woodtrolls' favoured timber.

Lower the *Galerider* came in the sky. As it did so, the Deepwoods revealed more and more tracks, each one leading off in a different direction. One veered off sharply to the west. A purple haze hovered there in the still air, far in the distance.

'See that?' said Quint, pointing.

Maris nodded.

'That'll be another settlement,' he told her. 'Woodtrolls build clusters of villages quite close to each other – any-thing from half a dozen to twenty or so. They're far enough away from one another to ensure they don't encroach on each other's land, or wood and water supplies, yet never further apart than a day's walk along those long winding paths of theirs – paths they never, *ever* stray from.'

'And they lead to the Timber Stands as well, do they?' said Maris.

'They certainly do,' said Quint, and laughed. 'Otherwise the woodtroll timberers couldn't get to them, could they?'

'Oh, look, what's that?' asked Maris, pointing as the *Galerider* swept low across a large square field, tracks criss-crossing the long grass and a basket atop a rickety pole at the very centre.

'A trockbladder pitch, I think,' Quint replied, 'though I haven't got a clue how you play the game.'

'Trockbladder!' Maris exclaimed. 'Oh, but *I* know! Nanny Welma told me all about it. You have to use this ball-type thing. It's made of a *hammelhorn bladder*!' she said, wrinkling up her nose with disgust. 'And stuffed with trock beans.' She looked at Quint, her eyes glazing dreamily. 'Sometimes Welma would lay out the balcony-hall with rugs and we'd play it together, her and me . . .'

Ahead of them now, Quint and Maris were able to make out the small woodtroll cabins themselves, straddling the branches of the grandest trees in the village and clinging to their mighty trunks. They were curious barrel-shaped dwellings set on jutting ledges, with round doors, smoking chimneys and spindly ladders, which offered access from the ground and could be pulled up to deter intruders.

Some way from the centre of the village was a massive

lullabee tree, its bulbous trunk gleaming, and a great caterbird nest hanging from one of its branches silhouetted against the orange glow of the late-afternoon sun. And beyond that were the docking-rings.

With great skill and pin-point accuracy, Wind Jackal brought the *Galerider* down out of the sky. It twisted slowly round, its lowered sails flapping, and came in to hover beside the jutting stanchions. As the mooring-ledge drew close, Steg Jambles seized the end of a tolley-rope, jumped over the balustrade and onto the platform, where he secured it to the gleaming metal ring.

'Ship tethered, Cap'n!' he shouted up to the helm, and Quint could see his father visibly relax for the first time in days.

'Crew!' Wind Jackal shouted. 'You may step down to earth . . .'

'I'll stay and tend to the Stone Pilot, Mistress Maris,' said Duggin, laying a hand on her shoulder. 'You run along with Master Quint, and explore.'

'And you join them, Tem,' said Steg Jambles from the fore-deck, pushing his young friend forward. 'Do you good to get the smell of burned tilder sausages out of your nostrils for a bit.'

'But what about you?' Tem asked, reluctant to leave his friend.

Steg shrugged. 'With Sagbutt gone, someone's got to stand guard,' he replied.

'With your permission, Captain,' said Thaw Daggerslash, stepping forward, 'Hubble and I should like to repay you and your crew's kindness by standing guard while you all step down to earth.'

'Thank you, Thaw,' said Wind Jackal, smiling. 'Most thoughtful. Keep the flight-burners lit – and look out for league ships.'

'Aye-aye, Captain,' said Thaw, with an easy laugh, and gave an elegant bow.

The crew of the *Galerider* disembarked. Beneath their feet, the firm earthen path which led back into the village felt strangely unreal after the rolling decks of the sky ship. As they reached the middle of the village, there came a shout, and the crew turned back to see the diminutive figure of Spillins the oakelf racing towards them.

'Wait for me! Captain!' he cried in his quavery voice. 'Wait for me!'

As if in answer, from the trees all around them, the circular doors of the lufwood cabins creaked open, and timid, frightened-looking woodtroll faces – with beady eyes, rubbery noses and dark hair in knotted tufts standing on end – peered down. The sound of an oakelf voice seemed to reassure the villagers, for they came out of their cabins, and soon the *Galerider*'s crew was surrounded by curious chattering woodtrolls.

A woodtroll elder pushed his way to the front and saluted Spillins with his carved blackwood staff.

'Greetings, friend of the forests,' he said in a gruff voice. 'I am Chopley Polestick, the timber-master. I see you travel with the sky pirates. What brings them to our village?'

'Greetings, Chopley Polestick, Timber-Master,' said Spillins, fixing the woodtroll with his large dark eyes. 'My captain's sky ship is empty and his purse is full. If you guide him to your timber stores there is business to be done.'

Chopley Polestick turned to Wind Jackal and eyed him up and down. 'Follow me,' he said.

·CHAPTER FIFTEEN·

THE BLOODOAK

Wind Jackal and Quint followed the timber-master down a track, half-concealed by wood chippings and clumps of moss. Through bevies of clucking woodchucks scratching for seed they went, past hammelhorn pens, patches of swaying nightkale and tripweed, and stands of coppiced lufwood.

Behind them, in the middle of the village, at a huge round table, Maris, Tem and Steg were the centre of attention at a grand outdoor feast. Spillins the oakelf had taken himself off at the earliest opportunity to pay a visit to the caterbird nest hanging from the ancient lullabee tree in a clearing on the edge of the village.

Chopley Polestick stopped at the end of the path and cleared the wood chippings and moss at his feet with the end of his blackwood staff. The old woodtroll then bent down and pulled a copper ring, seemingly embedded in the earth, to reveal a trapdoor.

'The timber stores,' he said simply, ushering them inside with a wave of his staff.

Wind Jackal and Quint ducked their heads and descended the roughly hewn steps that led down a broad, high-ceilinged, but shallow tunnel, and on into a vast cavern. The dark earth walls were latticed with glowing roots which cast an eerie light over the great stacks of logs, planks, decking and broad beams of the timber store.

Wood of all kinds, from towering heaps of roughly hewn logs to criss-cross stacks of seasoned timber, filled every corner of the great cavern. Purple-tinged lufwood, ringed lullabee and grey, featureless leadwood; stinkwood and scentwood, their vastly different smells competing with one another in the cool air; bundles of thick sallowdrop branches and huge boulder-like slabs of sumpwood; neatly cut boughs of blackwood and redoak and the opalescent knots from dried silverpine – and all gathered and graded according to quality and size.

Wind Jackal stood for a moment, scanning the array of different woods, gently stroking his chin. Behind him, Chopley Polestick tutted and shook his grey tufted head.

'Not you as well,' he grumbled in his gruff voice. 'You don't have to tell me . . .' he went on. 'Bloodoak timber. Am I right?'

'How did you know?' said Wind Jackal, turning and smiling down at the timber-master.

'Because that's all anybody seems to want just lately,' he said. 'Something's going on back there in Undertown . . . No, no!' The timber-master shook his head and wagged a finger at Wind Jackal. 'Don't tell me, because I don't want to know. What I *do* know is that the last of the seasoned bloodoak was shipped long ago.'

'Can't you get any more?' Quint blurted out without thinking – then wished he hadn't when he saw the look on the old woodtroll's face. It was a mixture of irritation and impatience, as if the timber-master was about to scold a stubborn hammelhorn.

'I'll tell you, young master, what I tell those pushy leagues types who come here wanting bloodoak,' he said, tapping his blackwood staff on the earthen floor. 'The bloodoak is no ordinary tree. It grows far from the well-trodden path. You don't chop down a bloodoak, you *hunt* it, with all the skill and cunning that you can muster. It can take years to tread a path to the glade of a bloodoak, and great courage to bring one down. Its wood – stripped and properly carpentered – is the finest in all the Edgelands for strength and buoyancy, and one tree can furnish twenty sky ships, but at a cost . . .'

The old woodtroll shook his head as if remembering some distant event, and was silent for a while. Wind Jackal reached into his greatcoat and took out a tilder-leather purse, heavy with gold pieces – the profits from the cargo of tallow candles.

'There is enough here,' he said coolly, handing the bulging purse to the woodtroll so that he could test its weight, 'to furnish the whole village with new cooking pots, to buy every matron a new tilder-wool shawl and every tree-feller a new axe – and still have enough left over for a full season of feasting!'

Chopley Polestick handed the purse back to Wind Jackal and, although he frowned, there was a twinkle in his small black eyes.

'And in order to earn this fortune?' he said, fixing Wind Jackal with a level stare.

'I have a buyer in Undertown who requires bloodoak, and I have entered into a contract to supply it. I *always* honour my contracts . . .' Wind Jackal's voice was calm and reasonable, but icily determined. 'Now, I could have sought out rogue timberers. Scoundrels who think nothing of laying waste to the forest and using slaves as tarry-vine bait, and whose services are cheap. But I wanted the best . . .'

'Then you have chosen well, Captain,' said Chopley Polestick. 'The Snetterbarks, the Snatchwoods and the Polesticks are the finest tree-felling families in the twelve villages, each six axes strong! But it is many seasons since any of us have trodden a new path in search of bloodoak. It'll take at least a year . . .'

Wind Jackal smiled and jingled the fat purse. 'Not,' he said, his eyes glancing upwards, 'if you *leave* the path . . .'

The sun was low in the sky and the trees cast long shadows across the great circular table, yet still the feasting continued. From the cabins all round, now lit from within by lufwood lamps, woodtrolls came and went, carrying trays, platters and earthenware jugs.

Maris sat between two elderly woodtroll matrons,

who both could have been her old nurse's sisters, so alike did they seem to her, with their small twinkling eyes and rubbery button noses. Across the great table of polished redoak sat Tem Barkwater and Steg Jambles, each flanked by excited young woodtrolls who kept pressing platters of woodtroll delicacies on them: sweetwood cookies, slippery oakelm broth, tilder-sausage pastries and huge steaming mounds of sour-smelling tripweed.

Steg laughed and joked, and even joined in the chorus of woodtroll songs that kept breaking out without warning. Beside the harpooneer, Tem Barkwater looked wary and pensive. He took sips from the huge tankard of woodale before him, but hardly touched the platter of roast hammelhorn steak – and all the while shooting worried looks into the shadows forming beneath the trees.

'Have another sweetwood cookie, my little sapling,' purred the woodtroll matron beside Maris. 'You look like you could do with some flesh on those delicate little bones of yours. Don't you think so, Felda?'

'All skin and bones!' agreed the second matron. 'Too true, Welma, dear.'

'My nanny's name is Welma!' cried Maris excitedly. 'At least, she used to be my nanny. She looked after me until my father died . . .'

'You had a woodtroll nanny?' cooed both matrons together.

'Yes,' said Maris. 'She was born out here in the Deepwoods. Welma Thornwood.'

'Thornwood!' gasped the matrons, almost upsetting a flagon of sapwine in their surprise. 'Why, we have Thornwoods in the twelve villages! At least three families – perhaps they'll know of this Welma of yours . . .'

Across the circular table, lit up now by glowing lanterns of all shapes and design, Steg leaned over to Tem, a look of concern on his face.

'I say, lad, are you all right? Not coming down with something, I hope. Woodfever? Or glade-fret?'

'No, no,' said Tem, trying to smile. 'It's just that . . .' His face clouded over, and he reached out and pulled a tall glowing lamp towards himself.

'Out with it, lad,' said Steg.

'Being here . . . In the middle of the Deepwoods like this . . . It brings back such memories . . .' Tem took a gulp of woodale and shivered.

Just then, wild clapping and cheering rang out as the timber-master, Chopley Polestick, appeared together with Quint and Wind Jackal. The old woodtroll grasped a bulging tilder-leather purse in one of his gnarled hands and waved his blackwood staff over his head with the other.

'Sharpen your axes!' he commanded, 'and send word to the Snetterbarks and the Snatchwoods! Tomorrow we and our guests here go in search of the bloodoak!'

Maris rushed over to Quint, who was smiling broadly.

'Quint! Is this true?' she said, her eyes blazing with excitement. 'Can I come, too? *Can* I?'

Quint looked to his father. Wind Jackal laughed, all the cares and worries of the last few weeks seeming to fall away in front of their eyes.

'Of course, Maris!' he said. 'Though there'll be no tramping along woodtroll paths for us, for on this expedition, the *Galerider* comes too!'

His words were almost lost in the tumult that had erupted at the timber-master's announcement as the great table was swiftly cleared and woodtrolls rushed to their cabins to prepare for the momentous event to come. Steg, Maris and Quint gathered round Wind Jackal as he issued instructions for the preparation of the sky ship.

'Steg, I want harpoons, cutlasses, saws and axes sharpened and greased. Maris and Quint, I want three hammocks strung up in the cargo-hold – and make sure the water butts are full. Tem, check the ropes and . . .' His voice softened. 'Tem?'

But the young fore-decker wasn't listening. Instead, he sat by himself at the great circular redoak, now cleared, his eyes wide with horror and his mouth twitching as he muttered the same word over and over in a quavering voice.

'Bloodoak . . . Bloodoak . . . Bloodoak . . .'

*

Spillins patted the soft weave of the caterbird cocoon and sighed.

'Well, Lorkel, I envy you your fine nest and beautiful tree. You've picked a wonderful spot, and no mistake.'

Lorkel the oakelf gazed into his new acquaintance's large dark eyes with large dark eyes of his own.

'You don't fool me, Spillins, my friend,' he chuckled. 'For all the storm-damage and worn weaves, you've never once regretted hanging your caterbird cocoon from a sky-ship mast ... This forest glade is far too quiet for you, and you know it.'

Spillins chuckled in reply. 'That's true, Lorkel. The *Galerider* will always be my home ...' His face darkened. 'And yet ...'

Lorkel gazed into Spillins's eyes. 'You are troubled.'

Spillins nodded. 'My captain's aura,' he said slowly, 'is cloudy and sick-looking. And as for the young sky pirate, Thaw, *his* aura is even more worrying ...'

Lorkel nodded and laid a wizened hand on Spillins's shoulder. 'Auras can be difficult,' he said. 'But always remember, Spillins, my friend, though someone's aura may sicken, it can also heal – given time.'

Spillins's large dark eyes seemed to glaze over. 'That's part of the problem,' he whispered. 'I think time is running out . . .'

By late morning, as the dappled sunlight was streaming down onto the mooring-platforms and docking-rings, the *Galerider* was packed up and ready to leave.

The goodbyes were a heartfelt affair for the woodtroll timberers. Members of the eighteen-strong band bade farewell to their families and friends, with young'uns clinging round the legs of their fathers, refusing to let go. After much kissing and hugging, tears and shouts of *good luck!* and *safe path!* – this last shout greeted by nervous looks and more tears from the matrons and young'uns – everyone finally climbed aboard.

Steg Jambles unhitched the tolley-rope and leaped back over the balustrade and – with Thaw Daggerslash cooling the flight-rock and Wind Jackal at the helm – the great *Galerider* slipped its moorings and rose gracefully into the air. Below them, the whoops and cheers of the waving crowd below grew faint as the ascent gathered speed, and the sky ship soared off above the trees.

Chopley Polestick extricated himself from the band of woodtrolls – who were sitting cross-legged on the deck in a circle, their arms wrapped round each other's shoulders and humming softly – and joined Wind Jackal at the helm. It was the first time the timber-master's feet had been so far from the ground, and he felt dizzy and slightly sick.

'Is . . . is it always this . . . this *shuddery*?' he asked, as the sky ship passed through a covering of low cloud.

'Shuddery?' said Wind Jackal, laughing out loud.

'It's . . . it's a woodtroll expression,' said the timber-master, reddening. 'How we describe standing on an unstable branch . . .'

Wind Jackal clapped his hands round the woodtroll's shoulder. 'You'll soon find your sky-legs,' he assured him. 'And once you do, who knows? – Maybe you might even prefer the *Galerider* to those well-trodden paths of yours.'

Chopley smiled queasily. 'I doubt it, Captain. Though I must admit, this view is better than any I've ever seen – even from the tallest ironwood pine.'

Wind Jackal's hands darted over the flight-levers, though his gaze remained on the timber-master.

'What exactly should we be looking for?' he asked, as the woodtroll scanned the vast carpet of treetops spread out below.

Chopley shook his head. 'Difficult to say, Captain,' he said, still wobbly on his feet and clutching the balustrade. 'Certainly it's impossible to spot a blookoak from above. Its glade is dark and concealed beneath the forest canopy. No, what we must look out for are the signs . . .'

'Signs?' asked Wind Jackal.

'Small, open glades. Perhaps a ring of them – although

sometimes, they may lie scattered in groups of two or three,' said the woodtroll. 'They're where the tarry vine ensnares its prey. The tree itself will lie some way off, hidden. To find the bloodoak, Captain, we'll have to hunt on foot. Only down there,' Chopley pointed a stubby finger down into the depths of the forest, 'can we hope to track it down.'

'More signs?' Wind Jackal smiled grimly.

The woodtroll nodded. 'Small but important signs,' he replied. '*Vital* signs!' he added. 'After all, our very lives will depend on them.' His face grew more serious. 'The first is a quality of the air. In our woodlore, it is known as *deathstillness* – a deep oppressive silence that surrounds the tree, devoid of birdsong or creature cry of any kind. Then there is the smell: the *underscent*. Thick, sickly, rancid, it is. Once smelled, never forgotten.'

'I can imagine,' said Wind Jackal, his hands running expertly over the bone-handled flight-levers.

'Oh, I don't think you can,' said the timber-master with a gruff chuckle. 'But you will, when the time comes.' He stumbled down the steps and joined his fellow woodtrolls huddled on the aft-deck.

'Master Spillins,' called Wind Jackal, 'you heard the timber-master, I trust? Look out for clusters of glades!'

'Aye-aye, Cap'n,' Spillins's voice floated back. 'That's just what I'm doing.'

Despite his best efforts, however, Spillins saw nothing that first day as the *Galerider* swept on over the towering Timber Stands and left the paths of the woodtrolls far behind. Yet later, when Wind Jackal brought the great sky pirate ship down to anchor above the treetops for the night, no one felt disappointed. Surely the next day would reveal signs of the bloodoak.

It didn't. Nor did the following day; nor the day after that. And as they sailed on – with Wind Jackal using the sun, his compass and the tranche of charts to navigate the sky – the woodtroll band became ever more nervous and jittery.

Throughout the day, the band of woodtrolls remained up on deck, clustered together as far from the balustrades and the terrifying view as possible. Apart from Chopley Polestick, only one other woodtroll gained his sky-legs. Plucky and young, Tuntum Snatchwood would leave the others and join the timber-master at the balustrade, where the pair of them ventured a brave look over the side – though never for long. At night, when the rest of the crew retired to their cabins, the woodtrolls trooped down to the three large hammocks slung the width of the cargo-hold and climbed in, six to a hammock. And all the while – day *and* night – the group gave off the same curious buzzing, humming sound like the noise of smoke-drowsy woodbees.

'Funny little fellows. What *is* all that moaning and groaning about?' Thaw Daggerslash smiled, nodding towards the cluster of woodtrolls.

Hubble grunted from the nest of sailcloth he'd constructed beneath the aft-deck gunwales.

'Some kind of chanting, I reckon,' said Steg. 'To ward

off evil spirits, or whatever . . . They're a superstitious lot. I mean, look at the way they're always rubbing those wooden amulets of theirs.'

'Well, I hope it works,' said Daggerslash.

'Me too,' said Duggin. 'Though I'm beginning to think we'll never find a blasted bloodoak, no matter how much they chant.'

'Have a heart,' said Steg. 'The woodtrolls are frightened, away from their paths.'

'Yes, and I know just how they feel,' said Tem, his voice quavering and his face ashen grey. 'Just the *thought* of them bloodoaks . . .'

'Don't worry, Tem,' laughed Thaw Daggerslash. 'We'll only use you as tarry-vine bait as a last resort!' Chuckling at his own joke, Thaw sauntered off towards the aft-cabins.

Steg glared after the sky pirate a moment before turning to his young friend. 'Just a stupid joke, Tem,' he said. 'Don't you go worrying yourself sick about it, there's a good lad.'

Tem shook his head doubtfully.

'When the time comes,' said Steg, '*if* it ever comes, and we're in that bloodoak glade, I'll be right beside you. I promise you, Tem, lad, old Steg Jambles won't let anything bad happen to his fore-decker.'

Down below deck, Maris and Quint were staring into the galley's store cupboards. With the *Galerider*'s quartermaster, Filbus Queep, gone, and Tem Barkwater hopelessly distracted, the pair of them had offered not only to prepare the meals, but also to manage the supplies. They were about to go into the second week of the bloodoak voyage and, with eighteen extra mouths to feed, the store cupboards were looking increasingly bare.

Quint sliced the last of the stale black bread while Maris diluted the already watery stew. She laid the ladle down.

'This is hopeless,' she said. 'When the stew's finished, all we'll have left are woodonions and glade oats.'

'Delicious,' said Quint with a laugh. 'Onion porridge, my favourite!'

But Maris was having none of it. 'This is no laughing matter,' she complained. 'How can we be expected to feed the crew if the store cupboards are empty, Quint? And your father won't stop the search for us to forage . . .'

'I've never seen our captain happier!' came a voice, and the pair of them turned, to see Thaw Daggerslash standing there, his hands behind his back. 'He's like a new sky pirate up there at the helm.' Thaw flashed them both one of his dazzling smiles. 'Give the woodtrolls watered-down stew,' he said. 'What do you say *we* have roast snowbird for supper!'

He brought his arms from behind his back and held up six plump snowbirds.

'Oh, Captain Daggerslash!' gasped Maris, flushing pink with pleasure. 'But of course we must share them with everyone!'

'Not only a beautiful cook, but a fair and honest

quartermaster,' smiled Thaw, handing the birds to Maris. 'Is there no end to your accomplishments?'

Now blushing furiously, Maris turned away and began busily preparing the snowbirds for the roasting tray.

'But how . . . ?' began Quint, who could see no telltale crossbow bolts in the birds.

'Simple,' said Thaw triumphantly. 'I simply coated a log-bait with tar and the nibblick seeds I feed my ratbird with, and the greedy things swooped down and stuck fast!'

'You have a ratbird?' said Quint, intrigued.

'Indeed,' said Thaw. 'From my sky barge – only thing left to remember the *Mireraider* by. Now, Maris, remember, plenty of woodonion sauce with those snowbirds!'

The following morning, the sun hadn't even risen above the horizon when Quint climbed from his hammock and made his way up to the helm. He emerged at the top of the stairs only to find that the sky ship had slipped anchor and was already in flight, with Spillins up in his caternest scanning the forest, Wind Jackal at the wheel, steering by the dim grey morning light and the hooded figure of the Stone Pilot supporting herself on crutches, tending the flight-rock once more.

'The Stone Pilot's up!' Quint exclaimed as he joined his father at the helm.

'Wouldn't stay in the infirmary cabin a moment longer. That roast snowbird certainly seems to have done her the power of good,' said Wind Jackal, adjusting the flight-levers as the wind caught the sails and the *Galerider* soared high up into the sky. All round them, the air filled with a mist of droplets as the dew-drenched sailcloth quivered and flexed. 'In fact, last night's supper has revived spirits all round,' Wind Jackal added. 'Even our woodtroll friends seem happier this morning.'

Quint looked down to the aft-deck where the woodtrolls clustered in groups of six, busily sharpening their axes and chattering excitedly. Just then, the great orange sun split the distant horizon to the east, casting shafts of light out across the sky. At the same moment, Spillins cried out from the top of the mast.

'Captain! Captain! There! A ring of glades!'

Quint stared over the balustrade. Sure enough, far below them was a telltale ring of glades circling a dark, dense mass of forest. The woodtrolls laid down their axes and danced in a circle, their arms round each other's shoulders. The droning hum was gone. In its place – echoing around the sky ship – was a loud, triumphant whooping that brought the rest of

the crew onto the deck to see for themselves what was going on.

A matter of minutes later, the great sky pirate ship was hovering just above the forest canopy, and Steg, Thaw and Duggin – at three points along its length – were lowering grappling-hooks. Ropes were let down and the crew and the band of woodtrolls slid quickly down them.

On the forest floor, in the dense undergrowth on the fringe of the sunlit glades, the bloodoak-felling party organized itself into three groups, as the lone figure of the Stone Pilot remained at her post aboard the *Galerider*. Wind Jackal, Quint and Maris went with the Polestick clan; Steg Jambles, a white-faced Tem and Duggin the gnokgoblin joined the Snatchwoods, while Thaw Daggerslash, Hubble and a frowning Spillins fell in with the six axes of the Snetterbarks. Chopley Polestick took command, raising his carved blackwood staff to gain the attention of the three gangs.

'Somewhere in there' – he jabbed the staff in the direction of the dense, dark forest on the other side of the sunny glades – 'lurks a bloodoak. Remember – look, listen and smell for the signs. Deathstillness. Under-scent. And out there in the glades, the tarry vine . . .'

Tem felt his knees buckle and his heart begin to race. Beside him, Steg reached out with a steadying arm.

'Easy there, lad. I'm with you,' he whispered.

'There are three axe-teams,' the timber-master continued. 'Enough for a classic death thrust. Snatchwoods approach from the east, Snetterbarks from the north . . . You must engage the tarry vine, and hold it off for as long as you can, while we Polesticks attack from the west. We'll do our best to bring it down before any of you are taken.' He looked round the circle of expectant faces. 'Attack on my signal.'

Tem felt cold sweat trickling down his back.

'And may the axes of our forefathers protect us!'

The timber-master waved his blackwood staff once more and the three axe-teams – with the *Galerider*'s crew falling in behind them – set off to take their positions on the edges of the glades.

A short while later, Quint and Maris found themselves crouched behind a thornberry bush beside Wind Jackal. There was no birdsong; no rodents scurried, no creatures cried. The three of them clutched razor-edged axes, each one sharpened by the woodtrolls of the Polestick clan, who were clustered round the timber-master. Putting his stubby hands to his mouth, Chopley gave a low hooting whistle that cut through the unearthly deathstillness of the sunlit glade in front of them.

At the sound of his whistle, Quint glimpsed the flash of sunlight reflecting off axe-heads between the clumps of trees and undergrowth as, from the north and east, the Snetterbarks and Snatchwoods dashed out into their respective glades.

'Wait!' Chopley growled to his axe-team as they tensed in readiness to spring forward. 'Wait till they engage the tarry vine . . .'

Suddenly, from the dense patch of forest in the middle of the ring of glades, came a whirring, snapping sound, as if a driver was cracking a hammelhorn whip.

Halfway across the eastern glade, Tem gasped in horror as a thick, green vine – with trailing tendrils and pulsating veins of sap – reared up from the lush meadow grass at his feet. A short woodtroll spun round just in front of the terrified fore-decker and swung his axe, and the thick, poisonous-green coil of vine exploded in a spray of stinking slime.

The severed stump flayed around violently before drawing back, rearing high in the air and sprouting three fresh, oozing tendrils that sprang out in opposite directions. All at once, Tem's ears filled with the whirring sound of the Snatchwood clan's axes hacking through lashing vine strands that slithered back, only to divide and lash out again.

Whirr! Splatch! Whirr! Splatch! Whirr! Splatch!

The hideous rhythm rang in his ears, freezing Tem to the spot.

'Swing that axe, lad!' shouted Steg Jambles beside him as the sounds of battle erupted in the glade to the north.

But Tem couldn't hear him. He was back in the past, in a far-off glade, tethered to his brother Cal, and being driven by slavers towards the terrible sound of thrashing mandibles coming from the shadows . . .

Just then, an intense jolt of pain shot through his body; shocking, yet horribly familiar. Looking down, Tem saw a sinuous coil of green vine wrapped tightly round his forearm, and beads of blood pouring down from the vicious barbs which had pierced the skin.

This was no dream; no buried nightmare. It was real!

'Steg!' Tem screamed in terror as, kicking and writhing, he was dragged across the glade towards the black heart of the forest.

'Tem!' Steg's anguished shout answered his call, as the harpooneer hurled his axe, end over end, at the retreating vine.

All over the glade, the six axes of the Snatchwood clan were engaged in equally desperate battles with vines of their own. Steg's axe blade whistled past Tem's head and sliced through the vine with a juicy splatter. Duggin was first to the fore-decker's side, pulling him back and holding a rag to his bloody arm. Steg stood over them, a wide grin on his face.

'Told you I'd look after you,' he boasted, turning to retrieve his axe.

At that moment, in a loud whirr, the vine stump reared up, seized Steg by the neck and shot back into the depths of the forest. With a scream of horror, Tem leaped to his feet, axe in hand, and tore after his friend.

Into the dark mass of undergrowth and tree-trunks he stumbled, fighting back briars and switching branches – and the rising panic in his chest. Suddenly the undergrowth gave way to rich dark earth from which, at every footfall, a thick rancid odour rose up and caught in Tem's nostrils.

It was the underscent.

Trembling with terror, Tem looked up. And there, at the centre of the gloomy enclosed glade, rising up from a hideous mound of white bones, was the monstrous bloodoak itself. Its gnarled and pitted trunk was encrusted with grotesque lumps and nodules that oozed and glistened, and from the middle of the circle of branches at its top came the grinding sound of its great mandibled maw.

The noise grew in intensity, and while Tem clawed his way across the stinking earth of the clearing, the tarry vine came lashing back through the treetops towards its roots in the branches of the bloodoak. As Tem looked helplessly on, the vine dangled the limp body of Steg Jambles over the bloodoak's gaping maw. A sharp jerk rippled down the vine as it released the body from its strangling grasp and dropped it into the tree's gurgling gullet. The bloodoak shivered and shuddered, the grotesque lumps and nodules on its trunk pulsating.

'No!' screamed Tem, and swung his axe, embedding it deep in the bloodoak's fleshy bark.

Suddenly, from the far side of the clearing, burst the Polestick clan, their axes swinging. The air filled with the whirring of razor-sharp axe blades and the massive trunk pulsated and groaned with each blow as the woodtrolls fell upon the tree. Thud after resounding thud filled the air as the axes hacked at the tree, eating quickly into its very core.

Above them, high in the branches above, the tarry vine seemed to go berserk – thrashing and flailing in the forest canopy and filling the air with falling twigs and leaves. Suddenly, with an ear-splitting scream that rose

up from the very roots beneath the axe-team's feet and burst from the mandibles above, the bloodoak teetered, toppled and came crashing to the forest floor.

Tem threw away his axe, his face streaming with tears, and raced along the up-ended tree. When he reached its gaping mouth, ringed by razor-sharp teeth, he dived inside, disappearing deep within – only to emerge moments later dragging the lifeless body of his friend after him. Both were drenched in sweet rancid sap that made the woodtrolls step back and hold their round button noses with disgust. For a few moments the fore-decker crouched, cradling the crushed body of the harpooneer in his arms, rocking backwards and forwards.

'You *did* look after me, Steg,' Tem wailed. 'You *did* . . .'

Wind Jackal stepped forward, his face an expressionless mask, but his eyes fierce and unblinking. He took Tem gently by the arm, raising him to his feet.

'We shall send him to Open Sky with his harpoon, Tem,' he said. 'And you will meet again in Open Sky – when your time comes . . .'

With the great bloodoak chopped into logs and loaded into the hold, the *Galerider* set sail. The voyage back to the woodtroll village was short, with Wind Jackal's charts and calculations proving as reliable as a well-trodden woodtroll path. The mood was sombre. Once again, the captain retreated back into the brooding presence he'd been on the voyage to the slave market. Three crew-members lost on that voyage, now a fourth on this.

The *Galerider* was desperately undercrewed now –

something the woodtrolls seemed to sense, for no sooner had the sky ship docked in the woodtroll village than they scrambled back down to earth and disappeared without a backward glance. After all, it wasn't unheard of for sky pirate ships – or league ships for that matter – to press a few unwilling recruits into their service when the occasion demanded it.

Chopley Polestick took Steg Jambles's death harder than most and, as timber-master on the bloodoak expedition, felt a heavy responsibility for the tragedy. Before the sky pirates left, he personally supervised the construction of a traditional lufwood funeral sky-raft for the fallen harpooneer, built from the finest seasoned timbers in his timber store, and then stood, alone, on the mooring-platform, waving his blackwood staff in farewell till long after the *Galerider* had become a distant speck on the horizon.

With the pathways of the twelve villages now receding into the dusk, and heading into a golden sun-set, Wind Jackal signalled for his remaining crew to gather beneath the flight- burners on the flight-rock plat-form. There, on the lufwood sky-raft, lay Steg Jambles, his harpoon cradled in his arms.

At the captain's signal, Tem Barkwater stepped forward and took a blazing torch from the hooded Stone Pilot. Gently, tenderly, he held it to the logs at his dead friend's feet. As the flames took hold, the sky-raft slowly rose, gathering speed as the purple fire gained in intensity until the sky-raft became a blazing star soaring off into the vastness of the darkening sky.

One by one, the crew left the platform to find quiet private places on the great sky ship, for none of them felt much like talking. Below deck, the cargo-hold was stacked full with bloodoak timber of the most exquisite quality – but acquired, as they all knew, at a terrible price. Back at the helm, Wind Jackal found Thaw Daggerslash leaning against the balustrade, a thoughtful expression on his handsome face.

'It's hard losing a crew-mate. Even harder sending them on their final journey to Open Sky,' he mused. 'Though there's one former crew-mate of mine I'd happily send on *his* final journey . . .'

'The sky pirate you recruited for your mire-pearling voyage?' said Wind Jackal, raising an eyebrow. 'Yes, I think I've heard you talk of him before, Thaw. But tell me, this rogue who festooned you – I don't think you've ever mentioned his name.'

'His name?' said Thaw Daggerslash, examining his fingernails. 'His name . . . He did tell me, though he seldom spoke much . . . Now let me see. He was an old quartermaster, down on his luck . . . Oh yes, that's right. His name was Turbot Smeal.'

·CHAPTER SIXTEEN·

THE GATHERING STORM

i

The Stone Gardens

For the first time since the terrible winter of the year before, there was frost in the air and a bitter wind was blowing. The great sphere of the full moon came and went as clumps of cloud were blown across her bright yet mottled face, like a vast shaggy herd of migrating hammelhorns sweeping across the Silver Pastures. Far below, at the furthest extent of the Edge, the Stone Gardens were one moment bathed in delicate white light; the next, drowned in shadow.

Weaving wormlike in and out of the tall stone stacks was the flickering golden glow of a dozen flaming torches, as a line of gowned figures made its way from the arched gates to the jutting lip of rock at the very edge of the gardens. Their progress – silent, secretive and unnoticed by a sleeping Undertown – was marked by the white ravens, that squawked indignantly and flapped their wings, high on their roosts at the top of the mighty stone stacks.

At the front of the column strode Imbix Hoth, High Master of the League of Rock Merchants. As a huge white bird, flapping and cawing, launched itself from the top of a stone stack above, Imbix glanced up. His high hat keeled to one side and tumbled to the ground.

'Imbecile!' Imbix Hoth snapped at his hat-tipper.

'I . . . I'm so sorry, sir,' the lop-eared goblin replied, leaping forward, picking up the tall hat and gingerly returning it to the high master's head. 'It won't happen again, sir . . .'

'Make sure it doesn't, Brummel,' Imbix Hoth rasped, his tone harsh and mocking, 'unless, that is, you *want* some more marks of my displeasure?' Metal finger-spikes glinting menacingly, he pointed to four angry-looking scratch marks on the lop-eared goblin's cheek.

'N . . . n . . . no, sir,' Brummel stuttered.

The high master turned impatiently away and strode on. The lop-eared goblin – tipping-pole in one hand and torch in the other – tripped along behind him, struggling to keep up.

'I trust all these months of waiting have been worth-while,' said Hoth, turning to the stone marshal, Zaphix Nemulis, who was walking beside him, a pair of large rock callipers under one arm.

The academic's violet and white robes flapped in the

cold wind. 'I think you will be more than satisfied, High Master,' Zaphix Nemulis replied proudly. 'You requested a flight-rock fifteen strides across . . .'

'At the very least, Nemulis,' Imbix Hoth broke in.

'Indeed,' said Nemulis, 'and as your Most Highness knows only too well, to grow a flight-rock of fifteen strides across is an almost impossible feat, and yet . . .' He paused for a moment, to savour the look of antici- pation on the high master's face. 'I have produced a rock a fraction off *sixteen* strides – and still growing.'

Imbix Hoth whistled softly. 'Impressive,' he said.

Nemulis nodded. 'But it must be harvested this night,' he said. 'Otherwise, by daybreak, with such a frost in the air it will surely break free and be lost to Open Sky for ever.'

The stone marshal and the high leaguesmaster strode on, side by side, at the head of the torchlit column, their words turning to coils of mist in the ice-cold air. Behind them, Brummel the hat-tipper skipped and bobbed in front of a hand-picked contingent of academics-at-arms from the Knights Academy, their armour and weapons glinting in the torchlight.

'Have you any idea what this is all about, Phin?' one of the academics-at-arms whispered to the young swordmaster in front of him.

The swordmaster shook his head. 'Only that the stone marshal has a rock that needs harvesting,' he whispered back, pushing the thick fringe of hair out of his eyes, 'and wants it to be done quietly, without any fuss . . .' He patted his jacket pocket, which clinked softly with the coins inside it, and grinned. 'And, Balfus, that he is paying us handsomely for our trouble.'

'I know that,' his companion persisted, 'but aren't there rather a lot of us to harvest just one flight-rock?'

Suddenly, up in the sky, far ahead of the column of academics-at-arms – twenty strong, and weighed down with rock callipers, flaming braziers, rock nets and fire-floats – the clouds cleared. The full moon shone down brightly.

'*That's* why,' said Phin, with a whistle of amazement.

A gasp rippled through the column. There, towering above them, at the top of the last stack in the Stone Gardens, was a huge pitted rock, silhouetted against the silvery sky.

'Truly outstanding,' Imbix Hoth exclaimed gleefully. 'I congratulate you, Stone Marshal.'

But at his side, the stone marshal had a tense worried expression on his face. 'We haven't a moment to lose!' he announced, hurriedly turning from the high master and gesticulating to the academics-at-arms. 'I chose you because you are the best,' Zaphix Nemulis told them. 'Don't let me down . . .'

At his words, the academics-at-arms sprang instantly into action. The young swordmaster, Phin, and his companion Balfus quickly scaled the rock stack, a great weight-fringed rock net in their hands. Scrambling up, agile as lemkins, they expertly dropped the net over the mighty rock to form a hanging canopy. Then the others – using their hooks and grappling-poles – eased the huge rock from its perch at the top of the stack and gently

guided it down to the waiting
rock-handlers with their
white-hot rock callipers.

'Carefully! Carefully!'
Nemulis clucked, like a
broody woodhen over a
newly-laid egg. 'Easy
with those callipers. I
want no chippings!'

From the rock stacks
nearby, the white ravens eyed them
suspiciously, flapping and cawing uneasily.

Normally the vicious birds would attack intruders
who dared to trespass within the Stone Gardens, keeping the place safe from robbers, vandals and vagabonds.
But not this night. Their flock-leaders recognized the tall
academic in his violet and white robes as the stone
marshal – and besides, the chunks of meat and offal the
academics-at-arms had been careful to place beneath
each stack they passed went a long way to compensate
for the disturbance in the middle of the night.

As the icy wind blew, the huge rock teetered and
tugged, threatening to break free of the rock net.
Nemulis flapped his violet and white robes desperately.

'The braziers!' he shrieked. 'More heat!'

In answer, the academics tending the sumpwood-
burning braziers raised them in gauntleted hands and
gathered beneath the huge rock. The warm air beneath it
brought the massive rock down and eased the strain on
the rock net and the academics-at-arms clutching it.

'Now we must get it to the carts before this wind gets any stronger!' the stone marshal commanded.

Struggling and straining, the academics-at-arms set off for the gates of the Stone Gardens as quickly as they could, tugging the huge rock after them. Even the High Master of the Leagues of Flight, Imbix Hoth, played his part, seizing a corner of the rock net with his razor-sharp finger-spikes and gripping ferociously. Having waited so long and paid so much, he had no intention of losing his precious flight-rock now.

At the gates at last, the huge buoyant rock was loaded up onto a waiting hammelhorn cart and bound tightly into place with ropes – and not a moment too soon, as the wind turned into a snow-flecked gale. The stone marshal ran round the cart, checking each of the knots, before declaring himself satisfied.

'Move it on out!' he bellowed, hands cupped to his mouth.

The mobgnome driver – a wagoneer who worked for the League of Rock Merchants, his eyes obscured beneath a low-brimmed cap – lashed his whip and the great bull hammelhorn trotted forward, with the exhausted academics-at-arms following behind on foot.

Back at the gates to the Stone Gardens, an ornate two-seater barrow pulled by two lugtrolls drew up, and the High Master of the League of Rock Merchants climbed in, his hat-tipper fussing behind him. Settling himself on a velvet cushion, he reached into his robes and drew out a small fromp-skin purse and handed it to a smiling Zaphix Nemulis.

'A little bonus for you, Zaphix,' Imbix Hoth grinned, his small eyes gleaming. 'The finest mire-pearls – for a job well done. You have done the Leagues of Undertown a great service tonight, Zaphix; more than you know!'

'The honour is all mine, High Master,' said Zaphix proudly.

Imbix Hoth raised a metal-spiked finger to the barrow-pushers – then paused for a moment.

'Just one last thing,' he said to the stone marshal, with a thin smile. 'If you're thinking of celebrating with a bottle of sapwine in one of our fine Undertown taverns, take my advice . . .' Imbix clicked his fingers, and the barrow jolted into movement. 'Avoid the Tarry Vine tavern tonight!'

ii
The Knights Academy

Raffix Emilius pushed his small round spectacles up over the bridge of his nose thoughtfully. He was standing in his chamber at the top of one of the thirteen towers, staring out of the open window. Ever since he'd been made a knight academic-in-waiting, he had spent most of his time in his quarters, reading, meditating, studying – awaiting the day when he would be called upon to embark on a stormchasing voyage to the Twilight Woods in search of sacred stormphrax.

Such a voyage would test him to the very limit, calling upon all the skills and knowledge he had gained in his time in the Lower and Upper Halls of the Knights Academy. Now those carefree days of model sky ships,

prowlgrin rearing and tilt-
tree practice were behind
him. The knight academic-
in-waiting's mission now
was to do just that –
wait. And while he waited,
to prepare himself for
the greatest test any
Sanctaphrax academic
could face: the quest for
stormphrax.

Yet, Raffix thought
grimly, this waiting was
hard. He was meant to be
clearing his mind, focus-
ing on the quest to come –
yet he couldn't stop thoughts from the past from flooding back. There was that extraordinary voyage into
Open Sky, the cloudeater, the battle in the inner courtyard, the winter knights and . . .

'Quintinius Verginix,' he whispered, the words lost to
the icy air outside.

Perhaps it was this biting wind, whistling through
Sanctaphrax with its promise of snow, that was bringing the
events of that terrible winter back to him. Raffix peered out
of his window, past the tilt trees and the West Wall of the
Academy, over the domed roofs of the Hall of Wind, past
Undertown and the bleached Mire beyond, and on towards
the horizon, far, far away above the distant Deepwoods.

'Oh, Quint,' he whispered. 'I wonder where you are now?'

*

Stope, the grey goblin forge-hand, raised the visor of his furnace hood and held the honed tip of the harpoon up to the light. It was magnificent, with long razor-sharp jags glinting in the golden light. Furnace-fired fifty times and hammered out on the armoury anvil, the massive harpoon's smooth surface was patterned with flowing swirls of exquisite beauty.

Since he'd first found a home in the foundry of the Hall of Grey Cloud, young Stope had built a reputation for fine craftsmanship and an eye for detail. The two furnace masters – hulking Clud Mudskut and diminutive Spedius Heepe – didn't know what they'd do without him. Now, instead of a bed of rags behind the main furnace, Stope had his own sleeping-closet in the hall's upper chambers and the furnace masters had even presented him with three cloddertrog stokers to fire up the furnaces – a job Stope had previously had to struggle with single-handed.

Of course, the furnace masters had ulterior motives for making their talented young forge-hand's life more comfortable. Freed from menial tasks around the armoury, Stope could devote his energies to forging the finest weapons and armour in the whole of Sanctaphrax or Undertown.

As his reputation grew, so both Spedius Heepe's order-book *and* Clud Mudskut's great chest filled, one with scrawled ink entries, the other with gold. As for Stope, so long as he was fed and watered, he seemed

happy to spend long hours in the heat of the armoury, forging weapons for his furnace masters to sell.

Stope placed the completed section of the great harpoon in the rack beside the cooling-trough and hung up his furnace-hood and gauntlets. He'd forgotten all about the time, and now, through the high narrow windows of the armoury, he could see a full moon.

Working on the harpoon – one of a whole flurry of commissions from Imbix Hoth, High Master of the League of Rock Merchants – Stope's head had been filled with thoughts of sky ships. A weapon as large and powerful as this one, he realized, could be destined only for the most magnificent of vessels. Oh, how Stope wished he could sail in such a ship! After his extraordinary adventure on board the old sky ship *Cloudslayer* in the terrible winter of the previous year, Stope's imagination had been filled with thoughts of sky-flight – and of his friend, Quintinius Verginix.

'I wonder, Master Quint,' he whispered to himself, 'exactly where you are now?'

*

Phin climbed out of the hanging-basket and followed the rest of the academics-at-arms across the West Landing, back towards the Knights Academy. It had been a long night and the muscles in his arms and legs were aching. But they'd managed to get the great flight-rock safely to the sky-shipyard without attracting attention – and had ten gold pieces each to show for it.

Although urged to celebrate their night's work, Phin declined – bidding goodnight to his comrades outside the Academy Barracks, golden light streaming through its great oval window – and crossed to the Lower Halls. Climbing the great Central Staircase of the Knights Academy, he reached the Upper Halls. Then, at the western end, he went up a second set of steps to the top of the tall gantry tower and – despite the lateness of the hour and his own fatigue – walked out onto the gantry platform. The old sky ship, the *Cloudslayer*, creaked and swayed from the tether-ring above as, with aching muscles, Phin climbed the ladder and boarded her.

'Phin!' came a voice as his foot landed on the fore-deck. 'Not you as well!'

Raffix Emilius, knight academic-in-waiting, strode across the deck and embraced his friend.

'What do you mean, not me as well?' Phin asked.

'This cold weather, of course!' grinned Raffix. 'The snow in the air . . . Don't tell me your thoughts aren't full of last winter and our incredible voyage . . .'

Phin smiled. 'Well, now you mention it, Raff, I *was*

thinking about the old times. That's why I came up to visit the old girl . . .'

'Me, too,' came a third voice from the prow and, emerging from the shadows, Stope stepped forward.

'Well, well, well,' laughed Raffix. 'If it isn't Sanctaphrax's most celebrated forge-hand! I'm surprised you had time to leave that armoury of yours, what with all the weapons you've been producing . . .'

Stope and Raffix shook hands warmly.

'It's true,' said Stope. 'I *have* been busy. Just finished a prow harpoon for a league ship – and if the size of it is anything to go by, then the league ship itself must be an absolute giant . . .'

'That's funny,' said Phin thoughtfully as the three friends stood at the prow of the old sky ship and looked out across the dark wintry sky. '*I've* just helped harvest the largest flight-rock I've ever seen and delivered it to a sky-shipyard in Undertown this very night.'

Raffix took his spectacles off and polished them with a spider-silk handerchief. 'Rumour has it the leagues are up to something,' he said slowly. 'Been refitting and repairing their league ships for months now – buying up all the timber they can lay their hands on. But this is the first I've heard of a giant sky ship . . .'

'The leagues, *pah!*' snorted Phin. 'Probably just fighting amongst themselves as usual. We all know what they're like.'

'Maybe so,' said Raffix, 'but if the leagues ever *did* manage to act together, then one thing's for certain . . .'

'What's that?' asked Stope.

'I wouldn't want to be a sky pirate,' said Raffix. 'Talking of which . . .'

'I know,' said Phin, with a faraway look in his eyes. 'Quint . . .' He sighed. 'I wonder where he is right now?'

iii
The Tarry Vine Tavern

Perched upon his high stool, Patricule the tavern-waif slowly rotated his wing-like ears. Fine as parchment and lined with a network of pale-blue veins that pulsed as they swivelled and fluttered, his ears listened to the thoughts in the great drinking hall of the Tarry Vine tavern, just as he did every night.

Although tonight was different . . .

The tables and drinking-benches were crowded as usual. Sky pirates of every description, from mire-pearlers to Deepwoods traders, Undertown sewer-skimmers to Edgeland pavement-poachers, sat slumped over tankards or troughs of foaming woodale. Their greatcoats were done up, their polished tricorne hats set at jaunty angles, with their swords, cutlasses and bludgeons at the ready. Though none of them moved so much as a muscle, they all sat in a curious expectant-looking silence, as if listening for something . . .

Patricule's great wing-like ears twitched. Up above the hall, beside the huge vats of woodale, he could hear the thoughts of the tavern keeper, Glaviel Glynte. Sharp, clear, cool thoughts, they were, full of calculation and cunning. High above him on the gantry, Patricule could hear Sister Horsefeather's clucking thoughts – agitated and fierce; barely suppressed excitement in her strange shryke head. But in front of him, in the crowded drinking hall, there was an eerie silence . . .

Crash!

Patricule stifled a howl of pain as the sound of the tavern doors slamming back on their hinges exploded in his ears. And there, standing in the doorway, was the portly gnokgoblin with the high-collared jerkin – the doorkeeper, Jaggs. He stared into the tavern, his eyes bulging and a bemused half-smile on his face.

Pity, but it can't be helped, Patricule heard Glaviel Glynte's thoughts above.

You'll pay! You'll pay for this! Sister Horsefeather's thoughts rose to a shriek that made the waif wince.

He stared across the tavern from his high stool. All at once, Glynte's and Horsefeather's thoughts made sense. The gnokgoblin doorkeeper's feet were hovering

inches above the floor, and
protruding from the centre
of his chest were three
glinting talons, each one
dripping with blood. The
next instant, the hapless
creature was tossed aside
like a discarded rag, and
replaced in the doorway
by a massive black-
feathered shryke, dressed
in a dark cloak, a gleaming
spiked helmet and breast-
plate. A spiked ball and
chain dangled from her
left hand.

With a shriek of rage,
the bird-creature launched
herself at the nearest table,
scattering the sky pirates
with her flailing claws.
Behind her, seven identical
black-feathered shrykes –
screaming with fury,
green bile dripping from
their beaks – came
bursting into the tavern.
They slashed and stabbed
with their vicious claws,
slicing through the heavy

leather greatcoats and staving in the bicorne and tricorne hats with axe, cosh and cudgel-blow.

At each swinging blow or dagger-like claw-thrust, blood sprayed into the air, splattering table-top and tavern floor alike. From his high stool, Patricule stared with horrified fascination, the hideous chorus of murderous shryke-thoughts clamouring inside his head . . .

Die! Pirate scum! Die!

Blood! Blood! Blood!

Rip and slash! That's it, pirate! Spill your guts!

Then, a moment later . . .

But wait! What's this? Tilder guts? Hammelhorn blood!

Looking up from the bloody mess of bodies around her, the black-feathered shryke leader's yellow eyes narrowed.

'*Waaaaach! Waaaaach! Waaaaach!*' she screeched, as she raced around the tavern, lashing out at the lifeless dummies at the tables.

Around her, her shryke-sisters let out similar shrieks of outrage.

A trick, sisters! A trick! their identical thoughts sounded in Patricule's head.

All at once, they stopped stock still, and eight pairs of yellow eyes turned on the tiny waif perched on the high stool in the corner of the drinking hall.

Time, sweet ladies! the waif's voice sounded in each bird-like creature's head. *Time . . .*

The waif's large pale eyes turned towards the gantry, high up above the massive woodale vats where Glaviel Glynte and Sister Horsefeather stood. The eight pairs of eyes followed his gaze as Sister Horsefeather reached down and, with both hands, grasped a thick, grooved lever attached to the gantry and yanked it as hard as she could.

As she did so, there was a series of creaks and cracks, followed by a loud whooshing sound, as the fronts of the huge woodale vats swung open and their contents gushed out into the drinking hall below in a tremendous roar. Gurgling with fear, shock and horror, the eight shrykes had their legs pulled away from beneath them and, along with the bloody sky-pirate dummies, the tables, the chairs, the stools and drinking-troughs, were washed across the tavern floor in the frothing torrent.

With a satisfied smirk, Patricule jumped from his high stool and pulled the draining chain. At the end of the hall, metal trapdoors in the floor slid open as the foaming tide of woodale reached the waif, then thundered down into the sewers beneath the tavern. Spinning round in the heady swirl, the shrykes tried desperately to hold their ground – lashing out

341

with their glinting claws and savage beaks – to escape the great rushing flood. But all to no avail.

Save me!

I'm drowning!

A-aa-aaa-aiih . . .

The shrykes' thoughts receded in the tavern-waif's head, to be replaced a moment later by Glaviel Glynte's ice-cool musings.

First blood to the sky pirates. Imbix Hoth will be in need of a new bodyguard . . .

iv
Palace in the Western Quays

Imbix Hoth stood on the balcony of his palace, staring out across the Undertown rooftops. On the other side of the Edgewater, far from the opulent palaces of the leagues, was that nest of sky piracy, the Tarry Vine tavern. For too long had that impudent sky vermin defied the power of the leagues. Now their time was up.

First, flush the sky pirates out of their filthy nest in Undertown! His beloved shrykes would see to that.

Imbix smiled as he looked down at the glittering moonlit waters of the Edgewater River.

Then draw them out into the skies in one stinking swarm, and . . .

But what was that? Imbix's eyes narrowed as he

leaned out over the balcony. It couldn't be . . . One, two
. . . four . . . eight shrykes floating down the Edgewater
River. Black, bedraggled – and very, very dead.

·CHAPTER SEVENTEEN·

THE SKY WRECK

The sky wreck hovered in the air, dark and brooding against a backdrop of billowing clouds. Far below lay the turbulent treetops of the Deepwoods forest, the windblown canopy moving like the swell of a mighty ocean. To the east, west and north, the forest stretched off towards the horizons, seemingly for ever. Only to the south – where the sun was already low in the sky – did the luxuriant trees thin out as they approached the rocky Edgelands, that barren strip of land, lashed by gales and wreathed in swirling mist.

It was there – now blurred by wisps of cloud; now stark against the yellow sky – that the ancient wreck of a once proud sky ship floated. The vessel had not turned turvey. Upright, but only just, its great hull tilted at a sharp angle, as if caught for ever in the act of tacking into the winds of the long-forgotten storm that had wrecked her.

Somewhere along the line, both of the sky ship's great ironwood masts had snapped off. One was now a blunted stump; the other had been left with a circle of jagged splinters of wood, like a crown worn with jaunty disrespect. Huge gaping holes lined the vessel's fore- and aft-hulls where the lufwood decking had fallen away. From every surface, every cracked panel, every shattered plank and shard of decking, there sprouted weird plants and fungal growths.

Some stood tall and jagged in yellow and orange peaks; some hugged the timber like ruffs of thick mottled fur; while some – resembling clusters of purple parasols – swayed delicately to and fro as wild winds buffeted the bows and the wreck rolled gently from side to side. Still more grew in the places where rain collected; clumps and clusters, like lowland shrubs and forest undergrowth. And in addition to all this, the entire floating vessel was fes- tooned in great diaphanous swathes of shimmering threads that flapped and trembled in the shifting air like tattered silken sheets. Even the hanging-weights were not spared, with the chains and pitted rocks themselves covered with sky moss and air lichen and great tongue-like fronds.

As for the flight-rock at the heart of the vast wrecked ves- sel, like all other buoyant rocks whose origins lay in the Stone Gardens, it had continued to grow. Once it had been enclosed by the spherical rock cage. Now, years after the sky ship had been wrecked and without a stone pilot to trim it, the rock was bulging through the gaps between the criss-cross lattice of riveted bars, pushing the torn and twisted metal out of the way in some places; swallowing it up in others.

Yet, despite the fact that the rock had swollen to almost twice its original size, very little of its surface was visible, for the curved contours were almost entirely obscured by jutting tiers of the giant mire-clams that now encrusted it. All round the rock, at regular intervals, these huge creatures opened their mouthlike shells wide to gulp greedily at the rich spore-laden air – only to expel it moments later, in curious spiralling wisps of warm steam.

Though the ancient flight-burners on the mossy flight-rock platform had burned out long ago, the giant mire-clams that had put down roots in the rock's porous surface, had kept the rock stable and warm for numerous years. Clinging on tightly, regulating the temperature as they did so, they had ensured that the sky ship maintained an even altitude, preventing it from either crash-landing or soaring off into the aerial graveyard of Open Sky.

Instead, as a final indignity, the hapless sky wreck had been forced to hover in mid-air, drifting this way and that across the Edge – now above the Deepwoods, now above the Edgelands or the Twilight Woods; now back above the Deepwoods – a haven to the countless seeds, spores and windblown creatures of the sky.

From an opening in the wrecked sky ship's once magnificent aft-castle, a long rope stretched off into the middle distance. There, like an obedient young prowlgrin at the end of its master's leash, a small vessel bobbed about. Though evidently deserted, this skycraft – a humble sky barge – was, in marked contrast to the wreck, clearly skyworthy. Its single mast was intact and its rubble cage undamaged – though how long they would remain this way, it was impossible to say. Since it was untended, it was only the thin rope tethered to the ancient sky wreck which was preventing the sky barge itself from spiralling off into Open Sky.

All at once, the quiet of high sky was shattered by the piercing shriek of a ratbird. Moments later, a tiny creature appeared through the clouds. With its wings beating furiously, it spiralled down towards the small sky barge that it knew instinctively as home. Around its middle was tied a length of twine which snaked out behind it.

Moments later, a third vessel – a fine sky pirate ship, heavily laden judging by its rolling gait, but sleek and well-maintained – appeared from the billowing clouds. It became immediately clear that the other end of the length of twine was attached to the jutting prow. This meant that, despite the swaying weights and billowing sails, it looked for all the world as though the great sky ship was being pulled across the sky by the tiny ratbird.

As the ratbird sped down to the sky wreck, the sky pirate ship went with it. The creature disappeared inside the sky barge – and the twine fell away. The sky pirate ship now approached the two deserted vessels – one huge and disfigured, the other small and lifeless – and hovered in mid air, its flight-burners flaring. From the helm, the tall figure of a sky pirate captain raised a polished telescope to one eye and took in the sight.

'Father.' Quint's worried voice sounded at Wind Jackal's side. 'Father, please, talk to me.'

'There's nothing further to say,' Wind Jackal replied icily, still holding the telescope to his eye. 'You have made your views quite plain to me. You wish to return to Undertown. I do not . . .'

'But, Father,' Quint pleaded. 'You haven't slept for

three days – ever since we left the Timber Stands. You're not thinking clearly.'

'How *can* I sleep?' Wind Jackal turned to his son, his eyes blazing, but his voice scarcely above a whisper. 'Knowing as I do that Daggerslash's ratbird is leading me to the one I seek . . .' His eyes narrowed. 'Finally!'

'But, Father, look! That's a sky wreck out there.' Quint shook his head miserably. 'Remember the cliff quarries? And the Sluice Tower? A sky wreck is a thousand times more deadly . . . Can't we just sky-fire a blazing harpoon at it, set the whole hideous thing on fire, and leave? After all, it's no more than that skycur deserves . . .'

'No!' This time Wind Jackal's voice was an im-passioned roar. 'Have you learned nothing, Quint? Fire is the weapon of the scoundrel and coward! No, Quint, I shall look into Turbot Smeal's eyes, face to face, as I kill him with my own hands!'

'And I would suggest we don't delay,' Thaw Daggerslash's voice, smooth and silky, sounded from the aft-deck stairs behind them. 'When he festooned me and stole the *Mireraider*,' he said, 'Smeal said he intended to go mire-pearling.' He snorted. 'Looks like he's found a fine wreck and is busy harvesting it as we speak.'

Wind Jackal nodded slowly as he glanced across at the sky wreck. Thaw smiled.

'Surprise will be the key to success,' he continued. 'I propose a small boarding-party, Captain. And I'm happy to volunteer. Poisoning Hubble, stealing my sky ship . . .' he muttered angrily. '*I've* got a score to settle with Smeal myself, don't forget.'

'Prepare a harness, Thaw,' replied Wind Jackal without another word. 'Quint,' he added, 'you take the helm.'

'B . . . but, Father!' protested Quint. 'I'm coming with you!'

'That,' said his father coldly, the words like a knife thrust to his son's heart, 'won't be necessary.'

A few moments later, Captain Wind Jackal and Thaw Daggerslash slipped over the port-side balustrade of the *Galerider*. They climbed down the hull-rigging and, with a soft *thud* and a grunt of exertion, dropped onto the deserted deck of the small sky barge. Then, crossing to the prow, they silently hooked their harnesses to the tolley-rope, which was taut and sloping down towards the floating wreck, and launched themselves off from the side of the sky barge. With a low hiss, they slid down towards the distant sky wreck, gathering speed all the time.

Up in the caternest, Spillins turned away and crouched down, moaning softly as he covered his eyes with his hands. Far below him at the balustrade, Hubble grunted uneasily. Tem Barkwater stood on the fore-deck beside the harpoon, biting his lower lip nervously, while Duggin stared out ahead, equally nervous, by his side. On the flight-rock platform, the Stone Pilot – impassive beneath the great conical hood – patiently tended the flight-rock, hobbling now on a single crutch, while up at the helm, Maris beside him, Quint fought back bitter tears.

'You did your best, Quint,' Maris said soothingly, though the look on her face showed she was as worried as the rest of the crew. 'He just wouldn't listen to reason . . .'

'It should be me, not Thaw, by his side, Maris,' said Quint, swallowing hard. 'But after all we've been through. All the horrors, the dangers, the deaths . . . I just wanted this voyage to be over . . .'

Maris laid a hand on his shoulder and squeezed it hard. 'I understand,' she said softly. 'We all do.'

Quint raised his telescope and trained it on the great looming wreck in the distance. Wind Jackal and Thaw were approaching it fast, each of them tugging on their harness ropes to slow their descent. And, as Quint looked on, first Wind Jackal and then Thaw reached the aft-hull of the ruined vessel and slipped inside through a cavernous hole. High above them, up on the flight-rock, the rows of giant clams opened and closed in great ripples, like some monstrous chorus, their steamy breath

wreathing the aft-hull in a ghostly mist.

The sight filled Quint with dread.

'It's no good, Maris,' he said at length. 'I just can't stay here and watch.'

Maris heard the misery in her friend's voice.

'Take the helm,' he told her. 'I must go to my father!'

Before Maris could say anything, Quint turned away and made for the stairs which led down to the aft-deck. Passing the anxious-looking young banderbear at the balustrade, Quint scrambled down the *Galerider*'s hull-rigging and leaped onto the sky barge. He looked about him desperately.

The small craft was open to the elements. A small lufwood awning covered the helm and rudder at the stern, between which the enclosed rock cage with its buoyant rubble and rock shards nestled. Rudimentary burners and cooling-levers sprouted from the rock cage's sides, within reach of whoever stood at the helm.

A sky ship this simple had no need of a stone pilot, Quint realized. In fact, there was barely room for two crew-mates, let alone a young banderbear. It was little wonder that Smeal had got rid of Thaw and Hubble at the earliest opportunity.

Smeal!

The very thought of the evil quartermaster chilled Quint's blood. He made his way across the deck, scrabbling over animal pelts, barrels of pine pitch and bundles of tilder leather – a meagre cargo, even for a rundown sky barge like the *Mireraider* – until he found what he was searching for: a coil of rope. Drawing his sword, he cut a length and tested it for strength.

From above, Quint could hear Hubble's worried call. 'Wuh-wuh. Wu-uu-uh!'

Yes, he *would* take care. The trouble was, there was no time to rig a harness. Quint knew he had to get over to the sky wreck, looming in the distance, as quickly as he could. Whatever happened, he was determined to be at his father's side.

Hurrying to the prow, Quint looped the length of rope over the tolley-line that would carry him across to the terrible wreck. Taking a deep breath, he climbed over the low prow-rail, wrapped the ends of the rope round both hands and – gripping for all he was worth – slid off into the yawning void.

The rope scritched, scratched and juddered as it hurtled over the taut tolley-line. If Quint had only thought, he would have smeared it with tilder grease. As it was, all he could do was hang on tightly and concentrate on bracing himself for what, without the control a harness would have provided, was going to be a very heavy landing.

Halfway across now, the wind roaring in his ears, his arms were already beginning to ache. Far ahead of him, towering in the sky, the wrecked vessel looked even more gigantic and ominous. The fungal forest that covered it swayed and shimmered and, as Quint peered through streaming eyes, half-closed against the onrushing air, it was as if the sky wreck itself abruptly burst into life.

A scattering of tiny translucent razorflits emerged from a moss-fringed scar in the hull; while further along the bow, two large vulpoons launched themselves into the air with haunting, sonorous hoots. From the flight-rock, the wheezing hisses of the mire-clams grew louder by the second and the air became tinged with a damp, tangy odour. Then all at once, up on the overgrown tangle of fronds and lichen that was the flight-rock platform, there came the flashing glint of metal.

Quint peered closely.

It was his father, Wind Jackal! He was standing by the shattered remnants of the main mast, waving his sword and shouting.

He must have spotted Quint approaching, for now Wind Jackal was gesturing and calling to his son. Quint struggled to hear, yet with the wind racing past his ears growing louder and louder as he gathered speed, it was all but impossible.

'Turbot . . . Smeal . . . is . . .' His father's words sailed out towards him.

'I'm coming, Father!' Quint bellowed into the teeth of the wind. 'I'm . . .'

Suddenly, from behind Wind Jackal, a second figure reared up. Dressed in a tall bicorne hat and dark, metal-studded greatcoat, the figure stared down at Quint's father, its demonic, scarred face a monstrous splay of jagged fangs below deep, dark eye-sockets.

'No!' screamed Quint as the figure raised a curved sword above its grotesquely grinning head.

But Wind Jackal hadn't noticed him. 'Not . . .' His voice reached Quint, just as the sky wreck's hull loomed up to meet him and the terrible scene disappeared from view.

Bracing his legs, Quint crashed through the jagged opening in the aft-hull into which the tolley-line went. The next moment he landed, striking a great smothering mattress of foul-tasting dust and fetid spongy softness. Flailing around wildly, Quint fought off the clinging strands of spore-coated fungus that seemed to have enveloped him in the eerie blackness of the sky wreck's interior. All around him, he could hear scratching and chattering as startled wreck-dwellers scuttled about.

Sword in hand, Quint struggled to his feet and sliced through the fungal blooms that flourished on the rafters and decking all round. He made his way towards a thin shaft of light breaking through from the aft-deck above his head. He had to get to the flight-rock platform.

Turbot Smeal *was* here! Even now, he could hear the unmistakable sound of metal on metal as two sky pirate swords clashed in battle.

Reaching the shaft of light, Quint found a ladder coated with white powdery spores leading up to the aft-deck. A small rat-like creature with huge, unblinking eyes shrank back into the mouldy shadows at his approach, and Quint clawed his way up the rungs of the ladder in a cloud of choking dust. At the top, he slashed his way through a forest of stinking toadstools, disturbing pale, bloated-bodied spiders on stilt-like legs as he did so, and emerged at the steps to the flight-rock platform. Gasping for air and coated in foul-smelling dust, Quint looked up to see his father staring down at him.

'Father! I . . .' Quint's voice choked in his throat, and hot stinging tears sprang to his eyes.

Wind Jackal was half-sitting, half-slumped against one of the moss-covered flight-rock levers. He was covered in the same powder of white mould spores that now coated Quint from head to foot, giving them both the appearance of ghostly figures on the dead sky ship.

As Quint climbed the steps to the flight-rock platform, the mark he'd instantly spotted on his father's chest –

bright red against the powdery white – rapidly grew from a tiny pinprick to a bloody blossom, to a great seeping stain . . .

Gasping with horror, Quint grasped his father's shoulders. As he did so, Wind Jackal slumped forward into his arms.

'No! No! No!' Quint wept, seeing the vivid wound between Wind Jackal's shoulder blades where a sharp blade had been driven.

Just then, between the wheezing of the mire-clams below him, came a hideous, chattering cry from inside the flight-rock itself. A moment later, it was followed by the sound of scuttling claws and leathery scales.

Looking down, Quint saw, with a sickening lurch of the stomach, that his father's blood was dripping from the flight-rock platform straight down into the flight-rock below. Quint laid his father gently down, climbed to his feet and brandished his sword – just in time to see first one viciously clawed hand grip the edge of the platform; then another.

With a wheezing grunt, the creature pulled itself up out of the rock. There was a low, rasping sound as its leathery wings scraped against the tunnel-entrance to its lair at the heart of the flight-rock. The next moment, the mutant wreck-demon climbed onto the flight-rock platform. It paused, and regarded Quint malevolently through six gleaming yellow eyes.

Shimmering, venom-tipped tentacles quivered at either side of its broad, fang-fringed jaws, and an evil-looking spur crowned its lumpen, misshapen head. Behind its thin, scaly body, a vicious-looking whiplash tail flicked menacingly backwards and forwards. The creature swayed from side to side – its tail hissing as it slashed the air. The scent of the fresh blood had awoken in it a great hunger; now it was sizing up the latest intruder to the sky wreck, preparing to strike.

Quint stood his ground, his back against the shattered mast; his front stained with Wind Jackal's blood. And as he stared ahead, a cold fury gripped him as all the trials

and tribulations of the terrible voyage he had endured seemed suddenly to be embodied in this loathsome, malformed creature before him.

'I won't leave you, Father!' Quint shouted defiantly, as the wreck-demon curled its lips and hissed. 'Not to this monstrous creature. Not like this . . .'

With a sharp crack, the razor-sharp barbed tail lashed out, ripping Quint's greatcoat at the shoulder as it whistled past him and sending a thin streak of blood out across the powdery white moss on the platform. Quint leaped to one side as the tail swung back a second time – and sent the wreck-demon scuttling back with a deft slash of his sword.

'I am a squire of the Knights Academy of Sanctaphrax,' he roared defiantly, rounding on the creature and releasing a volley of plunging sword-cuts.

358

The wreck-demon fell back, hissing indignantly.

'Schooled by scholars!' Quint bellowed, urging himself on.

The creature howled in pain as a clawed hand was severed at the wrist, twisted in the air and clattered down to the mossy deck.

'Trained by sword-masters!'

The barbed tail fell in three pieces.

'And raised by a sky pirate captain!'

Six yellow eyes, wide with startled amazement, stared back at Quint as the wreck-demon's head tumbled from its shoulders.

Quint sank to his knees, the tears coming thick and fast now, and sobs racking his body. He had slain the monstrous creature, yet this offered no release from the torment of grief that overwhelmed him . . .

'Magnificent swordplay, young Quint.' Thaw Daggerslash's voice sounded behind him. 'Just a pity it came too late for your poor father . . .'

Quint looked round. There was a hard, unfamiliar edge to Thaw's voice. Then Quint saw why. The sky pirate had a deep wound in his shoulder, dark red with blood, which he gripped with white-knuckled fingers.

'I saw Turbot Smeal,' Quint began, 'standing over my father, his sword raised . . .'

'Turbot Smeal is dead,' said Thaw. His face was drained of colour, his legs unsteady.

'How . . . how do you know?' asked Quint.

'Because,' said Thaw Daggerslash with a strained smile, 'I have just killed him.'

·CHAPTER EIGHTEEN·

SHRYKE TEETH

What followed was a blur for Quint – a blur of pain and movement, of shouts, cries and disturbing shrieks. The sky wreck had burst into life all around them, and he and Thaw Daggerslash had stood back to back on the mossy flight-rock platform and defended the body of Wind Jackal from the loathsome denizens of the dead ship.

There were transparent wind snakes, bloated hull-crawlers, gelatinous tentacle-spinners, and far worse. Not even the *Galerider*'s log-baits could have prepared Quint for the hideous, half-formed creatures that slithered, oozed and scuttled from the depths of the mighty wreck, up to the eagerly anticipated feast on the flight-rock platform.

Quint's arm ached now from the slashing cuts, parries and sword thrusts he rained down on anything that came near, while behind him Thaw's grunts and snarls told him that the wounded sky pirate couldn't hold out much longer. His own head was swimming, his eyes were blinded by sweat. He slumped back and, half-crouching, half-kneeling, supported his weight on his slime-flecked sword . . .

All at once, strong arms grasped Quint by the shoulders. Before he could so much as cry out in protest, he felt himself being lifted off the flight-rock platform and into the air.

'Wuh-wuh! Wuh!'

Hubble's voice sounded in his ears, followed, moments later, by Tem Barkwater's anxious call.

'Hold onto them, Hubble! I'm winching as hard as I can!'

Quint looked up. He and Thaw were enfolded in the arms of the great white banderbear, who was gazing down at him with sad eyes. Hubble was in a harness attached to a long rope which extended up to the *Galerider* hovering high above his head, and getting closer by the second. Below him, Quint saw that the flight-rock platform was now seething with wriggling, crawling life.

'Father!' he cried out, as pain worse than any sword wound exploded in his chest.

The rattle of the deck-winch grew louder. Suddenly Quint was being lifted over the balustrade and lowered, sobbing, on to the deck. For several minutes he was lost in a blind, hysterical grief, before he became aware of being carried to a darkened cabin, and gentle hands – Maris's hands – pressing a sedating wood-camphor poultice to his forehead.

Then, blackness . . .

*

Quint wasn't sure how long he slept, but when he awoke, he found himself in his own hammock. The fetid stench of wreck-mould still clung to his clothes. There were sounds of activity coming from the fore-deck and, pulling on his jacket with aching arms, Quint stumbled out of his cabin towards them. As he emerged onto the aft-deck, Thaw Daggerslash's voice rang out in the frost chilled air.

'FIRE!'

Quint started.

From the prow, a blazing harpoon soared off through the air like a great shooting star, hissing and spitting as it went. In a great fiery arc it flew, from the *Galerider* down towards the great sky wreck below. With a great splintering crash, the harpoon's flaming tip drove into the vessel's hull and continued right up to its shaft. Instantly, the wooden planks and beams burst into flame and, as the fire spread rapidly through the sky wreck, the air filled with a thick, pungent smoke.

Slowly at first, the sky wreck began to climb in the sky as the fire took hold and the buoyant wood blazed. Then, as Quint watched, its ascent slowed until, once again, the great vessel hovered motionless in the air. Realizing that the heated flight-rock was acting as a counterweight to the up-thrust of the burning timber, Quint gripped the balustrade and watched closely as the great ship – now parallel with the *Galerider* – shuddered violently, its rotten timbers ablaze.

The ancient bloated flight-rock grew hotter and hotter, and the mire-clams hissed and screamed as they sizzled.

One by one, the giant shells began falling, taking chunks of hot rock with them and tearing the heart out of the ancient rock. The next moment, unable to take the strain any longer, the flight-rock disintegrated in a blazing shower of white-hot rock shards and shell splinters, which hissed like woodsnakes as they plunged down into the forest canopy far below.

Freed from the great flight-rock, the blazing vessel soared off into the sky. The wood hissed and crackled – but the sounds were drowned out by the noise of the wreck's hideous inhabitants shrieking as they burned. Little by the little, the noise faded as the great fireball rose higher and higher. Quint watched as the blazing vessel became as small as a distant moon, a twinkling star, a pinprick of light that, in the blink of an eye, was extinguished.

'Fare well, Father,' Quint whispered.

He turned from the aft-deck balustrade, crossed the flight-rock platform – where the hooded Stone Pilot nodded silently to him – and climbed down to the fore-deck. There he was greeted by the rest of the crew.

Tem Barkwater stood by the prow from which he'd just launched the lufwood harpoon, Duggin – pitch-bucket and flaming torch in hand – by his side. An anxious, distracted-looking Spillins stood, cap clutched in his gnarled hands, and large eyes darker than ever, next to the huge figure of Hubble the banderbear. Maris stepped out from behind them and rushed over to Quint, tears streaming down her cheeks.

'We were going to wait for you, Quint, but Captain Daggerslash thought . . .' she began.

Quint handed her his handkerchief and turned to the sky pirate who stood tall and erect at the fore-deck balustrade, one arm in a sling.

'*Captain* Daggerslash?' he said, raising an eyebrow.

Thaw gave Quint a dazzling smile. 'Only of the *Mireraider* just now,' he said, 'though if the crew of the *Galerider* will have me . . .' His face grew serious. 'You've been through a lot, Quint. Without you, I wouldn't have survived on that hideous wreck. I'm only sorry that neither of us could save Captain Wind Jackal . . .'

Quint nodded slowly. 'Where were you, Thaw, when Turbot Smeal killed my father?' He tried to keep his voice steady.

'We'd split up to search the vessel,' Thaw said smoothly. 'I was in the fore-hold when I heard the clash of swords. I met Smeal coming down from the flight-rock platform. He ran me through with a sword-thrust,' he said, fingering his shoulder gingerly. 'But I managed to trip him as I went down – sent him hurtling to his death over the side, Sky curse him!' He shook his head at the memory of it all. 'Evil-looking creature, he was; a grin like a skullpelt . . .'

Quint shuddered as he remembered the hideous face he'd seen looming over his father on the flight-rock platform.

'I'm sorry for your terrible loss, Quint, believe me, but if it's any help, I have avenged his murder . . .'

Quint reached out and shook the sky pirate's hand. 'For which I thank you, Thaw,' he said. 'But my father always intended that *I* should succeed him as captain. He gave me a sky pirate name long ago. Cloud Wolf.'

'Captain Cloud Wolf,' Thaw smiled. 'It *does* have a ring to it, to be sure, but your father was a great one for tradition, was he not?'

Quint nodded.

'And in true sky pirate tradition, a captain has to be elected by his crew.'

Quint nodded again.

'Each crew-member draws a shryke tooth and has a full day aloft to present that tooth to his choice of captain . . .'

'A "shryke-smile",' Quint agreed.

'A shryke-smile it is, then, Cloud Wolf,' said Thaw, his own smile flashing brightly, 'and may the best captain win!'

As the senior crew-member, it fell to Spillins the oakelf to organize the drawing of shryke teeth, which he kept secure in a small bundle in the caternest.

'Never thought I'd live to see another shryke-smile,' the old oakelf muttered sadly as he counted out six jagged yellow teeth – one for each crew-member – and climbed back down the mast.

It rained heavily during the night. The following morning the decks were glazed with the recent downpour, and the sails and rigging dripped as the first blush of morning lit the sky. Spillins shuffled round the sky ship as the sun rose, pressing each tooth into the palm of every crew-member and keeping one for himself. He smiled at Quint as he passed him at the helm – but then his dark eyes clouded over and he averted his gaze when Thaw Daggerslash greeted him cheerfully on the fore-deck.

'Sky protect us!' the old oakelf muttered to himself, peering up at the misty, watery-coloured sun. 'Sky protect us all!'

As Quint left the helm and made his way to the aft-deck, Spillins met him on the stairs. The old oakelf was heading for the mast, and the safety and comfort of his caternest.

'If it was up to me, young master,' he said. 'If there had been *any* way that this could have been avoided . . .' He left the words hanging in the air. 'Unfortunately, tradition is tradition.' He shook his head unhappily.

'My father always spoke warmly of Thaw Daggerslash,' said Quint. 'A little too ambitious, he thought, but that's not a bad thing, surely?'

The oakelf shrugged, his dark eyes growing wider. 'Let's just say your father could always see the good in people, whereas some of us see a little more . . .'

Quint frowned. 'You mean, his aura?'

'I have never seen a more poisonous hue,' Spillins replied, and shuddered.

'And what does that mean?' Quint asked.

'It could mean any number of things . . .' said Spillins. 'Pain and suffering; sorrow in the past, causing black moods – or worse; thwarted ambition leading to evil thoughts . . .'

Quint hesitated. 'That doesn't sound good . . .'

Spillins stared into Quint's face with his huge dark eyes.

'I see the stain of sorrow in *your* aura, my lad,' he said with a sad smile, 'but also the golden glow of greatness – which is why I'm giving you this.' Spillins slipped his shryke tooth into Quint's hand, and winked. 'Good luck,' he said, softly.

Hubble was down in the aft-hold when Thaw Daggerslash caught up with him. Since Ratbit's untimely death, the number of scrabsters had multiplied a dozenfold. Hungry, now that the tallow candles they had fed on were gone, they had started making forays into other areas of the sky ship – the fore-hold, the food stores, the infirmary cabin, devouring anything they could find. It was when Thaw Daggerslash had discovered his tilderskin breeches half-consumed that he had announced that 'something had to be done' – and had volunteered Hubble for the task of eradicating the vermin.

'*There* you are,' he said.

Hubble, who was crouching silently by a small hole in a cross-beam of the great hold, a clawed paw raised, glanced round.

'Wuh-wuh,' he murmured.

'Never mind "wuh-wuh". You know what I want,' said Thaw. He stepped closer. 'Hand it over.'

'Wuh?' said Hubble, his great furry face creased with confusion.

'You really are a stupid creature,' said Thaw in exasperation. 'The shryke tooth. Hand it over!'

For a moment, Hubble did not move. Thaw Daggerslash reached towards his sword – a sudden gesture which caused the albino banderbear to yelp involuntarily.

'It gives me no pleasure inflicting pain, but you force me into it . . .'

The banderbear raised a great fist, as if to strike the sky pirate, only to open its paw and allow a shryke tooth to fall to the floor. Thaw Daggerslash snatched it and pushed it into the inside pocket of his jacket. Then, turning on his heel, he marched back towards the exit.

'Excellent choice, Hubble,' he chuckled. 'For such a stupid creature!'

As Thaw disappeared up the stairs, a scrabster poked its scaly head out into the hold and sniffed. Before it had a chance to determine what exactly it could smell, the banderbear's great paw descended, decapitating the creature with a single slash of a great claw.

Returning to the helm, Quint busied himself realigning one of the flight-levers. The lever cord was frayed and would need to be repaired by the look of it. Quint called to Tem on the fore-deck to join him. The young deck-hand climbed the stairs to the helm, two at a time.

'What seems to be the problem?' he said, cheerfully, peering over Quint's shoulder.

'It's the stud-sail lever cord. Needs replacing . . .' Quint muttered.

'Steg used to keep an eye on the lever cords,' Tem sighed. 'I do miss old Steg . . .' He swallowed hard.

Quint nodded and looked up. 'Why, Tem Barkwater!' he exclaimed. 'When are you going to stop growing? You were shorter than me when I first untethered you from that whipping-post, and as light as a vulpoon feather. *Now* look at you! Half a head taller and built like an ironwood privy!'

It was true. The thick jerkin, tilderskin jacket, heavy canvas leggings and stout boots that he had bought in Undertown were all now looking tight and skimpy – even the huge hammelhorn felt cap no longer looked too big for him. Tem smiled amiably.

'I reckon it must be all that good food Mistress Maris serves up,' he said. 'Here, give me that,' he said, leaning over and taking the end of the cord from Quint. 'I know how to fix nether-fetters. Steg taught me.'

With deft fingers, he twisted the frayed end of the cord, doubled it back on itself, and slipped the tide-ring into place.

'There,' he said, as straightened up. 'Try the flight-lever now.'

Quint did so. It worked perfectly. 'Excellent, Tem!' he said. 'Well done.'

'My pleasure,' he replied, beaming happily. The next moment, his face grew suddenly serious. 'You know that Thaw Daggerslash was down on the fore-deck this morning, complimenting me on my harpoon firing and ropecraft, and acting all nice and friendly like . . .'

'Thaw is always friendly,' admitted Quint.

'Yet behind those smiles,' said Tem, shaking his head, 'there's something else; something mean . . .'

'Mean?' said Quint.

'Yes,' said Tem, frowning. 'Like that time he was talking about using me as tarry-vine bait . . .'

'It was just a joke, Tem,' said Quint. He shook his head. 'Though it wasn't funny.'

'That's right,' said Tem. 'It wasn't funny. Not to some-one who's actually been used as tarry-vine bait. Not funny at all. And a captain of a sky pirate ship should know that . . .'

He reached into the pocket of his tight jerkin and teased out the shryke tooth wedged there.

'Here,' he said. 'For you, Quint.'

'Duggin! Duggin! Duggin!' said Thaw Daggerslash, laughing lightly. 'What a fine sky pirate you've turned out to be!'

The pair of them were on the fore-deck. Ever since he'd been brought aboard the *Galerider*, Duggin had spent his every spare moment working on his *Edgehopper* – moderating the sail/hull-weight ratio, adding adjustable cleat-mechanisms to the under-rigging and attaching jutting wind-spoilers to the aft-hull to reduce the risk of turning turvey in heavy winds. The vessel was sleeker, faster and more stable than ever before.

Now, with the *Edgehopper* finished and the *Mireraider* on board, Duggin had turned his attention and expertise to the sky barge. He had stripped the mast and rebuilt it at a ten-degree back-sloping angle. He had lengthened the prow, trimmed the boom and, at the stern, added a device all of his own design.

'So, what *is* it exactly?' Thaw asked, tapping the series of oblique pipes that had been attached to the stern on either side of the rudder.

'I call it a wind-lift,' Duggin explained. 'Sky barges are notoriously sluggish. This should exploit the wind-flow at the stern, thereby reducing the drag of the rubble cage – and double the *Mireraider*'s speed.'

Thaw laughed. 'Ingenious!' he said, and patted the gnokgoblin heartily on the back. 'Duggin, old friend, with your skills, you could have a glittering future. You just need a captain who appreciates your talents.'

'Appreciates them how, exactly?' Duggin looked Thaw steadily in the eye.

'By making you the present of his sky barge . . .' Thaw smiled, holding out his hand. 'After all, you deserve it for all the hard work you've put into the *Mireraider*.'

Smiling broadly, Duggin reached into his pocket, drew out his shryke tooth and dropped it into Thaw's waiting hand.

'It's a deal,' he said.

'My dear Stone Pilot,' said Thaw Daggerslash. 'I am so, so sorry.'

Crossing the flight-rock platform, he had knocked into the Stone Pilot – sending the dropped crutch skittering one way, and the Stone Pilot herself tumbling in the other. He quickly recovered the crutch, and stuck it under his arm, then turned to help the floundering Stone Pilot.

'Allow me,' he said, crouching down, pushing his arm under hers and helping her back to her feet. 'No bones broken, I trust,' he said, smiling winningly as he patted her down and pushed the crutch back into place. 'No lasting harm?'

The Stone Pilot shook her head.

'Well, thank Sky for small mercies,' said Thaw, straightening her crutch and smoothing her robes into place. 'I can be *so* clumsy sometimes . . . Still, so long as you're all right.'

Behind the hood, the Stone Pilot nodded curtly, and returned to tending the flight-rock. Thaw Daggerslash turned and, whistling softly under his breath, continued across the flight-rock platform.

He was on the other side before he opened his clenched fist and inspected the contents of his hand. Then, glancing back at the Stone Pilot, engrossed over the cooling rods, he tossed something yellow and glinting over the side of the sky ship, before sauntering off towards the infirmary-cabin, where he found Maris.

'Oh, Thaw,' gasped Maris, as he entered the small cabin. 'You look awful. Is it your shoulder?'

Thaw smiled bravely and nodded. 'If you wouldn't mind taking a look,' he said.

'Of course not,' she said. 'Loosen your shirt, sit down and let me see.'

Thaw Daggerslash did as he was told. Maris used boiled water and wads of wood-cotton to clean the wound. Then, wincing with sympathy as she dabbed at the vicious sword cut with hyleberry salve, she proceeded to dress the wound.

'It's a deep cut,' she said, 'but it seems to be healing well.'

'All thanks to these excellent treatments.' Thaw smiled at Maris, his head cocked to one side. 'And an even better nurse.'

Maris blushed.

'You like Quint, don't you?' Thaw continued.

Maris nodded, blushing even harder.

'And you want what's best for him?'

Maris stopped and looked at Thaw. 'Of course,' she said.

'Have you ever considered that becoming captain of the *Galerider* might not be what he wants?'

'But Wind Jackal . . .' Maris began.

'Yes, yes,' said Thaw, 'but what about Quint's academic career in Sanctaphrax? His hopes and dreams of completing his education in the Knights Academy and setting forth, as a fully-fledged knight academic, on a stormchasing journey to the Twilight Woods . . . Isn't that what he *really* wants?'

'Yes, but that was before . . .'

Thaw shrugged. 'Perhaps I'm wrong. After all, you know him better than I, Maris.' He frowned, his face a picture of concern. 'But just imagine how resentful he will one day feel if the death of his father leads him into a future he does not want, while his true goal in life remains forever thwarted . . .'

As the sun slipped down towards the far horizon, the crew of the *Galerider* assembled on the aft-deck. The helm was secured and the rock-burners locked into position.

'It is time to count the teeth,' Spillins announced. 'Thaw Daggerslash, how many do you have?'

The young captain reached into his pocket for the shryke teeth. 'Two,' he said, displaying them both for all to see.

'Quint?' said Spillins.

'Also two,' said Quint.

'Which means that two teeth have still to be cast,' said

Spillins. 'Whoever wishes to cast their teeth must do so now, before the sun sets.'

The Stone Pilot reached into the folds of her heavy coat, looking first in one pocket, then in the other. Despite the conical hood she wore, her confusion was obvious as neither pocket revealed the shryke tooth. She looked again. And then a third time, before leaning forwards and seizing Quint by the arm.

It was clear she wished to vote for him.

But Spillins shook his head. 'I'm sorry,' he said. 'Tradition is tradition. If you cannot find your tooth, then I'm afraid it cannot count.'

The Stone Pilot hurried back to the flight-rock platform and searched it for the elusive shryke tooth. But all to no avail. Finally, she sat slumped at the foot of the mast, her conical hood drooping dejectedly.

On the aft-deck, Maris stepped forward. She was about to make her choice when she caught Thaw looking up at the flight-rock platform, a look of malevolent glee on his handsome face. He noticed her glance out of the corner of his eye and instantly composed his features into a look of polite concern. Spillins looked up at her with his deep, dark, worried-looking eyes, and instantly Maris knew what she had to do.

'Quint,' she said, turning away. 'This is for you.' And with those words, she placed the shryke tooth in his outstretched hand.

A momentary look of absolute devastation passed over Thaw Daggerslash's face. The next instant, it was

gone, supplanted with an expression of brave disappointment.

'Well done, Quint,' he said, offering his hand to be shaken, 'or should I say, Captain Cloud Wolf!'

He flashed them all a dazzling smile and strode from the deck. Spillins stared after him, his eyes wide with horror. The aura surrounding the young sky pirate was now a hideous boiling red.

No one saw Thaw Daggerslash leave, but the following morning a disappointed Duggin reported to Captain Cloud Wolf that the *Mireraider* was no longer tethered beside his sky ferry.

Quint shook his head. 'I was going to offer him a position as my quartermaster...'

'I think it was captain or nothing for Thaw Daggerslash, judging by the look on his face,' said Maris.

All at once, there came a cry that dispelled all thought of Thaw Daggerslash. Spillins, up in his caternest with his telescope trained ahead, had spotted a sight to gladden all their hearts.

'Undertown!' he shouted out, his voice strident and cracked. 'Undertown ahead!'

The crew rushed from their posts to cluster at the balustrades on deck. And there it was, sprawled out beneath a grimy sky on the far side of the Mire – the great centre of commerce and industry: Undertown. A cheer went up, and Tem Barkwater lost his wide-brimmed hammelhorn felt hat as he tossed it into the air – only to have it snatched away by the wind.

The next moment, though, the atmosphere changed. Certainly it was Undertown that lay before them, but it was a very different Undertown from the one they had left all those long weeks before.

·CHAPTER NINETEEN·

CLASH OF THE SKY GALLEONS

In the great glass-domed chamber at the top of the magnificent Leagues Palace, Ruptus Pentephraxis, High Master of the United Leagues of Undertown Free Merchants, stared out across the rooftops. A pall of dark, swirling smoke hung over the city, cutting out the sunlight from above and casting everything below in ominous shadow. In places, the unnatural greyness was broken by pinpoints of dazzling light, glittering like marsh-gems in Mire mud, where great fires blazed.

'The Sallowdrop inn, the Hammelhorn tavern, the Fromp, the Sky's Rest and the most treacherous of them all, the Tarry Vine tavern . . .' Ruptus growled in his deep, rasping voice, counting off the blazing buildings he could see, one by one. 'Verminous nests of sky piracy cleansed! We have done well, my fellow leaguesmasters – putting aside our differences and acting together for once. But this great purge of sky piracy is not yet over . . .'

The High Master turned and, with his one good eye, glowered at the assembled high-hats seated around the huge circular leagues table. A massive figure, as tall as a banderbear, his mighty paunch encased in battle-dented armour and his shaven head criss-crossed with scars, Ruptus towered over his fellow leaguesmasters without the aid of his own hat – the highest of them all – which sat by his side.

'Even as their Undertown dens burn, the sky pirates are setting sail for the Edgelands and their impregnable stronghold at Wilderness Lair where they'll skulk, like storm-scattered ratbirds, until they judge it safe to return . . .'

All round the table, the high-hats nodded.

'Just as they always do,' muttered Padget Pyreglave, weasel-faced Master of the League of Rilkers and Renderers.

'Same after every purge – and I've seen a few in my time,' agreed the corpulent Renton Brankridge of the Wheelers and Wedgers, his chins wobbling.

'Our leagues fleet is assembling in the boom-docks and is preparing to set sail in pursuit. Every league of Undertown has suspended commerce and contributed their finest vessels to our cause.'

'But what's the use, if they won't come out of Wilderness Lair and fight?' Padget Pyreglave's whining voice broke in. 'They know we can't sail into the Edgelands after them. Our league ships aren't built for it, and our leagues captains lack the skill . . .'

'As we speak, the last sky pirate vessel has left for

Wilderness Lair,' Ruptus continued, glaring at the weasel-faced leaguesmaster on the other side of the table with ill-disguised contempt. 'Its young captain delivered a load of bloodoak timber to our colleague Thelvis Hollrig's sky-shipyard, perhaps the most important cargo ever carried. Now he is hurrying back to his fellow sky pirates at Wilderness Lair with news of our leagues fleet.'

'And you let him go?' gasped Padget in disbelief.

'Of course!' roared Ruptus, raising his gauntleted fist. 'We needed him to tell the others. The sky pirates won't be able to resist! When they hear that our leagues fleet has set sail, they'll come out to meet us in open battle, confident that, once again, they'll scatter our ships and bloody our noses with their sleek sky ships and superior skysailing skills.'

The high-hats nodded uncertainly. What, they wondered, was to stop that actually happening?

'As usual, those arrogant upstarts will expect us to flee back to Undertown to lick our wounds,' Ruptus went on. 'Then, little by little, the leagues' resolve will weaken and we'll begin to use their services again – just as we always have. And before we know it, they'll be back in Undertown, in their taverns, smirking at us behind our backs . . . But not this time!' he bellowed.

Ruptus brought his huge fist down on the table with a resounding crash that set the high hats of the leaguesmasters trembling on their heads like startled reed eels.

'This time it'll be different!'

'But how?' queried Renton Brankridge, his large

flabby face reddening. 'High Master Marl Mankroyd tried smashing the sky pirates in "the Battle of the Great Sky Whale", and perished in the attempt . . . *You* should remember that, High Master. After all, you were there . . . How will this battle be any different?'

Ruptus's own face reddened and contorted with suppressed rage at the painful memory of that defeat, and his own humiliation at the hands of the great sky pirate captain, Wind Jackal. His great fists clenched, his one good eye blazed – and Renton Brankridge's high hat trembled uncontrollably.

Just then, from the far side of the table, there came the teeth-jarring sound of sharpened finger-spikes being scraped across ironwood. All eyes turned in the direction of the appalling sound.

Ruptus's deputy, Imbix Hoth, the High Master of the Leagues of Flight, stood up and crossed the chamber to the tall windows and threw one open. Far below, from the direction of the sky-shipyards in Eastern Undertown, came the sounds of sawing, drilling and frenzied hammerblows as priceless bloodoak timber was fashioned and worked, and fitted into place.

'How will this battle be different?' Imbix Hoth sneered, his features twisted into an unpleasant leer as he pointed towards the great sky cradles in the distance with his long, cruel finger-spikes. 'Let me tell you . . .'

*

A short while later, the magnificent curved stairway was full of clamour and uproar as the high-hatted leagues-masters clattered down its steps, chattering excitedly.

'Plunder for all!' babbled Ellerex Earthclay, the young Master of the League of Melders and Moulders. 'The sky pirate armada to be split up between the leagues!'

'We'll smash a few,' laughed Rustus Xintax, a wizened master of a minor barrel and cask-making league. 'But the rest'll surrender. I've my eye on the *Fogscythe*. Make a perfect slave-rider!' He chuckled nastily.

'There'll be plenty to go round!' laughed his companion as they joined the high-hatted throng spilling through the great door of the Leagues Palace, down the statue-lined steps and off towards the bustling boom-docks.

From the doorway, Ruptus Pentephraxis and Imbix Hoth watched them go, looks of sly satisfaction on their faces.

'Stupid, greedy fools,' sneered Imbix, with a thin smile. 'Once the sky pirates are crushed . . .'

'We shall take the sky pirate armada for ourselves, dear Imbix,' growled Pentephraxis. 'And then our plans can *really* grow.'

Imbix followed the brutish leaguesmaster's gaze upwards towards the great floating city of Sanctaphrax, and stifled a high-pitched giggle.

'Indeed, Ruptus, and I look forward to that,' he said. He turned. 'Now, if you'll excuse me, I must gather my hatch-lings and prepare for our voyage . . . Brummel, my hat!'

Imbix's hat-tipper raised his staff and steadied the leaguesmaster's hat as he hurried down the steps after him. Ruptus remained for a moment staring up at the floating city, a faraway look in his eye, before a hand on his shoulder brought him back down to earth.

'Father!' came a gruff voice. 'There's someone I'd like you to meet.'

Ruptus turned to see his son, Ulbus – stocky, thin-lipped and hard-eyed – staring back at him. The lad was as brutal and cruel as his father but sadly lacked both his tactical brilliance and driving ambition.

'What do you want, Ulbus?' Ruptus snarled. 'The fleet's about to set sail.'

'Come with me, Father,' said Ulbus, eager as always to win his father's approval, 'down to the cellars . . .'

'The cellars?' said Ruptus impatiently.

'It'll be worth it, I promise!' urged Ulbus, pulling his father by the arm.

Grumbling in his deep growling voice, Ruptus followed his son back inside the Leagues Palace and down the steps into the vast kitchen in the cellars, where brow-beaten goblin matrons scuttled away into the shadows at their approach. In a gloomy recess by the great furnace, a figure in a heavy coat – collar raised and wide-brimmed hat pulled low over his face – sat hunched on a copperwood chopping-stump.

'Father,' said Ulbus, 'allow me to introduce Turbot Smeal . . .'

Ruptus stared at the shadowy figure, then recoiled as the flickering furnace light illuminated a hideous, pitted face – deep sunken eye-sockets and glinting fangs. As if aware of his disfigurement, the figure looked down, pulling his coat collar up further and hunching his shoulders.

'Torcher of the Western Quays!' Ruptus growled. 'What brings you back to Undertown after so many years? The smell of burning taverns?'

Turbot Smeal shook his head, reached into his great-coat and drew out a blood-stained bicorne hat. He threw it at Ruptus's feet. The High Master bent down and picked it up.

'Wind Jackal's hat,' he murmured, turning it over in his great gauntleted hands. 'This can only mean . . .'

'Dead!' rasped Turbot Smeal from the shadows, his voice muffled but distinct. 'By *my* hand.'

Ruptus smiled and nodded his great scarred head.

'I knew you'd be pleased, Father,' broke in Ulbus, excitedly. 'Turbot found me in the boom-docks, told me all about it! How he'd hunted Wind Jackal down, lured him to a sky wreck and cut him down! He's heard of the purge and the leagues fleet, and he wants to sail with us, Father . . .'

Ruptus raised his hand to silence his son, and turned to Smeal.

'Turbot Smeal, traitor, fire-starter and assassin . . .' he growled, his one good eye glinting in the furnace light. 'Most hated and reviled individual in all of Undertown . . .' Ruptus paused, then laughed unpleasantly. 'I like your style. Tell me, what price do you put on your services?'

The hunched figure rose, and once more shot a look of hideous disfigurement towards the High Master in the flickering light.

'The *Galerider*,' he rasped.

'The gloamglozer rock!' shouted Spillins from the cater-nest, as the sinister-shaped landmark came into view. 'Two hundred strides, and closing . . .'

The winds howled across the Edgeland pavement as the *Galerider* plunged into swirling cloud so thick that, for a moment, everything disappeared from view. At the helm, the young sky pirate captain swallowed anxiously.

'Father, watch over and protect me,' he muttered

under his breath. 'Protect us all . . .'

Quint let his fingers play over the flight-levers. He brought in the sails slightly so that they wouldn't become saturated. He raised the prow-weights and lowered those at the stern – all just as Wind Jackal had taught him. This was his first time without his father that he was attempting to enter Wilderness Lair on his own.

What if he judged it wrongly and the *Galerider* hit the looming gloamglozer rock that rose up from the very edge? Or worse, what if he set too much sail and the howling winds drove them far out beyond the edge and off to a point of no return?

Quint swallowed again. He was Captain Cloud Wolf now, young sky pirate captain of the *Galerider*, and his crew were depending on him. There was Hubble the banderbear, his new bodyguard, standing behind him – massive, yet still only half grown. Maris, quartermistress and ship's doctor, wise beyond her years, and faithful old Spillins, ship's elder, on constant watch above. Good old Duggin, now a deckhand and second-mate to young Tem Barkwater, the harpooneer. The Stone Pilot, behind her hood, was as inscrutable as ever, but now fully recovered, the most dependable member of the crew. And then there were the three new recruits . . .

Quint smiled and his heart leaped. Stope, Raffix and Phin. The Winter Knights!

When Quint had delivered the consignment of blood-oak timber to the sky-shipyard, honouring his father's contract, the sinister yardmaster, Thelvis Hollrig, had let slip that a purge of sky pirates was about to begin and that they should get out of town. Quint hadn't needed telling twice. He'd taken the *Galerider* – light now without its great load – up into the sky as the first tavern fires had begun.

Hollrig, counting out a fortune in gold, had gleefully mentioned the great leagues fleet gathering in the boom-docks, and Quint knew he had to warn the sky pirates fleeing to Wilderness Lair of its approach. It would be a hard, tiring flight out to the Edgelands, and the *Galerider*'s depleted crew would not be enough . . .

There was only one place to go.

Quint had flown up to the floating city and sought the help of his old comrades at the Knights Academy. Stope, master forge-hand, dropped his tools at once and came running. He would man the aft-deck and grappling-hooks. Phin, the academic-at-arms, left the Academy Barracks and took up his position beside Tem at the harpoon, with the great crossbow and fore-deck hooks now under his control. Then there was Raffix – proud young knight academic – as Quint's second-in-command, ready to take the helm or lead a boarding-party as the occasion demanded.

The three of them had come gladly and without so much as a backward glance, delighted to help an old comrade in his hour of need – even though Quint knew how much the great floating rock meant to them. He swallowed hard again as the clouds thinned. Whatever lay ahead, he was determined not to let any of them down. He would get the Winter Knights safely back to Sanctaphrax once this voyage was over.

'Father, protect us all,' he murmured again, fingering the blackwood amulet which hung around his neck.

'Wilderness Lair, thirty degrees to port!' Spillins shouted down from the caternest as the clouds continued to thin, the closer the *Galerider* got to the very edge.

Quint stared down at the scene below him as he brought the *Galerider* round in a sharp curve to port, his heart singing. It occurred to him that, with the exception of Spillins, he was the only one on board who had seen the sight of Wilderness Lair before – and what a sight it was!

Far beneath, where the rock cliff dropped away into nothing, was a great gathering of sky pirate ships. There were already over two hundred there, with more late-comers emerging from the boiling clouds. Some had already moored, attaching themselves to the great steel eyelets that had been sunk into the rock. Others were coming in to land, making pinpoint adjustments to their sails and hull-weights as they battled with the un-predictable winds and air currents that threatened at any moment to dash them against the rock face. Inching closer by degrees, they would nuzzle up close to the rock and lower themselves into any gaps in the great flotilla.

'Easy does it!' Spillins shouted down as Quint brought his own vessel down close to the others. 'Starboard a touch. That's it. A little more . . .' His voice was soft, encouraging. 'Right, now hard to port and down.'

Both Quint at the helm and the Stone Pilot at the flight-rock platform reacted to his sudden command. Quint shoved three of the flight-levers forward, lowering all the

port-hull-weights, while the Stone Pilot gave the rock a sudden blast of heat from the burners.

'Down, down...' Spillins coaxed. 'Lovely job. Mooring-ring directly in front,' he called out.

But Quint shook his head. His father had never used mooring-rings that were already in place in the rock face. It was too much of a risk, he'd always said. The spikes could have rusted beneath the surface; the hot and cold of night and day might have shattered the slabs of rock which, if untested, were likely to break off at any moment and hurtle down into the void – taking any hapless sky pirate ship with it.

Save a minute and lose a life. The words Quint had heard Wind Jackal say so many times now echoed round his head.

'Tem! Duggin!' he called. 'Fire the fasting-spikes!'

The pair of them primed and fired the crossbows, shooting long, sharp metal spikes at the wall of rock up above them. With a grinding thud, they both sank into the craggy overhang.

'Launch the grappling-hooks!' shouted Quint.

With pinpoint precision, the two sky pirates sent the grappling-irons soaring off into the air, where they caught hold of the rings at the end of the fasting-spikes. Then, with the pair of them tugging the tolley-ropes, they pulled the hovering sky pirate ship in, until the prow was snug against the jutting rock.

'Port-side secure,' shouted Tem.

'Starboard secure,' shouted Duggin a moment later.

Half-suspended, half-wedged against the rock, with the buoyant flight-rock maintaining the equilibrium of the vessel, the *Galerider* was as firm and safe as Quint could hope for. He looked at the great inhospitable setting all about him. Wilderness Lair. A name to conjure with, to be sure. It was a place more suited to spirits, wraiths and ghouls than to creatures with blood running in their veins.

And yet it was to this furthest outpost in the Edgeworld – a hideaway that the lumbering league ships had never managed to reach – that the sky pirates had withdrawn so many times before. It was a haven, a sanctuary; a place that they would head for in times of persecution and attack.

Now was just such a time. Quint placed his bicorne hat firmly on his head, straightened his greatcoat and looked around. There were sky pirate ships

on all sides, as well as above and below, their
decks teeming with heavily armed and greatcoated
sky pirates.

On one side was the *Fogscythe*, a heavy two-master
with four stone pilots and a complement of cloddertrog
log-hurlers. On the other, the slim and elegant *Iceblade*
was crewed by tufted goblins, and had a young spindlebug quartermaster who trilled a greeting across to Quint.
Close by, the *Windspinner* had a sturdy catapult and
wood-tar braziers, while the *Thundercrusher* boasted a
giant wrecking-ball.

The sleek white *Driftcleaver* – complete with plough-
shaped battering ram at its prow – which had been
known to cut a league ship in two, was one of several
sky ships with an all-female crew. Another was the
Mistseeker, captained by the sky pirate Storm Kestrel and
her second-in-command, Heg-Hut, together with a
hand-picked company of ferocious female hammerhead
goblins. From her decks, a visibly shaken Glaviel Glynte
and his partner, Sister Horsefeather, looked out,
bemoaning the cowardly burning of the Tarry Vine
tavern to any who would listen.

Quint called down to Raffix to take over, and climbed
down from the helm to the aft-deck. There, he met Maris
– resplendent in a new greatcoat and breast-plate.

'How do I look, Captain?' she smiled.

Quint was anxious and tired, but the sight of his friend
in full sky pirate gear made him smile. 'Perfectly dressed
for the occasion, Maris,' he said, taking her hand. 'Come,
follow me.'

Quint climbed over the balustrade of the *Galerider* and made his way across the various gangplanks and walkways that linked the sky pirate ships, one with another. Maris followed, her eyes growing wide with wonder at the various vessels and their extraordinary crews, who saluted, doffed their caps or grunted greetings as they passed. Finally ten ships along and four down, they clambered on board a black stormchaser, sleek and deadly-looking with the name *Maelstrom Seeker* in silver letters on her prow.

On board, her deck teemed with sky pirate captains of every description, deep in muttered conversations. Quint, who was by far the youngest captain there, pushed through the crowded Council of Captains. He was making his way to the helm, where the mighty

Captain Ice Fox – his once-black beard now silvery grey – stood with the most experienced of his colleagues.

Quint took off his hat and bowed respectfully. They were all there. Sleet Snicket, the great Mire specialist, with Slug, his trained mud-jackal, by his side. Flood Woodwasp, legendary shryke-egg smuggler. Cruld Spikefist, the grey goblin swordmaster, and Sister

Bloodfeather, lifelong friend of Captain Woodwasp and the only shryke ever to captain a sky pirate ship.

They had all obviously heard of Wind Jackal's death, for as he passed by, they took off their hats and murmured their condolences. Quint thanked them before stepping forward and whispering urgently to Captain Ice Fox, while the others gathered round. After a few moments, as Maris watched from the aft-deck below, Ice Fox raised his arms and addressed the other captains aboard the *Maelstrom Seeker*.

'Captain Cloud Wolf brings news from Undertown,' he announced. 'It seems our erstwhile friends in the leagues have grown bold. We were all fearing a long, hungry lay-up here in the Lair, waiting for things to settle down back in Undertown. But no! Apparently there is a leagues fleet coming to do battle with us . . .'

At this, a buzz rose amongst the sky pirate captains, along with muttered oaths and excited shouts.

'We shall set sail from the lair by first light and clash with this leagues fleet of theirs . . .'

More shouts rose up from the captains all around Maris, together with calls of 'Sky curse them!' and 'We'll feed them to the Mother Storm!'

'. . . And it will be a mighty clash, I promise you, comrades!' Ice Fox boomed. 'The greatest clash there has ever been . . .'

The captains hollered and bayed and roared their approval.

'The clash of the sky galleons!'

*

As a swirling bank of cloud scudded across the vast expanse of the Edgeland pavement, the great armada of sky pirate ships rose up over the gloamglozer rock. The air filled with the roar of flight-rock burners and bellowed commands.

'Raise the stern-weights!'

'Steady, five degrees to port!'

'Arm the catapults!'

In a graceful arcing line, the mighty sky ships swept out over the edge, their sails suddenly billowing, one by one, in a great spider-silk ripple as they caught the wind. Then, equally suddenly, the great armada was racing on the crest of the howling wind back over the Edgelands and towards the high peaks of the Deepwoods treeline far in the distance.

Like a mighty flock of migrating snowbirds, the sky pirate ships fanned out into a great arrowhead formation, with the slower, heavier vessels like the *Fogscythe* and the *Thundercrusher* at the ends of the line, and the sleek black *Maelstrom Seeker* at its tip.

Eighteen vessels along on the right-hand spur, the *Galerider* raced through the air under full sail. Just ahead of her, the *Mistseeker*, with her crew of hammerhead warrior maidens, was a magnificent sight, while behind, on *Galerider*'s shoulder, was the slim, elegant *Iceblade*, her decks teeming with tufted goblins armed to the teeth.

At the helm, Hubble the banderbear clasped the ship's wheel, holding a steady course, while Quint's hands raced over the flight-levers. Behind him stood Raffix in full armour, his great black cloak billowing out behind him, ready to take over at Quint's command.

'A sky pirate armada under full sail!' he called over Quint's shoulder. 'What a magnificent sight, Quint, old chap!'

Quint smiled. Raffix was right. The great armada, in its arrowhead formation, each wing numbering one hundred and twenty vessels, did indeed look magnificent – but Quint didn't have time to admire the view. As the *Galerider* sped on, his mind was racing. Any moment now, with the Deepwoods speeding past below them, the leagues fleet would come into view. Two hundred and forty pairs of eyes peered out from the armada's caternests, straining to spot their billowing sails and furnace smoke.

When they did, at the tip of the arrowhead, the *Galerider* was to follow the *Maelstrom Seeker* and thirty-eight of her sister sky ships – the fastest and sleekest in the armada – and slice through the league ship fleet. Once they had been scattered, the heavier sky pirate ships would close in and pound the league ships into surrender, while the *Galerider* and the attack ships cut off their retreat.

It had sounded so simple when Ice Fox had outlined the battle-plan on the map table in the cabin of the *Maelstrom Seeker* the night before. But now that they were actually racing through the bright, sunlit sky, Quint was not so sure. He could only hope that, as the youngest sky pirate captain in the armada, he wouldn't let everybody down.

'Stay close to the vessel in front . . .' he repeated to himself under his breath. 'Guard her mast; let the vessel behind guard yours . . . Steer straight, harpoon up, keel down . . .'

'Talking to yourself, eh, Quint? First sign of madness, you know?' Phin's laughing face looked up at him from the aft-deck.

'Make sure the crossbow bolts are greased,' Quint called down to him, 'and the . . .'

'Yes, yes,' laughed the young academic-at-arms. 'You steer the ship,' he said. 'Me and the lads'll take care of any unwanted guests!'

From the harpoon on the fore-deck, Tem Barkwater and Duggin turned and waved, while beside Phin, Stope the grey goblin forge-hand raised his polished helmet so comically that Quint had to smile.

Up on the flight-rock platform, Maris, in her greatcoat and breast-plate, and with the medicine chest strapped to her back, stood beside the Stone Pilot, her face drawn and anxious-looking.

'Leagues fleet on the horizon!' The shout went up from caternests all along the line. 'Thousand strides and closing! They've seen us . . . They're turning!'

Quint's mouth was dry, and his fingers trembled as they moved expertly over the flight-levers. This was it; the great clash of the sky galleons that Ice Fox had promised.

'Sky protect us,' Quint muttered, concentrating hard on keeping the *Galerider* in formation.

They must have been sailing fast for, moments later,

when Quint looked up, the league ship fleet was just ahead. The big, sluggish league ships had none of the elegance of the sky pirate ships. They had been built to haul cargo, and most had clusters of small flight-rocks or unwieldy rubble cages that made them slow and difficult to manoeuvre. They now turned their sides to the oncoming sky pirate ships, prow to stern in a wall across the sky.

It was a classic defensive formation that allowed the leaguesmen clustered round catapults, slingshots and log-hurlers on the decks a shot at the sky pirate armada as it closed in. It was the task of the sky pirate ships at the tip of the arrowhead formation to break through this wall any way they could.

'Light the harpoon, Tem,' ordered Quint as the forty sky pirate ships at the arrowtip raced towards the lumbering wall of league ships. 'Target the rock cage!'

At the prow, Tem, with Duggin by his side, lit the end of the great lufwood harpoon and took aim.

'League ships twenty strides and closing!' Spillins shouted from the caternest.

Suddenly, a great hail of missiles spat from the league ships out across the sky – burning deck-javelins, sumpwood-charcoal grenades, spiked lufwood logs and molten balls of ironwood sap.

'Take cover!' Quint shouted urgently and tensed at the helm.

In front of him, the great bulk of Hubble shrank down behind the wheel, pulling a fire-blanket up over his shoulders, while behind Quint, Raffix raised a large ironwood shield above their heads.

The next moment, the air filled with angry humming and whizzing bursts as fiery missiles raced past them. A sumpwood-charcoal grenade landed on the flight-rock platform with a resounding clang, only to be kicked angrily overboard by the boot of the Stone Pilot, where it fizzed and crackled as it exploded into a million buzzing fragments. On the port-side, the nether-sail fizzled as a javelin tore a fiery hole in its centre, Quint pulling back sharply on the flight-lever to set it fluttering free behind them, like a blazing woodmoth. The *Galerider* shuddered once, twice, as lufwood logs hit her sides and bounced off while, just above Quint's head, the ironwood shield rattled as a hail of flaming splinters rained down upon them.

'Prepare for keel attack!' Quint shouted above the din, praying silently that the crew's tethers were all secure.

Ahead, at the tip of the arrow formation, the *Maelstrom Seeker* must have reached the wall of league ships, for the unmistakable sound of sky battle rang out: a huge shattering thunderclap of sound – the *clash!*

Clash! Clash! Clash! Clash!

Ahead of the *Galerider*, sky pirate ship after sky pirate ship hit the wall of league ships in front of them, their razor-sharp keels up as their captains pulled hard on the flight-levers and their stone pilots doused their flight-rocks moments before impact.

Now it was Quint's turn. In front of the *Galerider*, like a monstrous bubbling cauldron spitting fire, the *Bane of the Mighty* – the league ship he'd seen being

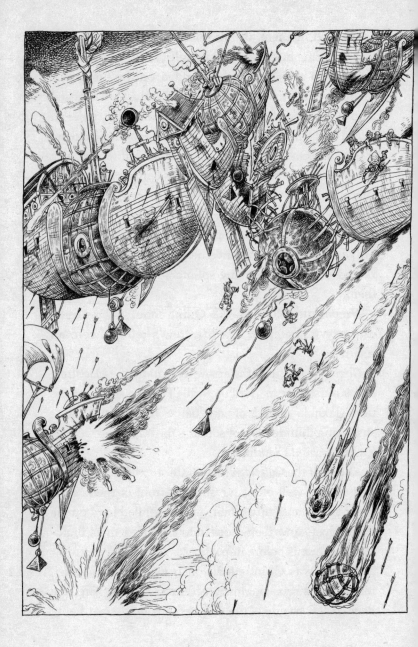

launched – filled the sky. Beside it, listing badly, its aft-hull shattered and flight-rock cage disintegrating, the league ship *Forger of Triumph* marked where the *Mistseeker* had just broken through. Over Quint's shoulder, the slim elegant *Iceblade* had taken a direct hit to its flight-rock that sent it spinning wildly as the hot rock sank.

'Fire!' Quint screamed at Tem, and the next moment, the *Galerider*'s harpoon rocketed from her prow and smashed into the rock cage of the *Bane of the Mighty*.

Seconds later, Quint flattened the flight-levers, and the Stone Pilot doused the flight-rock. With a shuddering *crash!* the *Galerider* reared up into the sky, its razor-sharp keel tearing through the aft-castle of the league ship as it did so. Quint glimpsed the ashen, terrified face of the leagues captain at the wheel of the *Bane of the Mighty*, as they hurtled past, and felt a sickening pang in the pit of his stomach.

The *Galerider* sped on into the clouds, part of a now ragged arrowtip formation which, Quint could see as he looked over his shoulder, had done its job well. The wall of league ships had split apart, vessels listing to one side, spiralling out of control, or disintegrating entirely and falling in fiery splinters from the sky. But it had not been without cost. At least ten magnificent sky pirate ships were ablaze. And as the *Galerider* joined the other attack ships and they fell into line once more, the *Iceblade* hurtled down into the Deepwoods canopy in a blazing ball of fire.

Quint swallowed hard, sickened and shocked by the terrible scene of carnage before him. The heavier sky pirate ships were moving in now, bearing down on the league ships that remained, scattered in twos and threes but still spitting forth a hail of missiles. The *Fogscythe* fired a great blazing ironwood ball that shattered a heavy league ship, the *Profit Bringer*, in one blow. Around it, the league ships now sent up signals of white smoke, signifying their surrender, as great flocks of distressed ratbirds spiralled round the battle, searching for new roosts, and leaguesmen clustered in tiny barges and lifeboats, or fell screaming down into the Deepwoods below.

'A magnificent yet terrible sight,' murmured Raffix behind Quint. 'Poor wretches.'

But Quint wasn't listening, for at his feet lay Hubble the banderbear, a great, bloody gash across his forehead where a shard from a sumpwood grenade had hit him.

'Take the helm, Raffix,' Quint ordered, dropping to his knees and cradling the young banderbear in his arms.

He was still breathing, but his eyes were closed and short soft whimpers of pain were escaping from his great tusked mouth. Maris appeared, her face flushed and her medicine chest open under one arm.

'Duggin's wounded in the leg,' she reported, 'and Phin has minor burns . . . Oh, Hubble!' Maris knelt down beside the banderbear and hurriedly began cleaning the wound. 'It's deep,' she said, her voice betraying her concern. 'I'll do what I can, Quint.'

Quint got to his feet and crossed to the balustrade, which he pounded angrily with a clenched fist.

'Why does there have to be such death and destruction?' he stormed. 'Such pointless waste . . .'

The words died in his mouth as he stared out across the sky. The sky pirate armada was regrouping around them, the *Maelstrom Seeker* holding its position at the head of the long line. But Quint wasn't looking at the sleek black vessel. Instead, his eyes were focused on a great dark bank of cloud to the west, out of which a gigantic vessel was emerging. It was like no sky ship he'd ever seen before. Quint's hands fumbled at his breast-plate as he unbuckled his telescope and held it to his eye.

'What the . . . ?' Spillins's astonished voice sounded from the caternest above.

The sky ship had six masts, a massive expanse of deck and a towering aft-castle. Its huge sails billowed out, sending the great vessel speeding towards the sky pirate armada at an astonishing rate. As it drew closer, Quint could see it was armed with weapons of every type. There were boarding-spikes, battering-rams, harpoons lining every one of the six tiered decks, catapults fore and aft, and crossbows, log-hurlers and deck-splitters everywhere.

As if that wasn't enough, this vessel had no ordinary crew. Quint scanned the decks. They were teeming with black feathered shrykes, clad in armour and bristling with murderous weapons. On its massive curved prow, the sky ship's name was picked out in gold letters.

The Bringer of Doom.

'A league ship . . .' Quint breathed.

As he watched, the mighty sky galleon's flight-rock burners flared, and as gracefully as a sky pirate ship a quarter of her size, *The Bringer of Doom* swooped down past the *Fogscythe*, the heaviest of the sky pirate ships. Suddenly, five flaming missiles – huge blazing logs – shot from the league ship and smashed into the *Fogscythe*, which exploded into flames. *The Bringer of Doom*, as if demonstrating its name, sped past the armada before it had time to manoeuvre and destroyed the equally heavy *Thundercrusher* in a matter of moments. It then circled round the mesmerized fleet once more, like a ravenous white-collar wolf circling a flock of frightened tilder.

Then the unthinkable happened. One by one – the smaller vessels at first, then spreading through the armada – the sky pirates began to abandon their beloved sky ships. The air filled with parawings as the sky pirate crews descended into the Deepwoods below.

Several, like the *Stormrunner* and the *Driftcleaver* tried to flee under full sail, but *The Bringer of Doom* ran them down in an instant, shattering the first with its enormous keel and the other with its catapults. The shrykes on board screeched and cackled, clearly in a blood-frenzy as the sky pirate ships went down, dragging several fleeing sky pirates out of the air and devouring them on deck.

Quint stood mesmerized as the nightmare unfolded, crew after crew abandoning their ships while the shattered remnants of the leagues fleet gathered greedily behind their monstrous saviour, *The Bringer of Doom*. Soon, with even the crew of the *Maelstrom Seeker* disappearing down into the green forest canopy below, the *Galerider* was alone in an armada of ghost ships.

'Quint, we can't stay,' Maris's tearful voice sounded in his ear. 'Duggin has the *Edgehopper* ready. We're all aboard . . .'

Quint spun round, as if suddenly awakened. 'What about Hubble?'

The banderbear lay on his side by the wheel.

Tears coursed down Maris's cheeks. 'There's nothing I can do for poor Hubble,' she wept bitterly.

'You go, Maris,' said Quint gently. 'I'll secure the helm and parawing after you . . .'

'But Quint! . . .' Maris protested.

'Please, Maris.' Quint's eyes beseeched his friend to understand. 'Go! I'll follow . . .'

They both knew he was lying; that he would never abandon his father's sky ship. What was more, if Maris gave him away to the crew waiting in the small sky ferry, then they wouldn't leave either – and Maris knew Quint couldn't bear that.

She nodded, tears running down her face, and her heart breaking.

'Maris. Please . . .'

She crossed over to Quint, took his head in her hands and kissed him gently on the lips.

Then she turned and ran from the helm. Moments later, the small sky ferry cast away from the *Galerider* and sped down towards the forest canopy, and not a moment too soon.

Quint stood at the helm, his hands poised over the flight-levers. The Stone Pilot had left the flight-rock burners at a quarter setting, and Tem had recharged the prow harpoon, ready for action. In the sky ahead, the massive league ship closed in on the *Galerider*. Its decks were bristling with screeching jet-black shrykes, and a boarding-party hurriedly lowered ropes and grappling-hooks.

Quint watched impassively, a deep sorrow welling up in his chest, making it hard for him to breathe. Yet despite this, he found himself fascinated by the most extraordinary feature of the monstrous vessel as it drew closer.

Its flight-rock.

It was the largest, most perfect flight-rock Quint had ever seen. No wonder *The Bringer of Doom* was so manoeuvrable and fast, with such an extraordinary flight-rock at its centre.

But how had the rock managed to grow so big before being harvested? Quint wondered, gazing at its surface, so smooth and unpitted – the clear sign of a freshly harvested rock.

The secret lay deep at the very centre of the enormous flight-rock. There, nestling in the heartrock, was the crystal of stormphrax in its sheath of glow-worm skin, which Zaphix Nemulis, the custodian of the Stone Gardens, had planted there. As the glow of the rotting skin dimmed, so the weight of the stormphrax had increased, weighing the rock down and allowing it to grow to its enormous size.

But now the rock had been harvested. Zaphix Nemulis had been paid and was back in Sanctaphrax, toasting his feet in front of a roaring fire. What did he care that the rock he'd nurtured with this clever technique over all those months had the seed of its own destruction at its very core? Zaphix had a full purse and warm feet – and better still, no spiky-fingered leaguesmaster bothering him all the time . . .

Meanwhile as the *Bringer of Doom* loomed up before the Galerider over the distant Deepwoods, the very last fragment of glow-worm skin fell into desiccated dust and its pale glow turned to pitch darkness.

At the helm, Imbix Hoth turned to Ruptus Pentephraxis with a look of exultant triumph on his cruel features, and opened his mouth . . .

What his final words were will, however, never be known, lost as they were in the roar of a gigantic flight-rock – suddenly the weight of ten thousand ironwood pines – hurtling down to earth and taking with it a fortune in finest bloodoak decking, not to mention a screeching flock of pedigree black shrykes.

CRASH!

Quint blinked, unable to take in what he'd just seen. One moment the *Bringer of Doom* had been bearing down on him; the next, the sky was empty and a great plume of smoke was rising up from the forest below. Around the *Galerider*, the abandoned sky ships bobbed on the stiffening breeze – although the shouts and calls coming up from the forest canopy suggested that they wouldn't remain so for long.

In the distance, a dejected gaggle of badly mauled league ships was snaking off in the direction of Undertown. And from the underside of the *Galerider* came a scratching, scraping sound . . .

Quint turned to see a tall figure in a heavy sky pirate coat and bicorne hat slowly hauling himself up from the hull-rigging. His sense of being in a waking dream intensified. First he was waiting for death as a monstrous sky ship bore down on him. Then it disappeared. Now a sky pirate was climbing aboard his deserted vessel.

Quint shook his head, and smiled, bemused.

'Greetings, comrade . . .' he called down, then gasped as the sky pirate straightened up and turned a hideous scarred face – all bared fangs and deep glinting eye-sockets – up towards him.

'Turbot Smeal,' he breathed.

·CHAPTER TWENTY·

OPEN SKY

Turbot Smeal! Turbot Smeal! Turbot Smeal!
The evil quartermaster's name screamed in Quint's head. Turbot Smeal – the malevolent monster who'd set fire to his home and killed his mother and five brothers in the blaze. Turbot Smeal – whose insane act of retribution had killed thousands in the great fire of the Western Quays! Turbot Smeal – murderer of his father, the great Captain Wind Jackal, on board that sky-cursed wreck! Turbot Smeal, who had haunted Quint and Wind Jackal's dreams ever since he'd first come out of hiding, was coming towards Quint across the deck of the deserted *Galerider* – not dead after all, but hideously, nightmarishly alive.

So this was how it was going to be, Quint thought grimly, the last Verginix facing his family's scarred nemesis . . .

'Yield the helm!' the quartermaster's rasping voice sounded as he climbed the aft-deck stairs, his sword glinting. 'The *Galerider* is mine!'

'Never!' Quint cried, drawing his own sword and stepping forward to meet him.

Their blades met with a clanging clash of metal, followed instantly by another and another as Quint deftly parried the quartermaster's frenzied sword thrusts. Smeal was strong, but he, Quintinius Verginix, squire of the Knights Academy, had been trained by the finest swordmasters in all Sanctaphrax.

As the sword blows rained down, Quint turned them aside, a cold dark fury growing from deep within him. Beneath the great bicorne hat, half-hidden by an upturned collar, Smeal's hideous face flashed, white and glinting, as he twisted and turned in his efforts to cut Quint down.

'You stabbed my father in the back, Smeal!' Quint shouted, blocking another thrust. 'A coward's blow for which you shall pay!'

Quint leaped low to the right and caught Smeal with a flashing sword thrust. With a muffled grunt of pain, the quartermaster fell back, his great curved sword flailing in a wide arc as he fought to keep his balance. The blade clattered against the flight-levers, shearing off half a dozen of them, and severing the connecting-cables of half a dozen more.

Instantly, the *Galerider* listed sharply to starboard as the port-side hull-weights broke away from the flight wheel and hurtled down to the forest below. Quint was thrown across the aft-castle deck, slamming into the balustrade with a resounding thud. His sword clattered

from his grasp. Before he could get back to his feet, Smeal was towering over him, sword raised, his scarred, fang-encrusted face leering down.

'I didn't want it to come to this . . .' Smeal's voice rasped, 'but you stood in my way. You stood between me and the *Galerider*. Now you must die!'

Suddenly, Turbot Smeal's bicorne hat flew from his head. He pitched forward with a gurgling cry of surprise, and crashed down on top of Quint. Over Smeal's heaving shoulder, Quint saw Hubble – the great albino bander-bear; groggy, shaken, with a heavy gash over one brow, fighting his injuries, determined to protect his young captain – looking down at him. Hubble reached down with the mighty paw that had felled the quartermaster and pulled the dying body off Quint.

The *Galerider* was tilting at a crazy angle, and its decks shook as it hurtled up into Open Sky. With difficulty, Quint climbed to his feet and looked down. The hideous face of Turbot Smeal stared back at him. Low gurgling sounds were escaping from the bare glistening fangs, as his eyes glinted out from the dark sunken eye-sockets . . .

But wait . . . What was this?

Quint reached down and traced a finger over the bony pitted surface of the quartermaster's face – except it wasn't a face at all. It was a mask. Quint could see that now, despite the wind whistling past, and the pitch and roll of the sky ship. A hideous mask of bone and fang it was, belonging to a skullpelt. In life, this evil creature was a hunter of dreamers in lullabee groves. Now, in death, its grinning face was a mask for Turbot Smeal to hide behind . . .

With trembling fingers, Quint reached forward and undid the straps that held the mask in place. Then, gently, hardly daring to look, he pulled the mask away.

Beneath, instead of the mass of flame-melted flesh and scar-tissue he'd been expecting, was the young fresh face of a handsome sky pirate, blue eyes clouded with pain.

'Thaw!' Quint exclaimed. 'Thaw Daggerslash . . . I don't understand . . .'

The *Galerider* gave a great lurching shudder and, over Quint's shoulder, Hubble growled with alarm as they hurtled ever higher into Open Sky. Not that Quint noticed any of this. His eyes were fixed on the

young sky pirate dying before him. His hands gripped the collar of the impostor's greatcoat and shook it.

'Why? Why? Why?' he wailed.

'Because . . .' Thaw's voice was a whisper; urgent, breathless, full of pain. 'Because I was young . . . ambitious . . . Because I wanted a sky ship of my own . . . I wanted . . . I wanted . . . the *Galerider*!'

'So you lied? You cheated? You murdered?' Quint's eyes blazed and his fists clenched as they gripped Thaw's collar.

'It seemed so simple . . .' A thin smile crossed Thaw's lips, along with a trickle of blood. 'The moment I saw her, I knew the *Galerider* had to be mine. But . . . your father stood in my way . . . So I set a trap and baited it with the promise of a showdown with his long-dead enemy, Turbot Smeal . . .'

'The slave market, the cliff quarries, the Sluice Tower?' Quint shuddered. 'All you?'

Thaw grimaced with pain, but managed to smile.

'. . . *And* the sky wreck, Quint. I finally got him there, and the *Galerider* was going to be mine, along with her crew. I would have been a great sky pirate captain, Quint. And you would have grown to love me, and serve me faithfully – all of you . . . And one day, *my* name would have been carved on the great table of the Tarry Vine tavern . . . Captain Thaw Daggerslash . . . Greatest sky pirate captain . . .' Thaw's voice faltered, his breath coming in painful gasps, his blue eyes clouding over. 'That ever lived . . .'

The *Galerider* gave another shuddering lurch as Quint released his grip and Thaw sank back, his dead eyes staring up into Open Sky; his dead hands gripping the aft-castle balustrade of the sky ship he'd schemed so hard to possess.

For a moment Quint just stood there on the listing deck, all emotion drained from him. Then, looking across at the flight-rock platform, he saw the flight-burners flicker and go out. Taking Hubble by one mighty paw, he braced himself for what he knew was coming next.

Quint didn't have long to wait. Moments later, with a great howling scream, the cold rock slammed against the rock cage, and the *Galerider* rolled over and turned turvey.

Suddenly, Quint and Hubble were falling away from her, down through the sky, as the mighty sky ship sailed up into Open Sky, for ever.

As the *Galerider* disappeared into the clouds, Quint felt all the cares and sorrows of his past disappearing with her – the horrors of the cliff quarry, the terrors of the Deepwoods, the dangers of the sky wreck and the senseless carnage of the sky-battle. They all soared upwards along with the sky pirate ship into the endless void of Open Sky.

Below him lay the Deepwoods, and the future – a future in the Knights Academy with his loyal friends; a future as a knight academic dedicated to the sacred search for Stormphrax . . .

Quint reached for the lever at his chest and pulled.

Behind him, his parawings opened with a loud clap, followed closely by those of his faithful banderbear bodyguard. Hand in paw, the two figures silhouetted against the setting sun swooped down through the air towards the tiny sky ferry in the distance.

EPILOGUE

EPILOGUE

'So, here we are,' said Maris, looking up at Quint, 'the gates of the Knights Academy . . .' Her voice trailed away and her grip on Quint's hand tightened.

They were standing by the old East Gate of Sanctaphrax's most venerated academy, the sun setting over the high gables of the Upper Halls and the wooden Gantry Tower with its ancient tethered sky ship.

Quint smiled. What a voyage they'd had. Before the final battle, Quint had deposited the small fortune from the bloodoak timber with the Professors of Light and Darkness. With it, Maris had been able to move back into her old apartments in the School of Mist, together with her family's old retainers: Tweezel the spindlebug and Welma the woodtroll matron.

Quint had also been able to look after the rest of the crew. Tem Barkwater, Spillins and the Stone Pilot had joined Duggin and his new fleet of sky ferries plying a lucrative trade over the teeming thoroughfares of Undertown – teeming even more than usual, because of the rebuilding of the burned taverns. There were rumours that Sister Horsefeather had plans for the biggest establishment yet, to be called the Bloodoak tavern. Hubble the banderbear, now recovered from his injuries, had joined Stope in the forge of the Hall of White Cloud here in the Knights Academy, where Quint saw him often. Raffix was in one of the thirteen towers awaiting the arrival of a great storm, while Phin – his burns fully healed – was back in the Academy Barracks.

Quint met them in the Eightways Refectory or up in the Gantry Tower, where they could watch the sky ships approaching Undertown from far destinations out in the Deepwoods. After the latest purge, it was business as usual for the sky pirates and leagues of Undertown.

But it was Maris that Quint saw more often than any-one else. Despite his arduous studies which one day would, he hoped, lead to a knighthood and a storm-chasing voyage, Quint always had time for her. Sometimes they would visit the deserted Great Library, or venture down in the sky cages from the West Landing, or climb to the top of the Loftus Observatory, reliving their past adventures.

But wherever they went, Quint and Maris always ended back at the gates of the Knights Academy as the sun began to set over their beloved floating city.

'Yes,' said Quint. 'Here we are . . .'

ABOUT THE AUTHORS

PAUL STEWART is a highly regarded author of books for young readers – everything from picture books to football stories, fantasy and horror. Together with Chris Riddell, he is co-creator of the *Far-Flung Adventures* series, which includes *Fergus Crane*, Gold Smarties Prize Winner, and *Corby Flood*, Silver Nestlé Prize Winner. They are of course also co-creators of the bestselling *Edge Chronicles* series, which has sold over two million books and is now available in over thirty languages.

CHRIS RIDDELL is an accomplished graphic artist who has illustrated many acclaimed books for children, including *Pirate Diary* by Richard Platt, and *Gulliver*, which both won the Kate Greenaway Medal. *Something Else* by Kathryn Cave was shortlisted and *Castle Diary* by Richard Platt was Highly Commended for the Kate Greenaway Medal.

THE
EDGE CHRONICLES
FAN CLUB

Join the FREE Edge Chronicles Fan Club:
read Paul and Chris's diary and find out how they
work together, check out the awesome character
gallery, wonder at the interactive map and download
wallpaper. Plus loads of other stuff to see and do!

www.edgechronicles.co.uk

THE EDGE CHRONICLES

THE QUINT TRILOGY

Follow the adventures of Quint
in the first age of flight!

CURSE OF THE GLOAMGLOZER

Quint and Maris, daughter of the most
High Academe, are plunged into a terrifying
adventure which takes them deep into the rock
upon which Sanctaphrax is built. Here they
unwittingly invoke an ancient curse . . .

THE WINTER KNIGHTS

Quint is a new student at the Knights
Academy, struggling to survive the icy cold
of a never-ending winter, and the ancient
feuds that threaten Sanctaphrax.

CLASH OF THE SKY GALLEONS

Quint finds himself caught up in his father's
fight for revenge against the man who killed
his family. They are drawn into a deadly
pursuit, a pursuit that will ultimately lead
to the clash of the great sky galleons.

'The most amazing books ever' Ellen, 10

*'I hated reading . . .
now I'm a reading machine!'* Quinn, 15

THE EDGE CHRONICLES

THE TWIG TRILOGY

Follow the adventures of Twig
in the first age of flight!

BEYOND THE DEEPWOODS

Abandoned at birth in the perilous Deepwoods,
Twig does what he has always been warned
not to do, and strays from the path . . .

STORMCHASER

Twig, a young crew-member on the
Stormchaser sky ship, risks all to collect valuable
stormphrax from the heart of a Great Storm.

MIDNIGHT OVER SANCTAPHRAX

Far out in Open Sky, a ferocious storm is brewing.
In its path is the city of Sanctaphrax . . .

'Absolutely brilliant' Lin-May, 13

*'Everything about the Edge Chronicles
is amazing'* Cameron, 13

THE EDGE CHRONICLES

THE ROOK TRILOGY

Follow the adventures of Rook
in the second age of flight!

LAST OF THE SKY PIRATES

Rook dreams of becoming a librarian knight,
and sets out on a dangerous journey into the
Deepwoods and beyond. When he meets the last
sky pirate, he is thrust into a bold adventure . . .

VOX

Rook becomes involved in the evil scheming
of Vox Verlix – can he stop the Edgeworld
falling into total chaos?

FREEGLADER

Undertown is destroyed, and Rook and his
friends travel, with waifs and cloddertrogs,
to a new home in the Free Glades.

'They're the best!!' Zaffie, 15

'Brilliant illustrations and magical storylines'
Tom, 14

421 514